BRIGHT FEATHER

BRIGHT FEATHER

A Novel by

ROBERT WILDER

G. P. PUTNAM'S SONS

New York

PRINTED IN THE UNITED STATES OF AMERICA
AMERICAN BOOK—STRATFORD PRESS, INC., NEW YORK

To My Son Bob
The Story I Promised to Tell You

BRIGHT FEATHER

1

THEY struggled with the deceptive fury of strong young cats at play. Clawing and snarling, their bodies spinning in a threshing tangle, the two boys beat a whirling course across the sandy hillock. Flying knees tore into the soft earth. Browning clumps of springy grass and the delicately green and pleated fans of young palmetto shoots were flattened by their rolling weight. Then, abruptly, and as though by prearranged signal, the contest ended in a series of sharp, whistling sighs and the heavy, panting gasps of labored breathing. Slowly, warily, the victor straightened his back. Leaning slightly forward, he rested, and with rigid arms pinned unresisting shoulders to the ground.

"Say uncle." The command was not much more than a relieved wheeze, uttered weakly and without authority. "Say uncle an' give up?" He forced a questioning grin to his strained features, waiting with hopeful apprehension.

The youth on the ground stared back into the face of his conqueror with unblinking gravity. His eyes, as brilliantly black as the tip of a ripe acorn, mirrored neither anger nor humiliation but only the calm acceptance of a situation now beyond control. His body was relaxed, sprawled easily on the warm and yielding sand. In defeat it somehow managed to give the impression that this position was the more comfortable of the two.

Clay Hammond cinched his knees, digging them roughly into the narrow waist. His movements were cautious; he took no chances on an unexpected renewal of hostilities.

"Say uncle." A weary note of exasperation crept into his voice. "Say uncle or I'll ride your belly like a burr."

There was no reply from the boy on the ground. The hot flush of furious encounter was draining slowly from his cheeks, but as it receded the natural color of the skin held the warm sheen of gently rubbed copper. A dark confusion of damp, heavily matted, coarse hair was pressed tightly to his forehead in a roughly scalloped design, blunting the clear oval of his face. His breathing was regular and unhurried as he waited, and he made no effort to

3

shift his head to dodge the drops of sweat that gathered on the nose and face above and fell with small spatterings on his chin.

Impatiently, Clay shot a tight spurt of air from the corner of his mouth in a futile effort to blow away a collection of pine needles, damp sand, and leaves clinging to his upper lip.

"God damn it!" The oath was only mildly explosive. "You gotta say uncle. You're licked an' so you gotta say it. Everybody knows that, otherwise how can a wrassle end? Only a knothead like you would hold out against sayin' it when he's been whipped fair." The statement was made in almost plaintive tones and he paused hopefully, waiting for the traditional admission of surrender.

Something close to a smile tipped at the corners of a solemn mouth and momentarily illuminated the eyes of the vanquished. Finally, the dark head, pinioned by rigid and unrelenting arms, moved in a small, negative gesture.

"I could sit on you like this all day." Clay urged the course of wisdom. "Only a fool would want to get sat on when all he has to do is say uncle. Come on, huh?"

He paused expectantly and then, with a grunt of disgust, drew back on his haunches and straightened up until he stood spraddle-legged above his companion.

"You're sure enough hell for bein' stubborn," he said with grudging admiration. "In all the time I licked you I guess you haven't said it yet. Come on." He extended a hand. "I'm hot an' filled with grit to my belly button. Let's go swimmin'."

With an easy, twisting roll that brought him to his knees without assistance, the boy rose from the ground. He wiped at a sand-smeared face with his knuckles and then glanced to where the sun was already half through the western segment of its arc.

"It's gettin' late," he said doubtfully. "I ought to be startin' back to the town."

His voice held a curious, almost passionate, resonance that seemed to spring from some fierce eagerness well hidden within the stripling frame. The words were edged with a rude accent, elusive and difficult to imitate. They were colored by the sounds of half a dozen dialects; the ancient tribal speech of the Creeks, the soft, liquid slurring of the Negro, the muted twangings brought southward by the angrily restless men from the mountains of Tennessee gave them life. The roaring sounds of sweating, cursing drovers from Georgia had left their vibrations, while seamen and planters, French and English, the soldiers of Ponce de León and De Soto, wandering braves from beyond the Mississippi, runaway slaves,

4

blacks from the West Indies, and fair-haired Scots and Dutch boys from New York and Pennsylvania had added their coloring and shading to the speech of the Seminole when he abandoned his native tongue and ventured into the white man's phrasing.

"A swim ain't goin' to take the rest of the afternoon," Clay urged irritably.

His friend hesitated. "Tommie Macon's goin' deer huntin' tonight an' I want to go along. He'll leave before sundown."

Clay refused to be impressed by such a shallow argument. "It's still early." He grinned with a quick, mocking friendliness. "Anyhow, if it wasn't that I ran out of patience an' maybe a little wind, I'd still be sittin' on your gut an' so you couldn't go anywhere even if you tried."

The boy Asseola smiled in brief tribute to the boastful jest. "I guess you're right," he admitted, "but just the same, Tommie Macon won't wait for me when he's ready to go. We've been in the river twice today."

They stood in a sun-dappled clearing, feeling the afternoon's heat ripple over their bare backs. Shoeless feet stubbed into the loose, sandy soil, piling it into small mounds over restless toes that burrowed, and, like small, frightened animals, seemed to seek a hiding place. The warm hush that tiptoes in the day's decline gathered in fragrant and drowsily murmuring clumps in the tangled oak and scrub. It drifted lazily between the jack pines and glinted on the high, varnished leaves of tall magnolias, trailing away to spread itself with shimmering brilliance along the dark and deeply wooded river.

Standing beside each other, bound for the moment in the silent and mysterious communion of youth that makes speech unnecessary, they listened and mentally catalogued a dozen small sounds of the brush, their thoughts darting from one to the other with the bright and flashing indecisiveness of excited blue jays. Save in the matter of their coloring the boys were much alike physically; slender and with the tough, whipping strength of saplings, they were as primitively self-reliant as the animals of the woods surrounding them. Clay, taller by less than an inch, wore a shock of sun-bleached yellow hair with the jaunty air of a cockatoo's crest. Heavy boned, broad of shoulder, he would be a powerful man when ripened by the years.

Asseola's eyes searched across the treetops, marking the dark, conical spires of pines drawn starkly against the horizon, the ragged, feathered branches of oaks, and the high, effortless wheeling of

5

the buzzards in a cloudless sky. The night would be clear and without a moon, the hunting good. Even now Tommie Macon might be calling his dog and setting out.

Half closing his eyes to the glare, Asseola tracked the wide, circular course of the evil black birds. Always these ugly hunters prowled above the land, tireless and insatiable. The years had been fat for death's scavengers. They grew bloated and lazy, and the carrion stench was in their droppings. In the gray skeletons of stricken trees they perched with sleepy noddings or danced with awkward flappings over and around the things they found upon the ground. Always, though, there were others to take their places against the sun, and the days were never without them.

The years had been fat as guns roared across bank and clearing or knives cut with deep and silent certainty. Men had fallen in the scrub and high flats to lie where they had crumpled or crawl away to rot on the swamp's edge, clawing in an agonizing frenzy as their guts spilled and left a bloody trail. Terror spread over the land, and no man knew where he could turn and call another friend. Always the buzzards roamed above, banking and watching with greedy interest the helpless antics of the specks below and gorging themselves at a never ending feast.

"I guess I'll go huntin', Clay." The Indian spoke slowly and with an unconscious gravity his companion found slightly comical. It was almost as though each word were weighed and assayed for its true value before the lips were permitted to form the sound. "We can go swimmin' again tomorrow."

"Well," Clay nodded amicably, "let's make some tracks then. I've got to get my shirt and boots an' have 'em on before I get home; otherwise Old Clay'll start yellin' again." He smiled with a warming friendliness. "Old Clay's always sayin' that I'm gettin' to be more like an Indian than you are."

The contempt was there, unconsciously expressed in the thoughtless parroting of an old man's words, lying between them as a thin, cold blade. This Asseola understood, and it no longer held the power to bring him to a quick, blazing anger. He knew also that if Clay thought at all about what he had said, he would see only something faintly humorous in his grandfather's comparison.

They had been friends for a long time, he and the grandson of Clayfield Hammond, whose plantation stretched and measured itself by the mile along the high, rolling banks of the Apalachicola River. It was a friendship so old, as measured by the calendar of youth, that they both took it for granted. It had survived the

6

senseless, tempestuous quarrels of childhood and the stout contestings of adolescence. It had overrun Clayfield Hammond's bitter and unreasoning scorn for all things Indian and flourished in the shadow of the glowering and silent hatred of Asseola's people for the white man and the corruption he represented.

Asseola knew Old Clayfield well, for the man had become a symbol to be muttered over and exorcised around the fires and passed from lip to lip at the council circle of every Seminole town and *istihapo* along the river.

"As far as I can tell," he had once shouted, "Indians ain't nothing but red Negrahs, an' any damn fool ought to know a Negrah can't own nothin', leastways not along the Apalachicola he can't."

Every Indian in western Florida knew how well the old man had fought to give the strength of truth to his words. With an effort Asseola shrugged away the resentment that gathered whenever he heard the name of Hammond.

"Let's go." His hand touched Clay's shoulder. "It's late."

They parted at a fork in an old cow trail. One branch led a wandering path into Clayport. The other straggled away and lost itself in the scrub. Beyond lay the Seminole town.

"If Tommie Macon an' I get back tomorrow I'll let you know or come for you."

Clay hesitated. He was always puzzled by these moments of reserve when the Indian seemed to draw within himself. "All right," he said, "do that. I'll wait to hear from you." He turned to the trail that he must take.

At the end of the open stretch, where a straggly timber line was loosely drawn, Asseola halted and looked back at the now distant figure. As though he had been hailed Clay also turned in his tracks, and the figures of the two boys were sketched against the darkening purple of twilight. Across the hazy barren they faced each other, and then their hands lifted simultaneously in silent understanding.

Moving now into the woods Asseola was possessed by the uneasy presence of Old Clayfield Hammond, for the man's evil had been summoned up by his grandson's careless words. With bitter clarity he could recall one of the few times he had been permitted to stand freely in Hammond's presence.

They had met by accident on the high bluffs far below Clayport where a great brown arm of the river flung itself out in a deep curve. Here Blount's Fort had once stood, and here a fearful and bloody page in Seminole history had been written. Abandoned by the British in 1815, the well-stocked, stoutly constructed, and

7

heavily magazined post had been taken over by the Indians. They lived peacefully and in an atmosphere of new security. Their well-tended fields rose in hardy abundance, cattle grazed in the pasture lands. The fort became a center, the hub of a well-managed order. Over the long years many slaves had fled from their owners and found shelter with the Indians. The planters wanted them back; wanted them and their descendants who had been born and reared in freedom among the Seminoles. All Negroes became game to be hunted down and captured. So insistent became the demands of the great plantation operators that Congress and the Secretary of War were forced to listen.

From Nashville General Andrew Jackson wrote to his old friend General Gaines, then commanding the Army of the Frontier in Georgia.

"I have no doubt of the fact," Jackson instructed obliquely, "that Blount's Fort has been established by some villains for the purpose of rapine and plunder and that it ought to be blown up, regardless of the ground on which it stands; and if your mind shall have formed the same conclusion, destroy it and return the stolen Negroes and property to their rightful owners."

Outnumbered and outgunned, the Indians and their black allies fought from scrub and swamp, pillaging and killing when and where they could. Small bands ambushed the sweating, cursing, over-equipped troops and cut them down in the high brush. They met in swamp and glade and battled through the clogging reaches of the rolling scrub.

They fought in the dark of the moon on the slopes and lay in wait in the bright day to cut down stragglers. At night and in the hot, brassy glare of noon, the shrill, defiant war cry: "Yo-ho-e-hee! Yo-ho-e-hee!" sounded and would not be stilled.

Slowly, driven and harried by a power that seemed to feed upon itself and grow stronger, the Seminoles were beaten back. Always the pressure was there, relentless and constant. The avenues of escape were pinched and squeezed into narrow corridors. Then, somehow, it was over. It ended in brief and terrible encounters on the Suwannee and the Mickasukie and at St. Marks, and died with brief but bloody engagements that flared with the hot intensity of exploding powder kegs.

The Indians were battered and disorganized. Most of their villages along the Mickasukie and Apalachicola were charred and smoking. Their fields were seared and blackened, their herds cut to pieces or driven away. Jackson and his volunteers from Ten-

8

nessee and Georgia began to withdraw, and Chief McIntosh, who had rallied to Jackson's call with his Creek warriors, was prepared to pull back from the Territory and return home. The campaign frittered out, and yet no treaty had been signed, no agreement reached, no issue settled. Those of the dead who could be found were buried; others rotted where they fell. Along the trails and roads miserable bands of captive Negroes were whip-driven by exultant civilian captors to the border and slavery. Buzzards wheeled lower and lower in the hot, burnished dome of the sky, and the stench of death lay as a heavy cloud over the land.

That was part of the story the old men told before the fires at night, and they would mutter toothlessly and stare with clotted eyes into the orange embers, shaking their heads and whimpering for their lost strength. For as long as he could remember Asseola thought he had heard the names of Clinch and Blount's Fort. They were stitched into the fabric of Seminole life, dyed in blood and indelible.

It never occurred to him to wonder or question the voice that had called. He had awakened suddenly and in full consciousness, and lay for a moment staring up into the rustling thatch of the lodge he shared with half a dozen boys of his age. The night was frosty, cold and clear, and in it the stars seemed to snap and crackle. Save for the fire tender, squatting just beyond the fluttering circle of light, the town was asleep. For what seemed to be a long time Asseola lay without moving. The thing that had called to him in his sleep spoke again, and then he knew it was true. He slid quietly across the floor and dropped the short distance from the raised platform of the lodge to the ground. The great tent of darkness was gathered tightly, and above the treetops a million brilliants throbbed and pulsated within its deep folds. Far away a wildcat screamed in sharp frenzy, and the startled whoo-whoo of an owl asked its melancholy question. A small fountain of golden sparks blossomed and fell to earth as the fire tender pushed the log spokes of the wheel, thrusting them toward the flaming hub as they burned away.

Moving silently and without hesitation Asseola had gathered the things he would need: a light blanket, his gun, and a pair of heavy moccasins. He halted near the fire, and without speaking to the old man who watched him with curiosity-filled eyes, he packed a greasy skin pouch with chunks of deer, squirrel, and turtle meat from the gently warming pot hanging from a tripod of slender poles near the cooking lodge. Over this he spread several ladles of *sofskee*,

9

the thick corn-meal mush, and then drawing a leather thong about the sack's neck he tied it to his belt.

At the river he paused, peering out into the darkness and listening to the gentle, liquid whisper as the water laid its mouth against the shore. Then he crawled into the narrow cypress dugout and slipped out into the stream with the silent movement of a snake darting from a bank. The prow of the slender craft swung down-river.

It took him two days to complete the journey, for he was in no hurry. The voice, having spoken, was silent now, and not once did Asseola question its wisdom or wonder at the call that had sent him on this lonely pilgrimage.

He had paddled leisurely or allowed the canoe to drift with the current. At night, blanketed against the damp and creeping chill, he would lie in the bottom of the grounded canoe, listening to the sounds within the darkness: the rustle of small animals, the nervous guzzling of the deer that came to drink, the bellowing woof of a mating alligator, or the crackling screams of a loon, absorbed in its own insanity.

The years had laid a merciful hand on the ground where the fort once stood. The brush and hardy tangle of creeping vines had stolen in to blot out the great hole that had welled with crimson when the powder magazine exploded. Violets and small red and purple flowers made a bright pattern in the moist depressions, and in the warm and reassuring sunlight the leaves of oak and bay were waxed and shining.

For silent minutes Asseola stood on the ridge while excitement, like the slowly accelerating beat of a muffled drum, thundered within him, catching at his throat and making it difficult to breathe.

He lifted his head quickly at the sound of distant voices and the crashing of a heavy vehicle as it lumbered and pounded over and through the light growth along the ridge. A few moments later he could make out a stout, boat-shaped carriage and two Negroes, walking ahead, leading a powerful team down the overgrown wagon trail. A liveried driver sat on the narrow box, holding the useless reins in his hands and trying not to clutch at the rails for support as the carriage heaved and rolled.

From the depths of the broad, cushioned rear seat Old Clayfield Hammond shouted curses at the uneven road, the unhappy driver, and the two sweating lead men who stumbled and clutched at the throat latches on the nervous horses.

"You keep pullin' them horses' heads like that, Jupe," the old man screamed spitefully, "an' I'll stake you out on a roof until you're cooked as dry as a dead bitch's tit. Watch what you're doin' now. Careful. Easy. Easy, by God, I said easy!"

Not until the heavily slung vehicle, cradled on thick springs of leather, had swung in a half circle and ground to a halt did Asseola see Young Clay. He was seated facing his grandfather, and cramped into one corner to allow a resting place for Old Clay's useless leg, which was stretched out on the forward seat. The eyes of the two boys met, and then Clay raised a hand in greeting, smiling with pleasure at the sight of his friend.

"Hi, Caccosoci," he called.

Asseola's mouth twitched lightly. Clay's use of the Indian word for child was a small, obscure joke between them. Neither could remember why or when Clay first started calling him that, but as they grew older they found a warm, personal humor in the term.

"Hi." Asseola made no move to walk toward the carriage.

Old Clay peered at him from the depths of his seat; his hawklike face turned in a gesture of alert curiosity, his bright, inquisitive eyes snapping with a cold brilliance as they were bent upon the solitary figure. Finally he raised his shaggy head, satisfied with the results of his inspection.

"Hey, you boy. Come here." His voice, sharp and shrill as a reed whistle, sounded angry and impatient. "Come here, you boy."

Asseola advanced slowly, and at his approach the bay team reared excitedly, dancing with quick, high, nervous steps and half pulling the clucking slaves from their feet.

"Hold them horses, Jupe, hold them horses good an' easy or I'll drag you back to Clayport at the end of a trace."

Asseola stood by the carriage and gave no sign that he caught the slight drooping of one of Clay's eyelids as the boy winked at the old man's vituperations and grisly threats. Finally his grandfather turned his attention from the horses and stared moodily at the slender figure, who returned his inspection with easy confidence.

"What the hell you doin' way down the river like this, Powell?" The question was explosive and querulous.

"You know good an' well his name isn't Powell." Young Clay spat the accusation with quick anger, and for a moment his features were twisted into a vivid miniature, molding with almost frightening naturalness into a mask of his grandfather's face. "It's Asseola," he continued, "an' you know it good an' well, as well as I do."

If Old Clay was surprised at the challenge, he didn't show it. Grandfather and grandson stared at each other, matching glare for glare in bitter and silent conflict. Old Clay's eyes became mere slits beneath the heavy, iron-gray brows. His head was thrust slightly forward, and his hair, the color of burned powder, seemed to rise as the hackles on a snarling dog. Young Clay's hands on the edge of the seat were balled into knobs, but his attention didn't waver. Finally the old man grunted, and something close to a flicker of amusement rippled lightly along the thin line of his mouth as he contemplated the sturdy defiance in the opposite seat.

"What the hell's the difference?" he muttered as he drew back against the cushions. "Osceola or Powell or Marmaduke Horse-manure. If I call him Powell his name is Powell. Anyhow, I say, what's he doin' way hell an' gone down the river this way?"

"Fishin'." Asseola supplied the answer, and at the sound of his voice the man turned as though surprised to find him still there.

"Hummph." Hammond, apparently, had no ready retort to such a simple answer. His eyes swept quickly over the boy and noted the gun, swinging easily in the crook of one arm. "Damn funny fish to be roostin' in trees, waitin' to get themselves shot out of the branches. What do you say to that, hey?" he concluded triumphantly.

Asseola ignored the mellowing attitude, made no attempt to reply, and by his silence managed to convey a mild contempt for the heavy effort at humor. He stood straight and unyielding, a quiet, self-contained youth who waited in pride and without arrogance. Old Clay's gaze sharpened itself upon him and for a moment there was no sound save that made by the bright, metallic jingle of polished fittings on the harness as the horses fretted and tugged beneath restraining black hands.

"Don't look at me like that, boy." The words of warning were softly drawled, deadly serious in their gentleness, and razor keen. "Don't stare at me, boy," Hammond almost whispered. "I'd flay the skin off a Negrah who looked at me the way you're doin'."

The pause that followed was alive with unmistakable danger. It lay coiled, ready to strike, and subsided as warily as a startled rattlesnake. Asseola recognized it and waited tensely, his fingers curling imperceptibly about the trigger guard of his rifle.

"Look." There was no disguising the anxiety in Young Clay's voice as he sought to distract his grandfather's attention. "You said you wanted me to see something."

12

Slowly, reluctantly it seemed, Hammond turned from his contemplation of the Indian beside the carriage. "There was," he said, and the announcement was without gusto. "Just stand up an' look around. I made this trip so's you could see it. This here was Blount's Fort. Twelve feet thick the walls was, an' packed with Indians an' Negrahs. Old Duncan Clinch took two eighteen-pounders an' just naturally blew 'em to hell an' gone. I figured you ought to see the place. If I had my way," he shifted his gaze and stared fiercely down at Asseola, "I'd bring every thievin', Negrah-stealin', God-damned Seminole in the Territory here an' rub their noses into the ground so's they wouldn't never forget what can happen to 'em when they step out of line."

"Well," Young Clay objected, "I still don't see what business it was of Andrew Jackson or the President, either, if the Indians wanted to live here. They weren't botherin' anyone, were they? Just livin' here an' mindin' their own business. Besides, you told me yourself it was Spanish territory. What right did we have down here then anyhow?"

Old Clay chuckled, a rasping, unpleasant sound. "We had the right of some big guns an' a lot of troops," he said with satisfaction. "A fella don't need much more than that." He leaned forward and thrust a broad spatulate finger into his grandson's side. "If you can't see that, then you've had too much or too little schoolin', I can't figure which. When a man goes to clear some land he don't have to make no excuses or give no reasons to the roots an' scrub an' stumps he tears out. It ain't hardly no different with the Indians an' their damn shifty maroons. The land is goin' to be cleared, an' if some people are damn fools enough to get in the way, then they surer'n hell are goin' to get chopped up some. I'd like for you to remember that." He looked squarely at Asseola, although the words seemed to be directed to Young Clay. "Now," he turned and shouted impatiently at the driver and the lead boys, "we're startin' back for Clayport. Get them horses turned around."

Not until the carriage had disappeared behind the screening woods did Asseola turn. Then he walked slowly down the slope toward the river. At the water's edge he squatted, gun resting across his knees and arms crossed on the long barrel. With somber, bitter eyes he gazed unseeingly at the opposite bank. Perhaps, he thought, this was what he had come for. It had been necessary for him to stand and listen to the words from the lips of a baleful old man so he should know the truth and never again believe the hopeful

13

cacklings of the old and timid who said there would be no more fighting and peace would come to the land. The weak and frightened would like to believe this, but he knew now that Clayfield Hammond and others like him would never have it so. This he had understood and would remember.

2

Trotting lightly, swinging with easy, effortless strides around the obstructing clumps of underbrush cluttering his path through the forest, Asseola took the ascent of the long, low ridge where lay the town without a slackening of pace. The woods thinned out rapidly here and the slope was dotted with high, bronzed pines in which the wind played with hurried whispers. For the past half hour he had been aware of the dogs as their sharp, nervous yappings fanned out to meet him. As he approached the community, Asseola smiled quickly to himself, wondering why the dogs of Indians were always noisier than those belonging to other men and able to work themselves into a snarling, staccato frenzy over the most commonplace things. A floating, twirling feather, the streaking, furry blur of a startled rabbit, or even the unexpected appearance of a familiar figure would set them off on a hysterical, racing course that no amount of clubbing or shouted orders could quiet. Without apparent reason they would charge through camp, darting between legs and over lodge platforms, yelping and baying. Then, as quickly and as mysteriously as the feverish excitement had gripped them, it would die. They dropped in their tracks, muzzles outstretched between their paws, heaving sides pressed tightly to the earth, feigning sleep or indifference to everything about them. Now, warned by their abnormally acute senses of his silent descent, they were communicating with each other, working themselves into an uncontrollable state of agitation. Through the broken ranks of the trees he could catch fleeting glimpses of the town and the shadowy, unreal movements of people in the distance as they moved from lodge to lodge or halted to exchange a few words with each other. The scene was contrived in miniature and the men and women were small stuffed dolls animated by concealed strings. Through the heavy green tops of the pines, slender, twirling ribbons of thin gray smoke unrolled themselves in the light air and scented the afternoon with a sharp and acrid perfume. As he ran he could hear the shrill calls of the children at play, their piping cries lifting clearly above the yammering nonsense of the dogs.

Standing tight and secure among the tall pines, the orderly community was not really large enough to be called a town, although the Indians in their pride spoke of it so. The great Seminole towns with their hundreds of inhabitants had been torn apart by the furious winds of a lost war. What remained were small colonies, *istihapos*, or camps. They dotted the banks of the long river and rose feebly from the ashes of destroyed towns inland to the east. They clung determinedly to little patches in isolated sections.

Islisemole. Runaways. Wild men. In the Creek dialect the word had several shadings; and the white trader and soldier, with his contempt for any language not his own, Anglicized the expression to Seminole, and so spoke of the tribe that had raised its towns in Florida. Almost three quarters of a century had passed since the great chief Secoffee had rebelled against Creek authority. From Georgia and Alabama he gathered the dissenters and led them into the long peninsula held insecurely by Spain. For close to seventy-five years these Islisemoles had pursued their way as an independent nation. As a gesture of defiance they accepted the scornful term of runaways and took it as their name. Their towns, embracing also those of the Mickasukies, lay along the rich bottoms of the Apalachicola and Suwannee Rivers, and the Islisemoles became wealthy in large herds and flocks as well as Negro slaves. Their trade was widespread and constant, and the river, with its mouth on the Gulf, provided the highway down which they sent their cotton, hides, dressed skins, sugar, and indigo.

The story of Secoffee's rebellion and the great hegira was celebrated in song and story, to be chanted in proud accents and re-enacted in warlike pantomime until every Seminole child was familiar with the theme of liberty. Asseola had heard it many times, voiced in melancholy but stirring accents.

As he dropped his pace to a slow jog, the pack of dogs charged out to meet him, milling, circling, snarling, and yelping in a false display of anger. It was always so when they ran together, and a man's own dog, delirious with the excitement, sometimes would pretend not to know his master and put on a fierce show of menacing fury until the self-induced intoxication had worn itself out, dwindling to a series of feints and throaty growls of warning. He stooped quickly and hurled a heavy pine knot into their midst. They scattered with high yelps of terror and then fell upon the wood, worrying and tearing at it with slavering jaws.

The town was laid out with economical precision on the bluff among the pines. Water drained from the high ground and the camp stood dry and snug even during the torrential rains of the equinox, and in the long, hot days of the summer months caught at every passing breeze. Near the center of the compound the community cooking house was ringed by half a dozen platforms bearing mortars for the grinding of corn and chopping blocks on which meat and fish were prepared for pot and spit. Around the rim of the cleared space the lodges, weathered to the colors of the surrounding woods, were open on four sides.

As he strode toward his lodge, Asseola saw the wrinkled, bow-legged figure of Tommie Macon as he squatted before his own house, carefully measuring out the charges of powder into a polished horn. The man, so old now that he no longer bothered about the years, was gnarled and worn to the color of a well-tanned hide. A short, almost grotesquely formed ancient who seemed to be on the brink of emaciation and barely able to totter, Tommie Macon was the greatest of all hunters.

Not by any sign did the old man indicate that he was aware of Asseola's arrival, but the boy knew he had been observed and that Tommie Macon, for reasons of his own, had delayed his departure these many minutes while waiting for him. They would fire-hunt tonight, carrying aloft the bright torches of fat and bubbling pine to reflect in the eyes of the nervously curious deer, which would stand in trembling fascination and make clearly drawn targets of themselves. In the dawn, while it was still not quite light and the sky held the silvery-gray color of a fired oak log, they would strike along the ridges where the flocks of turkeys roosted. The deer they had killed would be hung and marked to be picked up later, but a turkey they would share for breakfast, cutting only the thick, heavy breast meat and toasting the livers on the end of a stick while the dog worried the carcass as the breast was turned and cooked to a slow perfection. He quickened his step and carefully avoided Tommie Macon's eyes as the old man abruptly lifted his head.

On all sides, as he crossed the tightly packed floor of the open circle, picking his way through the scattering groups of children at their play, the quiet evidence of a secure and well-ordered life laid itself over him as a protective cloak, and he was warmed, as always, beneath its folds. In the high corn as it stood shimmering in the fields; the long racks of split and golden fish smoked in the curling haze of bay and hickory fires to a glistening and oily sheen; the huge storage jars, filled with coarsely ground meal; the rows of drying and stretching frames, each with its laced hide strung as tightly as a drum's head; the women shifting with silent attention about their tasks, and the men, asleep or seated cross-legged on their mats, talking gravely and marking diagrams on the floor to prove a point; where a deer had run or a tree fallen, there was contentment and the satisfaction of a full existence as the town closed itself in against the night.

Hurrying, he became aware of the small figure at his side. The boy, not much beyond the toddling stage, was having a difficult time as he attempted to force his unsteady legs to maintain the pace, and he stumbled frequently, his round, grave face upturned as he bargained silently for attention. Asseola halted.

"So, little brother?" He waited.

The child's mouth twisted, evolving a series of contortions as he sought desperately to form the words that would adequately convey the importance of the thing that had happened to him. His small, wistful mouth opened soundlessly a couple of times, and then, with a helpless smile, he gave up. The effort of speaking, of attempting to put into words the event of the day, was too great. With a pride he could not conceal he lifted a small brown arm for Asseola's inspection. The skin had been angrily clawed from rounded shoulder to elbow, and the furrows were darkly red where the blood had dried in the shallow channels. With a seriousness matched only by that of the little one, Asseola bent down and examined the marks. He nodded with exaggerated awe and, with an effort, sternly thrust a smile from his lips. The youngster submitted to the inspection, his chest swelling with pride and gratification at the impression he had created.

Still holding the arm, Asseola looked down into the shining face. "You must have been very bad, little brother," he murmured. "Such scratches could have come only from a great act of disobedience."

The child bobbed his head in instant and rapt gratification at the accolade and strained on tiptoes in an effort to push the arm closer to Asseola's eyes. He waited for additional comment. Asseola made small clucking sounds of admiration, knowing well the importance of what had happened. In every family lodge there hung a dried wildcat paw, bound to a length of stick, or a comblike instrument, fashioned from bone, the teeth of which were needle-sharp. For serious fractures of discipline the mother would rake the offender's arm into crimson furrows. He could remember his arm's being so treated and the pride, once the pain had been mastered, with which he bore the marks as signs of growing up. He blew softly between his teeth, expressing astonishment at the mag-

18

nitude of the offense. A broad smile of pleasure spread across the youngster's face and he laughed with a throaty gurgle.

"A great act of disobedience," Asseola repeated. "Probably no other boy in this town or along the river can show such marks." He sighed regretfully, implying envy at not having been the one to perpetrate the deed and receive such fearful punishment.

The child nodded; his eyes filled with worship, completely overcome by the understanding and appreciation. Then, thoroughly satisfied as to the enormity of his disobedience and the adult manner with which he bore the punishment, he wheeled from Asseola and raced across the compound, eager for another audience and additional testimony. He halted before a group of men and waited, fidgeting anxiously until one should notice him.

Still laughing to himself, Asseola vaulted to the platform of his lodge, where a dozen or so boys of his own age mauled and wrestled with each other or chattered aimlessly as they boasted of their prowess in woods and river or with the young girls of the town. As he stepped between or over them, they shouted aimless insults and ribald suggestions as to how he had spent the day and voiced open wonder that such a man as Tommie Macon would burden himself with a clumsy hunter. Dodging the outstretched hands that would trip and bring him crashing to the floor, Asseola jeered his replies, entering into the good-humored banter as was expected. Living, eating, sleeping, hunting, and fighting together, they were all bound brothers, although members of different families. Here in this lodge they would live beneath one roof until, growing older, they would marry and set up lodges of their own. If they took girls of the town, they would remain within the community; but those who married outside would go, as was the custom, to the homes of their brides. Running the wriggling gantlet, Asseola went directly to a far corner of the platform and knelt on his sleeping mats before a long, narrow box. He had made it himself, fashioning the sides of sand-rubbed cypress with inserts of red cedar, smoothing the whole with rocks and fat until it gleamed with the soft, dull light of stone. As he hunched himself above the box, he was aware that the noisy chatter in the lodge was abruptly stilled, and knew, without looking around, that a dozen pairs of eyes, filled with eager desire, were following his every move. Deliberately he raised the lid and reached in with both hands to lift out the long rifle in its protective sheath of soft, oiled deerskin. As a murmur he heard the quick, sucking intake of breaths behind him

19

and understood the envy as it rippled along the half circle drawn about the corner.

Not along the river, certainly, and perhaps not in the entire Seminole country was there such a rifle as this. That a boy of eighteen should own it was the more remarkable. Never had anyone seen a piece like it; and the pride of the town in its perfection was so great Asseola could leave it unguarded and unlocked with certain confidence that no one would dare touch it in his absence.

Peeling back the skin, he placed the rifle on the matting, and, as always whenever he came to the box, he thought of the strangely tormented man who had put the gun in his hands. Dimly, now, he recognized the silent despair of the white trader, Powell, who had married his mother. As he grew older and his knowledge increased, he understood, in a measure, the never ending struggle this Powell had waged with a stiff Scotch-Presbyterian conscience over taking an Indian woman as wife. Having looked upon the slow-burning contempt in the eyes of white men when they met or had dealings with his people, Asseola knew some of the bitterness Robert William Powell had fed upon. The man had never spoken of these things to the boy. Having made his decision, he endured the consequences with grim and unrelenting determination, exercising an unholy zeal in mental flagellation as just punishment for the transgression against his church and heritage. The anguish of outraged principles he endured until his spirit rebelled and left him broken and helpless, no longer certain of anything. Save at such a moment as this, when he held the shining and delicately balanced rifle in his hands, Asseola gave little thought to the man or his whereabouts. He was part of a distant and murky past when all that had happened was not quite real; a time as nebulous as a half-remembered dream in which a Creek woman had taken her child, abandoned the ways of her people, and joined her fate and body with an alien to live in a rude log house in Clayport as Robert Powell's wife.

That this white man should have vanished from their lives as quietly and mysteriously as he had come no longer was viewed as strange. It was a thing of the years. To the child Asseola, then only six, it seemed as though this man had always been with them, moving with silent purpose and speaking in an unfamiliar tongue, the sounds of which were without meaning or cadence. Yet, and this puzzled him then, there were times when, lying warm and deliciously sleepy on his pallet near the cabin's hearth, he could vaguely recall other days and times. What had occurred was in a different land and the people he recognized in his half dream were not those he now knew. There had been a man then also, tall and strong, whose skin had been the color of his own. This man, too, shared his mother's bed, but he had called him son with pride, tossed him high into the air, and sometimes placed him astride a horse before him and rode with the wind. Time plucked with uncertain fingers at the strings of memory; the sound was muted and indistinct but wavered persistently as a dying echo. Curious as he was, he had never ventured to ask his mother about this first man or of the people from whom they had come.

Although eight years had passed and many things had happened since they stood together, the image of Powell was clear. Bending above the rifle now, he closed his eyes and saw again the tall, gaunt figure as it filled the doorway or stooped beneath the lintel to enter the single room. He could recall without effort the deep, harsh, and accusing voice as it spoke the words read from a large, leather-bound book spread open across bony knees before the fireplace. Night after night, Powell would sit in the uncertain light of the fire. Sometimes, when the wind and rain scratched and tore outside, his voice would rise to a terrible but suppressed fury and the words from the book mounted one upon the other with frightening impact. What the man spoke of the boy could not know, but the tone was bitter with accusation and wrathful majesty. Huddled within his blankets in a corner, peering with fox-bright eyes from the shadows, Asseola would watch the man and listen, wondering at the thunder of his tones and the pain carving his features into deep furrows. There had been nights, also, when Powell would rise from his reading with a sharp oath, the book falling heavily to the floor, and he kicking at it savagely, striding out into the darkness, from which he would not return until morning had laid a brush across the eastern sky.

Yet, thinking of him, Asseola knew he was not a forbidding man. He could be surprisingly gentle and understanding. Now and then, returning from the frequent trips downriver, he would bring a small knife or a sack of brilliantly colored marbles or drop a bolt of gay cloth into his mother's lap. He would tell, in measured words, of what he had done, where he had been, and the things to be seen along the river and in the cities of New Orleans and Pensacola. Once, after being warmed by several long draughts from a wicker-covered jug, he had rummaged through a neatly packed bale. From it he took a short skirt of many colors, not unlike those worn by the Islisemoles in the neighborhood of Clayport. Fitting the garment

21

about his waist, drawing on heavy, patterned stockings and strange shoes with silver buckles, he roared with approval as the Highlander emerged, barbarically resplendent from the drab cocoon of a frontier cabin. To the wild shrilling of the pipes slung across one shoulder, he twirled and danced with the grotesque dignity of a giant crane. Asseola had screamed with delight at the spectacle, hugging himself in inarticulate rapture as the tempo of the fling mounted. Even the woman, usually silent and impassive, smiled and rocked gently back and forth on her stool, beady eyes following every measure of the dance. When it ended, Powell took several long pulls from the jug as if to keep from remembering he had played the fool. Then, almost regretfully, he divested himself of the fine garments and moodily repacked them in the bale. Never again during the years they were together in the cabin did Asseola or the woman see the costume, or did Powell make reference to it.

Frequently Powell had taken the boy into Clayport, and as they walked down the sandy length of the main street, churned into a spinning channel by horsemen, heavy wagons, and droves of cattle, Asseola marched proudly and did his best to imitate the gravity of the man. His eyes, though, grew wide at the spectacle of many people: Spanish soldiers in bright uniform, shouldering heavy muskets; hunters, traders, and frontiersmen lounging before posts and taverns; files of silent Indians moving in from the deep woods carrying small packs of furs, hides, alligator skins, egret plumes, baskets of grain, and freshly butchered carcasses of deer and pig for sale or barter; these provided a multicolored and ever shifting tapestry.

It was in Clayport, he thought, he had first heard the name of Powell and understood it belonged to the man. They had walked from the road, out of the bright sunlight, into the low, dimly cool room of the tavern. Here voices seemed unnaturally loud, and there was an odor, rankly sweet and perplexing, in the air. Men standing at a waist-high counter were drinking steadily and banging their mugs on the shelf as they were emptied. Other men sprawled in chairs, asleep or gnawing hungrily at huge chunks of meat and yellow corn bread. Powell walked purposefully to the bar, spoke, and received a measure of whisky. He downed it quickly as the boy watched, and then wiped at his mouth with sharp knuckles. A small pool of liquid ringed a spot where a cup had stood, and Asseola timidly touched it with a finger tip, carrying a drop to his tongue. The sensation was as though he had lifted a small coal to his mouth,

22

and he blinked with astonishment. Abruptly he was conscious of a roaring gust of laughter, and looked up quickly to see the fierce, strange men regarding him with bellowing delight.

"By God, Powell," a man at the bar yelled happily, "if that little son of a bitch ain't Scotch, he's sure enough all Indian. Look at him dip into that rum." He extended his cup invitingly. "Here, boy, take a swig. By God, there ain't anythin' funnier than a drunk Indian." He shouted with obscene hilarity as Asseola backed quickly away.

With a sweep of his arm, Powell had knocked the drink from the stranger's hand, and it flew in a bright crescent across the room. The laughter died immediately, and there was heavy silence along the bar. Then Powell did a strange and wonderful thing. He reached down and took the fingers of the frightened boy in his own. Asseola could remember with what confidence he had clung to them and glanced up with a quick, shy smile of gratitude. Then, stiffly and together, they walked from the room into the sunlight. The jeering, profane laughter following them rolled out of the door as a small enveloping cloud.

From this man, whose name he now knew was Powell, he learned many things. With painful concentration he had forced his tongue to master the unfamiliar sounds of the man's speech. The trader, returning from one of his trips, brought as a gift a tattered primer. Each night thereafter he would sit in the firelight at the man's feet to spell out the words and utter them as instructed. He could remember Powell shaking his head with bemused patience.

"Aye, lad," he said wonderingly, "I don't doubt you'll learn the language; but it is a remarkably fearful accent you're goin' to have at the end with a Scotsman's burr an' the Indian sounds maulin' like fightin' cats in the middle of the Queen's own English."

From Powell he learned to skin a deer, quickly and cleanly without tearing the hide. He had been shown how to pack a horse so the load would not slip and gall the animal. He mastered the trick of pouring the silvery, hot metal into molds and learned to file and smooth the bullets after they had cooled. He learned how to load and prime the long rifle and not to shut his eyes against its flashing roar. Sometimes at night, when the mood was upon him, the man would tell incredible stories of faraway places; of the great seas and the ships upon them, of towns and cities with strange names: Philadelphia, New Orleans, Savannah, Charleston. He learned of money, holding the coins and pieces of paper with which the white

23

men traded, and he wondered, a little, how such things could have a value comparable to the shiny softness of a doeskin or a measure of corn from which flat cakes were made.

They had hunted together, the boy trudging stalwartly beside the man, thrusting back his small shoulders against the weariness overtaking him on the long miles. There had been nights they spent along the river, sitting cross-legged within the opening of a lean-to hastily thrown together and looking out at the small fire as it tossed rippling waves of heat at them. At such times Powell would talk; more, it seemed, to himself than to the boy. Speaking softly, he would tell of how he had come first to the Creek country and then later to Florida. As the words gathered and flowed, a bitterness would creep into the voice, and Asseola could sense that some great shame and a feeling of guilt tore and wracked him. Later, long after he was supposed to be asleep, he would lie in the dark with wide-open and wondering eyes, staring at the hunched frame of the man, blocked against the dying fire, a picture of silent torment.

Left much to himself, Asseola went frequently to the settlement of Clayport. Huddled unobtrusively against the weathered side of a building, he listened to the speech of the white men, marveling at their sudden furies and unsuspected violence. He learned to look calmly upon their quick, roaring brawls as they catapulted from the tavern and beat each other into insensibility before the doors. He watched and became accustomed to the sharp report of pistol and the silent deadliness of a knife thrust. Life was vigorous and uncertain, and men's fears were set against their cupidity in bloody wrangles. Sometimes, waiting on the edge of the settlement beside the heavily rutted road, he would stand as a plodding line of Indians materialized from the deep woods. Bound with their goods for the trading post, the men and women walked, not in pride but as those already resigned to a system of inequity. Vaguely he knew these were his people; understood they belonged to him as he did to them, although he did not live in their town and even the clothing he wore was different. As they passed, he was conscious of quick, sidelong glances from beneath lowered eyes; but, when he once raised a hand in greeting, there was no reply. This, he thought, was because he lived close to the village and his ways were no longer theirs. They were suspicious and uncertain of his presence.

Of this and other things that puzzled him he tried to speak with his mother. Why did they live as they did, being neither Indian nor part of the white community? How was it that strange people in the village sometimes called him Powell, while others gave the sound of Osceola to his name of Asseola? Instead of satisfaction he received only a sharp rap across his hand and silence.

It was while they shared the cabin with Powell that he first saw the young white boy whose name, he later learned, was Hammond. He had been playing near the road when the magnificent, high red carriage, hauled recklessly by two charging horses, came sluing and whirling from the river trail. Striking a deeply rutted section, the vehicle jounced and skidded, plowing a sidelong course in a high shower of sand until it shuddered to a halt. From the cushioned seat a shaggy and terrifying figure screamed fearful curses at the unhappy driver, who was attempting to ease the trembling horses back on the road. Beside him, his eyes snapping with excitement, a young boy added his treble commands to those of the old man, bouncing up and down with demoniacal glee while the miserable Negro rolled his eyes in helpless fright as he attempted to obey the orders of both and at the same time unscramble the confused tangle. In exasperation, the old man gave the boy a sudden push, half thrusting him from the carriage.

"God damn you, Clay," he yelled furiously, "shut that monkey mouth. When I need any help runnin' my rig, I'll call for it."

Clinging to the handrail, swinging back and forth with unmistakable delight, the white boy paused as he saw the solemn figure of the Indian youth. For a moment they stared at each other with wary interest, and then young Clay grinned.

"Hello," he said suddenly.

Asseola was too surprised to answer, but his eyes lighted and he experienced a sudden warmth and a strange feeling of kinship. For the first time someone of his own age had spoken to him, and he wanted to treasure the experience.

"Ain't this the damnedest racket you ever heard?" Young Clay nodded his tow head in the direction of his infuriated grandfather and the bedeviled coachman, who couldn't make up his mind whether to soothe the horses or make quick replies to his master.

Clayfield Hammond's huge hand shot out and dragged the boy into the seat. A moment later the carriage was eased back into the ruts and spun away in the direction of Clayport. Asseola waited until it was out of sight before he could bring himself to turn away. Throughout the day, and until he went to sleep that night, the unexpected friendliness of the white boy remained with him, and he tried to hold the memory of it tightly to his breast.

25

Balancing the rifle now in his hands, Asseola was oblivious of the youths of the lodge gathered behind him. Almost caressingly he ran his fingers the length of the barrel. An engraved design of a twisted vine and slender leaves ran from lock to forward sight, and beneath his finger tips he could feel the sharp, clean marks of the artist's tool. The stock of black walnut was silver bound and on the butt plate the craftsman had set his name: John Altmus, Lancaster, Pa., 1790. For fifteen hundred feet the rifle would carry hard and true. He had seen this proved by Tommie Macon, who had drilled a roosting turkey at that distance. Many men had examined the rifle, openly coveting it and expressing surprise and wonder that a boy should own such a treasure. In the presence of white traders and hunters Asseola had held the rifle fearfully, refusing them permission to examine or even touch it. Tommie Macon had warned him many times that such was the nature of white men that they would accuse him of stealing it and so take it from him on the pretext of finding the rightful owner. Here, in his lodge, it was safe. This he knew. Envy might consume the bodies of the boys with whom he lived, but they would never lay hands on the rifle without his permission.

With a sensitive thumb he felt the spring of the hammer, recalling how the man Powell had spoken on the night years ago. He had been sitting in silent meditation before the fire, the big book unopened in his lap. He had not spoken throughout the evening meal, which they took, as he instructed, at a table, helping themselves to portions from the small pots and vessels in which he had directed the woman to serve food. Later he had filled his pipe, but it remained cold and unlighted, cuddled within his hands. From his place against the wall, Asseola had watched him, and somehow he was not surprised when his name was called.

"Come here, lad." Powell spoke softly. "I'd have a word with you this night."

As a puppy might answer a summons, uncertain but eager, Asseola crept to the man's side and waited while frosty blue eyes regarded him thoughtfully.

"I am going away," Powell said deliberately. "Of this I have already spoken to your mother, although I doubt she fully understands the reasons for my decision. 'Tis the way of a woman to believe only that a man becomes tired of her. This, I will say to you, is not true."

He held the blackened pipe bowl between his fingers and the

irelight reflected on its smooth and shiny surface. Asseola noted with wonder that the hands trembled slightly.

"Some of what I will say to you now," Powell continued with difficulty, "will make little sense, but 'tis of no matter between us. When a man does a thing, as I have done, outside his conscience, then the evil begins to live with him and becomes a black thing, chewing slowly at his insides and giving him no peace. There are those who have called me a fool for marrying the woman, saying it would have been a simple thing to bed with her and having no word of wife. In such a way," his smile was wintery and without humor, "a man thinks he can make a nonnie of his faith."

He bent forward and thrust a sliver of pine into the fire, carrying the flame to his pipe and drawing with deep satisfaction. The splinter curled and wasted and he waited until it had burned to his finger tips before pinching it out.

"The name of Powell," he said thoughtfully, "I could have given you, for already two great chiefs of your people carry the Scots' blood in their veins and bear the names of McIntosh and McGillivray." He chuckled mirthlessly. "It has been said that the only colonization the Scots have ever done has been in the wombs of their adversaries' women. But," he stretched out his hand and laid it for an instant on Asseola's head, "since Indian you are and likely to remain, I think 'tis better you should be called as one."

He sighed heavily and dropped his brow to bony, upthrust fists, resting there for a moment as though to ease some great pain. Asseola waited, wondering why the man should speak so.

" 'Tis no fine future you face, boy. There will be much blood spilt before this business between your people and—" he hesitated, "aye, I'll have to say it—mine is finished. When the weak have things coveted by the strong, the results have never been in doubt. So you'll fall upon each other with knife, hatchet, and gun, and they'll drive you out or reduce you to a pitiful handful of basket weavers and cattle tenders. While the hacking is going on there will be rare words of hypocrisy uttered in Congress and you will be told how the government seeks only your welfare and to effect the harmonious junction of those who have with those who have not. Not one syllable of right or wrong will be uttered, for that would serve only to tear away the bloody mask and reveal the truth, a thing inclined to give legislators a queasy feeling and spoil their suppers. I would like to leave you something better." He rose and reached up to the rack above the fireplace, lifting from its pegs the long rifle. "Courage," he continued, standing with his back against the fire and

27

holding the gun before him, "you have in good measure for a lad. Understanding will be thrust upon you. In the assimilation of the latter you will need something to lean upon." He extended the rifle.

Asseola raised himself slowly from the floor and stood before the man. Much of what Powell had said he could not understand, but he was filled with the solemn music of the words and his features were grave as his face tilted and his eyes met and clung to those looking down from the shadows.

"Take this now." The man laid the rifle across the boy's outstretched arms and smiled as they sagged a little beneath its weight. "It may serve you well in the years to come or find you a quick grave. In any event, it is yours, and there's no finer piece in the Territory. Take care of it, and—" For a moment he seemed to be on the point of touching him, then drew back. "Take care of it and yourself." He turned then and walked out and they never saw him again.

Though his mother did not speak of it in the days following, Asseola was aware she no longer intended to live in the cabin. For a week she dressed only in her oldest clothes, sitting silently before the cold fireplace, refusing food and his timid offers of companionship. At the end of the seventh day, late in the afternoon, she took his hand and they walked together to the road. By its side they waited until a small band of the Islisemoles, returning from Clayport, drew past. At the end of the file they stepped into the road and joined it. No one of the group spoke or appeared to notice their presence.

Stumbling a little now and then beneath the heavy burden of the rifle, Asseola forced his glance to remain on the back of the man before him, staring straight ahead and trying not to betray the excitement welling within his body. These were his people, and he walked with them as had his father and his father before him.

Within the circle of the town the group broke apart and scattered, and as yet no word had been uttered. His mother moved slowly toward the center of the compound and paused, her glance sweeping the lodges. Then, without hesitation, she walked to one, and with the boy at her side, stood waiting.

An old man was seated cross-legged on his mat, his hands dropped limply in his lap, his head drooping beneath withered shoulders. For a long time he remained so, as the woman and boy waited. Then, slowly, as though awakening from a deep sleep, he lifted his eyes and nodded.

"I am," the woman spoke clearly and at her words every sound

28

within the town seemed to be quieted, "I am Creek and was wife to the warrior Amaltha. This," she laid her hand on Asseola's arm, "is his son."

The old man didn't shift his position but his eyes swept quickly from the woman to the boy and rested upon him an instant. Then he lifted one hand slowly and nodded.

"You are one of us," he said. "We take back what is our own and you are welcome."

These things had, it seemed now, happened so long ago that they were without reality, yet never did he take the rifle from its case without the memory of them flashing sharply through his mind as a series of clearly drawn pictures. With an impatient exclamation he dropped the lid on the box. Already he had wasted much time. From a half crouch he turned and saw the bent figure of Tommie Macon disappearing past his lodge. The old man, he knew, would be angry over his impudence and the casual treatment of the honor to hunt with him.

Pushing aside the eager questions of his companions, he dropped over the edge of the platform and hurried after the retreating hunter, thinking rapidly of the subtle bits of flattery and acts of humility that would put the old man into a good humor before they should be gathered together in the night and come across their first deer.

3

REARED boldly against the dusky curtain of an untracked wilderness, commanding a sweep of the churned and rolling country that lay as a gray-green, static sea to the horizon, the Hammond plantation house stood as a challenge to those who would enter this new territory.

Old Clay scorned the architectural effects of Mississippi, Georgia, and Alabama. He built with a lavish but clumsy hand and created a fortified post out of his plantation and the trading settlement of Clayport, which had grown up outside its boundaries. From this remote bastion he was, he announced to all who would listen, prepared to stand off the Army of the United States, if it became necessary, as well as cope with the open hostility of the Indians and the predatory sorties of the organized bands of slave hunters who slipped into the Territory to hunt down and carry off the miserable, fugitive Negroes who had fled to the Seminole country.

To bolster his position he had searched the border towns along the Georgia line sixty miles away and sent word into the deep reaches of the Okefenokee Swamp. He picked and culled through the thieves, cutthroats, deserters from the Army, and assorted renegades he found there until he had selected twenty-five of the most vicious and unregenerate scoundrels to be gathered together along the eastern seaboard and hammered them into a Caesar's guard.

Having drawn his furtive legion, he set about whipping it into a semblance of discipline, holding the murderous band of dubious loyalty by his furious will, binding them to him through their common knavery and fear. He dressed, armed, and paid them well, allowing them to drink freely from the rum distilled from the acres of cane and to rut like eager hogs through the plantation's slave quarters. Their services and their mulatto bastards he took in fee, along with the other produce from the pens and acres, to be turned to his own profit. He imported rifles, side arms, swords, and uniforms of a sort, drilling the ill-starred lot in military maneuvers from an old Army manual in a shrill and vituperative tongue as he watched them wheel and form in sullen obedience to his commands.

"Someday you border scum may have to fight somethin' stronger than a bottle," he would scream, "an' when that day comes what I'm teachin' you here an' now may save your dirty hides!"

At the conclusion of each formation he forced the men to line up and pass in single file before the heavy litter on which he was carried to the field. There, beneath his burning eyes, they would stack their arms before him. Later the equipment was taken away and locked in the small arsenal he maintained in the big house.

"If you sons of bitches want to kill each other," he shrilled triumphantly once, "do it with your knives. I ain't goin' to have my good powder wasted."

Accountable only to the furious old man who, despite the twisted, withered leg that bound him to a chair or litter, ruled them with raging abuse, the tough and efficient guard swaggered through the settlement, fighting and brawling and holding the Indians, Negroes, and white traders in a tightening grip of fear and uncertainty.

The stories of Old Clayfield Hammond and the rumors out of Clayport were passed through every post and tavern on the coast from St. Augustine to Boston. They were carried by hunters and traders through the back country of Georgia and the Carolinas, spread into the ports along the Gulf from Pensacola to New Orleans, and repeated on the broad porches and around the fine tables of plantations in Louisiana and Mississippi.

Along the Georgia border, where the Hammond legend was a demonstrable fact, the name of Old Clay was mentioned in respectful accents. The citizens of the state were compelled to awe by what went on in Clayport and by an old man who feared nothing. The Georgia planters were not without their own fire, and to prove it they had once caused the sovereign state to declare war on His Most Christian Majesty Ferdinand VII of Spain, backing up their challenge with an invading army that marched into Spanish territory when that unhappy monarch could not or would not force the return of their runaway slaves. Old Clay's princely attitude appealed to both their imagination and their greed. In the Seminole towns and among the Indians who elected to live and trade along the fringes of Clayport, Hammond's reputation became an almost mythical fury, an evil spirit to be propitiated and avoided if possible.

"I kept my land an' stayed on it whilst the Spanish were here," he roared angrily at the reports that land grants were to be reexamined, titles searched and authenticated, and new surveys run. "I chased the Indians off it an' laid out my fields. I stayed here while the God-damned stupid British were hellin' around at the mouth

31

of the river. Now, it would be a thing, wouldn't it, if I was asked to whack it up by a bunch of fools in Washington who couldn't walk half a mile out of Clayport without havin' an Indian slit their throats?"

Clayfield Hammond had invaded the lush Territory of Florida with little more than a few head of livestock, a couple of wagons, and half a dozen slaves, all that remained after a charming but unstable parent had run through a huge Georgia fortune. With this meager equipment he set about the business of battering an untamed country and its resentful Indian inhabitants into submission. His enormous grant of land from the Spanish crown was of dubious value, for the transaction was effected between him and a short-termed governor at St. Augustine. Hammond outlined the acres he wanted and dropped a fat envelope on the official's desk. The governor, mentally estimating the amount before him, demurred half-heartedly over the extent of his visitor's desires.

"It is the custom, *señor*," he said, "in granting such an enormity of land, that His Majesty's Government stipulate a certain crop be raised."

Clayfield Hammond snorted impatiently. "By God, Your Excellency," he replied, "if that's all that's standin' in the way, let's get together. Suppose we say the principal crop is to be pine trees? That'll do it. Pine trees an' hell. One is there already an' the other I'll raise with the Indians."

The official shrugged and fingered the envelope. "It shall be as you say," he agreed softly, and then smiled tiredly. "Perhaps, though, His Majesty's Government would be as well satisfied if your ambition was limited to the pine trees already standing."

From time to time Hammond added to his stock of slaves through outright purchases at auctions across the border. Whenever possible, however, he stole the blacks, pursuing the fugitives with horse and dogs and contesting their ownership with gun and fist. Through furtive channels he managed to spread the word in the slave quarters on the plantations in Alabama and Georgia that a happy and bright haven awaited those who could make their way to his acres in the Spanish territory. Only Hammond ever knew how many Negroes were enticed and deluded by these fanciful tales and came willingly to place themselves in unending bondage behind the high barriers of his stockade. The threats and outraged screams for justice rising from over the border he heard dimly or not at all, and his villainy was difficult to prove. Searching parties never located their quarry on his land. Hammond saw to it that the slave hunters

32

were well fed and generously supplied with liquor, suggesting as they ate and drank that their Negroes were undoubtedly hiding with the Seminoles, by whom they must have been stolen.

Unscrupulous, fearless, and with an ambition suckled by a greedy wolf, Clayfield Hammond put everything to his use. When it suited his purpose he played upon the timorous, indecisive colonial policy of Spain, wrapping himself in that nation's flag and loudly calling upon Castile for protection. When the necessity for such measures was past he openly flouted its laws, backing up his decisions with his force of renegades.

Under the bright knives and axes of his blacks the clearings spread. Cane thrust its bright tops to the sun. Cotton flourished in heavy-bolled, luxuriant rows. Cattle moved in slow contentment across his range. Rice sprouted in the rich bottoms. Indigo and corn added their yield, and saws whined through the inexhaustible stands of pine. Outbuildings, storehouses, and mills rose and weathered to a silvery grayness in the gentle climate, and Clayfield Hammond's wealth flowed steadily down the Apalachicola and was funneled into ships and warehouses.

With the accumulation of a fortune, respectability of a sort came to Hammond. The dark and angry mutterings of slaveowners in neighboring states were quieted and dulled by time. The bitterly accurate epithets lost their sting. Hammond found and grasped the opportunity to make a few judicious loans to hard-pressed but socially prominent and influential planters in near-by Georgia and South Carolina. In the crisis of crop failure he extended a generous hand to the large estates in the neighborhood of Tallahassi and maintained an easy business relationship with the commercial houses in Mobile, New Orleans, and Charleston. These things he did, not out of any budding social consciousness but rather because he considered them to be politic. He maintained an open and hospitable house for the infrequent traveler of importance and made himself a gracious and entertaining host. As a result of these well-planned maneuvers he commanded a certain respect, if not admiration, in the tight circle of plantation aristocracy.

When the time came to raise a more elaborate dwelling place on his acres, Clayfield Hammond drew freely from his memory. Without the services of an architect he sketched his own plans, expanding or modifying them as the work progressed. He sent crews into the swamps to cut and inch out huge cypress trees. Tall, straight pines wavered and crashed and were dragged to the spinning saw of the plantation mill. Material for the foundation and a crew of masons and carpenters were brought up-river or made the long journey inland from St. Augustine over a rough and unmarked trail. Because the ornamental wrought-iron grillework on a balcony he had seen in New Orleans appealed to him, he bought the house and tore away such pieces as he desired. The flooring, entire room sections of exquisite paneling, delicately contrived mantels and door-frames, were ripped up and sent by sailing ship to Apalachicola Bay, where they were transferred to a river craft for the upstream voyage. Transportation was uncertain and the times turbulent, but the house rose steadily. Low and broad of room, a wide porch commanding an uninterrupted view of the gently rolling fields, the building was both practical and comfortable, and it lay under the warm sun, shaded by heavy, moss-draped oaks that flung their tattered gray beards with every passing wind. Well satisfied with what he had done, Clayfield Hammond crossed the border once again and returned months later with his bride.

Uncertain and frightened, Carla Lanceford Hammond lived only long enough to bear Clayfield a son. Suffering with the rude surgery of the frontier, for Hammond insisted that the baby be born on his land, Carla Hammond died in childbirth, leaving behind her a wracked and bitter man who cursed his own stupidity and the mewling red infant in the arms of a slave woman. When the child was old enough to travel he sent him with a nurse to the grand-parents in Mobile with instructions that the boy be raised by them, disclaiming all interest in his future. The name of Hammond he would bear, and when the time came a rightful share of inheritance would be his. Other than this, the man wanted no reminder of the boy upon whose small shoulders he had laid the responsibility for his own stubbornness and folly. With absorbing vigor he hurled the full weight of his energy into the development of the plantation, snatching greedily at every dollar, driving himself and his slaves to exhaustion. He became a scourge to the Indians and the small farm owners who dared settle within riding distance of him. In bitter loneliness he shut himself off from the small world and knew but one ambition, to become the wealthiest and most powerful man in Florida.

Then occurred the accident that struck at the deep roots of his self-sufficiency. He had gone into the darkened stall to examine the leg of a nervous, ill-tempered stallion whose limp had been reported by the groom. Without a preliminary stroking, which might have quieted and reassured the animal, he bent down and tugged at the injured leg. With a high note of terror and pain the animal lashed out, battering and cornering Hammond within the narrow box. When he was finally rescued his hip and knee were crushed and splintered into a hopeless pulpy mass.

Throughout the long, pain-shot days and nights that followed, Clayfield Hammond lay beneath the billowing canopy of his bed. In his torment he became shrill-voiced and vindictive, cursing the doctors who had made the arduous journey to treat him, a helpless fury eating away at his soul as a malignant tumor. When he understood he would never walk again but must drag out the balance of his life trailing a twisted and withered leg or being carried in a chair or on a litter, he screamed obscene blasphemy from a horrible, saliva-dripping mouth, beating heavy fists against the pillows and ripping the bed covers to shreds in impotent fury.

The years brought no surcease from the agony. The pain in the useless leg was constant, but more terrible was the searing torment of broken pride and the humiliation of having to be carried and shifted, needing assistance whenever he wanted to move. He had tried to prop himself with a crutch, but there came a day when the support skidded and he fell, face down in the dirt, and lay in stricken helplessness, unable to turn or rise. To the two yard boys who had run to his assistance he bawled frightening threats until the terrified Negroes backed away and out of sight of the insane terror on the ground. Inch by inch, blubbering and sobbing, his face tortured out of all human resemblance, he dragged through the clinging sand, crawling on his belly with the wriggling, twisting motion of an injured snake, while the house and yard servants watched with horror from behind curtained windows or at the corners of the porch. At the foot of the steps he collapsed, and for two days he remained in a state of wild delirium until the fever passed. His first act upon recovering was to order the plantation overseer to get rid of the two Negroes who had witnessed his debasement.

"Sell 'em or shoot 'em," he commanded from his bed, "I don't care which, but don't let me ever see 'em again. I'll have no one about who looked upon me as I was."

The years and loneliness hardened the soul of Clayfield Hammond. His will and imperious attitude toward everyone and everything were unbending. He tolerated no suggestion or interference as he drew his frontier acres about him and raised their barriers against the trickling flow of immigration into the vast, unsettled land. His wealth was without flavor but he was unrelenting in the pursuit of more. When he went outside the house he was borne

35

almost regally on a litter, supported by six slaves and transferred to the glittering magnificence of his red and gold landau, built to order by German carriagewrights in Pennsylvania and reassembled on the plantation.

He watched and waited with brooding indifference as the sporadic fighting crackled throughout the land and the border states, ignoring the protestations of Spain, sent hard-hitting raiding parties against the Seminoles and their Negro allies.

"Whenever shootin' starts," he instructed his overseer, Salano, "you shoot back. I don't give a damn if it's Andrew Jackson or the King of Spain who begins the trouble. They ain't goin' to use my land for a battlefield. If they want to kill each other, then let 'em do it down the river or over on the east coast. If any of them bastards from Georgia tries to lay a hand on a Negrah of mine, we'll get it chopped off for him."

Only when this vicious scrub-to-creek guerrilla warfare interfered with the orderly movement of his commerce down the Apalachicola did he display any interest in the outcome. At such times he dispatched scurrilous letters to Washington and the harassed Spanish governor at St. Augustine, ordering an end to the trouble and offering to handle the situation himself if it was proving too much for the combined efforts of the United States and Spain.

Powerful, defending itself against all enemies and the changing times, the plantation was without laughter and occupied only with the creation of additional wealth. It was the retreat of a man of desperate fortune who snarled and raged at his useless leg and the childish helplessness of a once vigorous body. Clayfield Hammond fed upon himself, tasting the full bitterness of seclusion. He was bound to neither friend nor charitable impulse, and the days were long wearing.

When the opportunity to ease the bondage of his own tyrannical fury presented itself, he reached for it reluctantly, not well understanding why. Along the distant Gulf coast yellow fever struck at the port cities, licking in and out as a hot flame. It disappeared here and flared up there, running with a maniacal lack of direction. In Mobile it cut through the city, racing along the crowded water front and through the residential section. Before the epidemic waned and died it wiped out entire families, among them that of Clayfield Hammond's son. During a quarter of a century the man's only contact with the child he had looked upon so briefly had been in the form of stiff, impersonal communications transmitted through a firm of lawyers. He had evinced no interest in his youth or manhood

36

beyond seeing that he was liberally provided for by an annual draft arranged through a local commission house. Now he learned with surprise and troubled emotion that he had been a grandfather these past six years and the boy was the only surviving member of the household.

Hammond never fully understood what prompted him to claim the child and arrange the details of his journey and care from Mobile to the plantation. Conscience he had put aside years ago, and he felt no kinship for the son he had seen but once. The grandson was nothing but a name; yet he extended his hand, and as the day of the child's arrival neared he found himself possessed by a strange spirit of elation and eagerness. Although he loudly cursed the madness that had resulted in his burdening himself with a youngster and declared his intention of shipping him off the plantation as soon as proper arrangements could be made, he knew he was only tricking himself. Alone, he mused on the novelty of companionship in the insufferable monotony of the days and years.

From his carriage at the plantation wharf he watched while a small barge put out from the sloop, anchored midstream, and was worked to the dock. He waited, his keen eyes following every move, as the strange man, dressed in extravagantly foolish city clothes, walked from the pier holding the small fingers of a sturdy figure. He smiled beneath the hard, drawn line of his mouth as he noted how the child's head swiveled from side to side and the curiosity-filled eyes tried to record every fascinating detail of this new and richly colored scene. He called no greeting, though, nor permitted any relaxation in his attitude of fierce aloofness. When the pair halted beside his carriage he waited for the man to speak first.

"Mr. Hammond, suh?" The stranger spoke with a soft richness and his bow was one of elegant deference.

Clayfield Hammond inclined his head slightly but made no reply to the greeting. The man paused half expectantly, and as the moments lengthened a little frown of surprise and annoyance flashed briefly across his face. He glanced down at the boy and then returned his gaze to the carriage and its occupant.

"I am Marcus Whitmore, suh," he continued, "junior partner in the firm of Claypoole and Whitmore, solicitors in Mobile. This," his slender hand rested lightly on the boy's shoulder, "is your grandson, Arthur Lanceford Hammond. I am bringing him to you in obedience to your request and as the child's only immediate relative."

"Arthur's a hell of a name for a boy," Hammond snorted with disgust.

37

Whitmore permitted himself the briefest of smiles at the unexpectedness of the comment. "Well, suh," he said gently, "I'd say that's a matter of opinion."

"The hell it is," Clayfield Hammond snapped. "I said it was a hell of a name to give a boy, an' so it is."

The Mobile lawyer shrugged, indicating his unwillingness to discuss the merits or demerits of Arthur as a name.

Clayfield Hammond peered down at the child, who was staring up, regarding him with an intent and speculative attitude.

"Get in, boy." He dropped his voice but made no effort to soften the tone or make an invitation out of the command.

The boy turned a questioning glance toward Whitmore, who nodded encouragingly.

"It's all right, Arthur." Whitmore was reassuring. "This is your grandfather. You remember, the gentleman I told you about on the boat. You are going to live here with him."

The youngster hesitated. "Are you coming too?" he asked.

Whitmore shook his head. "No, I won't be able to come with you."

"You'll spend the night with us, of course," Hammond rumbled.

"Thank you, suh." Mr. Whitmore permitted himself a slight sarcasm. "As much as I would enjoy the privilege and the pleasure of your company, I am afraid I must say no. The captain of the sloop wants to take advantage of the fair wind for the return run downriver." He reached out and swung the boy to the carriage. "Good-by, Arthur." He accented the name with malicious joy. "And to you, suh, my respects, and also good-by." He lifted his hat, turned, settled it at a jaunty angle on his head, and strode quickly toward the wharf.

Perched on the seat facing his grandfather, his small legs dangling and swinging with the lurching of the carriage, the boy solemnly contemplated the man who returned his stare with cold appraisal.

"If you're my grandfather," he said abruptly after five minutes of silence, "why haven't I ever seen you before?"

"Because I ain't been around." Clayfield Hammond clipped the words. "I still say," he added belligerently, "Arthur is a hell of a name to give a boy."

The youngster refused to be intimidated. He stared thoughtfully out from his side of the carriage at the passing fields, leaning slightly forward to get a better view of the hands bent at their labor. Finally he drew back and contemplated the toe of his boot.

"What's your name?" He lifted his eyes quickly.

Hammond shifted his weight in the corner cushion and regarded the small, determined figure with surprise. His lips rippled soundlessly before he spoke.

"Clayfield, Clayfield Hammond," he said and waited.

The boy digested this information and his eyes wandered up and above the man's tousled head. For a few seconds he stared at the tumbling white clouds.

"I don't think," he said thoughtfully, "Arthur's any more a hell of a name than Clayfield."

A quick, discerning interest leaped in the man's moody reflection of his grandson's person. He straightened from the slouching position and cocked his head with a quizzical attitude.

"You don't, huh?" he asked with unabashed surprise.

"No." There was no impudence in the boy's tone. He was only stating an obvious fact to an equal. "No, I don't, an' I'll bet if your name was Arthur you wouldn't think so either."

"Well, I'll be God damned." Clayfield Hammond leaned back. He sucked through the spaces between his teeth, making sharp whistling sounds. He pulled at his nose and then rubbed the knuckles of one hand to his ear while his glance sharpened and covered the boy for details he had missed.

"Am I goin' to live here always?" The question seemed plucked from nowhere and was asked without any particular animation.

Oddly enough, the permanent nature of the obligation he had assumed hadn't occurred to Clayfield Hammond until it was so simply voiced by the boy. He mulled over the implications of the query for a moment.

"I guess so," he said finally, and looked at his grandson attentively. "I hadn't thought much about it, but I guess you'll live here an' someday run the whole damn place."

"Can I have a pony? Will you show me some Indians? Can I have a gun, a little one?" The questions tumbled over each other in their eagerness to escape.

Hammond braced himself against the swaying motion of the carriage and moved in the corner to ease the tension on the outthrust, useless leg.

"You want them things real bad?" he asked.

The boy nodded and he jiggled on his small bottom, no longer making an effort to suppress his excitement. His lips were parted and he waited expectantly.

39

"Well, now." The man was close to embarrassment and he cut his eyes around quickly, almost as though he wanted to make certain his words would not be overheard by a third person. "That's a lot of stuff for one boy."

Disappointment threw an enveloping shadow over the young face and hope died slowly in the child's eyes.

"Oh," Hammond was reassuring, "I ain't sayin' you couldn't have 'em." His attitude became one of a conspirator. "The only thing I'm sayin' is that to get 'em a boy would most likely have to do somethin'. Now," he hesitated, "like I said: Arthur is a hell of a name to give a boy. If we could change it, make up a new one—say, maybe, like Clayfield—then I guess we wouldn't have any trouble in findin' the things you want around the plantation."

"You mean you want my name to be the same as yours?" The boy was genuinely puzzled. "How would people tell us apart?"

"I guess there wouldn't be much trouble about that. Not for a while, anyhow. Besides, I'll just call you Clay, like they used to call me when I was your age."

"What'll I call you?" There was a shade of doubt in the tone.

"Well, God damn it!" Clayfield Hammond was on unfamiliar ground and as shy as a skittish horse. "If you'd been brought up right you'd know to call me sir right off without any question."

The boy was momentarily confused by the man's abrupt irascibility, and then he intuitively realized it was a sham, one of the perplexing idiosyncrasies adults indulged in. His eyes twinkled brightly.

"Yes, sir," he said. "When can I have the pony?"

This new world into which he had been tossed unfolded itself slowly for Young Clay. His only friends were the house slaves, his only intimate companion the Negro boy of his own age who played the dual role of servant and confidant. The vast plantation with its manifold activities absorbed everyone on it as a great sponge until it became difficult to think of people or places outside its boundaries. The cities and towns of which he read as he grew older were small satellites revolving slowly and without much meaning about the orbit of the Hammond acres. The boy became accustomed to violence and the spectacle of his grandfather's armed guard, alert and watchful. At the age of twelve he knew that the welling fury in the border states had overflowed, spilling the troops of the American army and its Creek allies into the territory of Spain and to whirling, bloody conflict with the Seminoles. He heard, as a distant thunder, of the massacre at Blount's Fort and saw the smoke of burning Seminole towns rising as smudged plumes into the sky. From the porch he watched as files of troops moved down the river trace and disappeared into the scrub. The tides of conflict eddied and lapped around the Hammond holdings and then receded.

From a succession of tutors, lured into the wild territory by Clayfield Hammond's irresistible offers of high salary, he progressed haltingly through his letters and simple figures to a smattering of English, history, geography, and mathematics, but the constant danger and furiously erupting times finally exhausted the hardiest and most enthusiastic pedagogues. The history being written across the crimson sky made books seem pallid and mustily archaic, and so he experienced no regret when the last of the scholarly adventurers hastily packed and left for safer and more comfortable posts.

"You can always go to school," Old Clay philosophized. "Can't see there's any great rush about things. We'll get around to it one of these days when all this God-damned fightin' stops."

Between the two there had grown a warm understanding. There was respect, also, but a stranger might never have suspected its existence from the lusty contradictions they tossed at each other's opinions. The child's early independence flowered. He clung firmly to what he considered to be his rights and kept inviolate the things he held as his own. As he approached his thirteenth birthday Old Clay voiced his theory of their positions.

"You can stop callin' me sir," he shouted angrily in the heat of argument. "Don't be so damn respectful. It's just an accident I'm kin to you, an' if I tell you to do somethin' you know damn well you don't have to. I'm stuck with you an' I know it, so don't be so mealymouthed while all the time you're tellin' me to go to hell under your breath. If there's anything I can't stand it's a 'possum-eyed hypocrite."

The association with one of his own and the companionship of a growing boy had no mellowing effect upon Clayfield Hammond, nor did it dull the edge of furious energy that was transmuted into greater wealth and power. If, in his secret heart, he found pleasure in the boy's development, he kept the emotion there, locked away as a shameful evidence of weakness. He watched Young Clay's constant association with the Indian Asseola, or Powell as he insisted upon calling him, with deriding amazement. He knew that the boy moved freely and with sympathetic understanding among the Seminoles, ate from their kettles, sat easily and without self-consciousness in

41

their lodges. He knew also that nothing he could say would change this.

"By God," he muttered once, "I don't need to be told you're in the house. I can smell the Indian on you a mile off."

"Do you know how they call you?" Clay grinned at his grandfather's petulance. "The man-who-bites-himself."

THE high candelabrum laid a pattern of gently wavering light down the length of the table, touching with soft radiance the bright pieces of silver and starched white sheen of heavy linen. It fired the channels and facets of rock crystal with sparkling color and fluttered on the small pools of black coffee in fragile cups. Slender decanters of straw-yellow Spanish brandy stood at the right hands of the three men, and the misty-blue smoke from heavy Cuban cigars ran in quick twirling ribbons between their fingers. Behind the chairs of the four at the table the shadowy forms of the slaves were motionless; carved ebony in the deepening gloom outside the oblong of light.

Leaning slightly forward, resting crossed arms on the edge of the table, Young Clay hung upon the words of the man to his right. Throughout the long meal he had watched him covertly, admiring the proud carriage of his head and the simple, forthright attitude of his address. He was fascinated by the richness of the man's speech, the controlled resonance of the tones that throbbed and dropped away to a whisper as the distant running of a sea. More than anything else, though, he found himself becoming a little excited over the sentiments Colonel Gad Humphreys uttered so casually.

"By God, sir!" Old Clay made no effort to disguise his impatient disgust and he interrupted with conscious rudeness. "If I'm to believe what you, as Indian agent in the Territory, are sayin' as official government policy, then the country is bein' run by a pack of fools." He leaned back in his chair and glared ferociously at his guest.

Instead of taking offense, Colonel Humphreys smiled patiently. "I'll have to confess, sir," he said with gentle humor, "our policy toward the Seminoles is something we run up each morning like a flag; only," he paused, "we're not always certain of its design."

On the opposite side of the table the second guest permitted himself a quick grimace of rueful humor. He lifted his finely modeled face toward the speaker. For a moment his dark, intense eyes sparkled and his slender fingers played lightly along the delicate stem of his brandy glass.

"It's one thing," Colonel Humphreys added, "to call the tune and quite another to get people to dance to it. Governor du Val," he inclined his head across the table, "will bear me out in that, although we do not always agree."

Old Clay was not to be put off. He rumbled, growling from the depths of his huge chair. A slave materialized from the murky depths of the room, refilled his brandy glass with a swift, unobtrusive motion, and stepped back to lose himself in the half-light.

"If you're goin' to start givin' the Indians rights," he argued, "then you might as well go on and give 'em to the Negrahs. Let everyone in the whole damn country do just as he pleases. Let the ignorant an' the savage stand in court an' argue with their betters an' you're invitin' a bloody war."

Colonel Humphreys carefully examined the long silver ash on the end of his cigar and then lifted a quick glance in the direction of his host.

"In any such conflict, Mr. Hammond," he said silkily, "you are going to be outnumbered. Is that what you are afraid of?"

Young Clay unconsciously tightened the fingers of his locked hands. No one, certainly not in his hearing, had ever spoken to his grandfather this way. Anxiously he waited for the response certain to come from the head of the table.

"Colonel Humphreys," Old Clay was so angry that he measured the weight and quality of each word, "I'm not afraid of anything or anyone. These are my acres. I tore them out of the wilderness with my own hands, an' I defy the small things God has seen fit to put upon the earth to take them from me."

"Times are changing, Mr. Hammond." Colonel Humphreys touched the corner of his mouth with a napkin.

The explosion from the deep recess of the big chair was muffled.

"They ain't changin' so much I can't keep up with 'em, an'," the old man thrust his head into the square of light, "if you an' the government ain't able to keep step I'll march for you." He drew a deep breath. "There's only one solution to the problem: round up the Indians an' ship 'em back to the Creeks in Arkansas, where they belong. Then you'll have an end to this trouble."

Governor du Val lifted his hand in a brief conciliatory gesture.

"I'm afraid, Mr. Hammond," he said thoughtfully, "you oversimplify the problem. The Seminoles, independent for seventy-five years, are not going back now as members of the Creek nation. The solution, as I see it, and," he hesitated, "as it is viewed in Washington,

44

is to fix firmly and for all times the boundaries within which the Indians may live and act as a sovereign nation."

"Hummph!" Old Clay belched his disgust.

"Sir." Colonel Humphreys shook his head, almost in sorrow. "It is easy enough to fix the boundaries for the Seminoles, but," he lifted his brandy glass and tilted the liquid into his mouth, "who is there to place a mark on the white man's acquisitiveness? Today you place the Indians there." He furrowed a line across the tablecloth with his coffee spoon. "Tomorrow you have half a dozen new settlers who want land, and they press across the border we have drawn." He turned his gaze to Old Clay. "What happens then? Do we stop the immigrants or do we push the Indians farther south?"

"How the hell do I know?" Old Clay bellowed. "That ain't my business."

"What, Mr. Hammond," Colonel Humphreys pressed the question, "do you suppose the Indians will say in the face of such dealing?"

Old Clay hunched his shoulders, leaning out of his chair, and pointed his cigar at his grandson.

"Ask him your questions," he rumbled. "God knows he spends enough time with them stinkin' savages to know what's in their minds."

Young Clay experienced a quick flush of embarrassment. Throughout the table conversation he had sat wonderingly, disturbed and excited. For the first time he heard a white man speak as Colonel Humphreys had, talking quietly and dispassionately of the Indians as though they were human and entitled to a measure of consideration. He ducked his head and pretended not to know that the Indian agent was turning his attention to him.

"Well, sir," Colonel Humphreys spoke without condescension and addressed him as an equal, "what will the Seminoles say?"

"They'll fight." Young Clay looked up and took confidence from the eyes regarding him with pleasant speculation. "They'll send their women an' children into the swamps an' they'll fight inch by inch, foot by foot, across an' down the peninsula."

Colonel Humphreys nodded. "I agree with you. And," he shifted his gaze to Hammond, "when that happens, then neither your plantation nor that of any other white man in the Territory will be far enough removed to be safe from fire, plunder, and bloodshed."

Old Clay thrust out his lower lip and his eyes tightened. "Sir," he answered, "I'll keep what is mine. Them that ain't able to do as much deserve to lose their holdings."

There was a moment of silence. Old Clay dropped his chin, sink

45

ing it to his breast as he peered out at his guest with the baleful expression of a cornered lynx. William du Val toyed absently with a coffee spoon, twisting it in his fingers to catch a beam from the candles. His attitude was one of detached interest.

"There are others," Colonel Humphreys suggested, "who are not so fortunate in their determination or so strongly situated."

Old Clay's laughter was without mirth. "Then, by God, they ain't entitled to nothin'. There's only two kinds of people in the world: them that can take an' keep an' them that should never have."

Colonel Humphreys nodded as though it was the reply he expected. "What," he asked thoughtfully, "do you suggest we do about our treaty with the Seminoles?"

"It shouldn't have been made." Old Clay's sledgelike fist thumped the table. "There's treaty enough in the rifle barrels of my men for me. Why should we deal an' treat with a pack of dirty Indians any more than I'd argue with a half-acre white settler if he was squattin' on a piece I wanted? I'd run his ass off or fill it full of lead. This ain't no country for little men or halfway measures."

The Indian agent didn't attempt to suppress a bitter smile. It was an argument he had heard many times from the people with large holdings, and, unfortunately for the nation's honor, it was echoed far too often in Congressional halls.

"Let me tell you what has happened." He placed his cigar at the edge of a saucer. "We made a treaty with the Seminoles at Fort Moultrie, setting aside certain lands for their exclusive use. Now," he paused reflectively, "we were not dealing with a defeated people but members of a free tribe with a just and prior claim to the land they settled. Despite this, we said: 'Within these limits you may live. We will protect you and restrain all white persons from hunting, settling, or otherwise intruding upon your preserves.'"

Governor du Val made a restless gesture and his chair scraped lightly, breaking abruptly into the words of the speaker. Colonel Humphreys raised his eyes.

"Am I boring you, Governor?" he asked gently.

Governor du Val flushed. "I am," he said stiffly, "familiar enough with the terms of the treaty."

The Colonel's eyes brightened. "But not," he suggested, "with their fulfillment, perhaps." Before the Governor could reply, Humphreys directed his next words to Young Clay. "We also," he continued, "agreed to pay the Seminoles one thousand dollars a year for twenty years and to defray the expense of a gun and blacksmith shop within their land. To the responsible chiefs—Phillip, Wokse Holata,

46

Tusteneck, Hajo, Micanopy, and others—we told these things. We said, further, that their people might not venture outside the reservation without special permission. The Indians kept their part of the bargain. Unfortunately, our own citizens have not been so meticulous in the preservation of their word. Day after day white hunters have crossed the boundary. White settlers have pushed in and raised their cabins, appropriating land belonging to the Indians. Slave-hunting parties repeatedly enter the Seminole country and carry off any Negro they can catch without regard to ownership. Demands upon the government for the return of more and more Negro slaves are constantly being raised by the plantation owners in Georgia, Alabama, and South Carolina, although most of the Seminoles' slaves are now second generation, born and reared among the Indians. Every time a horse wanders, a pig dies, or a cow bogs down in a swamp and is lost, a white man turns up at the agency at Fort King and complains to me that the animal has been stolen by the Seminoles. For how long a time do you suppose the Indians will be content to share in this unequal distribution of justice?"

"Who wants 'em to be content?" Old Clay pursued his theme doggedly. "Let 'em get so damn discontented they'll move out. If they won't go, then send a couple of Creek war parties down to fetch 'em."

Colonel Humphreys laughed with honest amusement. He touched his glass with a finger tip and waited until the slave refilled it before he replied.

"Let me tell you, sir," he chuckled throatily, "our Creek allies in an earlier conflict now view us with a certain amount of well-founded suspicion. Representatives from Georgia brought so much pressure on Congress for reimbursement for runaway slaves that the legislators succumbed to their demands. Getting the money was quite a problem, but casting about for a solution, Congress remembered the Creeks. The argument was simple. Since the Seminoles were alleged to have stolen the slaves and the Seminoles were once part of the Creek nation, what should be more natural than to levy upon the Creeks for an indemnity? That is exactly what we did, to the tune of two hundred and fifty thousand dollars, and the Creeks paid. Well, sir," he paused, enjoying the humor, "after all possible claims had been settled and every plantation owner in Georgia had been given each cent he asked for, it was discovered that there was a surplus of a hundred and forty thousand dollars. Quite obviously this money should have been returned to the Creeks, since there were no unpaid accounts left. Do you suppose the government of the United States turned back the money? I'll tell you what happened. The moment the Georgia planters heard about this surplus, they demanded every penny of it, basing their action on the slender theory that if their original slaves hadn't run away and found shelter with the Seminoles, they probably—and that is a pleasant qualification—they probably would have had children, and the value of these unborn children, by a miraculous coincidence, came to exactly a hundred and forty thousand dollars. No, sir." He shook his head resignedly. "I wouldn't count too heavily on the Creeks for assistance."

Only Young Clay seemed to share the Colonel's amusement. The laughter bursting from him was prompt and immoderate, but catching his grandfather's gaze upon him he forced it to subside quickly. Governor du Val snapped open the case of his watch, consulted the hands gravely, and replaced the timepiece in his waistcoat pocket without comment.

"Doubtless," Colonel Humphreys said mildly, "I make dull table conversation. The story, though," he continued, "is not without a moral, but then, perhaps, we have reached a point where morals are of little interest. My apologies." He thrust back his chair and rose, bowing to the head of the table. "A pleasant and generous meal, sir, for which I am grateful. My compliments, but since I must be on my way early in the morning for St. Augustine, I beg you excuse me."

Old Clay grunted ungraciously and made no move to stay his guest. Governor du Val stared pensively at the empty glass before him. He was disturbed and a little angry over Humphreys' open baiting of such an important Territorial figure as Clayfield Hammond.

Oblivious or indifferent to the silent antagonism flanking him at the table, Colonel Humphreys smiled. Turning to Young Clay he said, "Perhaps you would be kind enough to take a turn outside with me before we retire. I find the need of a bit of fresh air."

Young Clay almost bounded from the chair in his eagerness. "I'd be honored, sir." He bent his head to Du Val. "You will excuse me, Governor?"

Du Val glanced up, smiled pleasantly, and nodded. Old Clay growled something unintelligible, which Young Clay took as grudging permission to leave the table. From long experience with his grandfather's temper he knew how thoroughly aroused the old man was by the open heresy voiced within his house. For weeks he would chew and mutter over the words, inventing all manner of excuses to repeat them and hold the ideas they carried up to ridicule. At the moment, he expressed his contempt by silence.

"If you'll follow me, sir," the boy stepped away from his chair, "we'll go out this way."

From the depths of the broad porch the night unrolled itself as a heavy-piled blue-black carpet, moving up in wide, gentle swells across the country to meet the sky. No sound intruded upon the hour and the plantation seemed locked within itself, asleep and untroubled. Clay knew, though, that in a dozen strategic positions men were alert. On the high platforms of wooden towers scattered about the acres they would stand until relief came at dawn. Rifles were primed and ready, eyes and ears sharp and curious. The trouble being brewed in a hundred *istihapos* rose fitfully and subsided, but always the white people knew it was there, lying hidden and close to the ground as a trailing mist, refusing to be blown away. Behind the house, at the far, lower end of the plantation, the slave quarters huddled toward each other in slatternly rows of rude cabins. The half-dead embers of small fires glowed fitfully as they were sighed upon by the wandering night wind. Behind the sagging, strap-hinged doors the Negroes lay upon their pallets and whispered to each other of what was to come, for they sensed, somehow, the slowly accumulating evil, and knew instinctively it could not long be denied. By word and sign, brought mysteriously to them by Indian and maroon, they knew that the time of this uneasy peace was running swiftly to a close. It was a thing a man could hear and almost feel if he stood quietly at night and listened. The whites might not know or believe, but the blacks wondered and waited, putting their fears to melancholy song before the cabin fires or in the fields by day as they bent between the rows.

Standing at the edge of the porch Colonel Humphreys finished his cigar, appreciatively savoring the rich leaf and reluctant to toss the butt aside. Clay waited, uncertain whether to suggest a walk. He wanted to talk with the Indian agent about the Seminoles but didn't know how to begin.

"I'd like to have you visit me at Fort King," Colonel Humphreys said. "You'd find it interesting and the journey isn't too difficult by way of St. Augustine."

"Well, sir," Clay replied, "we don't travel much. My grandfather's leg bothers him on a long trip. I don't guess there's much chance of my gettin' off the plantation for a while."

Colonel Humphreys smiled briefly. "I wasn't including Mr. Hammond in the invitation," he said, without rancor. "I'm afraid my company and his leg would prove a double irritant."

Young Clay laughed. "Yes, sir," he agreed. "The combination would likely enough be too much for him, or," he added, with a grin, "any of us, to stand. He's real upset tonight—the Governor too, I reckon."

"I'm sorry." The man expressed honest concern. "It is an unhappy faculty of mine to annoy people. Somehow, though, I can't reconcile myself to the idea that the way to be rid of a trouble is to shut one's eyes to its existence." He paused. "Do you know the Indians hereabouts well?"

Clay chuckled at the idea. "I have a friend, Asseola. He's about my age an' the only real friend I have, I guess. We see a lot of each other. As for the others—well, they speak to me when they feel like it, let me eat from their pots when I'm hungry, an' so far no one has raised a gun in my direction when I've been alone in the woods. That's about as well as a white man can know a Seminole." He hesitated. "There's a town southwest of here, down the river a piece."

Colonel Humphreys examined the remaining two inches of his cigar and then tossed it from him to the ground below. He was thinking of a map hanging on the wall of his office at Fort King. It was a good map with fine, clear lines marking off the Indian territory. Also it was an optimistic fraud, and no one knew this better than the agent.

"They'll have to come in, all of them," he said, and added ruefully, "eventually."

"I don't know, sir." Clay pictured the town, secure and prosperous, high along the pine ridge. "It'd be pretty hard to make them see why."

"Damn it, sir—" Humphreys was instantly sorry for the explosive words and he continued in a milder tone, "I can't protect them if they insist upon scattering all over the Territory."

"Can you if they come in, sir?" There was no implied disrespect in the question. It was honestly voiced.

Humphreys regarded him with shrewd speculation. He knew Clay wasn't being impertinent. "I don't know," he said sadly. "I really don't know."

"Well, sir," he searched for the proper words, "I guess they feel the same way, and they'd rather take their chances as they are."

"They can't stay and take their chances." With a certain amusement Humphreys realized he was on the defensive before this teen-

50

age boy. "The land has been set aside for them. It's good country, good land, and it will be theirs."

"For how long?"

Humphreys laughed unashamedly and he turned to Clay with friendly understanding. He liked the boy and the way his mind leaped ahead to the ultimate question.

"Sir," he said soberly, "I think we had better go to bed." He touched his companion's shoulder with an affectionate gesture. "You are beginning to ask me the questions I ask myself and for which I have no answer. You mustn't embarrass people by being direct."

They turned together and walked inside, through the broad hall, and to the wide staircase. Behind them a slave secured and bolted the door. They could hear him fumbling with the heavy chain and the thud of the crossbar as it dropped into place. A second Negro, holding aloft a branching candelabrum, waited at the foot of the stairs to light their way.

They paused at the base of the stairway and Colonel Humphreys glanced humorously at Clay. The house was without sound, carefully barred and guarded against intrusion. It was also, the man thought, safely closed to all unpleasant ideas. Old Clayfield Hammond and the Governor had either retired early or elected to remain in tight seclusion at the dining table as a method of avoiding further contact with the heretic. Some of the amusement he felt must have filtered through to his eyes.

"My grandfather has probably gone to his room, sir." There was embarrassed apology in the words. "If there is anything you want or need?" Clay waited.

Colonel Humphreys shook his head. "A good night's sleep will more than do for me. If—" he hesitated, "if you are an early riser, then perhaps we shall meet in the morning. In any event, my invitation to visit at Fort King is standing."

"I'd sure like to, sir." Clay's pleasure was frank and spontaneous. "I'll talk it over with my grandfather."

Humphreys' chuckle was softly audible. "Then," he said, "I'm afraid I shan't be seeing you unless Mr. Hammond has a special charm or incantation to protect you from the devil." Still laughing over the notion, he turned and started up the stairs. "Even so," he threw the words back over his shoulder, "I'm afraid there is a certain element of risk involved. An idea can sometimes be more dangerous than all of hell's imps. It can also be catching. At the moment, I am the uneasy custodian of one."

They parted in the long upper gallery and the agent was still chortling as he entered his room. Apparently the brief skirmish with Hammond had put him in high good humor and he was relishing every moment of it.

For a long time after he was ready for bed Clay stood by the open windows in his room, staring out into the moonless night. There was a fresh, crackling chill in the air, the wind of a new season, and he drew the heavily brocaded China robe closer about his shoulders and lifted his head to sniff, animal-like, at the winy fragrance as it was released from the day's heat. There was always something mysteriously exciting in this subtle change of year after the rains of October, and he looked forward to the bright, hard days to come.

Unconsciously he kept turning over in his mind some of the things Colonel Humphreys had said at the table. This puzzled him a little when he thought about it, for he had never bothered to measure the quality of justice before. Probably, he thought, I'm growing up. Old Clay had once said, "You'll get old in a hurry or die young in this Territory." Maybe it was part of growing up to be puzzled about things. Laughter was a flicking shadow on his face as he recalled Governor du Val's well-bred annoyance and his grandfather's outraged growls. A man like Colonel Humphreys, he mused regretfully, wasn't going to last very long in Florida. They, such people as the Governor and Clayfield Hammond, would have his hide scraped and drying before he knew he had been skinned.

The damned part of the whole business, he admitted, was that behind Clayfield Hammond's stubborn vindictiveness there lay a certain honest realism. The new white settlers who pulled up at the border and gazed eagerly at the lush acres being opened would never be satisfied to share them with the Indians. It had been so before and would be true now. Even with the best intentions, the government was going to find itself in constant trouble as it tried to maintain peace with a Seminole reservation set squarely in the path of land-starved immigrants. When the shooting started, and it would start, every time a white man wanted something owned by an Indian, then the Seminoles were bound to get the worst of it. They couldn't hope to survive. The cause was lost before it was stated. This being so, and it troubled and worried him now to admit it, then it might be better to get the Seminoles out, force them to rejoin the Creeks and settle in Arkansas as had been proposed. His grandfather, of course, offered a more direct solution, the one of extermination.

As though in response to a call, his eyes turned to the south and followed the line of a distant river. Beyond lay the Seminole town. He wondered if the people there slept uneasily this night. Did the bronzed old man who tended the big fire hunch his sagging buttocks closer to the ground as his eyes lifted to search the sky for a sign of what was to come? Was it true, as was whispered, that the Indians were counting the short sticks in every ragged Seminole town and *istihapo*, taking a census of the young men who could and would fight, when and if the war cry should stab again at the night?

Of such things he and Asseola had never spoken. The Indian knew, though. Already he was old enough to be permitted a silent place in the councils. Clay knew he sat with the men and listened to their talk, yet, old friend that he was, he had never revealed to the white boy a word of what had been said. In this he was completely Indian, remote and fatalistic. With a sudden shock Clay realized for the first time that when the bitterness should finally erupt, Asseola's hand would be among those to put a torch to the Hammond plantation or lay his cheek to sight along the long rifle at those who lived there.

The possibility, he knew, had never entered their minds; yet it was there, stark and uncompromising. It startled him now to admit that Asseola might one day kill him, or at least make the attempt. He would go about the deadly business with the same silent perfection as he now tracked some wary animal on a hidden ridge. It amazed Clay that he could think of this without a feeling of resentment or a sense of betrayal. His friend would do what he must, coldly and impersonally. He would shoot at Clay Hammond because certain lines had been drawn and it was in the nature of things that they should stand on opposite sides. No one could help this, nor could he avoid the consequences.

"By God, Caccosoci." There was a certain grim amusement in Clay's voice. He spoke aloud and without being aware of the surprise in his tone. "That would be one hell of a note, now, wouldn't it?"

5

TIME was a lazy spinner, drawing slowly at the thread of the years; yet the wheel turned and the skein thickened, piling upon itself with many colors.

Along the Apalachicola the days of late December hung as a bright canopy, collecting its frosty ornaments in the silent hours before dawn and yielding them reluctantly to a touch of sun. The woods changed imperceptibly and the cold ground seemed to crackle with a crisp and brittle sound when trod upon. It was a period of movement and migration. Great flights of geese and ducks were inked in long streamers against the gray of morning; vain and handsome turkey cocks strutted on the pine knolls; the doe and the buck raced together and nuzzled each other with trembling affection. Young squirrels hunted and played in the high branches, and in the scrub flats the quail drummed and launched themselves into sudden whirring flight. A fresh vitality crept across the land and there was an abrupt awakening to the magic of a winter that returned each year without the harsh terror of the North. This was no time to be spent in drowsy hibernation, but a season of activity, charged with energy and new meaning.

Only on the plantation did the tempo of life slacken. Wheels within the mills were stilled and the blacksmith's forge was allowed to cool. On the almost boundless sections the brown and dying cotton stalks were stripped of all but a few scattered wisps, left to flutter and blow away by the eager, questing fingers of the pickers. The billowing white crop, long since ginned and baled, had gone downriver in the flatboats along with kegs of molasses, barrels of coarse sugar, heavy sacks of rice, and casks of rosin and turpentine. Now the soil lay at rest, waiting for the deep bite of a plow and a new planting.

Along the narrow street of the slave quarters the men and women lounged in the faint warmth of a metallic sun. They leaned weary backs against the sides of their cabins or sat in narrow doorways, smoking the acrid, badly cured tobacco from small back-yard patches. In the open spaces the children tumbled and played, shrill and tireless at their games. No one noticed or made a distinction between those of blue-black coloring and the bright-faced, clearer-featured youngsters. It had always been the way of the white man to find a Negro girl at the lonely end of a field or to call to her from the darkness behind the cabins at night. No one expected it should be different.

Half or three quarters of a mile down the plantation road were the houses of Salano, the Hammond general overseer, and the small frame buildings in which lived his four white assistants and their families. Beyond, at the edge of a cleared and packed square, stood a low, single-storied barracks for the use of Old Clay's militia. Here his ruffians ate, slept, drank, and wenched in noisy confusion.

There was little intercourse between the plantation whites and the big house save when Old Clay was brought down to direct and watch the drill or halted his carriage to speak to one of the foremen in the fields. Once a month Salano, freshly shaven, hair greased and slicked, stiffly uncomfortable in his best clothes, came to talk over plantation affairs with his employer on the front porch. Every four months they went over the books and accounts and finished the examination with a glass of whisky in mutual dislike and suspicion. Of obscure Spanish parentage, Philip Salano had been brought to the Territory by Old Clay, who found him on a small farm in St. Marys, Georgia. The overseer was a sharp and envious man who constantly nursed the galling delusion that he had been cheated of his birthright. The malice burned at him as a strong acid. He remained in Hammond's employ only because of the large salary the position offered and the infrequent opportunities for petty larceny. His speculations were small and he writhed inwardly over the old man's outspoken contempt.

"As long as I can't figure out what you're stealin', then you're safe." Old Clay was brutally direct. "A boar here, a few shoats there, an' maybe a cow or a steer, you can get away with. I can't keep track of 'em all. Don't," he warned, "'never let it get so big I start missin' things."

Salano protested, lifting expressive shoulders with the gesture of a misunderstood but loyal servant. "You make," he whispered, "a small joke, Señor Hammond." The smile he forced to his lips was evil.

"The hell I make a joke." Old Clay bared his teeth in a snarl. "If I didn't let you steal some you wouldn't stay, an' even if I wouldn't trust you at my back you're a good man with the crops an' the Negrahs. Just remember this." He paused, expelling his breath

55

with gusty emphasis. "If there's any good thievin' to be done, I'll do it. Don't you never forget it, neither."

Salano nursed his hatred, making of it a living thing as a companion. He carefully stored away the grudges, the real and fancied insults, against a day when they should be presented for payment. He expended his anger on the white foremen and slaves, driving them with unrelenting determination, and unwittingly contributing to the ever swelling Hammond fortune by forcing the land to yield abundantly from the seeds of his fury. He shunned association with those of his own color. At night he drank heavily and abandoned himself to the guardedly scornful affections of the two young Negro wenches who served him. Fearfully the girls listened to his mumbled schemes and alcoholic ravings of the time when something would happen to Old Clay and the plantation would fall into the hands of a youth who, Salano never doubted, would be easily led. To this end he cultivated Young Clay. Affable, courteous, and displaying a lively sense of humor, Salano rarely missed an opportunity to fish or hunt with Hammond's grandson and make of himself a good companion.

Clay was riding into Clayport, his horse trotting with muffled thuds in the loose sand of the wagon road. Christmas was but two days away, and although he knew it was a ridiculous fancy, Clay thought he detected a holiday spirit in the air as though the world unconsciously yielded to the season. The clumps of holly seemed brighter, the waxy green and white of mistletoe, bunched solidly in the high oaks, more abundant. For the past week the slaves had been decorating the big house. Boughs of fir and pine were laced above the windows surmounting enormous wreaths of holly. A bushy blue cedar towered in the center of the living room, strung with gleaming white lengths of popped corn and dotted with candles of many colors. In the long kitchen, separated from the house by a covered walkway, the spits over the half-dozen fireplaces had been filled with the dripping richness of hams, haunches of venison, and whole suckling pigs. Puddings and pies, cakes and small sweet biscuits stood in rows on the shoulder-high shelves. Old Clay looked upon these preparations with silent derision, yet, oddly enough, he made no move to halt them.

"Don't never think I can't see what's goin' on." He spat on the floor beside his chair at the corner of the porch and eyed his grandson morosely. "Fillin' the house with pine knots an' the stink of brush an' not a hand on the place doin' a lick of work. You been inchin' up on me with this Christmas thing for years. Why don't

56

you say right out you want me to lay a little sugar-tit present underneath the tree for you to come down an' find Christmas mornin'? Who," he demanded after a moment, "who the hell is goin' to eat all the stuff they been fixin' in the cookhouse?"

"Santa Claus." The boy had grinned with disarming brightness. His grandfather's assumption of anger no longer fooled him. They were too much alike.

"Well," the old man bent his head, "he better get here early. Otherwise every Negrah on the place will have a ham tucked underneath his tickin'."

Clay nodded and bounded down the steps to where his horse was being held. He knew these holiday preparations were a little childish and that the big house this year, as in the past, would not awaken to a holiday spirit. The huge amount of food would be distributed to the white families on the plantation and much of it would find its way to the slave quarters. Old Clayfield and his grandson would eat in silence and the day would pass as any other. For as long as he could remember this had been their custom, and there was no reason to believe it would, or could, be changed now.

Salano's mount danced with sudden skittishness out of the deep sandy rut and bounced playfully against the rump of Clay's mare. Startled, she reared, and Clay gave her her head. With a long leap she stretched out, flashing over the stubbly ground, working into long strides that left the surprised overseer far behind. Clay allowed her to run without check, glad of the opportunity to be rid of the man. He neither liked nor trusted Salano and had tried to avoid his company.

With a whirling flourish he turned down the main road, bisecting the cluster of low, weathered buildings making up the settlement of Clayport. The community was growing. Every few months a new cabin would be raised or another small frame dwelling added to the straggling line. The pulse of the territory was quickening as more and more outlanders and eager settlers pushed their way across the border.

Tying the mare to a hitching rail, Clay was secretly delighted by the fact that a half-dozen men gathered before the open door of the tavern had been on hand to witness his spectacular display of horsemanship. He felt he had created something of a fine and dashing figure for a moment there. Trying to appear casual, he nodded with easy friendliness as he passed them on his way to McCollum's trading post, but the eyes meeting his were without recognition. They regarded him with blank, impassive faces, and his jaw tightened slightly at the frank hostility. This was nothing new. Long ago he had become aware of the truth; few persons, if any, could be counted as friends of the Hammonds. Old Clay's contempt for the small farmer and new settler was open and vicious. He snarled at their attempts to settle a land over which he assumed dominion and sought to block their progress, encouraging his men to pick quarrels with the newcomers and run their cattle and live-stock whenever an opportunity presented itself. Wrapped in their small hopes and fears, the immigrants were wary of the old man's antagonism and tried to avoid all contact with anyone from the plantation. Clay forced a small and not very jaunty whistle and strode on through the clinging sand.

As indisputable evidence of his prosperous state and standing as Clayport's first merchant, Andrew McCollum had laid a narrow length of platform before his establishment. His was the only build-ing displaying such a modern convenience, and the strip of boards achieved an immediate popularity; not as a walk, as he had intended, but rather as a novel seating arrangement that permitted a man to rest on his hams in comfort and from a gratifying elevation watch a portion of the world go past. By an unvoiced rule the ends and the outside edge of the boardwalk were reserved for the exclusive use of the whites. Farmers, traders, roaming pedlars, idlers, and an occasional drunk from Ben Brady's tavern made a social center and forum of the spot. Ranging themselves on the planks' ends, they dug heavy-booted feet into the loose sand, argued politics and current events with lean-jawed intensity, and dotted the ground before them with dark round blobs of tobacco juice.

Behind the whites, pressed against the pine-sheathed front of the store, a scattering of Seminoles daily took up their less favored positions. They drifted in from the woods, seemingly without purpose, to stand in silent discomfort throughout the long day. They stood straight and unbending, their eyes staring blankly out across the narrow road and their passionless faces reflecting no interest in the scene. Now and then, one or two would glide away and their places would immediately be filled by others who waited patiently at the sides of the building. Ignored or roughly brushed aside by McCollum's white customers, who had to force their way through the thin lane opening to the doors, the Indians flattened themselves to the warm boards until they seemed to be part of the structure itself.

A little angry and still smarting from the studied insulting silence that had challenged his greeting to the men in front of the tavern,

58

Clay deliberately skirted the narrow opening at the far end of McCollum's platform where he could have squeezed his way through to the entrance. Perversely he kept to the road until he was directly opposite the doorway at the center of the boardwalk before he turned. The row of seated loungers confronting him was without a break, and Clay, with a curious feeling of tightness in his throat, moved purposefully forward. As he paced off the short distance he had time to wonder at his action. A hundred times he had entered McCollum's, and always, as custom and courtesy dictated, he had threaded his way along the meager aisle. Now, without reason and only because he was annoyed, he was on the point of creating a small scene. It was a senseless and unnecessary action. By God, he thought with sour amusement, this is something Old Clay might do just because he is ornery and likes to have people know it, but I sure don't know why I'm acting like him.

Not until he was a half-dozen steps away did any of the men glance up, and then their faces displayed only a mild curiosity, as though they wondered at his unexpected appearance. Straightening his shoulders, Clay focused his eyes on the back row of immobile Indians, and he had the feeling that the Seminoles were watching him with quickening interest. Strangely enough, this irritated him. You're making a hell of a show of yourself, he thought. There was no turning back, though. He couldn't just pretend he was sauntering up to join in the conversation. As his shadow fell across the group the men looked up as one. Their packed bodies left no space. Without pausing, Clay set the toe of his boot on a finger of an outspread hand, but before his weight came down, the owner snatched it out of danger. Roughly Clay pressed forward, his knee following the foot, forcing a space between touching shoulders, and he leaned into it as he stepped to the platform, thrusting the men apart as he cleared a path and making them shift to either side. There was a quick and angry exclamation.

"You near to stepped on my hand." The speaker glared at him, turning to look up.

"Keep it out of the way, then." Clay swung around. His voice was hard and cold. This, he thought, is the way trouble starts, and I'm going out of my way to look for it.

The offended man half rose, his eyes traveling swiftly over the tall, heavy-shouldered youth, and a slight rippling murmur ran lightly along the seated ranks.

The man, a stranger to the settlement, rapidly calculated the risk. "If you wanted to push in, why didn't you say so?" He glanced about, seeking encouragement. There was no way of telling how things might split up in a brawl.

Clay wondered at the veiled apology. I'm damned, he marveled, I'm damned if he isn't scared. This was a new experience and one that, oddly enough, gave him no satisfaction. The decent thing would be to meet the man halfway and let the incident dissolve.

"You saw me coming." Obstinately he pursued the quarrel. "Why didn't you get off your butt?"

Somewhere down the line of seated figures there sounded a low, short whistle of surprise, and an uneasy movement touched the nudging shoulders. Without waiting for a reply, Clay turned and walked to the doorway, the muscles in the small of his back gathered in a prickly bunch of nerves. If he jumps me now, he thought, I'm licked before I start, an' it'll damn well serve me right. He was ashamed of his part in the scene. This, he told himself, is how you turn out to be a son of a bitch like Old Clay. With every instinct drawn to a singing tautness, he tensed himself for the attack. Then, without looking back, he sensed that the man had reseated himself and the moment had passed. Something, an almost audible whisper from the row of seated spectators, told him so, but he could feel the anger and hatred as a solid wall pressing against him.

As he crossed the boards the head of every Indian swung with a steady movement, pulled by an invisible force, to follow his course. Bright black pebbles of eyes regarded him with hot excitement. The scene had been to their liking and there was a deep satisfaction in witnessing the humiliation of a white man even when it had been brought about by one of his own race. It would have been better if the men had fought.

Pausing at the entrance, Clay spoke rapidly in the dialect to a youth standing near the doorway. He recognized him as a member of Asseola's *istihapo*, a lodge brother.

"Where," he asked, "is Asseola?" He knew that every Indian was listening and heard the question passed down the line for the benefit of those who had not caught the words.

The young Seminole shook his head. "He went ten days ago but would not tell us where."

"Down the river?" Clay was curious. He had not seen his friend for over three weeks.

The Indian shook his head. "He took only his rifle and would not say."

Clay nodded. "Tell him I would talk with him when he returns."

60

The Indian ducked his head in assent and Clay pushed past and into the store.

McCollum's was a dim and cluttered retreat packed with the sharp odors of molasses and coffee, the musty smell of cloth in bolts, the scent of baled pelts, smoked meats and fish. They ran together, accented by the strawlike aroma of dried beans and the pungent perfume of salt pork and sun-cured beef. As the only post of importance between Pensacola and Fort King, the store had to stock a little of everything from pieces of harness to candle molds, plow points to boots, all hung and stacked in pleasant confusion. Waist-high counters, darkly stained and rubbed to a leathery sheen by countless greasy arms and hands that had leaned upon them, ran around three sides of the long room. Indians, in pairs, wandered slowly through the maze of assorted merchandise, fingering strips of bright cloth and gazing with silent wistfulness at the jugs and small casks of whisky stacked on shelves beyond their reach. Few of them made purchases, but they arrived punctually each morning to feast their eyes on this wonderland of unattainable treasures, padding softly from display to display beneath the watchful scrutiny of McCollum.

The brisk, ruddy-cheeked little Scotsman was measuring a length of red and white checkered cotton against a rule set in the counter. "Ten yards it is, ma'am," he chatted as the fabric slipped between his fingers, "an' there'll be no finer curtains in the Territory, I'm thinkin'." He chuckled and glanced up at Clay. "If the truth is to be told," he added, "it will make the only window curtains on the Apalachicola, save, pairhaps, those o' the Hammond plantation." He nodded amiably in Clay's direction.

The girl turned with open curiosity at the sound of the name and stared with unabashed interest at Clay, who flushed uncomfortably beneath the cool, almost impudent inspection of the gray-green eyes meeting his.

" 'Tis the young Muster Hammond," McCollum continued with easy informality, and then added for Clay's benefit, "This would be Miss Rogers an' a newcomer to the Territory with her brothers." Having discharged the amenities of the moment, the man returned his attention to the business at hand. "Now," he spoke persuasively, "there would be other things you are needin', miss?"

The girl unhurriedly completed her survey of Clay, who made a stiff and awkward bow.

"Servant, ma'am," he muttered.

61

"Mr. Hammond." She spoke softly, acknowledging the casual introduction, and ignored McCollum's question.

For what, to Clay, seemed an almost unbearably long interval her glance swept over him with lazy and deliberate attention. Suddenly she smiled; a darting flicker of amusement danced briefly at the corners of her mouth as his embarrassment spread itself for all to see.

Unhappily Clay fumbled for additional words. With a mounting feeling of uncertainty he realized that for the first time since he could remember he was speaking to a white girl of his own age. The situation was new and perplexing. There must be, he thought miserably, something you said to a girl when she kept looking at you the way this one was.

"I—I hope you'll like it, ma'am." He stumbled with the words and they fell heavily.

"What?" She posed the question with wide-eyed innocence and seemed to wait breathlessly for his reply.

"Why," vaguely he realized she was deliberately prolonging his discomfort, "why, Florida."

"Oh, that." Airily she dismissed the entire peninsula. "We'll do our best."

Clay experienced the sharp pricking of gathering anger. For reasons of her own this girl was trying to make a fool out of him, treating him like a backwoods lout. It seemed a pretty silly piece of business.

Confidence returned with a gratifying surge. "I'm certain, ma'am, the Territory will be grateful for your efforts."

Her laughter was spontaneous and friendly, and at the sound several of McCollum's customers turned to stare. For a moment she seemed to light the room, a slender, vivid sprite poised on tiptoe.

"You bleed easily, sir," she said, and stilled her quivering lips with an effort.

Clay didn't attempt to stifle an appreciative grin. He was no longer angry. Something close to intimacy touched the encounter.

"That depends on who handles the goad, ma'am." Deliberately he exaggerated a drawling inflection. The reply both surprised and pleased him. I'm damned, he thought wonderingly, I'm turning into quite a wit.

With an extravagant gesture of appreciation she dropped the merest suggestion of a curtsy, indifferent to the surprised stares of McCollum's patrons.

"Mr. Hammond," she murmured with mock humility, and there was the hint of a flutter in her lowered eyelids.

Clay glanced up as a shadow fell across them and a man moved to the girl's side. She turned at the touch of his hand on her elbow.

"Oh!" she said happily. "Are you finished?"

The man nodded, but his attention was directed at Clay, who returned his stare with easy self-possession. For a moment they measured each other. There was no hostility in the inspection, but rather a careful estimation. No taller than Clay, the stranger was several years older and held himself with simple confidence. His eyes, like those of the girl, were grayish green, steady, and penetrating.

"Had," the girl lifted her face, straining to catch the newcomer's attention, "this is Mr. Hammond. Mr. Hammond, my brother Hadley Rogers."

"Servant, sir." Clay experienced a pleasant sensation of relief at the identification.

Rogers nodded, and then, as though conscious of an unintentional rudeness, he permitted himself a faint smile and thrust out his hand.

"Pleasure, sir," he said gravely. "I've heard the name."

For a moment Clay thought he detected a subdued note of sarcasm in the statement, but decided quickly he must be wrong. The grip meeting his was frank, almost cordial, and Rogers' features were without guile.

"It's a small community, sir," he said. "I guess everyone's name gets heard sooner or later."

Hadley Rogers turned to his sister. "Will is outside with the wagon. Are you through here?"

She gathered up her purchases and thrust them into her brother's unwilling arms.

"Don't look so glum," she laughed at his expression of distaste. "Your masculinity will not be offended by carrying a few paper packets." With a confidential air she directed her attention to Clay. "I'm buying the carriage before the team, window curtains before we have windows. When they are up you must ride over sometime and see them. Mr. McCollum assures me that between us we will possess the only curtains in this part of the Territory."

Clay flushed with pleasure. "I'd be happy to, Miss Rogers." He was reluctant to have her leave and wondered if it would be presumptuous if he moved to accompany her to the door. "I—" He hesitated, desperately seeking an excuse for prolonging the conversation. "I guess," he continued, "it would be easier, though, if I knew in advance where to look for you."

Any reply she might have made was forestalled by Hadley Rogers'

63

interruption. "We're going to clear and raise a house on a river section; Elbow Bend, I think they call it. Anyhow, it was marked so on the Land Commission maps at Pensacola."

Clay couldn't contain his surprise; it flashed across his face with unmistakable clarity and he stared almost stupidly at Hadley Rogers. The land around a sharp crook in the river had always been held to lie within the Hammond plantation boundaries. The acres had never been cleared or the soil put to work, but Clay knew his grandfather claimed it as his, and heretofore no one had disputed him.

"It's a good piece," he said slowly.

Rogers nodded agreeably. "The surveyors at the Commission told me the same thing when I bought it in. There were other sections for sale, but this looked best—on the map, at least."

Clay understood well enough that Rogers was deliberately feeding him this information piecemeal, tempting him to voice what was in both their minds. The man knew, he must have heard, that Elbow Bend had long been considered a part of the Hammond holdings. Clay wondered how it could have been put up for sale by the Territorial Land Commission, the body that had been established for the purpose of bringing some sort of order out of the many overlapping titles resulting from British and Spanish patents. Unconsciously he allowed a long, low whistle of astonishment to escape his lips. Old Clay, he thought rapidly, will tear up the Territory, section by section, when he hears about this.

Hadley Rogers was watching intently. "Are you surprised at the selection, Mr. Hammond?" He spoke with a gentle encouragement.

Clay couldn't hold back a grin. The more he thought of his grandfather, the more monumental the possibilities of an explosion became. Actually, the land was of little value to the plantation as it was organized. It ran parallel to the river and far outside the areas under cultivation, but Clayfield Hammond was not a man to relinquish a square inch of soil he claimed as his own.

Regarding Hadley Rogers with an almost friendly interest, Clay shook his head in reply to the question. "No, sir," he said thoughtfully, "I'm not particularly surprised, but," he chuckled, "my grandfather's sure going to be. Yes, sir, there probably won't be a more surprised man in all of Florida when he hears about it."

"When you mention it to him," Rogers spaced his words carefully, "you might say the sale and my papers are in order and the record is on the Commission's books. We are not looking for trouble."

Clay was enjoying the humor of the situation. "I don't think," he said slowly, "you'll have to hunt for it. More than likely it'll come

64

right up and peek through those new curtains Miss Rogers is going to hang."

Hadley Rogers was frankly puzzled. He hadn't expected the younger Hammond to treat his announcement so lightly. Through carelessness the section had not been included in the claim filed by Clayfield Hammond after the Territorial purchase from Spain. When the new surveys had been run, it and hundreds of other sections throughout west Florida were offered for public sale. Hadley and his brother, Will, had purchased the land in good faith, but ever since their arrival in Clayport they had listened to whisperings of the old man's fury and predictions of his rage to come when he learned what had happened. Now, at his first meeting with a member of the Hammond family, he found the matter being treated as a joke.

"I hope," Rogers was serious, "I hope it can be avoided." He eyed Clay expectantly.

The younger man nodded. "So do I, sir," he said. "If it was a proper sale, then I guess there isn't anything anyone can do about it." His face lightened momentarily. "But," he added, "that won't keep Old Clay from trying."

Susan Rogers made a small sound of impatience and tugged at her brother's sleeve. The man turned and look down at her with quick consideration.

"My goodness, Had," she protested, "I wish you'd stop talking about trouble. First it was the Indians who were going to scalp us in the night, now it's something else. Do you and Will have to be fighting something all the time?"

"There's not much fight left in the Indians, ma'am," Clay reassured her, "and I don't think there is anything else to worry about."

"Well," the girl seemed doubtful, "I hope you are right, sir." She smiled. "Anyhow, come and see us before it has a chance to start."

Clay stared after them as they left the store. It had never occurred to him that a girl, well-bred and gently reared as this one undoubtedly had been, could be so casually friendly and still hold herself with dignity. His only contact with young women had been through the medium of books, and there they had been portrayed as artificial, given to inexplicable fainting spells and brittle coquetry. I guess, he mused, there are a lot of things outside of Clayport I can learn.

He turned and realized McCollum was regarding him with a shrewd, sidelong glance that held amused speculation. The little Scotsman cocked his head to a shoulder and peered brightly through thick-lensed spectacles.

"An' now, Muster Hammond?" He waited expectantly.

In desperation Clay tried to remember what had brought him to the post. Certainly there must have been something he wanted to buy, but for his life he couldn't remember what it was. He stared helplessly at McCollum and his short laugh was uncertain and embarrassed.

The trader sighed commiseratingly. "Aye, lad," he said patiently, "let's forget about the business. 'Tis not the first time a man has been muckled by the sight of a pretty face. Doubtless, in a day or two, you'll be able to recall what it was you wished to pairchase. Until then, you'll forgive me if I don't remain a party to your moonin'." He bustled off behind the counter to attend to the wishes of other customers.

For a moment Clay remained where he was, trying to recall the laughter of a girl, the sound of her voice, or how a touch of color had crept shyly along the gentle curve of a satiny cheek. With an effort he roused himself from these pleasant speculations and moved slowly and thoughtfully toward the entrance.

Bright sunlight made a yellow oblong of the door framing McCollum's boardwalk, the rounded, hunched backs of the sitters, and the clustered group of buildings beyond. Later, when he tried to reconstruct the scene, Clay had the strange conviction that he knew what was going to happen even before the first move was made. One of the men rose from the outside edge of the walk, stretched regretfully, and moved out of sight down the road. For a moment his vacated space gaped, an irregular hole in a dingy, serrated row. Before it could be filled the Indian youth Clay had spoken to slid from his place against the wall and dropped into it, hunching himself tightly against the certain consequences of his effrontery.

At the doorway Clay heard a quick intake of breaths run down the line of Indians as they looked upon the reckless intrusion, and Clay could see the backs of the white men stiffen as they realized what had happened. For a moment there was no sound, but the silence was heavy and ominous with the charged violence of a gathering storm. Then, and Clay had the sensation of looking upon the movements of actors who automatically took their places upon a stage, one of the white men rose and stepped back on the platform. A heavy musket dangled in the crook of his arm, and as he turned Clay saw the small muscles in his face leap and twitch with anger. There was no movement along the ranks of the seated men. The figures, sketched against the hard sunlight, waited, and their eyes sought the opposite side of the road with fixed intensity.

Slowly the man took the few steps necessary to bring him to the

Indian's back. Clay watched him, powerless to halt what he knew must happen. It's my fault, he thought unhappily. If I hadn't been so cocky, forcing my way through the way I did, letting the Indians see a white man humbled, then this would never have happened. They saw a custom flaunted, a taboo mocked, and now this damn fool thinks he can do the same thing. The man paused and Clay expected to see him reach down, grab the Seminole by the back of his shirt, and pull him from the seat. Instead, his roughly booted foot swung back and then out in a vicious kick which sent the intruder sprawling face down in the sand. There was no outcry or other movement. The youth lay prone, arms and legs outstretched, as though delivering himself for additional punishment.

His training and every instinct warned Clay he was being a fool, and yet he could not stay his action. Searing rage enveloped him at the spectacle of the brutality, senseless and unnecessary. He stepped across the doorsill, and as the man turned he hit him furiously with every ounce of power knotted in his shoulders. The solid fist caught the man full in his face and he spun in a half circle, lost his balance, and toppled with a muffled thud to lie beside the Indian.

As though someone had blown upon the feathery puff of a dandelion, the file of seated men scattered, whisking out in a tumbling motion and fanning away to leave a cleared space.

The man rose slowly from the dirt, streaming blood from his mouth and nose clotting with the sand that smeared his twisted features. He stared drunkenly at Clay as he stood outlined against the doorway, and then his thumb drew deliberately at the lock of his musket. Clay heard the sharp click, harsh and spiteful, as sudden terror gripped him. I ought to run, he thought. By God, I've sure got to do something other than stand here. Every face was turned to the man in the road as the musket came to his shoulder in an easy, swinging motion. Something, almost a sigh, welled with a small bubbling sound from the spectators. He's going to kill me, Clay thought, and I don't even know his name. In the scant second left he thought this was the oddest part of a nightmare incident, to be shot by a man whose name he didn't know.

The knife, as it flashed past his head, sang with a deceptive gentleness as though someone were whistling upon its edge. Instinctively Clay ducked, and his eyes caught the gleam of bright steel as it hurtled through the sunlight. Then he heard the blade go home and thought the sound it made was not unlike that of an overripe melon being cut. Behind the musket's dark stock the face of the man seemed to rest tenderly against the wood. His cheek caressed it. Then, as

Clay watched, surprise and stunned bewilderment flooded the eyes, and for a moment the man seemed to be appealing for help. Even as his body sagged and his knees buckled he appeared to lower the firearm with profound regret, dropping it from his shoulder with an apologetic air. Briefly, he supported himself in an attitude of dejected weariness, and then a rushing crimson flood spewed with horrible suddenness from between graying lips and he pitched forward, his head gouging a deep furrow in the ground as he slid to rest.

Clay was not conscious of any outcry from the crowd. It advanced almost timidly, peering down at the stricken man as though unable to accept the spectacle of death come riding with such silent certainty. Clay wheeled. The boards of McCollum's store front were bare, the row of Indians swept up as though gathered in a giant hand to be stuffed out of sight. Quickly he turned his gaze up and down the road. The pitted, uneven track was empty and bare of life. The Seminoles had vanished, disappearing into the scrub and woods, losing themselves with chameleon cunning and fleeing from the wrath to come. Clay paused to wonder at what moment the Indians had known what was to happen. When, sensing the onrushing violence, had they faded from their places, leaving a vacant wall to confront their accusers? Whose hand, he mused, had hurled the knife, and why?

Reluctantly Clay crossed to the still figure, bent down, and turned it over. For a moment he stared at the bloody mask of a face, obscene, somehow, in death, with its brown caking of sand, bits of grass, and dried manure flakes pressed tightly against mouth and chin, plugging the flaring nostrils. Hesitantly his fingers closed about the knife's hilt and he withdrew the steel. It came easily as from a well-made sheath, and he held it point down as a tiny carmine rivulet trickled on the blade and dried.

An excited crackle exploded around the semicircle of men at the sight of a small, looped thong of beaded rawhide dangling from a hole in the haft.

"Seminole." The word bounced from mouth to mouth.

Without comment, Clay handed the weapon to the man nearest to him. It hadn't occurred to him to think anyone might believe the blade to be his or suspect he had hurled it with such accurate deadliness. The knife passed from palm to palm and the muttering gathered volume. Without a word Clay pushed through the crowd and walked without haste to where his horse waited.

6

OLD CLAY was sprawled in a heavy, fan-backed chair, staring with milky-eyed contempt at the three men who stood in uneasy silence at the bottom of the broad flight of steps. With flinty deliberation he forced them to wait in attitudes of supplication below his porch while he looked down upon them with unmistakable disdain. They shifted uncomfortably in the sun, muskets cradled in their arms, hats thrust back from their foreheads, faces upturned to search his face. One of the trio rolled and coaxed a quid of tobacco from his cheek and then looked quickly at the ground for a likely place to spit it. The soggy ball was between his lips when he caught the full impact of Clayfield Hammond's glare. With a small choking sound he sucked the tobacco back and out of sight, working unhappily over the offending weed with broken and yellowed teeth.

"So." At the sound of Hammond's voice the men stiffened into attitudes of alert attention. "So a white man gets himself knifed an' you all are hot to go out an' kill yourselves a few Indians an' burn a town or two?" He paused and the men held themselves expectantly. "Well, go ahead. Who the hell's goin' to stop you? Not the government of the United States."

"But," the spokesman for the three grasped at the opportunity, "we got to have some help. You can see that. There ain't enough of us to take on that Seminole town an' do any good. You got the only real fightin' men in west Florida outside a few troops. We figured you'd want to come in with us before them Indians get to be a real danger."

Old Clay blew soundlessly through his sagging lips. "If," he said faintly, and the men strained to catch the words, "if you need help, then you surer'n hell ought to get out of this Territory. There's mighty little space save maybe a hole in the ground for them who got to yell for help whenever they get in trouble."

With surprising boldness one of the men stepped forward. "We figured you'd want to come in with us, Mr. Hammond." He hesitated. "Seein' as how you've got more to lose than anyone else if them Indians run wild."

"I ain't countin' on losin' anything." Old Clay slid his twisted leg into a more comfortable position. His voice was modulated and persuasive, almost friendly. "But," the words grated suddenly and his shoulders shot forward, "if I was, I wouldn't want to take up with no squatter scum to help save it. Now get off my plantation an' don't never put a foot on it 'less I send for you. It'd suit me right down to the ground if you an' them God-damned Indians were to cut each other's throats to the last man. Move off my land!"

As though thrust back by the impact of the words, the men shuffled away from the porch, but the lines in their faces were drawn heavily and their eyes cold. For a moment they stared at the figure in the chair and then slowly turned their backs. At the second pace one of them swung about slowly and with calculated insolence spat the dripping tobacco lump to the sheer white of the steps. It spattered and clung to the boards, tracing a spider-like design of dirty brown across the paint.

Old Clay didn't move. He watched the retreating men through squinted eyes and then bellowed a command to a house slave standing just inside the door.

"Get someone out here. There's mongrel dirt on my porch to be cleaned up."

For a long time Old Clay sat in the warming sun, peering out across his acres and mulling over the impending violence. Clay had reported his part in the affair and the old man had listened with growing anger. When his grandson finished he snorted with impatient disgust.

"It ain't bad enough," he said, "for you to dirty your hands on the scurvy rabble in Clayport, but by God, I never figured one of my family would get into a fight for the sake of an Indian."

"I wasn't fighting for an Indian," Clay protested. "I just don't like to see anyone get kicked around. There wasn't any need for it."

Old Clay ran a hand wearily through his tangled shock of hair. Long ago he had given up trying to understand his grandson's peculiar mental processes.

"You got the soul of a Bible-whacker," he muttered. "If there is anything I can't stand it's a fella who's got an itch to do good. A kick in an Indian's ass ain't worth bruisin' a knuckle on. That's what an Indian's got a butt for; it was made to kick. Now—" he paused thoughtfully, "you've likely enough stirred up trouble. Some of those fools'll go out and kill a couple of Seminoles an' we'll have a first-class shootin' match on our hands."

Clay was silent. He knew better, probably, than his grandfather how close to the surface an open conflict between the whites and the increasingly resentful Indians was. It wouldn't take much to touch it off. The Clayport killing could well be the match to kindle the fire.

Now, from his porch chair, Old Clay meditated and checked over his precautions. The tower guards had been doubled, quantities of powder and freshly run bullets were strategically stored. Under Hammond's prodding, Salano had tightened the discipline of the men in the barracks. Their Negro wenches had been sent back to the slave quarters, rum and whisky jugs confiscated. Rifles were stacked for instant use and the plantation was as safe as he could make it.

Probably, he thought, nothin' will come of it. I don't figure the Seminoles got the stuff yet to start a real good fight. The camps and towns were too widely scattered for there to be any real unity of action. Yet he knew the Seminole chiefs were holding their people with difficulty. Every move the government made to force and compress them into a reservation was being met with sullen resistance. The agitation within the Territory to compel a mass migration of the Indians to Arkansas was constant, but the Seminoles opposed the pressure. Responsible Indian leaders refused to attend the parleys, and the government was forced to deal with minor chiefs whose words were of dubious value and whose authority extended no farther than the limits of their small camps.

Staring up into the cloudless sky, the old man coolly weighed the risks of lending his aid to the angry settlers around Clayport against the possible gain of an Indian massacre. It might well be the opening shot of a war that would force the government to action and result in clearing all Florida of the tribe. There would be fine, rich holdings to be picked up and added to the Hammond acres at the successful conclusion of a war. The bloodshed and terror that would be unleashed throughout the peninsula were of minor importance. He whistled softly.

"It takes a little thinkin'," he said aloud. "It takes a little thinkin' an' some schemin'."

For several minutes he explored the possibilities of aiding and encouraging a clash of arms, dangling the fruit of such an action as a tempting morsel to be appraised and considered. There ain't, he pondered moodily, any use of breakin' your neck to get an apple that's full of worms, an' right now, from where I'm sittin', I can't be sure somethin' like that wouldn't happen. . . . He scowled, troubled by his inability to reach a decision, and then called impatiently for his litter.

Borne aloft by six heavily muscled slaves who struggled to maintain an even pace as they bent slightly beneath the carrying poles, Hammond toured the heart of the plantation on a swinging course that brought him eventually to the barracks. At his approach several men who had been lounging on a bench just outside the doorway straggled to their feet and waited until the chair was lowered gently to the ground. A visit from Old Clay, they knew, never meant anything but trouble. He whipped them with a relentless and vituperative tongue, and his scorn was molten. Contemptuous of their potential villainy and indifferent to their bloody records, he moved among them with the shrewd judgment of a trainer in a cage of snarling but uncertain animals. They endured this unending degradation only because they were safe on the Hammond plantation, out of reach of the laws, civil and military, which would have hung them collectively or individually from the handiest tree.

When the litter had been carefully deposited on the ground and the slaves deferentially gathered at his back, Old Clay allowed his eyes to roam along the short, glowering line.

"Well," he said finally, "get 'em out." The words cracked explosively. "I've a mind to look at all of you at once, though God knows it's sometimes more than my stomach can bear."

One of the men jumped for the doorway, and from his chair Old Clay could hear the shouted commands as he prowled through the rooms, routing men from their beds and breaking in upon card and dice games with hurried explanations. One querulous and sleepy voice, unconsciously raised higher than the others, floated clearly from the depths of the building to the compound.

"What," it demanded waspishly, "does the old bastard want now?"

Old Clay allowed a smile to hide behind his full, pursed lips while the men before him looked uneasily at each other or pretended not to have heard. A little spirit was a good thing, and he wondered idly who among this ruffian guard had the audacity to risk his displeasure.

When the men were drawn up beneath his critical eye he allowed them to stand without comment. They were a vagabond detail, he thought; the malcontents and stupidly brutal, envious and greedy, the back-door sweepings of half a dozen states. Unshaven, tousle-haired, bleary-eyed, or soggy with hidden liquor, they had but one thing in common: the conviction that life was a cheap thing at its best, and it was better to be quick than dead. With this philosophy they were admirably suited to the purposes of Clayfield Hammond.

They would fight to save their own skins, but in so doing would serve as his shield and spear.

"You know," the old man's voice purred, "what happened yesterday in Clayport. I don't need to tell you if trouble starts you're goin' to be dab in the middle of it."

One of the men weaved slightly, the dregs of whisky clouding his eyes. His head twisted with a foolish motion and a weak grin spread across his sharp mouth. Old Clay's finger stabbed out and quivered on the target.

"Take that man out of line an' lock him up till he's sober." He held himself without impatience until the fellow had been hauled protestingly away by two of his companions. From within the barracks there came the sound of a brief struggle, a sudden, clubbing thump, the muffled crash of a falling body, and then silence. A minute later the men reappeared and took their places on the hard-packed square before the litter.

With a nod of approval Old Clay made a further inspection of his mercenaries. Only two or three of the men dared to meet his eyes. The others twisted uneasily, their darting glances searching the sky and field and their hands alternately locking and unlocking behind their backs. The sun had beaten their faces into a deep tan, but around the shirt openings at their throats the skin showed a sickly, unhealthy white. Their features seemed to have been cast from a common mold and displayed a general characteristic of vulpine savagery and feral cunning.

"If," Old Clay's voice rasped, "a mob in Clayport tries to shoot up the Seminole town down the river, then hell is likely to break out. A man in a bed tangle with a Negrah wench or peerin' down the mouth of a whisky jug ain't goin' to be no good to this plantation. So," he deliberated, "the next of you I find drunk will get ironed up an' marched across the border into the law. If that's what you want you'll sure enough get it, an' don't never think for a minute I'm foolin'. All right, you, Race, Plummer," he motioned to two of the waiting slaves, "get this chair up an' back to the house."

When he had again been hoisted into the air he stayed his bearers for a final word.

"Keep your arms clean an' ready, because an Indian ain't goin' to stand around an' wait while you look for somethin' to shoot him with. If trouble comes to the plantation we'll take care of it." He hesitated, frowning thoughtfully. "An' if I decide we're to go outside an' look for trouble, well, we can do that, too."

73

Along the high, shelving banks of the river a heavy tangle of forest all but shut out the sun. Here, with the scale of great age upon them, the twisting trunks and tortured branches of gray oaks flung themselves upward as though seeking release from the clinging shrouds of wavering moss. Such light as filtered through from above was without warmth, and there was a perpetual chill in the air that stilled the songs of birds and caused them to dart from tree to tree with the silent urgency of bats. Here, also, the river flowed rapidly but without sound; a darkly mirrored tide, hurrying through the twilight cavern, anxious to escape.

Keeping to a badly defined deer run, Clay walked without haste or purpose. Now and then he kicked savagely at a dead branch or an exposed root, experiencing a stubborn satisfaction in the shock of pain racing from toe to hip when his foot encountered an immovable object. The surroundings were in keeping with his mood and he absorbed the melancholy.

Trouble in Clayport was spreading with the frightening strength of a poisonous growth, and the seeds for the planting had been carelessly strewn by his own hand. The white man who had been knifed was unimportant. Almost unknown in the settlement, he was one of the many adventurers who drifted restlessly through the community, pausing for a while and then disappearing as mysteriously as they had come. To Clayport he meant nothing as an individual; yet he was white, and the arm behind the blade that had struck him down was Indian. There lay the tragedy and danger, for it was agreed that as long as white fell upon white and Indian killed only Indian a safe balance in the scheme of things could be maintained. The rule, though, had been violated, and in their fear and insecurity the whites wanted not revenge but a reassertion of authority. So the talk and threats boiled and bubbled. The Seminoles remained within their town while in Clayport small groups of men argued, embracing muskets and rifles, waiting hopefully for courage and a leader to whip them into action. Avarice hid itself ineffectually behind the lofty sentiments of indignation. The Indians held rich and desirable land and there were slaves, the solemn black men, to be taken and claimed. In the measurement of justice these things weighed heavily.

Irritably Clay recalled his grandfather's words. The old man was right. A do-gooder, he thought grimly, never accomplished much but trouble. It would have been better to let the kick at an Indian go unnoticed; certainly the Seminoles would think so if they were forced into a local war and saw their town destroyed, their people killed. No voice would be raised in the council to hail Clay Hammond as a bright and shining champion of the oppressed. He smiled unconsciously. Probably, he thought, he would be the first to have a hole blown in his head by a Seminole bullet.

The sharp, dry whirring of a rattlesnake's warning brought him up shortly, one foot raised a few inches from the ground. He stood, rigid and alert, his eyes sweeping a half circle, on each side of the trail. Cautiously he began to lower his foot, and at the slight movement the unmistakable sound, the purr of sand and pebbles being shaken in a gourd, chilled him into immobility. Once again he inspected the brush on each side and the trail ahead; then he set his foot to the ground, ignoring the high, rasping threat. The only place a snake could be was behind him, and no rattlesnake ever hatched sat in the middle of a trail and sounded its terror after a man or animal had passed. With a grin, Clay felt the leaping of his heart subside. His eyes now sought a higher level, peering at the shadowy trees.

"Even a dumb Indian," he called, "wouldn't be fooled by that for long, not even one as dumb as Asseola."

He hoped there was a proper note of scorn in the declaration, but his confidence was shaken by the certain knowledge that the Indian had been laughing at him from his hiding place while he stood on one leg like a thoughtful crane.

"Come on out," he shouted boastfully. "I see you." The lie, though, was in his eyes as they roamed through the brush and over the trees. Instinct rather than any betraying sound caused him to whirl, but not before Asseola was close enough to place a hand on his shoulder.

"White man catch big snake?" There was an expression of hypocritical concern on the Indian's face. Deliberately he mimicked the stilted phrasing and guttural tone so often adopted by the whites when they talked with the Seminoles.

"Indian'll catch big stick across big ears one of these days." Clay's expression was sheepish. "That was a sure enough crazy trick." He shoved playfully at Asseola's chest and then suddenly they were both laughing. "I thought," Clay admitted, "I was in a whole nest of the things. Where did you come from?"

For a moment they stood regarding each other with undisguised affection. Time had filled them out, modeling their disciplined bodies to a man's stature. Somewhere the juvenile, coltish alertness had been lost and replaced by an adult carriage and demeanor. They held themselves as men, with pride and confidence. Clay had grown taller, and by comparison now the Indian seemed heavier, broader, and

75

almost squat. Much of his rangy litheness had vanished with childhood and he appeared older and possessed of a grave wisdom. The bright, full shirt he wore was bound at the waist by a colored sash, forming a loose blouse and a skirt reaching to his knees, where the high leggings of buckskin were tied. The effect was to make him seem shorter than he actually was. Over the flowing scarves falling from his throat he wore a chain of small, crescent-shaped silver plates that glittered softly. At the back of his head, held there by a beaded band, the snow-white, feathery plume of an egret, its tip dyed a royal purple, erupted in dazzling color. Standing within the shadowy reaches of the forest, one arm hooked around the long rifle, the Indian was barbarically resplendent.

Surveying him critically, Clay whistled with a prolonged, expressive note of appreciation. Unmoved by the implied amazement, Asseola bore the inspection without embarrassment or concern.

"Goin' to a fancy ball?" Clay couldn't resist the gibe.

For a fraction of a second there was something savagely unpleasant in the Indian's expression. It fired his eyes with sharp brilliance and then disappeared as quickly as it had come.

"It is the dress of my people," he said simply. He spoke in the Seminole dialect, and Clay understood he had done so deliberately and in a spirit of short rebuke.

"That was a dumb thing for me to say." Clay apologized willingly and with spontaneous grace. "Sometimes I forget you're Seminole."

"I also," Asseola continued in his own tongue, but his hand moved out and closed with understanding about Clay's wrist. "You are my brother," he said with quiet dignity. "That would be hard to forget and something that should not happen between us."

Clay nodded, impressed and sobered by what he had seen momentarily in his friend's eyes. Vaguely he sensed the reason behind the Indian's sudden return to the dress and speech of his tribe. It sprang from the uneasiness of the times, as though he found an old strength and comfort in the customs of his own people.

"Where have you been?" Clay asked.

Asseola replied readily, anxious to change the subject, "Fort King, St. Augustine, along the Big Swamp, and among the Mickasukies." The names rolled rapidly from his tongue, but he now spoke in English. "I have sat, without speaking as yet, in the council circle, and listened to the chiefs. I talked long with the Negro Abraham, who interprets for our people in their dealings with the whites. I crossed the Ocklawaha River and spoke with a young warrior known as Wildcat, a man no older than I. The things I have heard were not good. Here also," ne paused and studied Clay intently, "there is trouble and words of fighting."

Clay nodded. "Let's take a walk," he said. "I'll tell you about it. It was a damn fool thing to do, I guess."

They moved together along the narrow path and Clay recounted what had happened in Clayport. Asseola listened without interruption. The story had already been told him upon his return, but he wanted to hear it again from his friend.

"So," Clay concluded unhappily, "I guess it is like Old Clay says. Everyone would have been a lot better off if I'd just minded my business."

Asseola shook his head. The same thought had been expressed by the old men of his town. They mumbled and whined or in shrill, fear-accented words declared the abasement of one young Indian was not worth the destruction of their crops, the killing of their people, the burning of the *istihapo*. These things would surely happen if the aroused white men came again in force. The youth had transgressed against white customs and had been punished. There the matter should have been allowed to rest. In their tired and faded eyes lurked the memory of terrible days, of Jackson's troops and the bloodshed they had brought. They were too old and weary to fight for such a flimsy thing as a young man's pride. Asseola listened to their lamentations and found himself growing impatient. He had made no attempt to learn the identity of the Indian who had thrown the knife and saved Clay Hammond's life. Such a secret was better shut away in one man's knowledge, but he felt a fierce elation in the act. It was a good thing to have done.

"We grow older, Clay," the Indian said thoughtfully and glanced up to scan his friend's face, "and honor is a thing to be satisfied. I have seen in my own people how, when it is put aside, they become little better than animals, living in filth and like dogs, without nobility. The man Powell once spoke so to me and I have never forgotten. What you did was brave and fine, a thing I would like to have done myself even though it brought great trouble to us all."

They crossed a small gully, cut by a little stream in its effort to reach the river, and clambered up the opposite bank. As they walked, Clay wondered if he should say anything about the delegation that had called upon his grandfather.

"How," he asked abruptly, "are you fixed at the town?"

"We have guns and, perhaps, men to shoot them," Asseola replied with a slight hesitation. "The dogs," he smiled a little, "will sound a warning long before anyone can get within musket shot."

77

Clay made his decision. "Some men came to see my grandfather. They wanted help, our men."

The Indian turned questioningly. "Did they get them?"

Clay shook his head. "No. I guess Old Clay couldn't figure anything out in it for him." He grinned and there was something of an apology in the expression. "That's a hell of a way to talk about your kin, isn't it?"

The woods thinned abruptly, and from where they stood they could follow the sharp angle of the river as it swept in to form Elbow Bend. Faintly, the sound of steady, solid blows of an ax on heavy timber drifted up to them. Asseola listened and turned with an unspoken question.

"New settlers," Clay said. "Didn't you know about them?"

The Indian shook his head. "I have been away," he said, then motioned with his head in the direction of the bend. "Isn't that part of the Hammond plantation?"

Clay, trying to imagine what was going to happen when the old man heard about the Rogers men and their sister, chuckled, and Asseola regarded him with surprise.

"I guess Old Clay sure thought so," his grandson replied, "but if what these new people say is true, an' I suppose it is, then the section was never included in the Hammond claim when it was filed. The Land Commission at Pensacola just put it up for sale along with a lot of other stuff, and it was bought in. Mighty pretty girl goin' to live there, too," he added irrelevantly. "Suppose we take a walk on down an' visit our neighbors. I figure on gettin' a little better acquainted before the shootin' starts."

7

Mistress Susan Rogers rested her rough and reddened elbows on the edge of a leaky wooden tub and groaned. The sound was dismal and unladylike but satisfying. She tried it again, this time louder and with more feeling. Her arms and slender hands were dead white and puckered from long immersion and the strong, lye-filled soapsuds drifted in a scummy crust on top of the lukewarm water. At the bottom of the tub lay a sodden mass of heavy clothing, which for all her scrubbing seemed not one shade cleaner.

With an effort she straightened her back, half expecting it to creak, and wiped wrinkled palms across the front of a soggy apron. Resignedly, she pushed a sweaty lock of hair into place and stood, hands on hips, in an unconscious attitude of belligerent defiance. Suddenly she grinned with a puckish and impudent expression, realizing the picture she must present.

"Well," she said to no one in particular, "I wanted to be a pioneer woman, didn't I?" She waited, as though half expecting an invisible confidant to agree with her. "Providence was dull and a servant to do the washing and cooking namby-pamby, wasn't it? I had to be one with this brave new band to conquer a territorial wilderness, didn't I? I had to leave Rhode Island and come to Florida." She finished her catechism on a note of exasperation. "Well, my pretty," she glared at an inoffensive clump of sea myrtle, "here you are."

The washtub was balanced on the level base of a huge stump in the center of a small clearing where the long, russet pine needles made a carpet inches deep. To the left, a short distance away, two tents had been neatly raised and tightly staked and before them a banked and smoldering fire had drawn a charred black circle. Behind the tents the Rogers brothers had built a corral of saplings within which their two horses cropped with melancholy frustration at the sparse clumps of tough grass. Beyond the fenced square a lone cow at the end of a long tether rippled its hide and swished its tail at the persistent flies and lowed unhappily into the distance. Such was the barrier the Rogerses had reared against their primitive surroundings.

Sue glanced up at the declining sun, tentatively poked a finger into her unfinished washing, and wondered whether her brothers would prefer clean shirts to having their evening meal on time. Abruptly she felt ashamed of herself. With saw and ax the men attacked the forest from the moment the first streaks of dawn were laid against the sky until the sun sliced deeply into the smoky-blue cloud bank on a far horizon. They fell into their tent at night too weary for talk but arose each morning with renewed enthusiasm, stamping impatiently about the cherry-red fire as she hurried their breakfast. The clearing spread as their blades bit into the high, straight pines and brought them to earth and the piled split logs dried and seasoned throughout the long, warm days. Soon they would be able to start on the cabin, building it timber by timber. Not until the first logs were laid, however, would Susan be able to believe that the whole business was anything more than an outrageously fantastic camping trip on which she was humoring her hulking brothers.

When she thought at all about the neat white house with its prim green shutters and orderly flower beds they had left behind in Providence it was as though it were but a scene from a story, read long ago and half forgotten. The markets and the shops; the fine brick mansions on George Street with their ivy and boxwood; friends and the small gossip around tea tables; the excitement of a new frock or hat; all these things had achieved a dreamlike quality. It was difficult to recall her brother William as he had appeared behind his drawing board in the long, low room of Brown's Shipyard or to remember the sober elegance of Hadley Rogers as he strode up Exchange Place on his way to the bank, where he was considered to be a steady and dependable man with a bright future. More impossible to recall, though, was grim but efficient Martha, who cooked and cleaned, washed and sewed, and never—well, hardly ever—complained at the multitudinous tasks of the small household. Sometimes Susan dreamed of Martha. It was a pleasant dream in which the servant appeared miraculously out of the forest and hurried them all off to home and bed as she had when they were children.

Frequently Susan would try to retrace the first conversational steps that led them from Rhode Island to Florida. They had begun, she thought, shortly after the death of their father; a quiet, scholarly, and ineffectual man who had done his best to cope with three motherless children. Hadley read aloud each evening from the news, and it was he who mentioned the new territory of Florida for the first time. They talked of the country in the same manner in which they might have discussed China, as a faraway and improbable land. Then, and none of them was ever sure how it had come about, they were discussing the nation's latest acquisition with great seriousness, arguing the merits of its east coast over the Gulf of Mexico side. Had and Will pondered over such matters as acreage and Indians, horses and mules, plows and crops. Before their sister knew what was happening they had both given up their positions and made arrangements to send her to live with a maiden aunt.

The household storm that followed, later to be referred to in quotation marks as "Susan's Rebellion," was short-lived but fierce. When it abated the girl stood triumphantly on the deck of the coastal schooner with her brothers and looked southward where lay Savannah to mark the first part of their journey. There were times later, during the long arduous trip across the Territory from Jacksonville to Pensacola, when Susan Rogers regretted ever having heard of the peninsula. She was appalled by the dreary waste and ramshackle huddle of buildings at Jacksonville; the settlement having but recently changed its name from the unlovely but more appropriate designation of Cowford. The vast stretches of scrub-studded prairie, desolate pine flats, and murky, untracked swamps that stood between them and the west coast filled her with unspeakable terror. Insects and reptiles, sand and a shriveling sun that seared and tortured, made the word Florida seem something in the nature of an overstatement. Pensacola was a bawdy, roaring town booming with the seamen of the world. Speculators, thieves, adventurers, merchants, slave hunters, and soldiers fought and roistered, gambled and wenched. Fancy girls paraded their wares openly on the streets or leaned from balconies and doorways to expose their dubious charms to anyone who cared to look. Fights and murders were commonplace, and to Susan Rogers, huddled fearfully in her bed behind bolted doors and latched windows, the port town was the gateway to hell itself. When Had and Will announced they had purchased land far up a river known as the Apalachicola she was packed and waiting long before they had finished describing the state of their new home.

Knowledge had been rudely thrust upon the sixteen-year-old girl, but with wisdom had come confidence. She learned to take the long days in a jolting wagon beneath a blazing sun. She trained herself to load and fire a musket, to sleep in the open, to cook and wash and fend for herself when necessary. With the elasticity of youth she adapted herself to the wild frontier, flushing with pleasure and gratitude when her brothers finally accepted her as a full partner in their venture instead of an awkward and unnecessary appendage. Now she was almost as self-reliant as they and shouldered her share of the work, danger, and hardships without complaint. In the beginning Had and Will talked hopefully of purchasing a slave or two, but good Negroes were expensive and the bad ones weren't worth what they cost. The men took the brunt of the heavy work, but the days were chore-filled and never ending for the girl. She cooked and cleaned, sewed and washed, with monotonous regularity. The sun hammered her skin into a dusky copper tone and the strenuous labor hardened and refined her slender body, lending it grace and beauty. Now and then she thought a little wistfully of other days and times, of parties and beaux and the excitement of being sought after, but for the most part the hours between sunrise and sunset were too packed to make room for dreaming. Now the most important thing in the world was the completion of the cabin, a room of her own, curtains on the windows, a fireplace with spit and kettle rod to cook on, a door to close and lock, a solid roof overhead.

Turning, she looked to where Will and Had were working. They were never far away, and the sight of them, bending their broad backs and thrusting their strength against the wilderness, filled her with a tender, almost maternal pride. She was continually surprised by their knowledge and the quiet certainty with which they went about the unfamiliar job of raising a home. Once she left her tent and crept into theirs, nestling down between them with the furtive air of a puppy. When Will awoke, grunted in sleepy surprise, and looked at her in amazement, she threw an arm around his neck.

"Oh, Will! I'm so glad I'm your sister." A flood of affection engulfed her and she felt, at that moment, she would never love anyone quite so much. "I don't ever want to go away from you and Hadley."

With rough but understanding affection he had laid a heavy hand on her head, rumpling her hair and drawing her within the curve of his arm.

"I guess we're stuck," he whispered. "Who'd want a skinny little thing like you? Go to sleep before you wake Had an' he throws you out."

Without enthusiasm now she returned her attention to the tub of unfinished washing. The water cooled rapidly and was slimy to the touch, but she plunged hands and arms into it and sloshed vigorously at the weighted garments.

"I'll give you one more chance," she warned the soiled mass. "Get clean now or I'll toss you away for good."

With a heave and an inexpert twist she wound a dripping shirt into a rope for wringing and glanced up across the tub. Her eyes widened and she stood transfixed for a moment, the length of cloth stretched between her hands. With a stifled yelp she dropped the garment and raced toward one of the tents, screaming at Had and Will as she ran. Canted against the tent's wall was a primed and loaded musket. She snatched at it.

"Will, Had!" Her cry had lost its original panic. "Indians!"

From the distance she heard her brothers' reassuring shouts and knew they were coming. Suddenly she began to feel a little foolish. At first glance she had seen the two figures approaching through the woods, caught a glimpse of the Seminole, and her imagination, set afire by the Clayport rumors of trouble, peopled all of Elbow Bend with hostile savages bent upon destruction. With the musket held across her body she took a calmer view. The men were walking openly, casually toward her, and only one was an Indian. She heard her brothers' pounding feet slow to an even stride as they also appraised the situation. With a small hysterical giggle she replaced the musket and stood uncertain and half angry at having made a fool of herself.

Clay and Asseola had witnessed the consternation their appearance created, heard Susan's scream of terror, and watched her whipping skirts fly as she ran. Clay grinned and flashed a sidelong glance at his companion. He thought Asseola was smiling, but it was hard, sometimes, to tell when an Indian was amused.

"By God," Clay murmured, "I knew you weren't pretty, but I never figured you were ugly enough to scare the girls an' make 'em cry."

The Rogers men stood side by side, muskets hanging from their arms, displaying neither curiosity nor alarm at the unexpected visit. Doing her best to appear unconcerned, Sue joined them and pretended not to see the bantering expression on their faces. She recognized Clay now and thought unhappily of her frumpish appearance, stained apron, and stringy hair. Illogically, she found herself growing angry with him. Stalking and sneaking out of the woods this way, she thought, and bringing an Indian along to frighten the wits out of people. Having justified her alarm, she drew herself up in an attitude of proud aloofness.

At the far side of the tub Clay and Asseola halted. The Indian waited unconcernedly. His detachment was complete and he left the burden of the moment to his friend.

"Hello." Clay nodded pleasantly, his eyes skipping quickly over Sue and fastening themselves on Had. "We heard your axes," he continued, "an' thought we'd stop by to see how you were getting along."

The Rogers men relaxed slightly. Hadley stepped forward and extended his hand.

"We're glad to see you," he said. He indicated Will. "This is my brother, Will. You've met my sister."

"Servant, sir," Clay said, trying not to look at the girl. "This is my friend Asseola."

The Seminole barely nodded and Clay understood that in an obscure Indian fashion he was enjoying the moment. The girl was regarding him with something close to fascination, taking in every detail of his savage finery, and, womanlike, already wondering how the bright egret plume would look on a hat. The men were less obvious but their interest was apparent.

"You'll have to forgive Sue." Will spoke slowly but with relish, and his words might have been directed to either of the visitors. "She's a little skittish sometimes." A smile puckered his mouth at his sister's angry gasp.

"I'm sorry we frightened you, ma'am." Clay turned his glance full upon her and thought, She's a mighty pretty thing. About the prettiest thing I ever saw.

"I wasn't frightened." Sue was not to be placated so easily. "We're —we're just not used to visitors way out here, that's all."

There was an awkward pause, which Will finally broke. "Will you stay a while?" He looked hopefully at his sister. "Sue here will be glad to fix something to eat." He made a slight motion toward Asseola. "What do I say to your friend? I mean, we'd like to have him also." The hospitality was there but crudely expressed.

"Oh!" Clay was unperturbed but he didn't dare look at Asseola. "You just say Ug! or How! to him." He bit fiercely at his lip, chewing back the laughter that threatened to explode in their faces. In dialect he spoke rapidly to the Indian. "Don't stand there like a silly fool. Say something."

Dreamily, Asseola considered a distant point above their heads, but one eyebrow twitched spasmodically. His features were frozen and without expression. Finally he lifted one hand, palm extended, in a gesture of salutation.

"How!" he grunted, and the sound bogged down deep within his throat.

Clay was forced to turn his face away. If he does that again, he told himself, I'm going to have to yell right out. He caught the girl's glance as it wavered from the Indian to him. A tiny puzzled frown crinkled her brow. She's smart, Clay thought quickly. She's pretty an' smart, too.

"We wouldn't want to put you to any trouble," he said lamely in reply to the invitation. "We were out this way an' I thought we'd stop by an' see if you were all right. Neighbors are kind of scarce," he smiled, "an' I figured we ought to take care of those we have."

"Ug!" Asseola gulped the sound and then wheeled abruptly, striding off along the way they had come.

Too surprised to speak, Clay watched until his friend reached the fringe of pines. He, the girl, and her brothers unconsciously formed a tableau as the Seminole merged with the forest. Clay could stand it no longer. Laughter overwhelmed him as he thought of Asseola's grotesque performance. He howled, tears streaming down his face, doubled in uncontrollable mirth. Every time he looked up and saw the astonishment written on the faces of the Rogerses he whooped with delight until, weak and shaken, he staggered limply and collapsed at the base of a stump.

"Are you quite sure you're all right, Mr. Hammond?" Susan Rogers watched him suspiciously and her enunciation was unnecessarily prim.

Clay nodded feebly, wiping at his eyes and trying not to remember the expression of grave stupidity on Asseola's face.

"That crazy Indian," he gasped, "that fool of a Seminole. He speaks English as well as—probably better than—I do. Ug! How!" He shouted happily at the sound and then lay back against the stump, his chest heaving, his sides sore.

The Rogers brothers, who had watched his antics with an expression of patient bewilderment, grinned appreciatively at the jest. Will chuckled, a real concession, but his sister, for one reason or another, seemed to be annoyed.

"Indians," she said thoughtfully, "must have a strange sense of humor."

Clay nodded. "Yes, ma'am, they do. I never thought much about it before, but that is just the sort of thing they would enjoy." He rose from the ground and dusted at the clinging pine needles on his trousers. "He'll be laughing about this to himself for days."

"Huh!" She sniffed.

Clay regarded her sharply. "Don't you really think it's funny, ma'am?" If, he told himself, she doesn't see anything comical in this, then you've sort of made a mistake.

Sue smiled at the unmistakable anxiety with which the question had been phrased. There was something appealing in his concern. The tip of her tongue rippled inside her cheek and she gazed up at him.

"Ug!" she said.

Suddenly they all were laughing with a companionable understanding as though they had known each other for years. Had Rogers kicked a pine cone and sent it flying across the tub. His customary seriousness magically swept away, he looked at Clay and chortled, sharing the memory of a ludicrous moment.

"You'll stay and eat with us now?" Sue addressed Clay.

"Ug!" he replied, and again they all seemed to find something inexpressibly ridiculous in the sound.

While Sue hurried through her washing, stringing it out on a line behind the tents, Clay and the Rogers men walked back to where they had marked out their homesite. Axes and saws lay as they had dropped them at Sue's screams. With habitual neatness, Had set the ax blades into a log and carefully propped the saw against their shafts. It was a long and backbreaking job the two men had set themselves; felling trees, splitting, smoothing, and stacking the timber for curing, underbrushing the tract.

"I'm damned," Will said with a touch of exasperated weariness, "if that scrub doesn't seem to grow back overnight."

They grouped around a broad stump and each of them elevated one foot, leaning forward and resting crossed arms on upthrust knees. Solemnly they stared at the cabin's floor plan as it had been staked out in the black dirt, as though by the power of imagination they could cause the walls to rise. All over the long peninsula, Clay thought, men like the Rogerses were battering against the wilderness, crowding their hopes and ambitions into small clearings and cabins. The land hunger gnawed at them, driving them to almost heroic measures in a never ending battle for survival. Many, he knew, must fail, but the tide was irresistible. For those who dropped out of the contest there were a dozen to take their places. Against them, seeking to block their way, were the swamps and flats; the terrible heat of midsummer, which brought maddening swarms of mosquitoes and flies; the clogging scrub and forests; the Seminoles and, Clay mused, such men as Clayfield Hammond, who would devour the Territory,

86

gorging themselves upon it, seeking always to add to their already large holdings.

Clay rubbed thoughtfully at his chin, glancing at Hadley Rogers out of the corners of his eyes. A half a dozen slaves, he thought, could have this section cleared and a house up in thirty days.

"You know," he said reflectively, and wondered what prompted the words, "I could get a few Negrahs over here an' have this done in a month for you." He laughed without mirth. "I'll swear, though, Old Clay'd run me from here to Alabama an' beyond if he ever heard about it."

Will and Had Rogers were surprised and they turned to stare at him, perplexed by the suggestion and curious as to the motive behind it. Nothing they had heard led them to expect a generous gesture from the Hammond plantation.

"We sort of thought we might hear from your grandfather before this." Had watched him, cocking his head to one side like a man hard of hearing.

Clay nodded agreeably. "You know," he admitted, "I've been wonderin' some about that myself ever since I met you an' your sister in McCollum's. There's a chance he doesn't know you're here, but it isn't likely. Maybe he's had other things on his mind. Besides, we—he holds an awful lot of land. No one knows for sure just how big the plantation is. You could lose a hundred families on the place."

Will dug a piece of turpentine gum from the stump and kneaded it thoughtfully between his fingers.

"I'd just as soon get it over with. We're not," he added defensively, "squatters."

Clay experienced a momentary feeling of helplessness in the face of such innocence. The Rogerses had an idea they would be dealing with an ordinary man, logical and open to reason. Clayfield Hammond would be something new. They had never encountered anyone like him and had no way of judging his capacity for savage ruthlessness. He felt a little sorry for them.

"I don't know," he said doubtfully, "if I'd rush things. If you bought the Elbow Bend tract in as you say an' it's proper and legal, then I'd sort of wait for him. You see," he tried to explain, "there isn't much law in the Territory yet except around the fringes. My grandfather's been here a long time and he's sort of used to runnin' things his own way." He shook his head, halting the objections which sprang to their lips. "You could show him papers an' deeds an' whatever else you have, but he wouldn't give a damn." Although the Rogers men were his seniors by at least ten years, he felt older and wiser than either of them.

Had clicked a thumbnail against his teeth, playing it back and forth with a small snapping sound.

"You know, sir," he finally said, "I find what you have to say a little strange, coming from one of the Hammond family."

Clay smiled, frankly and with a disarming warmth. "I guess so. I'd probably feel the same way. Only—" He hesitated. "There isn't any Hammond family, just my grandfather an' me. That makes a difference. We don't always see things the same way. As far as I'm concerned, the plantation could have spared you this tract and more. We don't need it, probably won't ever use it. I'd be glad to see people, nice people like yourselves, come in. I'm not tryin' to hold anything for a Hammond family. There isn't any." He shrugged, unable to translate his thoughts into words. "I don't know whether that makes any sense," he concluded.

Had dropped his foot from the stump. "I'm sorry, sir," he apologized generously, "for the suspicion my statement implied. It didn't seem reasonable, after the stories we've heard, that the grandson of Clayfield Hammond could be as open and friendly as you offered to be. I was rude." He held out his hand.

"That's all right." Clay was embarrassed. "I suppose I'd feel the same way." They shook hands gravely.

Will tugged at the handle of one of the axes, wrenching the blade out of the soft wood and swinging the tool up and across his shoulder. "Let's get clean and see what Sue has for supper," he suggested practically.

By the time they had taken their turn at the washing bucket, snorting and splashing in the cool water, Sue had laid out the evening meal of fried salted pork, beans, and hot corn bread, baked in a covered iron skillet set in the ashes. Somehow she had managed to find time to change into a fresh dress, and her hair was brushed and drawn loosely about into a swirling knot at the nape of her neck. Moving unhurriedly and with a certain deft economy of motion, she served their plates, shifted the blackened coffeepot to the edge of the coals, and then, with a small sigh of pleasure, seated herself on a log just within the wavering pool of light. Her face was gently flushed and her lips slightly parted in an expression of pleased excitement.

"I feel like it's a party," she confessed happily.

Seated across the fire, balancing the warm plate on the palm of his hand between outstretched knees, Clay watched her over the low

88

flames. Now and then she glanced up and their eyes met, clung to each other, and dropped away reluctantly. Will and Had ate in silence, refilling their plates and heavy mugs, then stepping back to their places in the shadows. They moved slowly and as though a great weariness were upon them.

"Sorry we couldn't put a better meal before you, Mr. Hammond," Will apologized for the plain food. "Sue does the best she can but there isn't much variety. The Indians used to bring over fresh meat, fish, and vegetables for sale, but they just stopped coming. Had and I don't get much time off for hunting, and when we want anything fresh we have to go into Clayport."

"I like beans fine," Clay assured Sue. "As a matter of fact, I like everything."

She smiled at him across the crumbling fire and bent forward, locking her hands about her knees, staring contentedly into the dancing heat.

Had and Will leaned back against a supporting log, pipes in their mouths, long legs stretched comfortably before them. The night gathered itself about the group as the shadows merged and became one. A thin segment of lemon-yellow moon hung low in the west and the stars brightened, winking on one by one as though kindled by an invisible taper. In the high pines the wind was a restless hunter, speaking softly as it hurried along. There was a feeling of peace and security in the murmur of its passing.

"It's a fair land." Had's voice was muffled. "There's a rare beauty here, although at first it takes a bit of looking and knowledge to find it." He seemed to speak to himself.

"Will there be fighting, do you think, Mr. Hammond?" Will Rogers blew into the bowl of his pipe and the glow lighted his face for a moment.

Clay shifted uncomfortably. It would be hard to explain to the Rogerses. He compromised.

"If you mean tonight, tomorrow, or the next day," he said thoughtfully, "I don't think so."

"What about the day after the next day?" Sue raised her head and looked squarely at him. The question cut through to the core.

"It's hard to tell, Miss Sue." Clay ventured to address her informally. No one seemed to notice the presumption. "If you mean, will there be an Indian war with peace one day and some sort of a formal declaration the next, it won't happen that way. If it comes it will be like a brush fire, scattered and small at first, springing up an' then

89

dying down in half a dozen places but all the time working toward the center."

"What is it the Indians want, Mr. Hammond?" Hadley's words came from the darkness.

Clay experienced a touch of exasperation. "Why," he said shortly, "just about the same things the white people are after—something of their own, peace, a chance to live quietly, raise their children." He kicked gently at a charred length of wood, edging it back into the live coals. "Old Clay says I'm an Indian lover, but he's wrong. I don't think they're all noble or generous or honorable." A smile hovered about his mouth. "They're pretty much like us. Some of them are dirty, thieving, and without decency; they're shiftless an' sly, greedy an' dishonest. The pattern's much the same whether you cut it in red or white."

"If trouble comes," Hadley seemed to be pursuing a thought of his own, "surely it can't last long. The Indians will never be able to stand up against the Army of the United States."

Helplessly Clay wondered if the man had the slightest idea of what he was saying. Most of the whites talked the same way, repeating identical words.

"Well, sir," he answered thoughtfully, "they did pretty well the last time. They fought Andrew Jackson an' his troops along with McIntosh an' some Creeks for two years, an' when it was over they still hadn't signed a treaty. The Seminoles learned a lot. They won' fight with the Army's rules an' the Army won't be able to fight their way. It'll be the damnedest killing you ever saw."

"Isn't there any other way?" The girl lifted her head and looked over at Clay. Her voice was troubled and her question carried a note of sadness with it.

I'm doing an awful lot of talking, Clay thought. Old Clay ought to be around to hear me flappin' my tongue this way. The ideas th questions provoked, though, were stimulating. There was an exciting novelty in being asked for an opinion. He'd never been able to talk this way with his grandfather.

"There was a man once," he said slowly, "a Colonel Humphrey He spent a night at our place three years ago. He had another way Colonel Humphreys thought if we kept our word the Seminole would stick to theirs. He even had the crazy idea that if the Unite States made a bargain we ought to keep it even if we were only dealing with Indians. I don't guess Colonel Humphreys lasted ver long. He wanted me to come an' visit him once. I wish now I had.

Hadley Rogers tapped a pipe bowl against the toe of his boot an
90

the insistent knocking was that of a woodpecker at work on a hollow tree. Sparks from the tobacco scattered brightly and died quickly.

"You know," he said thoughtfully, "the things you say, the way you talk, they all sound a little strange, coming as they do from a— a—" He paused.

"A Hammond?" Clay suggested helpfully.

Will chuckled, amused at his brother's predicament. Sue looked across at Clay and smiled understandingly.

"Well, yes, sir." Hadley was abashed but determined. "I know it's impolite, but I couldn't help but wonder."

"You an' my grandfather ought to know each other." Clay was amused. "He wonders about the same thing, only his voice is louder. You see," he tilted back his head and stared at the sky, "there haven't been many white people in this part of the Territory. I never had much company; a Negrah slave boy was the only thing I had to talk to. Then Asseola and I got to be friends. He's the only real friend I've ever had. We grew up together, played, fought, and argued with each other. I learned a lot from him, a lot about him an' all Seminoles; what they want, how they think."

Hadley seemed to be digesting this, slowly and completely. When he spoke again it was as though he was still puzzled.

"Feeling the way you do," he worried the notion with an orderly mind, "where will you stand if trouble breaks out?"

Clay's surprise was immediate and genuine. "With my own people, of course," he said quickly. "Maybe I won't like it an' maybe I won't believe in what we are doing, but," his shoulders lifted expressively, "there isn't much choice."

"And," Sue was watching him, "your friend, what's his name, Osceola?"

Clay didn't bother to correct her pronunciation. He laughed good-humoredly and leaned forward, the better to see her face.

"Why," he said, "he'd shoot at me as quick as he would a soldier; quicker, maybe. Things would just be that way an' neither of us could change them."

Will rose, feeling at the muscles of his aching back. He stretched and looked seriously into the fire.

"It's late," he said. "If there was a war tonight I'm too tired to help fight it." He stared down at Clay. "You make a lot of sense, Mr. Hammond, even if some people wouldn't think so."

Reluctantly Clay rose. "I'd better start back," he said without enthusiasm.

Hadley joined his brother at the fire. "Why don't you spend the

91

night with us? It isn't much," his head jerked toward the tent, "but we can let you have some blankets, and it's a long walk in the dark to your plantation." There was sincere hospitality in the invitation.

Clay didn't attempt to conceal his pleasure. "I'd like to," he said, "and thank you, but I won't need to crowd into the tent. A couple of blankets out here by the fire will suit me fine."

"Whatever you say." Hadley didn't press the point. "At that, you'll probably sleep better. It takes some time to get used to Will's snoring."

Will yawned, his eyes heavy with sleep, and looked up at the sky. "If it rains," he suggested, "come on inside. The snores are dry." He turned to his sister. "Coming, Sue?"

"In a minute," she replied. "I'll get some covering for Mr. Hammond. You're sure you'll be all right out here?"

"I'll be fine," Clay answered quickly. "Don't worry about me."

"Well," Had turned away, "good night and we'll see you in the morning. Sue puts out a pretty good breakfast, for a girl."

The brothers stooped to enter the tent, dropping the flaps behind them.

Clay pushed a couple of pine chunks into the red embers and the flames licked with quick greediness at the seams of pitch. Sue watched him in silence until he sat down.

"You're our first visitor," she said. "It's sort of fun to have company even if we haven't anything to entertain with. Wait until the cabin is up and we'll have a real housewarming."

Clay looked over at her, experiencing a pleasant excitement at the intimacy of the moment. In the soft firelight she seemed almost incredibly beautiful and young. I guess, he told himself, I've been missing something living alone with Old Clay all these years. There are probably a lot of things goin' on in the world I ought to investigate an' know about.

"You know," he confessed, "this is the first time I ever talked with a girl, a white girl."

Her laughter was a low, throaty bubble that burst with amusement. "Do you find it such a terrifying experience, Mr. Hammond?"

"Not exactly," he grinned. "But I just keep wondering what to say."

"Oh!" Her eyes were bright with mockery. "I imagine you'd say the same things you would to an—" she hesitated, "an Indian girl."

Clay could feel the heat of a slow flush as it rose to his cheeks. She said the damnedest things for a nice girl; like telling him in McCollum's he bled easily. Wasn't that a hell of a thing to say?

92

"Of course," she continued, "you'll have to say them in English."

"I'll try an' remember," he said. "It sounds like good advice."

They sat without speaking for a moment. A lulling warmth from the blazing logs flooded out to envelop them. Clay peered steadily at the bright tongues of fire, conscious that the girl was watching him from beneath half-lowered eyes. She sighed with a small sound of pleasure.

"Tell me about the plantation," she urged, "how you live, what you do."

"There isn't much to tell. Old Clay an' I live pretty quietly. At least, we do when he's not yelling about something, which isn't often."

"Is he really as terrible as people say?"

"Probably." Clay had to smile at her wide-eyed seriousness. "Anyhow, a lot of folks have been bruised some trying to find out."

"What about you? Don't you think it strange never to have been off the plantation or out of Clayport?"

"Well," Clay maintained an attitude of sober reflection, "I didn't until you came along. Now I begin to see that I've been sort of backward."

"Sir," she rose with a smile, "I think it is time you went to sleep. I'll get some blankets, although it occurs to me that your imagination is sufficient to keep you warm."

"You know," Clay couldn't resist the opportunity, "you say some mighty funny things for a girl."

She laughed. "That's the result of being the only girl in a household filled with men. It gives one little opportunity or reason to be a fluttering dove. Besides, I play the role so badly."

"Are all girls in the North like you?" He watched her as she moved away from the fire.

"With minor variations." She touched his hand lightly in passing. "But you ought to go and see for yourself. I may be prejudiced."

She returned with three blankets draped over one arm. "If I were completely domesticated," she said, "I suppose I'd make up your bed, but I honestly don't know how to turn a corner or tuck in a sheet on the ground. You'll have to use one blanket for a pillow."

"I'll get along fine," he assured her.

A sudden awkwardness held them for a moment as though they had abruptly become aware of each other and recognized the attraction. She looked up at him, her lips parted slightly, her eyes deep and serious.

"I'm—I'm glad you came calling, Mr. Hammond." Her voice was little more than a whisper.

"So am I." The words seemed strained. "Would—" he hesitated, "would it be all right if you called me Clay, and I—" His mouth was mysteriously dry.

"And you could call me Sue?" she prompted.

"I had it in mind."

Her finger tips rested on his wrist and then withdrew reluctantly, it seemed, and with the gentleness of a caress. Clay was startled by the action.

"I think I'd like that," she murmured. Then, with what Clay thought was unnecessary haste, she added, "Good night." At her tent the girl turned. She was laughing again and the old impudence was in her manner. "Clay," she called softly, "maybe it wouldn't be such a good idea for you to go north and investigate those other girls."

"I gave up that notion about five minutes ago." He hoped the Rogers men weren't listening to this nonsense.

Waiting until she had closed the fly of her tent, he dropped the blankets to the ground and tossed together a bed of sorts. For a long time he lay on his back, arms crossed beneath his head, staring up at the sky. The heat from the fire crept out as small waves, lapping over him with a gentle persuasiveness. Sleep was an illusion and he didn't bother to seek it.

"I wonder," he said doubtfully to the night, "what Old Clay would say if I turned up with a girl, especially one from a family that has just snatched a piece of land from beneath his feet."

8

SALANO stood at the bottom of the steps, hat in hand, obsequious in attitude. A web of concern was drawn about his forehead as he looked up at Old Clay.

"It is as I have said, señor," he said softly. "A family has moved to the property and a house is being built. When I heard of it I moved with dispatch, calling upon them in person. The name is Rogers, and a deed, signed by a commission in Pensacola, attests to the purchase. How could such things be?" He lifted expressive eyes as though imploring heaven for the answer.

The old man didn't move in his chair, nor did he appear to have heard the overseer's words. Chewing thoughtfully at his lower lip, he stared over the man's shoulders. There was something frightening in his calm, and Salano shifted uneasily.

"We could," the Spaniard suggested, "have them moved."

Old Clay looked coldly at him. "I figure to have them moved. You don't suppose I'm goin' to sit by an' see my land overrun with Yankee squatters. Things are just gettin' too damn legal in the Territory when a fella thinks all he needs is a little piece of paper to set up housekeepin' on Hammond acres."

Salano nodded. "They could be made uncomfortable."

With a clawing motion of his fingers the old man tugged at his mouth, drawing away a tenuous thread of spittle.

"How come I didn't know about this until now?" He dropped the question almost listlessly at Salano's feet.

The overseer had been dreading the inevitable. "It but came to my attention. As you know, the section is two miles up-river. We go to it rarely. Only by accident did I hear of the family."

"They buildin' a house, you say, on my land with my timber?"

Salano raised his shoulders contemptuously. "It is but a cabin. It was told to me your grandson was a visitor there."

Old Clay lifted his head. "You're a no-good son of a bitch," he said mildly. "Don't lay the blame on Young Clay for not knowin' what's goin' on. My grandson ain't paid to tell me things. You are."

95

Salano flushed. "Yes, señor."

"I was just thinkin'," the old man whispered, "things bein' un-settled like they are, some drunken Indians might set fire to a cabin before it was finished."

Salano brightened. "It could be arranged, señor."

"I'll think about it some. In the meantime, you just go on about the plantation's business. Keep our men away from the Bend."

Throughout the long morning Old Clay remained on the porch, chin sunk to his chest, hands folded placidly in his lap. Not until the slaves came to carry him in for the noon meal did he rouse himself or indicate he was other than a weary man, drowsing in the sun.

Seated at the head of the long table, he looked thoughtfully at Young Clay's vacant chair and then carefully began filling his plate from the platters and dishes as they were brought to him for in-spection. He ate slowly and without relish, and when Clay came into the room he barely glanced up.

"You're late," he said.

The younger man nodded. "I was riding. The dogs jumped a bear in the scrub. Biggest, blackest bear I ever saw." He attacked the food with complete absorption. "Lit out like he wasn't goin' to stop this side of Savannah. Old Belle is still on his tail, I guess. I couldn't call her off."

"Belle's a good bitch. I wouldn't want to lose her."

Young Clay regarded his grandfather with surprise. "I didn't even know you knew she was on the place."

"Why the hell shouldn't I know what's goin' on? It's my plan-tation, ain't it?"

The younger man was startled by the sudden truculence. Holding a fork with a thick piece of ham on it an inch or so from his open lips, he stared down the table. Finally he thrust the meat into his waiting mouth and chewed pensively, his eyes never leav-ing his grandfather's face.

"That's a funny thing to say," he said thoughtfully.

"Why didn't you tell me there was squatters on the Bend?"

Young Clay's face cleared and he laughed. "I had an idea you were leading up to that. I didn't tell you because I didn't want to hear you yell the way you're goin' to do any minute. Besides, they aren't squatters. They bought the land."

"My land ain't for sale." The old man's voice shook.

"The Commission at Pensacola says it never was included in your claim, so it was free an' was sold as such. Anyhow, it isn't something you need."

"I'm the only one who'll decide such things." Old Clay's mouth trembled. "If you'd ever turned a spade of earth on the land you might feel different about it."

The grandson spooned up a large helping of thick and dripping preserves. "Well, sir," he asked with hypocritical meekness, "would you like to have me drive a mule or chop some cotton?"

"I'd like you to keep a civil tongue in your head." The answering roar almost shook the table and the slaves instinctively backed away from the chairs, making themselves inconspicuous against the wall.

"You're setting a hell of an example." The younger man's shout matched Hammond's bellow.

At opposite ends of the table they leaned forward, their tempers clashing, beating furiously at each other. If he cared to, the old man could gaze upon his image of over half a century ago. The resemblance was unmistakable in the powerful sloping of the broad shoulders, the challenging lift of the head, and the determined jaw line. Instead of being pleased with what he saw, Hammond was only irritated by the reflection. That was how he had looked before being reduced to a crawling, useless thing, trailing a withered leg.

"I had to fight for this land," Old Clay's voice was sharp and spiteful, "an' it ain't going to be given away. If you've got the idea things ought to be divided among the Indians an' squatters so's everybody can have a half-acre patch to raise beans on, then go out an' get your own to whack up with the dirty savages an' stinkin' immigrants. You ain't goin' to lay a finger on mine; not while I'm alive."

"I haven't given anything away." Clay tried to inject a quiet note of reason into the oral conflict. "I only said the section the Rogerses moved to wouldn't make any difference to the plantation."

"It makes a difference to me if I lose a piece of toenail." Hammond would not be soothed. "I aim to keep what I have," he snorted. "I aim to keep it against fools an' them with the ideas of fools. If you'd take some interest instead of whelpin' around with them Indians, maybe you'd feel the same way."

The old man gulped for air, breathing heavily, and his hands quivered as though his whole body was in the grip of a fanatical excitement. There was fever in his eyes. Looking at him, Clay realized for the first time that his grandfather was an old man. Always he had seemed ageless, untouched and indifferent to time, a huge gray oak against which the winds of the years hurled themselves and were defeated. Seeing him this way, Clay experienced a quick tug of compassion. The old man had beaten away his life in the Territory, building the fortune that lay in distant banks and counting rooms. Here in the wilderness the money was without significance and brought no comfort to the man who collected it so determinedly. Without friends, scornful of the helpless, suspicious, alert to encroachment, Old Clay had only one weapon against loneliness, power, and for it he had sucked himself dry.

With a brief nod Clay indicated a decanter to one of the slaves and waited until it had been placed before his grandfather. The old man didn't appear to notice the brandy. The breath whistled from his nostrils and he gave the appearance of an enraged stallion, frustrated but unbroken.

"Let's have a drink." Young Clay made the suggestion quietly.

Anger died slowly in Hammond's eyes. For a moment he seemed almost childishly uncertain, unable to follow the abrupt change of mood. His glance wavered from the hand of the slave to his grandson, as though he were trying to place them. There was something pathetic in his glazed stare and Clay was shocked by the spectacle of disintegration. He'll drop dead one of these days, he thought. I never knew he was old, not that old. No man with so much time on his shoulders can work himself up an' yell so often without gettin' winded right down to his toes.

With a palsied hand he strove to control, Hammond lifted the brandy glass to his lips and gulped at it. The rim of the crystal clattered against his teeth. The film lifted slowly from his eyes. When the glass was refilled he emptied it, swallowing the strong liquor without haste as color returned to his face. He watched as Clay drained his glass.

"I never knew you to drink before."

The younger man smiled. "Don't know as I ever did." The brandy ran in a fiery rivulet to his stomach. "Hot, isn't it?" he observed wonderingly.

"How come you're doin' it now?" Old Clay wouldn't have his curiosity put aside.

"It seemed like a good idea. And," he couldn't hold back the grin, "about the only way I could think of to stop a ruckus. We'd have had the table over on us the next thing."

Old Clay selected a fat smooth cigar from a silver box and a slave came forward quickly with a taper. The aroma of the fine

Cuban leaf filled the room. Through the blue-gray haze grandfather and grandson looked at each other.

"It ain't hardly possible." Old Clay was thoughtful. His choler had departed, his hand was steady, his eyes were clear, and he was as close to being jovial as his grandson had ever seen him. "It ain't possible," he repeated, "for you to be as dumb as you talk sometimes. So," he paused, "I got to put it down to ignorance."

Clay refused the invitation, allowing the words to pass without comment. The point, he understood, would be reached sooner or later. The brandy was soothing his insides and filling him with a lazy sense of well-being.

"I figure you're ignorant," Old Clay continued, "because you never been off the plantation or much out of Clayport." He tapped his glass with a spoon and rolled the liquor over his tongue. "Maybe the notions you got come from associatin' with that Indian, Powell, or eatin' with Seminoles where everyone sticks a hand into the same pot. Well, by God," his voice rose, but not in anger, "things ain't that way. If you got a filled pot the only way to keep it is to be damn sure no one else's fingers get in the stew."

Clay knew it was foolish to interrupt but the words came automatically. "If you've got more than you can eat an' another man is hungry—"

His grandfather gave him no opportunity to finish. "If another man's hungry, then he better go out an' get his own pot an' piece of beef. Once you let him come dippin' he'll end up by bringin' all his relatives, an' you'll finish with a cold tail an' not even able to get near the fire."

The old man's attitude was something new. He'd never bothered to discuss anything with him before. Clay wondered and waited, taking more brandy while his grandfather studied the tip of his cigar.

"I figure," the voice droned on, "you ought to get out an' look around. Take a trip, visit some, see how people are gougin' an' scroungin', clawin' an' bitin' to hold what they got or add a little more. Once you see it you ain't goin' to be so anxious to give your own away. It ought to do you good. You may have to fight one of these days to hold onto what I put together. I'd like to have you get an idea why you're fightin'."

It was the longest speech Clay had ever heard the old man deliver, and certainly more words than he had ever spoken to him before at one time. Also, there was a new note in the voice, almost as though the man at the other end of the table was pleading

99

to be understood. I must be gettin' drunk, Clay thought. He never asked anyone for anything. The way he talks now sounds as if he was makin' a will an' was scared.

"I'd like fine to go off an' see some things." He pushed away the remaining brandy. The idea was stimulating enough.

"Well, then," Old Clay was sharp, "why don't you go? Take a Negrah; I'll let you have Santee. He ain't too bright but he's able to learn. You want to go east or west or north? Take your choice to start with."

Clay suddenly felt as though a map had been unrolled before him on the table. In his mind he measured the distance between the plantation and Fort King. I'll go see Colonel Humphreys first, he thought. Abruptly he checked himself on the point of speaking. Old Clay would only have to hear the name of Humphreys and they would be back at the table-throwing stage.

"I guess," he said slowly, "I'll go east an' start with St. Augustine. I always wondered what the ocean was like."

"It's salty." The old man grunted. "I don't give a damn where you go. Just come back with some sense." With powerful hands he shoved away from the table. "Get me carried upstairs now," he commanded, "where I can take a nap. It ain't likely you'll start before the next couple of hours." Amusement illuminated his features, but he growled angrily as the slaves carefully lifted his chair and moved him toward the front hall and staircase.

Long after the clumsy sounds of movement on the upper floor had quieted, Clay sat at the table, his thoughts wandering without direction through an entire new world. It was startling enough that the old man had been the one to make the suggestion. Equally incredible was the fact that he was actually going away. Already he felt the journey begun; he and the big Angola buck Santee were on their way. By God, he thought with quickening interest, what do you suppose the people in a place like New York would say if I turned up with a Negrah the size of Santee? The next mental step was short and natural. He took it without conscious effort. Santee isn't goin' to be much company, not to talk to. How about Caccosoci? The brief whistle escaping his lips was automatic. They'd cut a figure, wouldn't they; he an' Asseola with Santee to fetch an' do for them like a couple of South Carolina bloods? Old Clay wouldn't ever have to know a thing about it. Ten minutes later he was astride his horse.

On the ridge, when he was close enough to see the Seminole town through the trees, Clay dismounted and, as a matter of simple courtesy, prepared to enter the *istihapo* on foot. In a wide circle the dog pack yelped and snarled, made frantic by the sight and smell of man and horse. Clay swung a heavy club in one hand and put his weight into checking his nervous and rearing mount. With their wicked red eyes on the club the dogs made no attempt to close the distance but ran in idiotic frenzy, snapping and screaming at each other. The Indians, having already identified the visitor, took no further notice of him. Clay led his horse well inside the camp and tied him securely to a lodge upright. A man, seated cross-legged on mats beneath the crisp and yellowed palm thatch, rubbed industriously at a white length of bone, shaping it into an ornament. Not until Clay spoke to him did he bother to look up.

"I would talk with my brother, Asseola?" The statement in the dialect came naturally as a question.

"He went two days ago, taking with him his long rifle and blanket. His place in the lodge is vacant."

"Is he hunting?"

"It was not told so to me." The Seminole was indifferent. "Do you have tobacco?" The voice held a whining note of complaint and the words were those of a beggar who knows no good will come of his plea.

Clay turned from the man and allowed his eyes to roam around the *istihapo*. There were evidences of neglect and slovenly disorder; a hole gaped in the thatching of a lodge, logs were laid carelessly to the fire, a blackening, fly-covered carcass of a small pig lay unattended on a chopping block near the cooking lodge, a stretching frame was tumbled and broken on the ground as though such things no longer mattered.

"Do you have whisky?" The Indian whispered the words slyly.

Clay wheeled. "It is known to you who I am," he said sharply. "I come not as a stranger to this town."

The Seminole dropped his eyes. Black, rancid hair tumbled over his forehead, and in it the lice crawled thickly. The single garment he wore was filthy and there was a greasy, sour stink upon him. Listlessly he turned the piece of bone over in his fingers. His shoulders hung without pride. He gazed at the ornament as though he were trying to remember what it was he intended to do with it. Clay's rebuke was unnoticed; comment was not worth the effort.

Wherever he looked Clay saw the same signs of apathy and neglect. This had been a prosperous camp, disciplined and happy. The people had been clean, bathing often in the river, proud of their appearance, and scornful of other *istihapos* not so well managed. Now the compound was littered, unswept for days. A kettle had broken from its tripod and lay on its side in the black ash. No hand had bothered to set it right. Men who should have been hunting, trapping on the river, or working in their fields lay sprawled on foul matting. Before the lodges women squatted in the dirt, their clothing spotted and torn, hair unbraided, hands in their laps. Even the children went at their play without zest. Nowhere could he see the orderly bustle that arose out of men and women engaged in the simple task of living. It had been almost a year since he last visited the town with Asseola, and what he looked upon now was foreign. A slow blight was eating into the community and its inhabitants seemed without the will to cleanse themselves of its poison. Nothing mattered.

"What has happened here?"

The Indian shrugged, lifting dull eyes. "Who knows?"

Clay untied his restive horse and swung into the saddle. Touching a heel to the willing mare, he charged at the dog pack and saw it scatter. What he had witnessed troubled him. These were not the people he had known since childhood. They were whipped and dispirited with little more than the will for animal survival. A stranger, reared with the certain knowledge that all Indians were shiftless and dirty, would have noticed nothing unusual in the town. Here was living confirmation of his belief. Clay knew better. That which had happened was not something brought with one night. It had been a long time coming. He wondered if it were so in all the Seminole towns. They had fought once, defending their lands and possessions. The years had brought nothing but further encirclement, and along the border more whites stood poised, ready to swarm over the Territory. In the face of this knowledge had they given up, satisfied with the scraps and a portion of the swamps?

Cantering along the ridge, following an old trail worn smooth by countless shuffling feet over many years, he thought of his last meeting with Asseola and how the Indian had spoken as they walked together on the riverbank.

In his memory now the words came clearly. "Honor is a thing to be satisfied. I have seen in my own people how, when it is put aside, they become little better than animals, living in filth and, like dogs, without nobility."

This, then, was what he had meant. This was why, for many months, he had not asked his friend to eat with him in his lodge or sit with the men at night about the fire as before. He was ashamed of what was happening to the people of his town.

Where the ridge sloped away and the trail bent as a tossed ribbon in the direction of Clayport, Clay turned the mare's head up-river, allowing the animal to select her own pace.

He understood better now the savage and traditional finery in which Asseola had clothed himself. There was defiance in a return to the old things. It was as though the Indian, looking upon the spiritless crumbling of his people in this isolated camp, reached backward into time for strength and courage. There had been pride in the spotless leggings of buckskin, faith in the softly falling long shirt with its bands of red, yellow, green, and brown, a challenge in the silver gorget and the bright feather of egret. In such a manner had his people before him faced the white men, and so again would he stand.

Riding easily in the saddle, Clay wondered at the action of one he had known all his life. The fires burning within the Indian had been well banked, their existence unsuspected. Not even the closest friend had been permitted to glimpse them. If Asseola had left his lodge, leaving it and the people of the town behind him, then it could only be for the purpose of seeking out those who thought as he did. If somewhere the Seminole men still walked with dignity, holding to ancient truths, he would find them. Clay wasn't surprised that Asseola had left without a word of farewell. To the Indian's mind the custom had no meaning. A man would do what he must, and if it was willed they should meet again, then this would happen without the aid of foolish pledges.

As he rode into the Elbow Bend clearing, Sue Rogers rose from a seat before her tent, shaded her eyes, and then recognizing him, walked forward with an expression of pleasure. She moved with the easy, free stride of a boy, but, Clay thought with a curious feeling of excitement, no one would ever mistake her for anything but what she was.

"Hello," she called. "No Indians today?"

He dropped to the ground and stood looking down at her. I'm a sure enough fool to go away an' leave all this, he told himself. Some scamp'll turn up while I'm gone.

"No." They walked, leaving the mare to follow. "I thought I'd try it alone this time."

"Had and Will will be glad to see you."

"I didn't come to visit your brothers."

She halted and tilted her face upward. "You're improving, Mr. Hammond," she said with critical approval.

"I've been practicing." His glance covered her boldly from the sleek softness of her hair to where the bodice of the dress of light gray wool held the round, hard firmness of her breasts.

Color brushed lightly at her cheeks, and small white teeth rested on her lower lip. "Don't become too proficient, Mr. Hammond," she murmured.

"I thought you were going to call me Clay." His swinging hand touched against hers as they walked again.

Her muted laughter was half giggle, a provocative and altogether feminine sound. "Not when you look at me that way, sir."

"I've sort of come to say good-by." He hadn't meant to blurt the words out this way.

"Oh?" Her step lagged and she half turned, lifting questioning eyes. "Isn't this sudden?"

"I guess so." The heavy trunk of a felled pine lay at one side of the path. He motioned toward it. "Could we sit down for a while? I expect I want to do some talking."

Without comment, waiting for him to speak, she settled herself on the log. He stood before her, kicking aimlessly at the soft black dirt, his features screwed into an expression of puzzled concentration. It was funny, he thought, how hard the simple things were to say sometimes.

"It's Old Clay's idea," he explained. "I don't exactly know when or where he got it, but I expect I plague him some. I guess he looked for a different sort of grandson. Maybe there isn't enough Hammond in me to suit him."

He looked at her and then sat down abruptly. She swept the broad folds of her dress in, making room between them, and waited while he laboriously put his thoughts in order.

"He figures I ought to get off the plantation and see what's going on."

"I don't think that's unreasonable. You can't spend all of your life in the backwoods."

"I suppose not," Clay agreed. It was damn funny, he thought angrily, but going away didn't seem half as much fun now as it did two hours ago. That was what happened when you got yourself mixed up with a woman. It fixed you so you didn't know what to do.

"Will you be gone long?"

He shook his head. "I don't know. In the first place, I'm not sure where I'm going or whether I'll like it after I'm there. Maybe I won't get any farther than Tallahassi."

He grinned ruefully. How to put into words the things that puzzled him? His fingers forced a brown flake of pine bark loose and thoughtfully crumbled it to bits, scattering them aimlessly on the ground. It was sure enough time he got out and learned to talk with people.

"I'm mixed up about a lot of things, I guess," he continued. "Maybe Old Clay is right, thinking an' acting as he does, but I'm getting close to twenty-one an' I better find out for myself."

"We'll miss you," she said simply.

His smile was brief, almost worried. "I was coming to that. I feel the same way. The trouble is I don't know if it's because you're the first girl I've ever known or something else."

She didn't laugh as he half expected she would. It was a fool thing to say.

"Will and Had will want to say good-by." She rose.

Clay hadn't half finished what he had come to say, but he stood up. Girls had a way of putting an end to things when they were ready.

As they walked toward where the Rogers brothers were working, Clay thought they must be at their labor from dawn to dark. Already one small field was cleared, the earth churned and furrowed. Stacks of yellowing scrub palmetto fans and their long, red, spongy roots, which must be chopped and dug out one by one, dried in the sun. The soil lay black and warmly naked, ready to receive the seed of a first planting. The shell of the cabin was taking shape, the logs now marking only a low fence about the design, but the dwelling rose as with adz and saw the men beveled and notched the timbers, fitting them with tight security.

When they saw him approaching the brothers dropped their tools and strode across the clearing. Already, Clay thought, they had the certain confidence of men born to the woods. It was hard to think of them as city people, and he wondered, a little enviously, at their quiet assurance. Without experience, they seemed to know exactly what they were about and what they intended to wring from the wilderness.

"Hello, Mr. Hammond." Will thrust a forearm across his sweating face, wiping at the beads of water.

"Clay's come to say good-by, Will," Susan explained, and he smile twinkled. "He's off to see the world."

"Not all of it," Clay amended good-humoredly, "just a piece here an' there. I hear some of it's different from Clayport."

Hadley stretched, working his shoulder muscles forward with a sigh of relief. "We're discovering that," he said. "Different and easier. I always thought that felling a tree was only a matter of an ax and a little muscle. I can see now it's a personal contest between man and his Creator."

"It looks pretty good." Clay indicated the beginnings of the cabin.

"It'll be tighter," Had said, "by the time it's chinked with some mud and the Rogerses' lifeblood. That," he added, "isn't much of an exaggeration."

"I just rode past to see how you were getting on and to say good-by." Clay filled in an awkward pause. "By the time I get back you ought to have the cabin up an' a crop in."

"Your grandfather's overseer came around yesterday," Will said conversationally.

Clay nodded. "I heard about it." He had guessed it was Salano who told Old Clay of the family.

Will continued, "We looked for some trouble but I guess everything is going to be all right. We showed him the deed. Had was for throwing him off the place at first, but we decided later he had a right to see the proof of ownership. Afterwards he rode away, so I suppose it's settled. He knows we're here to stay and not squatters without a title."

"Well," Clay was uneasy, "I guess I better say good-by an' get along." He thrust out his hand gravely.

"Come and see us when you get back," Hadley said agreeably. "Sue'll have her curtains up before the roof is on."

They shook hands solemnly and Clay felt a little foolish over the ceremony. He and Sue turned and started to retrace their steps, and then he wheeled impulsively to call to the men, who were already returning to their work.

"Mr. Rogers." Had and Will swung about. "Don't—" Clay hesitated, "don't take too much for granted, will you? I mean about Salano, or Old Clay either, for that matter."

"Why, no, Mr. Hammond," Will replied, "we hadn't intended to." He smiled. "Thank you just the same, though."

Clay had coaxed his horse in with a gentle clucking sound and stood with hand on bridle before Sue spoke. She looked up into his face, her level gray eyes seeking his.

"I think," she said softly, "I'll say it again. We'll miss you. Come back soon, Clay."

9

OCHLOCKONEE. The word chuckled and sang, humming the music of the river as it poured out of Georgia in a sweeping arc across the narrow northwestern shoulder of Florida and spilled into the Gulf's blue water. Suwannee. Ochlockonee, Ouithlacoochee, Ocklawaha, the sounds formed a liquid chant, primitive as the stamp of bare feet on hard-packed earth or the tinkle of hawks' bells.

With his back resting against the rough surface of an oak, Clay spoke the rivers' names aloud. Behind him the sun hurriedly made way for the night, swinging low like a tangerine-colored paper lantern in the smoky wisps of purple clouds. Through the trees he could glimpse the crimsoning river and hear its murmur. Ochlockonee. The sound was the call of a lonely bird.

Beyond his outstretched legs the coals of a small fire caught the drippings from an improvised spit and licked upward with hot greediness as the glistening beads fell upon them. Earlier in the afternoon the Negro Santee had knocked a plump and careless 'possum out of a tree. Now it broiled slowly above the even heat and the fat ran in shining rivulets down the crisping meat.

Through half-closed eyes Clay watched the black as he hunkered down on the opposite side of the fire, staring with brooding patience at their supper or reaching forward every now and then to scoop the live coals into a neater pile with his bare hands. Even in repose the thick ropes of muscle lacing his chest and arms seemed to writhe and creep over each other, moving ceaselessly beneath the light cotton shirt. Huge and powerful, Santee stood almost seven feet tall and would have been a prime field hand save for the grace of Old Clay, who kept him in the house as a personal servant. The slave's incredible strength came in handy when the old man wanted to be moved, and he could lift both master and chair with an innocent casualness, transferring the burden from room to room or porch with catlike ease. Old Clay bred Santee with the same thought and care he would have given a prize animal. From his litter, planted squarely in the street running through the slave quarters, he would select the girls, calling them to his side and feeling their breasts, width of pelvis, length of leg and buttocks before marking them for service. Clay always suspected the old man was stimulated by the knowledge of Santee's prowess. He was sure of it when his grandfather took him to a cabin where, from his chair at the open door, he watched the slave in the act of copulation, yelling obscene encouragements to the straining buck.

"By God," Old Clay chortled, "he roars like a bull when he's at it. Damnedest sound I ever heard."

Santee's offspring were valuable and numerous and grew like their sire, tall, heavily muscled, and tireless workers. Their skin was the shiny black of wet coal. Watching him now, Clay wondered whether he had any fun out of all the girls and women the old man picked for him. I guess, he decided, he must, otherwise he wouldn't be able to do it so often.

The warmth of the fire and the rich odor of roasting meat made him drowsy and he thrust back his head, scratching the scalp against the abrasive bark. It was pleasant to lie here, feeling the night as it gathered, knowing food was on the fire and shelter at hand. Tomorrow, lying somewhere beyond the eastern horizon, would come upon them quietly, and they would move through it without haste, untroubled by the necessity of reaching an unmarked destination.

This was the third night out of the plantation. Traveling eastward, they crossed the Taluga River, riding into the rolling country of pine and scrub where scattered groups of cypress threw their ragged crests against the sky. It was a wide and open land, warming itself beneath the winter sun, shot with pastel tints of gray, brown, and green. Where the pines and cedars rose they made somber splashes of blue shadow across the flats, and in the deep coolness of the swamps the great silvery trees seemed to strain upward on their spider-like roots to catch a glimpse of another world.

Clay and Santee had ridden off the plantation at dawn. The ground was crisp, sprinkled with the white powder of a light frost, and the chill in the air bit sharply. From the cabins in the slave quarters the smoke seemed balanced atop the canted chimneys, and behind the windows, with their oiled paper shields, the single lights of wicks in tallow were buttercup yellow. As he trotted ahead, leaving the mounted slave and a pack horse to follow, Clay regarded the plantation with a new interest. For some strange reason it seemed unfamiliar. The warehouses, the blacksmith's shop, the cotton gin, and the sugar factory reared themselves in bulky irregularity upon a slate sky. Within their shadow the smaller establishments, boot and harness shops, repair depots, and turpentine still, seemed huddled for protection. Far beyond and to his left were the houses of the overseer and his assistants, and past them the barracks squatted on a barren square. Looking over his shoulder he could see the plantation house itself, half concealed by a broken circle of trees. As he left it all now, riding away without actual destination or purpose, it occurred to him for the first time that his life was inextricably bound to this land. It was a part of him. The feeling of possession, of ownership, was something new. He was Clayfield Hammond's grandson and, without his lifting a hand, the enormous wealth and sprawling acres of the plantation would fall to him through the inexorable working of time alone. The knowledge made him vaguely uncomfortable and he shifted in the saddle as though to unseat an invisible companion who rode with him.

The parting with Old Clay had not been marked by any display of emotion. No word was passed of his departure. They sat at the evening meal without conversation, as was the custom. Not until the table had been cleared and decanters of port placed at their hands did the old man speak. He drew thoughtfully at a cigar, rolling the fat cylinder in his mouth, enjoying the flavor of tobacco. Finally he took a packet of letters and a heavy leather wallet and tossed them the length of the table.

"I tried to figure out where you might be goin'," he said, "an' provide for it. There's gold an' notes in the wallet, an' the letters will get you more money an' credit when you need it."

Clay turned the letters over in his hand. They were addressed in his grandfather's heavy, sprawling script, and he noticed with surprise that they were directed to persons from St. Augustine to New York, Pensacola to New Orleans. No matter where he went he would know someone. The letters were intended for individuals, banks, and commercial houses spanning the eastern seaboard. He examined them with surprise, realizing the extent of Clayfield Hammond's business connections.

Something of what was racing through his mind must have communicated itself to Old Clay, for he grunted impatiently and moved to favor his useless leg.

"I can't say they are all friends of mine," he admitted with a bleak smile, "but most of them owe me money or wish they could. Call on' em when you need to an' don't hesitate to ask for what you want."

Clay nodded, stacking the wallet atop the letters. By God, he thought, I'll have to do a sight of traveling to get around to all of them.

"I figure," his grandfather continued in a flat accent, "this is about as good an idea as I ever had, an' I don't want you to go spoilin' it for me. All I ask is that you don't stand on no street corners, beatin' a drum an' tryin' to save the world. Mix with your own kind, get to know what's in their minds, for it's your equals you got to look out for in this world. The other kind don't matter, they're too busy steppin' on each other's faces to look up out of the gutter. It's the man who sits at your table you got to be careful of." He nodded to the waiting blacks, who came forward swiftly to carry him upstairs. From the second-floor gallery he yelled, as an afterthought, "Take care of yourself."

The course they followed eastward after leaving the Apalachicola was part old Indian trail and part untracked wilderness. Even without a compass Clay was able to head almost due east, using the morning sun as a guide. I might not hit Tallahassi, he argued with himself, but I sure as hell can't miss the whole Atlantic Ocean if I keep going in this direction. Time enough to worry about where I am when I get there. This third nightfall found them on the banks of the Ochlockonee. Tomorrow they would have to strike a fording place, although he had been told a ferry was operated for the convenience of the post and occasional travelers along the rude highway connecting Tallahassi with Pensacola. He and the black would locate it or get across the river some other way in the morning.

With indolent pleasure he watched while Santee mixed corn meal and water, flavoring the dough with salted pork drippings, and spreading the mixture in a shallow pan for baking in the ashes. The slave had superintended the packing of their supplies, and he continually surprised Clay by the variety of foods he had stuffed into the heavy leather bags. With a smoked ham, preserves, a small sack of sweet potatoes, a thick, moist fruitcake, flour for biscuits, coffee, dried beef, they fared almost as well on the road as they would have at the plantation.

The Negro crouched at the fire's edge, his broad bare feet forming a solid pedestal for his great frame. Clay noticed how the strong toes dug and clung to the soil, and in this position, his body washed by the copper glow of the fire, he was the figure of primal man painfully drawing himself out of the earth.

"Ready soon, Marstah." Santee touched the roast with a knife point. His voice was soft with the deep, lustrous quality of blue velvet, and there was an animal shyness in his eyes as he glanced across at the white man.

Clay nodded and straightened up, drawing his legs inward and reaching down to tug at the heavy boots into which his trousers were tucked. He grunted. A moment later Santee was kneeling before him and with the gentle touch of a mother undressing a child he had the heel of the boot in the crook of one arm and was sliding the footgear off with a steady, even pressure. Clay peeled away the thick woolen socks and wriggled his toes delightedly in the cool air.

"If there's a trading post in Tallahassi," he said, "I'm going to fit out with some buckskins. This stuff is too heavy for travel." He regarded Santee with a grin. "I don't know what the hell to do about you. There's no ready-made shirt ever cut that'd go over those shoulders."

The slave ducked his head and rolled his eyes upward in happy embarrassment at the reference to his size. He smiled with an alert, watchful expression.

"Hit'd take a big buck, sure enough, Marstah." He spoke with a throaty chuckle as though the pleasure of exchanging this easy banter with a white man was too exquisite to bear.

He backed away, his eyes still on Clay. Then, without instructions, he moved quickly to the saddlebags and withdrew a bottle of dark plantation rum. With hot water and coarse brown sugar he prepared a toddy. Clay watched him with undisguised surprise and took the steaming cup.

"Hit'll keep d' night meggums away," Santee explained. "Sleep by d' rivah, wake up in d' mornin' filled wid meggums. Hahdly move d' han'."

Clay drank slowly, the heady concoction trickling in a deliciously warm stream down his throat. He wondered idly what the hell a meggum was.

Working swiftly, the black brought the pot of coffee to a boil and set it to one side. He snaked the pan of corn bread from the ashes, uncovered a mound of sweet potatoes, and cut the 'possum from the spit. He brought the meat to Clay, who divided it into two equal pieces, splitting it as he would a rabbit. After Clay had taken what he wanted of the other food, Santee filled his own plate and backed away. He paused by the embers to toss on some fat pine knots, and when the flames caught, slipped into the shadows on the opposite side of the fire. When the light breeze now and then twisted the blaze away Clay could see his dimly outlined bulk, hunched over the food in his lap, eating with the hurried concentration of an animal.

The brief twilight faded and night was upon them by the time Clay had sucked the last bit of juice and flavor from the small bones. Regretfully he tossed a white sliver into the fire and watched as it charred quickly in the heat. Along the river he could hear marsh hens as they spoke in short, harsh cries, and the rusty cackle of the loons made idiotic reply. The woods awoke with a muted babble of sound and the tethered horses snorted nervously now and then at the unfamiliar noises until Santee walked among them and with gentle, reassuring nickerings quieted their restless fears.

As he watched the slave Clay caught himself marveling at the ease with which the Negro adjusted himself to freedom. It was a strange thing, he thought, to see a man born. From the moment of his first step on the plantation Santee had been taught but one thing, to move when ordered and do what he was told. In his association with his masters there had been no need to think for himself. Now, after three days in a wild and unfamiliar country and under what, to his mind, must be curious circumstances, he no longer waited for orders. He did what seemed necessary at the moment, adapting himself to the immediate problems. Clay wondered what excitement must be stirring behind the black mask. Along with his rifle Clay had brought a light fowling piece, and although the law prohibiting the carrying of firearms by slaves was carefully observed in the Territory, he had allowed Santee to bear the gun, riding with it in a leather sheath at his saddle. He smiled to himself in the darkness, recalling the incredulous delight on the Negro's face as he held the piece in his hands and understood he was to care for it. Several times Clay had noticed how, on the pretext of securing the scabbard, he had reached forward and touched the stock, his broad face reflecting astonishment, his hand seeming to pet the wood with childish pleasure.

Behind the screen of fire the Negro blended with the darkness. Only the broad outline of his shoulders, black against black, marked where he sat.

"Santee?"

The shadow moved. "Yes, Marstah?" Intuitively the slave seemed to know there was curiosity rather than a command in the calling of his name.

"What do you think about, Santee?" Clay, as he spoke, wondered what prompted him to ask such a fool question.

In the silence it was almost possible to feel the slave struggling with the unexpected query, wondering if he were supposed to reply or whether it were just another of those obscure jokes with which the white people indulged themselves every now and then.

"I think about the mornin's, Marstah." The heavy, rich accent floated on the night.

Clay hadn't really expected an answer beyond a self-conscious, embarrassed grunt. He was surprised and it took him a few seconds to recover.

"What about the mornings?" he asked.

Possibly because his face was hidden, or perhaps because he was gaining a new confidence, the slave didn't hesitate.

"I like to think about the mornin's, Marstah. Hit's d' time o' day to like bes'. I git out an' dere ain' nobody on d' plantation up but me. I walk ovah d' groun' like I was d' only man in d' whole worl', like Adam only my name Santee. I say good mornin' to d' Lord; heah I am, Lord, movin' along all alone like You figured. Hit's a good feelin', Marstah. I say, I ain' lonely, Lord, so don't put no more peoples on d' earth to plague me. I ain' need a woman or a dog to talk wid. Jus' leave me by myself, Lord, to walk ovah d' earth." He chuckled and Clay understood he was enjoying the speech and his fancy. "Den," he continued, and there was no regret or malice in the tone, "den' d' Ol' Marstah yell. 'Santee,' he shout, 'where d' hell is you? Fetch my brekfus, lif' me to d' chaih, wheah d' hell you been?' Dat's when I know I ain' Adam."

Clay was silent. He had no inclination to laugh. There was something almost frightening in the simplicity of the slave's words. He felt a little ashamed at having heard them. It was like eavesdropping on a man at prayer.

The pine in the fire burned quickly into crumpling black fragments. Clay watched the heat in the coals die and then rose stiffly.

"We've got to get across the river in the morning," he said.

"Yes, Marstah." Santee stood, waiting.

"Maybe," Clay smiled, "you better get up early an' have a word with the Lord."

Beneath a tree the Negro had laid a thick bed of bough tips, sheeting the pile with freshly cut palmetto fans and securing the bundle with a length of canvas, pegged at the corners. The couch was high, springy, and fragrant, and Clay sank into it gratefully, drawing a blanket over him against the creeping chill.

Sleep raced ahead of him and he lay without moving, listening to the night. His lids were heavy with weariness but the image in his eyes persisted. Try as he would, he could not rid himself of the picture of a huge black man who walked in the mornin' an' talked with God.

Hadley Rogers awoke so abruptly that it was difficult for him to believe he had been asleep at all. Only by raising himself on one elbow and staring out through the tent opening at the remnants of the fire could he make a rough guess at the hour or so that had passed since he and Will turned in. He wriggled his shoulders in an effort to shrug off a vague uneasiness. On his side Will snored with gentle wheezes of contentment. The small camp was secure and quiet. Hadley stiffened. It was too quiet. When he had dropped off to sleep the woods had been filled with small sounds, the snapping of a twig, the soft brushing of wings in the air, or the furtive rustle of a branch in the scrub. Near by a whippoorwill had been sounding its plaintive call and waiting for a distant reply. It was the last thing he had been conscious of. Now there was no sound. It was as though the birds and questing animals had withdrawn, hiding themselves against an alien presence, watching from the trees and brush until the intruder had passed.

Hadley sat up, reaching to the tent's wall for his rifle. He held the gun across his lap, listening. Finally he bent over and shook Will.

"Will." His hand was rough and urgent on his brother's shoulder. "Will. Wake up." He kept his voice to a harsh whisper for fear of alarming Sue. "Will. Do you hear me?"

The brother grunted, tried to slide out from under the nagging hand, then his eyes snapped open and he lay rigid and alert.

"What's the matter?" He joined Hadley in a sitting position and then, seeing the gun, stretched over for his own.

Hadley shook his head. "Listen."

Will leaned forward, his head tilted to one side. "I don't hear anything," he said finally.

"Neither do I." Hadley didn't relax. "That's the trouble. It isn't right. All of a sudden everything has gone dead. Something out there has scared everything else."

"Bobcat, maybe?"

Hadley's head wavered thoughtfully. "It isn't likely. Smells more like a man."

Will kicked at the blanket wound at his feet. "Let's go out and take a look." He began crawling toward the open triangle of the tent. "Keep away from the fire and let me get out first."

The scream was lifted on a short, savage note and rose in a treble frenzy that pierced the ears. It was a shrill cry, sharp as a claw, raking at the brain.

"Yo-ho-e-hee!"

Rifle flashes bloomed in small crimson rosettes, flowering at scattered points within the darkness. Will and Hadley threw themselves to the ground, pinned helplessly there by the fire. Then the arrows came, their pitch-bound heads flaming, marking a wriggling, fiery course as they sped through the night to strike the tents and set them blazing. The two men retreated on their bellies, drawing away from the consuming flames. Will had a moment to see the form of his sister as she stood in terrified confusion before her shelter and shouted at her.

"Get down, Sue! Down on the ground!"

They fired and reloaded, aiming at the red and angry will-o'-the-wisps that appeared with crashing abruptness from behind the trees. As they fought back against their invisible attackers Will could hear his brother cursing in a terrible, impotent fury. Outside the brilliant pool of light now they could see past the burning tents to the long walls of the cabin. Shafts of fire were drilled into the timbers and the flames were running over the uncompleted structure, lapping at the veins of pitch, and racing along the fat wood. Above the barking sounds of musketry the brothers could hear the maddened cries of their terrified horses as they threw themselves against the light timbers of the corral and a low, steady moan of fear was loosed at regular intervals by their cow. Always when the brothers attempted to rise and fight back they were beaten to the earth by the shots stabbing out of the blackness. The tents collapsed into small mounds of rapidly dying flames and the fire spread toward them, feeding on the grass and pine needles.

"I can't see the bastards," Hadley sobbed.

Half concealed by the low clumps of palmetto scrub, Will shielded his eyes against the brilliance. For a moment he thought he had caught the shadowy movement of a figure behind a distant pine. Digging his elbow into the earth, he waited, the muzzle of his rifle nosing out. There was no saving the cabin. He could hear the crackle and gusty roar of the flames as they ate into the tumbling logs. All he wanted now was to kill someone. He waited, straining his eyes. There it was again, the brief outline of a shoulder.

"Don't shoot, Had," he cautioned his brother. "Let 'em think we've pulled out. I'm going to get one of the sons of bitches in a minute."

Made bold by the faltering defense, the enemy behind the tree stepped into the open. For a moment the black outline of his body was in Will's sights. Gently Rogers squeezed against the trigger. The belch of crimson smoke obscured the target for a moment, but as it cleared the brothers saw the shape turn slowly in a drooping and graceful movement as though executing the deliberate measure of a dance.

"You got him. By God, you got him," Hadley shouted exultantly.

The attack ended with the same startling suddenness with which it had fallen upon them. One minute the woods had been spewing destruction and the threat of sudden death and then the terror was lifted. The brothers waited.

"Sue?" Will called. "Sue, are you all right?"

"Yes, Will." The girl's voice came from somewhere behind them. "I'm here." Her words quavered.

Stiffly, and with the reluctance of men with the weight of years upon them, the brothers rose and looked about them. Where the tents had stood only small mounds of feathery ash remained to tremble and sift in the light wind. The cabin was a huge bonfire, the flames shooting high into the night, straining for the pine branches that curled and withered above the heat.

The men stood watching, unable to tear their gaze away. There, in the bright orange and red monster, their hopes and labor were being consumed. Timidly Sue wedged herself between them. She was weeping with the small, terrified sound of a frightened and lonely kitten. Will put his arm about her, drawing her close to him and feeling the trembling of her body.

"Who?" She looked up at her brother. "Who, Will, and why?"

He shook his head somberly. "I don't know, baby," he said gently.

"Indians." Hadley spoke. "Didn't you hear the yelling? Seminoles."

"Maybe." Will was thoughtful. "Anyhow," he paused, "one of them didn't get away. We can find out easy enough."

Followed by their sister, the two men moved toward the outer rim of light cast by the blazing cabin. At the base of a tree was the body of a man, sprawled face down, the arms outstretched, fingers dug into the soil. For a long moment the three of them stared down at the prone figure, and then with an angry curse Will bent and savagely flipped the corpse over, flinging it roughly by one arm. The dead face was that of a white man, the cheeks and sharp chin black with the heavy stubble of beard.

"There's your Indian," Will said.

"Hammond?" Hadley glanced at his brother, the question on his lips.

"If I had to make a guess I'd say so." Will nudged the corpse with the broad toe of his boot. "No one else would have a reason. It was just good luck I got this one. Otherwise, the whole business would have been blamed on the Indians an' no one could have said it wasn't so."

He turned away and stood gazing at the heap of glowing embers and dying flames, marking where the half-finished cabin once stood.

"Might as well get ourselves warm by it." Hadley, following the direction of his brother's glance, almost choked on the bitterness of the words. "That's a real, special bonfire." Without waiting for his brother and sister he walked slowly toward the lighted clearing.

Dawn smeared itself across the sky with the color of a polished shell. The Rogerses watched it creep up from the east and found no comfort in the arrival of a new day. Throughout the night they had sat without speaking, hunched within the waning circle of warmth, staring fixedly at the blackening mound.

"What are we going to do, Will?" Susan shivered, drawing her arms about her shoulders.

"I don't know." He spoke with a heavy, flat tone. "Try it again, maybe."

"What for?" Hadley tossed a small branch into the smoldering fire, experiencing a malicious pleasure in keeping it alive. "So Hammond can burn us out again?"

"But it's ours, the land. We bought it." There was a fierce rebellion in the girl's words. "There must be some protection, some law in the Territory."

"There is." Will laid his big hand over her trembling fingers. "The name is Hammond."

"You ready to quit?" Hadley shifted his gaze and stared at his brother.

"I don't know." He nodded toward the charred cabin site. "This would only be the beginning. The next time one of us would probably be killed. I keep wondering if it's worth it. You can't fight what you can't get near enough to touch."

"Couldn't we go to the courts?" Sue regarded him with amazement. "You don't mean to sit there and say this can go on? There's a government and officers to see that it is administered. Take Clayfield Hammond into court."

Will's laugh was short and harsh. "We'd be years getting there, and how would we prove that back there," he jerked his head over his shoulder, "was one of Hammond's men? He'd just say the fellow was a renegade white who'd run away to live with the Indians. Meanwhile we'd be moving about like gypsies without anything to call our own."

"It'll take some thinking." Hadley rose. "We'd better see if we can find the horses. They broke through the fence. God knows where they ran." His eyes roamed past the clearing to where the tents had been raised. "I guess," he made an attempt to smile, "a man shouldn't be hungry at a time like this, but I am." He reached for his sister's hand and pulled her gently to her feet. "How about it, Cook?"

"The supplies we bought in Clayport yesterday are still in the wagon. They weren't unloaded, and," she forced a tone of banter, "contrary to all New England precepts, there is a reward for shiftlessness: bacon, grits, and coffee."

The brothers found the cow still within the small pen they had raised for it. At their approach the animal lowed with a tone of injured reproach and regarded them with the sad eyes of disillusioned trust.

"There's milk for the coffee, anyhow." Will slapped the animal's rump affectionately.

They located the horses about half a mile away. Once freed from their panic of the fire, the animals had stayed their flight and were cropping docilely at the heavy, dew-laden grass.

"Right now," Hadley said, "I think I'd like to be a horse."

Bacon was spluttering and curling in the pan and a steaming fragrance rose from the soot-encrusted coffeepot. The white grits bubbled and spouted small geysers of steam at the side of the fire. The brothers rode into the clearing and tied the horses. Sue straightened up from the breakfast preparations.

"I salvaged the tin plates and cups from the ashes," she called. "They're a little twisted and black but good enough to start housekeeping over again." She smiled. "All your clothes were burned up, and so," she made a brave attempt at an impudent grin, "I won't have any washing to do."

"We're all right, then." Will bent down and flipped a piece of bacon from the skillet and tossed it from one hand to the other until it had cooled. "Hadley wants to be a horse."

"What about you?" Sue watched him as he crouched at the fire. For a moment the man chewed stolidly at the piece of half-cooked bacon, stripping away the thick brown rind as he ate. He looked up at his brother.

"I have an idea," he spoke thoughtfully, "I'd like to visit the Hammond plantation. I don't figure it will pay much except in satisfaction, but this morning I could use a little of that."

10

CLAY and Santee crossed the Ochlockonee at daybreak, stumbling upon a natural fording place where the current had thrust a sand-spit halfway across the dark and sluggishly twirling stream. The woods grew thickly to the river's edge in a matted tangle and they had to dismount, leading the horses and working their way foot by foot through small natural avenues. Now and then Santee was forced to take a sharp-bladed underbrushing tool and hack out additional yards to link a corridor before they could proceed.

"There's probably an easier way to get around here," Clay remarked as he had to turn back and edge out of an impassable lane to try again at a more favorable spot. "No Indian would go to all this trouble every time he wanted to get over the river. There's a trail somewhere, but we'd spend the rest of the day lookin' for it."

"We get across, Marstah." The slave was perspiringly cheerful and he swung the sickle-shaped knife with triumphant grunts as though he were falling upon a personal enemy.

They came upon the sandbank suddenly. It stretched in a high, golden triangle out from the dense willows. Around its tip the current raced with bubbling eagerness, forming small, spinning whirls that sucked at floating leaves and branches, pulling them beneath the mahogany-colored surface and releasing them suddenly yards distant downstream.

"We're goin' to get wet." Clay eyed the water skeptically.

"Yes, Marstah," Santee agreed happily.

Clay grinned. Nothing bothered the Negro. He acted and talked as a free man should, and the journey was high adventure. The untracked country was a constant challenge and he met it with the easy assurance of an animal, delighting in the strength of his broad back and powerful arms.

They made the crossing, clinging to the bridles of the horses, holding guns and powder above their heads and with the saddle-bags secured high on the backs of the animals, out of reach of the lapping water. When they finally stood on the opposite bank, dripping but triumphant, the Negro and the white man smiled at each other, sharing a sense of great achievement.

Looking back over his shoulder Clay surveyed the stream. "It doesn't look like much now," he admitted, "but I feel like Christopher Columbus."

They rode steadily throughout the morning, following a course slightly to the north of the climbing sun. Now and then they crossed an Indian trail, but always the paths ran in directions opposite to the route Clay had decided they should take. The woods broke away at intervals, leaving great cleared patches in which the high brown grass rose waist high and every few yards the horses kicked out coveys of quail that beat a drumming flight to safety. Without leaving his saddle Clay had knocked a half dozen of the birds down with the fowling piece, and they were strung now to his pommel, flapping limply against the leather. Turkey, deer, rabbits, and plump doves crowded the brush. The soil was rich and generous. No wonder, Clay thought, the Indians fought against being forced off of it. There was room to spare here for both Indian and white, but Clay knew the flood of immigrants would never be satisfied to share it. Better that thousands of acres go untenanted and emptiness stretch to the far horizon than to allow one Indian family to remain within sight of a white settler's cabin.

At the edge of a clearing they came suddenly upon a group of Indian hunters. The four men squatted about a small, smokeless fire. Near by lay the carcass of a freshly killed deer, and over the hot coals the hunters were toasting slices of liver, pieces of the tongue and heart. Their eyes lifted with brief curiosity at the approach of the strangers, but they made no sign of greeting, chewing stolidly on the half-raw meat and speaking to each other in low, confidential tones. Clay guessed they were Mickasukies from some near-by town.

"We seek the trail into Tallahassi," he said and waited.

None of the group appeared to have heard. With careful deliberateness they continued to turn the small pieces of meat on the ends of sticks, holding them deep within the heat. One of the men, much younger than the others, spat a piece of bloody fiber to the ground. The gesture carried with it both contempt and hatred, and in the lusterless, sullen eyes raised to his Clay saw a mocking scorn. Quick, flashing anger swept over him and for a moment he had the furious desire to spur his horse through the insolent band.

"It has been told to me," he said slowly, "that the Mickasukies are ill-mannered, thinking only of their bellies like dogs." He shifted the rifle athwart his saddle, purposely exaggerating the movement.

An old man, his skin as wrinkled as a dried grape, crossed his arms on his knees and peered up into the sky. The others appeared to wait for his reply.

"You speak well," he said finally, "but with a sharp tongue."

There was a low murmur of agreement from his companions, as though they had chanced upon some profound truth and were passing it from one to the other for examination.

"It is edged only for my enemies," Clay retorted shortly.

The old one nodded, satisfied with the answer. "How is it," he asked, "that the words come so easily to the white man?"

"I am called brother by the Seminoles on the Apalachicola." Clay made a token gesture and thrust his rifle, barrel down, in the scabbard.

Carefully the old man hacked a small sliver of meat from the heart and fitted it to the point on his stick. Then he raised his head and met Clay's eyes.

"The trail," he said, "lies to the north but a short distance. Ride as the head of your horse is now turned."

Clay touched his heel to the mare. "Eat in peace," he said, "and may the hunting be good."

They struck the trail two miles distant; a broad, well-used high-way, it displayed the wear of years of travel. The hills grew shorter but steeper now, mounting like the choppy waves of the sea, leading into the settlement of Tallahassi. The new seat of Territorial government was but five years old and had been hacked out of the wilderness as a compromise between those who wanted to re-tain the ancient town of St. Augustine as the capital and others who insisted it be located in Pensacola. Around the log house in which the Legislative Council had held its first meeting there arose a town, vigorous and testing its strength against the Indians, who watched with sullen amazement as the whites crowded in, thrusting their streets and buildings out in an ever widening circle.

With Santee and the pack horse bringing up the rear Clay rode slowly along the ridged center of the deeply rutted main thorough-fare of the capital. Try as he would to pretend he was unimpressed by the scene, he unconsciously shifted his gaze from one side to the other, absorbing the sights, sounds, and smells of this metropolis. Dirty and crude and with the gusty emphasis of the frontier in the air, Tallahassi was a teeming world center compared to Clay-port. Wagons and oxcarts pounded and creaked, slamming into holes and hub-deep ruts with protesting groans and thumps. At each side of the road groups of Indians shuffled through the dust, pausing to stare hungrily before saloons and sniff at the rank odor of raw whisky. White people, men and women, formed a continual and ever shifting file on the narrow paths, and before taverns and trading posts small knots of brisk, hawk-eyed men in booted trousers, elegantly brocaded vests, and gleaming beaver hats talked hastily and compared land figures from small notebooks. Men in buckskin and broadcloth, Indian squaws and ladies in flowing flowered dresses rubbed shoulders and jostled each other on the walkways. To Clay's untutored ears the air seemed to be filled with a senseless clamor, rising and falling from dozens of tongues all attempting to speak at the same time. He turned in his saddle once and glanced back at Santee, wondering what effect this spectacle was having upon the slave. Instead of displaying surprise, the Negro rode with a stiff black majesty, looking neither to right nor to left, indifferent to everything about him and intent only upon following the dusty path of his master.

Before a broad, single-storied, log building that bore a freshly painted legend, "McSwain's Tavern," Clay pulled up his horse. Through the half doors of the building he could see a long bar stretching the length of the room, and even from this distance the establishment seemed to hum and buzz with the angry sound of bees disturbed in their hive. Stout, empty whisky casks provided seats on either side of the doors, and the outside walls and roughly hewn posts, supporting a sloping wooden canopy over a length of board-walk, offered lounging rests for those who were not fortunate enough to find a sitting place. A constant stream of men shuttled in and out of the wide entrance, shouldering their way through the groups crowding the narrow boards. In the moment before he dismounted at the hitching rail Clay wondered what it was that everyone found to be so brisk about. They acted like a pack of dogs unable to make up their minds about a scent, wheeling, turning, and yapping out of sheer excitement for the chase.

When Santee and the pack horse drew alongside, Clay handed the reins of his mount to the Negro. He was conscious that the eyes of the men before him were turned with envious speculation on the powerful figure of the slave.

"Wait here for me," he said. "I want to find out about lodgings."

He pressed through the crowd and was halted by a voice.

"That there your nigger, mister?" A lanky, sharp-featured man in faded homespun jerked his head in the slave's direction.

"Yes." Clay paused.

"Would you think about sellin' him?" The stranger's words were coarsened by a rasping, unpleasant accent that grated harshly on Clay's ears.

"No." Clay moved forward.

The man cackled with the sound of two files being drawn across each other. "Well, mister," he said with a grin, "that's a good thing, because I couldn't buy him anyhow, but if he was for sale it'd be worryin' me considerable that I couldn't have him." He whacked at his rump with a broad hand and howled appreciatively at the jest, his bright eyes darting about the crowd, inviting others to join him in the display of wit. The lusty guffaw rising from the loungers set him to doing a quick jig-time step of delight.

"You're a card, Deke. I'll swear if you ain't, an' that's a fact," one of the men yelled.

Clay grinned at the idiotic display and pushed his way through the yielding ranks to the doorway. At the long bar men were crowded, elbow to elbow, and behind the unpainted and knotted pine counter four sweaty attendants moved with a steady rhythm, their hands rising and falling ceaselessly as they drew whisky from tapped kegs or set out heavy jugs of rum, slopping the liquor into mug and beaker and tossing coins and paper money into a bulging flour sack nailed to the wall. Swarms of whining flies whirled in restless clouds over the heads of the patrons or drowned themselves eagerly in the pools of whisky or foul-smelling ale on the bar. The room was filled with the dank and musty odor of an earthen cave and Clay found himself breathing with difficulty as nausea crowded into his throat. Littered tables, bearing scraps of food made black and crawling by the flies, were scattered over the floor, and at them other patrons wolfed their meals with greedy, sucking noises. Clay watched one man raise a crimson joint of venison. The flies made a thick, moving crust on the meat. The diner whacked the bone against the table, and as the insects swirled off in a startled cloud he set his teeth into the flesh and ripped at it with savage contentment before the pests swooped down to resettle themselves. Through the confusion a half-dozen Indian girls, clothed in faded and shapeless cotton, padded from table to table on bare and slapping feet, collecting platters and mugs or standing with expressionless patience as heavy, playful hands whisked up their single garments and pinched or slapped affectionately at their buttocks or slid with hot inquisitiveness over belly and breasts. The girls waited stolidly, displaying no more emotion than a cow who feels her teats between stripping fingers.

124

At the near end of the bar Clay paused, his eyes and senses trying to adjust themselves to the clamorous scene. From behind the serving shelf a man leaned forward. He was stripped to the waist and his thick breasts, heavy as a woman's and as hairy as those of a gorilla, almost touched the boards. His small red eyes took quick and accurate stock of Clay.

"Well, mister," he called encouragingly, "what's your pleasure?" With his fat, maggot-colored hands he thrust an opening between a couple of drinkers, making a place at the bar for the newcomer.

Clay hesitated. By God, he thought quickly, my pleasure sure isn't here. He blew through his nostrils, trying to rid them of the stench.

"Name's McSwain," the half-naked man continued invitingly. "Landlord an' jolly host," he sniggered complacently. "We aim to please our customers whether it be a meal, a fight, or a piece of Indian girl. Name your fancy." He rested his ham-sized arms on the bar and grinned with yellow teeth.

"I was thinking about lodgings for the night." Clay admitted his purpose doubtfully.

McSwain's animal eyes lighted. "Now you changed your mind?" he asked persuasively.

"I guess so." Clay looked about him, unable to hide his displeasure.

"It ain't good enough for you?" McSwain's round face seemed to beam.

The men near by turned slowly from their cups, their glances shifting rapidly from the tavern keeper to the stranger. Now, Clay thought rapidly, what the hell am I getting myself into? He looked about in a narrow circle and felt the muscles in his stomach contract.

"No, by God," he said deliberately, "it isn't."

McSwain's tongue, surprisingly small for the size of his mouth, licked across thick lips. His features assumed a babyish expression of wonder and his gaze traveled over Clay from waist to broad shoulders, leveled off several inches above those of the men near him. Then he laughed and his breasts jiggled crazily beneath their matting of sweaty hair as he leaned forward confidentially.

"Mister," he said in a hoarse croak, "I'll let you in on a secret. It ain't good enough for me neither, but I guess you're the only man in the room with guts enough to say so to my face." He thrust out a moist hand. "Name's McSwain," he added unnecessarily.

With an inward sigh of relief Clay reached out to take the

proffered hand. One of these days, he thought, someone is going to beat my fool head in. Abruptly his eyes lost their friendliness. The fingers of the tavern keeper curled about his with the crushing power of a trap. Automatically his muscles responded in quick defense. McSwain's face didn't change its expression of bland delight as he leaned on the bar with a lazy, indolent pleasure, but beneath the pink flesh of his rigid arm Clay could see the cords of a terrible strength gather. Without moving, his lips set, Clay countered the bruising grip, thrusting down from his shoulder, feeling the muscles rise the length of his arm and pull in tight ridges beneath his shirt. His fingers were becoming numb, feeling as though they had been bound with wet strands of rawhide and exposed to the sun. The men about them, unaware of what was happening and seeing only a friendly exchange of handclasps, turned again to their drinks. Tiny pearls of sweat gathered along the soft skin at McSwain's forehead but his mouth still smiled. His chest pressed against the bar's edge and a small roll of rosy fat bulged over the boards. Clay's toes curled within his boots as he dug earthward for support and made a desperate effort to draw the final ounce of brawn from his legs. He was breathing with heavy regularity and could feel the perspiration gather on throat and chest as he stood locked in this stupid, silent combat. The hand bound to his quivered sharply but would not yield, and the tavern keeper's eyes flickered briefly with respect.

"Name's McSwain," he whispered.

"Name's Hammond." Clay's words almost whistled between his teeth.

With a nod the innkeeper's grip relaxed, the hand seeming to dissolve between Clay's fingers, and they drew apart as a pair of bucks whose horns had been tangled in primitive struggle.

McSwain examined his whitened joints and blew upon them softly.

"It's a silly game," he said musingly, "but I don't get much fun in this place. Usually I can bring a man to his knees."

Clay grinned and massaged his throbbing fingers, into which the blood was rushing with stinging force. He felt no anger, no resentment.

"You're sort of hard to amuse," he replied. "The wear an' tear on the customers must be something awful."

McSwain ducked beneath the bar and Clay could hear him grunting and rooting in the recess. When he reappeared he clutched a bottle of Spanish brandy. Stripping away the bright yellow covering, the man set out two mugs and cracked the neck off of the bottle with a sharp rap against the counter. He filled their cups, the brandy pouring in a golden stream over the jagged lip of glass.

"Drink," he offered.

The effect of the liquor on Clay was almost magical. He could feel it running through every vein in his body, warming and assuasive. When he put down the empty mug his head was swimming, paddling through soft and downlike clouds. He watched while McSwain replenished their cups.

"Somehow," he rested his linked hands on the bar, "this place don't seem to stink so after a measure of that."

The landlord's fingers were searching through the hair on his chest, nipping away a large gray louse, which he cracked carefully on his thumbnail.

"It smells worse the next mornin'," he admitted cheerfully. "That's what makes daytime business so good. The customers can't seem to stand it without drinkin'." He glanced sharply up at Clay. "Any kin to the old man on the Apalachicola?"

"Grandson." Clay held to the bar's edge to keep from floating away.

"I hear he's the meanest son of a bitch in the whole Territory?" There was no rancor in the question, only a friendly interest.

"We get along all right," Clay replied.

McSwain splashed the palm of his hand with brandy and rubbed the liquid into the whorls of hair on his chest. "It don't kill the little bastards," he explained, "just sort of stupifies 'em for a while. I tried shavin' it off once, but when it started to grow back I couldn't get a girl to sleep with me. They said it was like boar bristles an' tore the hide off 'em."

"Why don't you set fire to it?" Clay was having a little trouble with his tongue, but he lifted his mug when McSwain had again filled it and drank solemnly.

The landlord's face creased with a delighted smile. "Now, that there's an idea," he said with admiration. "It ought to burn off soft an' good like a new field." He stretched out his hand with a gesture of appreciation.

Clay shook his head quickly. "The hell with you," he said. "We've been through that once today."

McSwain nodded regretfully. "If you're the old man's grandson," he asked, "what you doin' way up here?"

"Seein' the world. By God, that's strong liquor. I expect a man could get drunk on it."

"If he set his mind to it." McSwain examined the empty bottle and tossed it beneath the bar. His eyes swept along the length of the room and came to rest on a group at the center of the bar. "There's some fellas there," he flipped a thick thumb, "who'd be mighty happy to meet Clayfield Hammond's grandson, figurin' it would get them an introduction to the old man."

A little hazily Clay's glance followed the indicated line. The half-dozen men stood out sharply from the others in the room. From the silky tops of their rubbed beavers to their varnished boots they were the ultimate of elegance. Their cheeks were freshly shaven, beards trimmed, and their ruffled, spotless stocks gleamed in soft magnificence at their throats. As they talked and drew at long black cheroots they fingered thick gold chains or toyed absently with the seals on ribboned fobs. They seemed oblivious of the rude and boisterous character of the tavern, drawing a protective wall of supercilious indifference about them.

"There's a dozen more in Tallahassi like 'em," McSwain explained, "roostin' here like hawks, waitin' for someone to start another Indian war. After the government sends in troops an' does the killin' they'll grab every piece of land in the Territory. They've bought up most of it now from discouraged settlers for fifty cents an acre or less. Once the Indians have been run off an' Florida's safe they'll make themselves millionaires by resellin' it."

"What's that to do with my grandfather?" Clay was staring at McSwain.

"Well," the landlord thrust out a puffy cheek with his tongue, "from what I hear the old man has pretty much the same idea. An Indian war would suit him right down to the ground, an' if a lot of people get killed doin' the dirty work it'd just be tough titty."

"You're a liar." Clay's fingers tightened along the bar's edge, his head suddenly swept clear of alcohol. "I'll say it again an' mean it. You're a liar."

McSwain refused to take offense. "I'm only tellin' you what I hear."

"Well, then those who say it are liars."

"Maybe." McSwain's glance idled over the packed room. "It could be I heard wrong. This place gets noisy now an' then."

Clay's defensive anger melted quickly. There was no sense in starting a brawl in which he was bound to take a licking, and anyhow, the uneasy suspicion that McSwain was probably right nagged at his insides. It wouldn't be beyond Old Clay to encourage a war if it meant the slaughter of all Seminoles, and if a lot of white settlers were burned out or killed it would be, as McSwain said, just tough titty to be so unlucky. He rattled a handful of coins down on the bar and shoved them toward the man.

"I'll pay for the brandy," he said.

Indifferently McSwain gathered the money and flipped the pieces into the sack. "If that's the way you want it," he said. "You figurin' on lodgin' for the night? It ain't real bad if you get to bed first an' them Indian girls are accommodatin'. A few of them, I guess, got the claps, but it ain't really nothin' much more than a mild winter complaint."

"I still say it stinks." Clay's irritation smoldered. He turned away.

"Well," McSwain called agreeably, "keep your hair."

Outside, in the hard sunlight, Clay paused. Santee had not moved from his horse but sat easily in the saddle, staring blankly before him as though the crowd in front of the tavern did not exist. Clay blinked his eyes. His mouth felt dry. Damn that brandy, he thought. It sure makes a man feel and talk foolish.

"Santee."

The Negro looked up. "Yes, Marstah?" There was a note of relief in his voice.

"We're going to get on." Shoving his way through the loungers, he strode down the dusty road, hearing the soft clop of the horses as the Negro wheeled and brought them about to follow.

At a trader's Clay outfitted himself with buckskins, soft, creamy leggings and shirt with high moccasins to take the place of the heavy boots and dark, thick clothing. He changed in the back of the post, shucking off his old garments and feeling an immediate sense of freedom and relief in the light cotton shirting and loose trousers. Wriggling his shoulders happily, he tossed his stained clothes to the counter.

"You can throw these away or burn 'em up," he said. "I'll buy a compass if you have one an' be grateful for some information on the trails to Fort King."

"Hell, mister," the trader looked at him with amazement, "you ain't figurin' on trackin' to Fort King by yourself?"

"Why not?" Clay fingered the blade of a heavy knife on display. "People make it every day, don't they?"

"Some of them." The trader counted out his change. "Others end up staked out in the scrub for the buzzards to pick at."

"I'll take a chance." Unreasonably, Clay was annoyed by the man's solicitude. The brandy was wearing off, leaving him with a headache and making him jumpy and contentious.

"That's sure as hell what you're doin'." The trader handed him a compass, fitted into a metal watch case with cover. "This is reliable," he said. Spreading a crude map on the counter he bent over it, studying the plottings for a moment, and then traced a wandering line with his forefinger. "You can pick up an Indian trail about a mile to the southeast of here that'll run to the Econfina River, an' if you keep movin' south by a little east you're bound to strike the Suwannee. Over here," he held the nub of his finger on a spot, "is a lot of lake country an' wild as hell with the imps on a holiday. If you ain't been bushwhacked by Indians by the time you get there I expect you could find a trail into Fort King. I made the trip once but I sure wouldn't do it again. If a man wanted to keep breathin' for a long time I'd advise him to strike for St. Augustine first an' then cut back across again to Fort King. It's some farther but a fella'd be likely to live longer."

"Thanks," Clay said shortly. "The map for sale?"

"If you want to buy." The trader folded the cloth-backed paper. "I wouldn't say it's too accurate, except along pretty general lines." He waggled his head wonderingly as he studied Clay. "That yellow hair," he said admiringly, "is going to look handsome hanging from some Indian's belt."

Clay laughed at the dismal croaking. He was beginning to feel better. The loose and comfortable casualness of the buckskins gave him a gratifying sense of freedom and confidence. He was part of the country again and out to see the world, or some of it. Indians he had known all of his life, and, he reasoned, they couldn't be much different between here and Fort King than they were along the Apalachicola.

"I'll take the map an' the compass an' keep my hair, too," he said.

From the doorway he called to Santee and they made additional purchases of bacon, beans, coffee, corn meal, and, finally, two additional horns of powder. As the Negro packed the leading horse Clay could see him glance from the corner of his eyes now and then at his master. Also, and not without pleasure, Clay was conscious that the townspeople regarded his tall and rangy person in the new buckskins with more than passing interest. I'm fool enough to like it, too, he told himself. Next thing you know I'll be primpin' before a mirror. When the bags had been secured he swung into the saddle.

"Let's ride," he ordered, and grinned at Santee.

At a fork, where the road crossed the Indian trail the trader had spoken of, he reined up. To the south lay many miles of country that few white men had penetrated. It stretched away in tumbling hills and sudden plains, losing itself in the bending sky.

Glancing back over his shoulder he called to the slave, "Santee, you're likely to be a mighty dead Negrah before we get to Fort King."

"Yes, Marstah." The black was unmoved, but Clay could see the beginning of an embarrassed smile at his eyes. He was enjoying himself, tasting the heady wine of freedom. If this cherished thing should end abruptly, then the few hours would be worth what they cost.

Clay's glance fell upon the tightly curled, kinky hair, forming a spare cap on the slave's broad skull, and he chuckled. "Anyhow, that scalp of yours is goin' to be a hell of a disappointment to the Indian who takes it."

The iron tires of the wheels chewed into the sandy ribbon of the plantation road and an ungreased axle squealed with a high, dry note of protest with each slow turning of the hub. On the narrow board seat Sue Rogers sat stiffly between her brothers and tried to hide her bare feet beneath the folds of her dress. Like her, the men were shoeless, and they wore only trousers and shirts, the clothing in which they had gone to bed the night before. There had been no time to salvage anything from the burning tents, and everything they owned had been consumed in the hungry flames. In her moment of panic the girl had snatched at a dress and she wore it now, acutely conscious of the fact that there was but a light shift beneath its gray and stained length. Unaccountably she giggled, and Will glanced across at her, the question in his puzzled stare.

"Something tickling you?" he asked mildly.

Sue nodded. "I was just thinking we certainly look ragged to be calling on Clayfield Hammond." She thrust her naked feet out and surveyed them solemnly.

"It isn't what you'd call a social event." Hadley stared straight ahead, his features drawn, his eyes worried. They were courting trouble. Will knew it too, but he refused to be moved by his brother's arguments.

"I want the old man to know we know," he repeated doggedly when Hadley attempted to dissuade him. "It doesn't make sense and may just let us in for more trouble, but I've got to do it. I'll go alone. You and Sue wait here for me."

In the end his stubbornness prevailed. The brothers had loaded the stiff and grotesquely sprawled corpse into the back of the wagon, where it rolled and thumped with every turning of the wheels.

They had passed unchallenged through the open gates of the Hammond plantation; the guard on the tower platform hadn't even glanced down at them as the wagon drew abreast of his post. Watching the solitary figure with open curiosity, Sue had the feeling that they were passing over the drawbridge of a medieval fortress and with a little shiver of apprehension pressed her shoulder against her brother.

"Looks as though we might even be expected," Will remarked thoughtfully as they creaked through the opening.

"Probably." Hadley slid the reins through his fingers and the small muscles at the line of his jaw tightened.

The road followed a winding and seemingly aimless course across the Hammond acres, and Sue wondered why no one had ever bothered to straighten it. As their wagon crept forward she permitted her eyes to wander and caught herself thinking that this was where Clay Hammond had lived and played and grown to manhood. She wondered if he had known what his grandfather had intended to do and, for this reason, had left so suddenly. Quickly she thrust the idea away and felt ashamed at having entertained it even so briefly.

"Hadley?" She turned to her brother. "When this is over, when we're through here, what then? Are we going back to Providence?"

The man shook his head. "I don't know. Maybe it would be easier for Will and me if you went home until things could sort of get straightened out. A girl isn't too handy at a time like this. I'd feel better knowing you were in Rhode Island."

"I won't leave without you." She set her small mouth into a firm line.

Hadley sighed wearily. "I didn't think so," he said unhappily. "You and Will are too much alike. Stubborn."

"I'm not afraid of Clayfield Hammond, if that's what you mean." Will snapped the words angrily.

Hadley smiled but there was no humor in the expression. "Well, I am," he admitted frankly, "but I'll fight him just the same if that's what we decide to do."

From where the road swung sharply to pass before the house the Rogerses could see the old man seated in his chair within the shade of the porch. Below, at both sides of the steps, two figures squatted in the sun. Rifles lay across their laps and their hats were pulled down as a shield against the glare. As the wagon ground to a halt the men thrust up the broad brims of their head coverings and stared at the visitors with steady watchfulness. Old Clay might have been asleep for all the attention he paid to the arrival of the team.

For a moment time hung suspended in a bright vacuum and the world was without movement or sound. The two Rogers men were motionless on their seat and between them the girl, frightened now, tried to hide herself. Finally Hadley sighed and dropped the loose reins.

"Let's get it over with," he said wearily.

At his words the men near the steps stiffened, their hands tightening about their rifles, and they rose in a half crouch as the muzzles of their pieces swung in a slow arc until they covered the brothers. Ignoring the threat, Hadley and Will slid across the board to the back of the wagon, where they bent down and lifted the dead weight of the body. With a heave they swung the corpse into the air and sent it flying across the narrow space separating wagon from porch. The thing, rigid and unwieldy, spun once in the air and landed with a solid crash, sliding feet first across the boards and coming to rest only inches from Clayfield Hammond's chair. The old man didn't move, but his eyes were flecked with yellow fury and the upper lip pulled away from his teeth.

"Your men forgot that last night." Will was breathing hard and spoke with difficulty.

Old Clay refused to dignify the charge with a reply, and only by the slowly spreading flush of anger on his face did he indicate he was aware of what had happened.

Legs apart, their feet planted solidly in the bottom of the wagon, the brothers waited. As the moments dragged they both began to feel a little foolish. Their challenge was being met by a contemptuous silence, their presence ignored. Will started to speak again and checked himself. Anything he might say would only sound like the empty threats of a schoolboy, hurled outside the hearing of a teacher. Reluctantly he turned away from the figure on the porch.

"Come on, Had," he muttered. "Let's be going."

Old Clay watched the retreating wagon, waited until it had passed beyond the line of trees. Then he leaned forward and spat full into the upturned face of the dead man at his feet.

11

From the little Chipola to the river of St. John the drums throbbed with the feeble persistence of a flickering pulse. A slow-burning fever sweated the Seminole nation and the patient tossed and muttered with hot restlessness. At night, along the Territory's central ridge and dotting the sloping flatlands, the flames of many fires shot straight into the windless sky, and in their copper light the faces of men were grave and drawn.

At the high council, his voice sharp and clear, a chief, John Hicks, addressed the silently attentive circle of his peers.

"No longer do we meet at Fort King, in the white man's house, which, he says, was built for us and where we might take our just grievances. As our fathers before us we sit beneath the ancient trees to decide what must be done. A great evil has been loosed among our people, and under its spell we die slowly. The evil is whisky, not in the jug or gourd of white trader or hunter, but in a quantity that would destroy us. Who sends it here? Who gives it so freely to inflame our young men to acts of violence? Under its influence our braves barter or gamble away their guns and land, trade their women for an additional cup. Then, with sodden heads and tortured brains, they seek to regain what they so foolishly threw away. In desperation they steal a white man's cow, drive off his horse, burn his cabin, or do quick murder on the lonely trail. These things the whites pile before them as evidence. See, they say to the Father in Washington, the Indians are but thieving, murdering dogs. Send the soldiers quickly or we are lost. It is no accident that the whisky comes to us, and its cost is small to those who would have us driven from our lands like slaves and transported to the country beyond the river Mississippi."

Ringing a hundred smaller fires throughout the Territory the older men of minor authority held talk while the youths mocked their words with silent laughter. No longer did their elders bind them with traditional discipline and authority. They roamed the broad lands in small, fierce bands, falling upon isolated cabins, murdering and raping, scalping and mutilating, laying the torch to house and field.

On every side they saw the authority of the government derided by white settlers whose hunger for the Territorial acres knew no satisfaction. Wealthier and more powerful landowners in the border states ceaselessly demanded the return of more and more Negroes, sending spies and agents to seek out the identity of the blacks and then making formal documentary claim for their return. When the fugitive slaves or their descendants could not be delivered, the annuity guaranteed the Indians was levied upon and the people grew hungrier and more desperate without corn for planting or grain with which to feed themselves. Rarely now was the sky unclouded by the smoke rising from the burning cabin of a white settler. Inadequately guarded storehouses were broken into, their contents stolen, scattered, or destroyed. The sporadic raids crept to within ten miles of St. Augustine itself, and the searing breath of hate blew across the land.

On the long journey southward from Tallahassi Clay could almost feel the malevolent vapors creeping over the land and see the fury behind the eyes of Indian and white alike. Time after time he and Santee had encountered stray Seminoles, Mickasukies, nomadic and straggling Cherokees from Alabama, or furtive Spanish Indians from the great swamp of Okeechobee. Ragged and with the indelible stamp of poverty and frustration upon them, they displayed a snarling suspicion of a friendly greeting, gazing upon the white man and his Negro companion with undisguised hostility. When offered meat or tobacco they snatched at the gifts with savage hunger, but there was no gratitude in their speech or courtesy in their manner. Only the fact that they were inadequately armed or lacked the courage of sufficient numbers prevented these desperate wanderers from making an attack, but always the threat was there.

At the scattered white villages, where three or four badly constructed log cabins huddled together for protection, Clay found the settlers being slowly consumed by an unreasoning hatred. Crowding in upon the Indian lands, arrogantly appropriating what they wanted without regard to prior ownership, the immigrants screamed their fury to heaven. They banded together to hunt down or lie in wait for a lone Indian or to attack small shifting groups, slaughtering the men, women, and children. Hacking, slashing, and cutting their dead victims, they fed an insane rage. Thus the bloody orgy spread. Not yet had it gathered violence enough to be called an open war. In neatly bound theory the government and its Indian wards were at peace, but in the sky the buzzards wheeled lower and lower and the sweet, sickening stench of death was in the air.

Three weeks had passed since Clay and Santee had ridden out of Tallahassi, and the marks of travel were upon them and the horses. Clay's fine buckskins were torn and stained, grease-spattered and smoked to the color of an old hide. A heavy reddish beard bristled on cheeks and chin, and fine lines of weariness pulled at his eyes. The long days in the saddle, or, more often, afoot, as he and the black forced their way through limitless stretches where the high, thick scrub and clustered sapling pines formed an almost impenetrable barrier, had worn him down to the tough resilience of a hickory shaft. As the days lengthened he frequently wondered if the white people who were crying so loudly for action against the Seminoles had any idea of the country in which troops would have to fight. Properly armed, and when the time came they would have the guns and powder, a couple of dozen Indians could harass and weary, snipe at and destroy, a company of soldiers. Able to live in the swamps, moving swiftly, the Indians could prolong the conflict for years, until the United States sickened of it.

This was a new and curiously frightening land he and the slave now looked upon. Swept away were the soft rolling hills of the Apalachicola district. The dusty red soil that tinted the fields and forests, springing into brilliant color at evening time, had yielded to sand with marbled streaks of black dirt. Vast stretches where the high, reedlike grass of greenish yellow stood chest high frequently spilled into the distance as far as the eye could mark. Small streams, dark of color and draining from the swamps, laced their path, trickling through a lush, tropical, and deathly silent panorama. Small lakes, held captive by constricting circles of bent and twisted trees from which long streamers of death-gray moss trailed to the water, sprang with mysterious suddenness from the forest to block their way. Here thick fields of waxy water lilies shifted and wavered beneath the light touch of a breeze. Along the scant shores alligators stretched their scabby length in the sun, hissing and snorting at their approach, and then waddling with quick awkwardness into the water. Barely rising above the riffled surface, their bulbous eyes watched with implacable enmity. Slipping from the cool tangle of vines and roots, slender cotton-mouthed moccasins cruised through the shallows, their heads lifted inches above the water and, stick-like, forcing silvery ripples on each side. Tall gray cranes and flocks of pure-white egrets fished in the swamp grass, rising in mottled clouds at the approach of horses and men. The sky was a hot and cloudless saucer pressing upon every living thing, and the sun beat down with a frightening and breathless intensity that sapped the strength and made breathing difficult. In the scrub flats, where the knee-high palmettoes grew brown and scorched, the angry whirring of rattlesnakes tormented the nervous, rearing horses, while sudden flights of quail or the bounding race of panicked rabbits set them to plunging and wheeling in snorting uncertainty. Only in the scattered stands of pine, where the ground was cool and the air fresh, did Clay and the slave find refuge from the oppressive heat and the ever present threat of coiled death underfoot.

Early in the journey Clay had discarded the light jacket and shirt. He traveled now only in the discolored leggings and worn moccasins. The sun had hammered the upper part of his body into a mahogany brown against which the blue of his eyes and straw-bleached hair made a strange contrast. Astride his horse or thrusting ahead on foot he made a compelling, primitive picture. The coarse beard gave him a new appearance of maturity and his glance, sharp and discerning, roamed ceaselessly. No longer did he laugh and joke with Santee. The trader at Tallahassi had been right. If a man wanted his scalp he had to keep moving fast and with his eyes open. The ashes of an isolated settler's cabin, the mutilated body of a careless trader, staked out beneath the blazing sun, over which the buzzards hopped and tore, the hatred on the faces of the few Indians they had encountered were constant reminders that he no longer traveled along safe and familiar paths. At night he slept fitfully, dividing the hours of darkness into watches with Santee. In the brightness of noon they halted briefly to build a small smokeless fire and cook their meal, putting aside enough for the evening. After sundown the warming luxury of blazing wood was an invitation to attack. The danger didn't display itself openly, but Clay could feel it in the air.

If Santee was disturbed or apprehensive as they moved deeper and deeper into the Indian country he never permitted Clay to suspect the existence of such emotions behind his placid black face. In the performance of his duties there was an expression of simple trust and complete confidence. What the white man decided to do must be the proper thing, otherwise he couldn't have said it was so.

"God damn it," Clay once snarled with exasperation, "I wish you'd stop acting as though I was Moses leading the children out of the wilderness, or whatever the hell it was he did. I get just as jumpy as you an' you know it."

Santee smiled with a disarming gentleness. "When you yell like dat," he said happily, "hit soun' jus' like Ol' Marstah, an' so I know everythin' comin' out good."

Clay stared at him for a moment and then laughed. He did sound like the old man. Sometimes, he suspected, he even felt the way Old Clay did as he raged against the obstacles in their way and sought to push them aside by the sheer power of his fury and will. This, he thought ruefully, was a hell of a way to see the world; dodging Indians, living off the country, eating half-raw meat, clawing his way through scrub and swamp. I sure hope it's worth looking at, he told himself. Right now I'd trade it all for a small piece of the plantation or a cabin in Clayport.

Always their course wound southward, the sun crawling up each morning out of the east on their left and dying in a crimson flood to their right in the evening. They skirted the big Indian town of Micanopy on the clustered lakes near Lochloosa, picking up an old trail, straggling off in a southwesterly direction. Each morning, as Clay looked about him in the smoky dawn, he experienced a curious sensation of frustration. Always the landscape presented the same familiar picture and he felt as though they had not moved from the site of camp two days back. During the brief moments of twilight, as they prepared to bed down for darkness, he would stare at the map and silently wonder where they were. The chart wasn't much help, since he had no way of knowing the distance covered each day. Now and then he could fix a rough approximation through information gathered from the inhabitants of a small settlement, but for the most part he had to make his own guess. For the past week they had encountered no one.

"Some evening," he told Santee, "we're likely to step right off the peninsula into the Gulf of Mexico. When that happens we'll at least know where we are."

Despite its inadequacies, he clung to the map with an obstinate faith, and after several minutes of perplexed study would press his finger to a spot.

"I guess we're about here," he would assert. "If we aren't here, then sure as hell we're someplace else."

Looking over his master's shoulder, Santee would peer solemnly at the indicated section and nod his head as though the mysterious piece of paper and Clay's finger contained all the magic necessary to solve their problems. His confidence in the map cheered Clay immensely, and he always felt better after witnessing the slave's mulling amazement and childish happiness in the crudely drawn lines. Maybe, he thought, all you have to do is believe.

Food was becoming a problem. The stores that had seemed more

138

than adequate when they were packed at Tallahassi were dwindling rapidly to a few handfuls of beans and a small measure of corn meal. Days back, when he tried to purchase salt pork and grits at a settler's cabin, he had been met with a sullen refusal. The man seemed almost desperately intent upon hoarding his stores against what emergency he would not say. Although he was reluctant to discharge a rifle, Clay was forced to shoot now and then. Once, after killing a young buck, he and Santee spent the day roasting and smoking the meat, packing it away for future use. As time lengthened the improperly cured venison developed a ripe and pungent odor that brought persistent swarms of flies swirling about their heads and over the greasy saddlebags.

Clay examined the meat with a wrinkled nose. "I guess," he admitted, "you've got to have salt to cure meat." He slapped at the flies and tossed the graying chunk to Santee. "Maybe if we cook it up some more it'll be all right. One good thing, we probably stink so by now that not even an Indian would bother with us."

On a small stick Clay marked the days as they passed, adding a notch each evening. At the twenty-ninth cut out of Tallahassi they made an early camp on a high pine knoll. There was a gentle roll to the country again as though long ago the sea had passed this way and left its imprint on the land. Wherever they were, Clay decided, many men had traveled before. Throughout the afternoon they had crossed half a dozen trails. They were footpaths, with no sign of horse or wagon travel. Some were so old as to be barely discernible, showing only faint traces and losing themselves abruptly in the ever encroaching scrub. One was fresh, swinging in a wide circle around their camping site and turning eastward.

"I don't give a damn if there are fifty Indians to the square foot on that trail," Clay said, "we'll hit along it tomorrow."

Santee located a small stream near by and took the weary horses down for water. Clay unpacked the remaining pieces of venison and then quickly dug a small hole and buried the stinking hunks. The meat was squashy between his fingers, seeming to dissolve into a bluish slime. He wiped the putrid stuff on his filthy leggings and with a sudden decision reached for the fowling piece. Indians or not, he'd get a couple of rabbits before it was dark. His belly ached for fresh meat.

Something caused him to lift his head. It wasn't a sound, more of a feeling. In a half crouch, fingers locked about his gun, he waited. Slowly he pivoted, his eyes wary and probing. A moment before the narrow space between two pines had been vacant; now it was filled.

The Indian stood with hands crossed on the rifle barrel, resting his weight on the stock. For a long moment they stared at each other, and then a grin of relief and recognition twitched at Clay's lips. With an exaggerated display of indifference he examined the flint on the light piece, muttering over it as though he had discovered an irritating fault. When he spoke it was to the firearm.

"I knew an Indian to get shot once," he said, "slipping up on people that way. Fella got nervous an' blew his head off before he knew what was happening." He rose and stretched negligently, staring up at the sky. "Now what," he said musingly, "do you suppose a child from the Apalachicola would be doing way down here?"

"I wondered about that, too." Asseola shook his head and stepped forward.

With a quick stride Clay met him, throwing an arm exuberantly about his shoulders.

"By God," he yelled happily, "but I'm glad to see you. I'll swear," he backed away, "if you weren't so ugly I'd be of a mind to kiss you." He expelled his breath with a gusty emphasis. "For a minute I could feel the scalp lifting right off the top of my head. How did you get here? Where you been?" The questions tumbled over each other.

Asseola leaned the rifle against a tree and regarded his friend with grave appraisal. He smiled a little to himself, thinking of what Clayfield Hammond would say if he could see his grandson. Bearded, dirty, naked to the waist, his sun-burnished skin as dark as that of a Seminole, Clay, in appearance, was one of the breed of tough frontiersmen who moved through the Territory at will, indifferent to white and Indian alike.

"I heard about you three days ago," Asseola answered slowly. "It was said a white man, tall and with hair the color of ripe corn, traveled with a Negro. It was also said he was either a very brave man or a great damn fool." The solemn eyes brightened. "The more I thought about the words, the more I was sure it must be you."

"Where the hell am I?" Clay managed an embarrassed grin.

Asseola squatted close to the ground, poking at the dirt with a twig. "I guess that depends on where you want to go."

Clay joined him in the crouch, their shoulders touching. "I was figuring on Fort King," he said humbly.

Asseola glanced at him and nodded with approval. "You've done pretty well for a white child," he said. "The fort lies a day's ride to the east."

Clay breathed deeply and then chuckled, not attempting to hide the satisfaction he felt. "I told that trader in Tallahassi I could make it," he boasted.

The Indian continued to make little marks in the dirt. Finally he snapped the piece of wood between his fingers and rose.

"You're a great fool, Clay," he said flatly.

Deflated, Clay also stood up. "I guess maybe you're right. Anyhow, there have been a lot of times when I would have agreed with you. Right now," he picked up the fowling piece, "my gut is crying out loud. Let's see what we can get."

They hunted the scrub, painted in soft heather colors by the twilight. Clay shot at anything, as though the pleasure of firing again at will was too great to resist. Catching Asseola's amused glance, he whooped without restraint.

"I been afraid to do this for days," he confessed.

With the limp carcasses of half a dozen rabbits dangling from their fingers, they made their way back to the camp. Santee regarded the figure of the Indian without surprise. If he was astonished at his master's companion, he refused to allow the white man to know it. Without comment he took the rabbits and went back to the stream to skin and clean them. His mind never troubled him beyond the immediate moment. Tonight they would have fresh meat. What might happen later could be waited for.

The fire burned with a high, bright warmth. Clay, stretched on his back, head pillowed on his arms, stared up through the trees at the stars. They had stewed the rabbits slowly until the meat fell from the bones at a touch. Into the rich broth Santee had dropped their remaining cupful of rice, and the stew simmered and bubbled to a thick richness. Clay and Asseola had eaten, Indian fashion, from the pot after a generous portion had been ladled into a pan for Santee. As the small white bones mounted before them in little piles they grunted with satisfaction, licking the gravy from their fingers.

"I've always wondered," Clay sighed happily, "how a rabbit can taste so good and still stink the way it does when you gut it. Nothing, I guess, smells worse, except maybe a squirrel. God, but a squirrel stinks."

They rested now, warm and contented. Asseola sat cross-legged on the ground, occasionally tossing a small knot or a ruddy pine cone into the fire.

"It's been a long time since we've done this together, Caccosoci."

Clay's voice was muffled and he turned his head slightly to look at his friend.

"The years are at a run." Asseola kept his gaze on the fire.

"Where have you been?"

"Listening to much talk and watching an evil thing grow."

Clay propped himself on one elbow. There was a disturbing bite in the words. This was a new and strange Indian, who resembled his friend of childhood only in form and feature. The easy freedom they had once known together had vanished and restraint lay between them.

"Why is it," he asked abruptly in the dialect, "we no longer speak to each other as we once did?"

For a few seconds the Indian was silent, and then he reached down and, with a rough jerk, pulled Clay's loose legging above the ankle. Where it had been protected from the sun the skin was startlingly white. Asseola laid his dark hand against it and the contrast was there for both of them to see.

"Some would say the reason lies in a color," he spoke softly, "only you and I know this is not so." He tugged the legging down and with the same hand touched his forehead. "I think it rests here, and no one can say why. It was not always so. Perhaps the fault is mine. We grow older, Clay, and as the years gather I become more Indian and you more white. We cannot escape our destiny. I have sickened over this many times, for it is not an easy thing to lose a brother, and I have had none but you."

Clay stirred restlessly. There was a melancholy in the words that tugged at him, opening the gates to a flood of memories. He waited, making no reply. The Indian would say what he must.

"A man should hold the truth in his hands and examine it," Asseola continued, his voice barely rising above a whisper. "Something burns within me and I do not know if it be good or evil." He turned his head and there was a smile on his face. "I do not even know why I should have traveled two days to make our paths cross here at this spot."

"You looked mighty good to me, child." Clay was embarrassed.

"I have been many places," Asseola turned his face away and addressed the fire, "and always I listen. The sounds your people make are ever the same. Now there is talk of sending a Seminole delegation to a land called Arkansas. It is the idea of the whites that if these chiefs like what they see, then the Seminole nation will move as a whole across the great river and settle there. Why is this so?" A fierce rebellion shook his voice. "If this country of Arkansas is so good, why do not the white people who crowd upon us go there themselves? We have no need of a new land. This," he thrust his fingers into the soil, "is ours. I will die here."

"Where have you been living?" Clay was troubled by the anger he was witnessing. God help the whites, he thought, if this spark finds the tinder.

Asseola's smile was the expression of a man who cherishes a joke. "Much time I spend at Fort King," he answered. "I am a trusted messenger between the agency and my people. I interpret in the small disputes. Osceola," he mimicked the whites' pronunciation of his name, "is a good Indian and does many services. He arranges for fresh meat for the garrison, finds corn when there is no corn, settles many little arguments. Permit him," sarcasm flicked the words as he spoke with the condescension of the whites, "permit this Osceola, who is a good and humble Indian, to travel freely within and outside the boundaries we have marked off for the Seminole."

Although he well understood the implications in his friend's speech, Clay couldn't resist a chuckle. Asseola glanced up, surprised by the sound.

"The agent," he continued after a moment, "is a good man. Colonel Humphreys. But," he hesitated, "this man's own people make a fool of him. This we will do, they tell him from Washington. In such a manner will we be generous to the Seminoles. Take them our word. In his innocence this Colonel Humphreys believes it is so, but when the time comes to fulfill the promises he is helpless. He will not last much longer and the Indians will have lost a friend."

"I will visit him at Fort King." Clay partly explained his journey.

"Also," Asseola continued as though he had not heard, "there is a maid of my people at the fort who looks upon me with favor." He ducked his head with an expression of sheepishness.

"Well, I'll be damned." Clay snapped upright. "I never knew you to look at a girl."

"I found it strange at first." The Indian refused to raise his eyes and Clay understood he was in a delicate torment. "Now it is pleasant."

Clay laughed, not quite understanding why the words of his friend should sound so funny. There was something silly on the face of the Indian, and the contrast between this low moaning and the fierce words of a few moments before was ludicrous.

With an assumption of wounded dignity that sent Clay into another spasm of hilarity the Indian rose. He stood looking down at the white man.

"It would be a good thing if we slept now," he said soberly. "In the morning I will take the child who lost his way to Fort King."

"Yes, Papa," Clay hooted. "I'll be ready."

12

INDIFFERENT to the amused stares cast his way by an occasional pedestrian or the frankly curious glances from the occupants of slowly moving carriages, Clay stood wide-legged on the wall's irregular parapet and listened. To his ears the deep-throated running of the sea beyond the low, heavily wooded spit of sand across the river made a strange and disturbing music. Now and then he cocked his head from side to side with the quick, nervous jerking of a puppy trying to identify a new and interesting sound.

At his back lay St. Augustine, stretching its length along the narrow unpaved street running parallel to the water front. At the north end of the town the great gray pile of Fort Marion thrust its battlements out in sharply angled design and the grim black snouts of cannon covered the city's approaches by land and sea. On the high bulwarks the figures of sentries were dwarfed to doll-like proportions and the flag, snapping brightly in the purpled haze of late afternoon, was no more than a hand-sized piece of gaily striped and starred bunting. Even as he watched Clay heard the padded roar of the sunset gun and watched as the banner ran slowly down the staff to the accompaniment of a bugle's sweet, sad notes.

Beside him, at the base of the sea wall, Santee waited patiently, his bare toes digging into the dust as he hauled against the fretting horses. As the cannon's echo rolled over the town and lost itself along the shore the slave's glistening face lifted again in wonder. The sound that came to them from a distant beach carried a powerful magic, awakening a primitive response within him. He was listening to a great drum, beaten upon softly by countless sensitive fingers.

Reluctantly Clay turned to look at the town. The twilight wind was moist and cool, and when he touched the tip of his tongue to his lips he could taste the salty freshness in his mouth. Somewhere beyond the row of houses, cut by cramped streets running at right angles to the wall, a bell began to toll with heavy solemnity. The air was weighted with the scent of many flowers and tidal muck, still warm and rich from the day's heat. Behind curtained windows candles sprang into wavering life and traffic on the road dwindled to a solitary horseman or a hurrying servant. Above all other sounds, though, that of the restless, murmuring Atlantic persisted.

Earlier in the day Clay had become conscious of it. A new wind, slipping through the interminable stretches of scrub and pine, brought with it a stimulating freshness. The horses felt it and lifted their heads. Reining in, Clay halted and listened. It came faintly but would not be denied, the whisper of a sleepy giant, tossing restlessly in uneasy slumber. Hearing it for the first time, Clay felt he was upon the point of a great discovery, and he urged his mount forward, eager to look upon this tumbling phenomenon.

The parting with Asseola at Fort King was two weeks behind him, as was Gad Humphreys' sincere but harassed cordiality. The years had not brushed lightly over the Indian agent. New lines of concern and the marks of baffled integrity had been graven upon his face, but his welcome was genuine and spontaneous. With sincere hospitality he had insisted that Clay put up at the Humphreys house and had set aside all but the most pressing matters in order to be at the disposal of his guest. He took Clay on a personally guided tour of the small settlement, introduced him to the citizens and the commandant and officers at the lightly garrisoned fort. He had even seen to it that the visitor was outfitted with new buckskins after Clay had insisted that was what he wanted.

"I'd advise, sir," the Colonel regarded him with an amused twinkle, "that one of your first places of call in St. Augustine be a good tailor. If, as you say, your purpose is to see the world, then you'll find that costume is regarded with more than passing interest outside the Territorial borders."

To Clay's eyes, grown sharper and more critical, Fort King seemed pitifully inadequate for all its high stockade and brave clashing of military trappings. The troops sweated uncomfortably in heavy uniforms and equipment designed for a different climate. The men were restless and bored, cursing and railing at the loneliness and lack of women. At a luncheon where he and the Colonel were guests of the commander, Clay found the officers blithely unaware of or indifferent to actual conditions outside the fort's walls. They spoke contemptuously of the Seminoles, serenely confident that any war between the Indians and the whites would be conducted by the book, drawn in an exact and familiar pattern in the maneuvers of a field manual. Silently Clay wondered what strength they would draw from the textbooks while floundering waist deep in the swamps or slogging through the sandy reaches of clinging scrub.

On the eve of his departure for St. Augustine Clay and his host sat late at the table while the Colonel asked him many questions concerning the temper of the Indians on the Apalachicola and those encountered on the long journey southward.

"You find me, sir," Humphreys touched the end of his cigar to the port in his glass, "not quite so certain of many things as I once was. It is an unpleasant thing to say, but I no longer trust the word of my government, and what I cannot believe, I cannot honestly expect the Indians to accept."

"We haven't had any trouble along the Apalachicola," Clay said thoughtfully, "but it looked to me as though they're clawing for each other's throats in the interior."

"There's an Indian here from your district." The Colonel raised his eyes. "Asseola or Powell, he is called by different names. You know him." He concluded with a statement, not a question.

"He's my friend," Clay answered with simple directness.

"I know." The Colonel smiled. "It is my business to learn such things. Also," he paused, "although he has no authority and speaks without the voice of a chief, he is dangerous. He has the ear of the Pond Governor, Micanopy, a man grown fat and lazy with many slaves. This I know, for in my talks with Micanopy I hear the words of Asseola, goading, prodding, and angry. I should confine him, but," he shook his head with weary humor, "under present conditions I am afraid to take such a step."

"What about this talk of sending an Indian delegation to Arkansas to examine new land?" Clay deliberately shifted the conversation from Asseola.

"A pleasant dream," the Colonel tapped nervously on the table's edge, "which only the very old chiefs share with us. These, tired and weary of bloodshed, eager to spend their remaining years in peace, are the ones who listen. The others, young and vigorous men— Coacoochee, or Wildcat, as he is called, Holartoochee, Tiger Tail, Jumper, Alligator, Little Cloud, Chekika, and," he glanced sharply at Clay, "your friend Asseola, who has no standing yet commands attention and respect—these are the ones who will force a war rather than yield."

Long after he had said good night to his host Clay tried to reconcile the Colonel's estimate of Asseola with his own. It had never occurred to him that the Indian with whom he had played since childhood could appear as a formidable figure in other eyes. He smiled to himself in the darkness. It was difficult to accept his friend in the role of a dangerous and desperate character, challenging the might of the United States government for a principle.

His parting with the Indian had been simple and without any display of emotion. They met, as agreed, on the road outside Fort King.

"I don't know when I'll see you again, child." Clay held the Indian's hand in his own. "Maybe you'd better come with me."

Asseola shook his head. "We will meet. This I know without question. How, where, or when I cannot say."

Clay grinned. "I've been hearing things about you. For a dumb Indian from the Apalachicola you seem to be causing a lot of talk and maybe trouble."

"The trouble is not of my making." The quick withdrawal within the Indian shell was sharply apparent, then his grip tightened on the white man's fingers. "Nor of yours either, Clay. It will be good for us to remember this." He smiled and their clasped hands fell apart.

Looking back as the road turned sharply to the east, Clay saw the Indian standing in the middle of the trail. He flipped a farewell salute and the Seminole's arm came up stiffly, raising the long rifle high above his head in reply.

Clay dropped lightly from the sea wall. At an angle from where he stood he could see the sign and inviting lights of a tavern. The building was low and weathered with a narrow balcony and leaded windows looking out upon the river. Leaving Santee to follow with the horses, he strode toward the entrance, stopping once in the middle of the road to examine its powdered surface and sift the gritty dust and small particles through his fingers.

"What the hell do you know about that?" He spoke aloud. "Making roads out of oyster shells. I wonder who figured it out."

Slater's Tavern was cheerfully warm and inviting with the glow of many candles set in heavy wrought-iron sconces high on the walls of paneled cypress. From a ceiling beam a huge ship's lamp of polished brass dropped a shining pool of light on the sanded floor. The public room was spotless, bearing its years with a gracious and friendly dignity. Metal tankards winked on a shelf behind the damp bar as the candlelight caught their burnished surfaces, and below them the bottles and jugs of green, blue, and colorless glass were set in an orderly and shining line. At the far end of the room, crouching in almost devotional attitudes before the soot-blackened fireplace, two slaves worked patiently at the spit handles, turning with slow care a dripping roast and crisping fowl. Sniffing at the musty coolness, the sharp scent of tobacco, and, above all, the odor of cooking food, Clay brightened. Whatever Slater's antecedents, he thought, he could be no kin to McSwain in Tallahassi.

Stout oaken tables were spaced through the room's center, and against the wall a row of high-backed booths offered private retreats for more leisurely dining and conversation. Well-dressed, carefully groomed, and, to Clay's inexperienced eyes, foppishly tailored men occupied the chairs, their hands moving with light elegance to pipes and glasses. Others stood leaning against the small bar talking quietly in a curious mixture of Spanish and English. At a center table a younger man caroled happily to himself in a tenor voice, fuzzed slightly by alcohol. He paid no attention to his tavern companions. Glittering, calf-length boots and slim, tightly trousered legs were outthrust on a second chair, and the face rising above the intricately ruffled stock was one of dark arrogance. A thin sneer played along his lips as though he understood he was disturbing and inconveniencing the others in the room and didn't give a damn.

At Clay's entrance the orderly hum of voices was suddenly muted, and many heads turned slowly to view this tall, bearded stranger in the soiled buckskins who moved with such quiet assurance and whose skin was almost as dark as that of an Indian.

"God's blood!" The exquisite blade dropped his feet to the floor with thumping astonishment and stared owlishly. "It's the ghost of Daniel Boone."

Slater himself, hands tucked neatly on a comfortable paunch beneath the snowy apron, padded hastily across the room in Clay's direction. His face wore a curious expression of determined geniality and apprehension as his keen eyes took in every detail of the stranger's unkempt appearance.

I guess, Clay thought quickly as he waited for the landlord, I do look like hell. When the tavern keeper halted and peered up expectantly but with an attitude that plainly told Clay he was out of place, he smiled.

"I'd like supper and lodgings for myself an' Negrah."

At the mention of an attending slave Slater's features abruptly lost their worried frown. Obviously this was no brawling backwoodsman or trouble-seeking drover, for all his crude appearance. Such characters didn't travel with a personal servant. He beamed upward into the visitor's solemn face.

"The finest, sir." He spoke with a heartiness that gave the impression that his entire life had been directed toward the moment when this stranger should enter his establishment. "Nothing but the finest and a clean, sweet bed of hay for your black." His head bobbed up and down as though it had been set on springs.

Clay nodded indifferently and his eyes swept lightly around the

149

room. Beneath his easy stare the other occupants suddenly remembered their manners and turned to their drinks or made embarrassed attempts to pick up the loose threads of conversation. Only the young man in the center of the room was undaunted.

"God's blood," he repeated, "how virile!" He peered at Clay with incredulous interest. "God's teeth," he muttered.

Clay chose to ignore his insulting amazement and turned to the waiting host. "My Negrah's outside with the horses. Will you have someone see to him?"

"Immediately, sir." Slater clapped his hands with a peremptory slap and, when a slave came forward in quick response, gave the necessary instructions. "Have no further concern, sir," he assured Clay, "your stock will be taken care of. Now," he became attentive, "to your immediate desires?"

Clay grinned, thinking to himself that the landlord would be standing on his head next. "I guess I'd like a drink first."

While Clay found room at a corner of the bar Slater busied himself with a large mug, hot water, rum, pinches of spices, and finally a thin slice of orange, which floated on the steaming mixture.

"Traveler's Delight," Slater said proudly as Clay buried his nose in the fragrant warmth and allowed the liquid to trickle down his throat. "A boon to the weary."

"Hah!" the young man sprawled at the table shouted approvingly. "God's teeth, but you're a wit, Slater. A Boone for the weary. Gad, but that is good. A Daniel for the lion and a Boone for the weary."

Clay turned slowly. His eyes were suddenly hard and he stared at the man, his glance moving with deliberate insolence over every extravagant detail of his dress. Unperturbed, the other submitted to the inspection, and then, surprisingly enough, winked at Clay with an expression of complete amiability.

"Now, Mr. Beulow, sir." The landlord hurried from behind the bar. His hands fluttered as though to clear the air. "No trouble again this evening. You promised, sir."

The young man sighed resignedly. "You're an old woman, Slater, who would keep a man to an oath taken in a moment of weakness." He swung his attention again to Clay and bowed his head with a small jerk. "My apologies, sir," he said. "I was rude, but," he whistled between his teeth, "God's blood, I'll say it again, you are a fearsome figure, Slater or no Slater, fight or no fight, insult or not." He banged his glass on the table. "A drink, Slater, and quickly."

While the harassed tavern keeper edged himself between them, Clay moved around to his place. I'll never get to see much of the world if I stop along the way to fight with every drunk I meet, he thought, and leaned his elbows comfortably on the bar. His mug was empty and he waited without comment as Slater brewed a second portion. The man clucked with the small sounds of a disturbed hen, glancing up now and then to scan Clay's face.

"You musn't mind Mr. Beulow, sir," he whispered confidentially. "He's wild and impetuous but with a heart of gold. Yes, sir, a veritable heart of gold." He made the pronouncement hopefully.

With the threat of a brawl removed, the room quickly reverted to its air of quiet order. Conversation was resumed where it had been interrupted, accompanied by the musical tinkle of glass and silver and the whispered shuffling of two blacks who moved from kitchen and spit, laying tables with fresh white cloths and setting the services for the evening meal. Clay locked his hands about the warm tankard and, without being obvious, studied the men at the bar, and listened, without understanding, to their rapid, expressive speech. St. Augustine, he knew, was still predominately Spanish, and members of the old families who had elected to remain after the Territorial purchase were fiercely antagonistic toward the Americans who were crowding into a land they still considered to be their own by kingly grant.

"Will you honor us by taking dinner here tonight, Mr. Spain?" The landlord directed his words to one of the men at the bar, and the tone and attitude were obsequious, almost fawning.

At the sound of the name Clay glanced up. It had a familiar ring. Suddenly he remembered. One letter in the packet given him by Old Clay bore the inscription "John Spain, Esquire, St. Augustine, Florida." Covertly he looked at the man. Tall, clean-shaven, and of middle age, John Spain was a commanding figure. His features were chiseled into rocklike angles and there was cruelty cut into the thin line of lip and chin. Slender fingers, ring encrusted, moved restlessly between each other as the hands lay upon the bar. He either had not heard or elected to ignore the landlord's question. Looking at him, Clay wondered how he happened to fall within his grandfather's list of acquaintances. With quick, sniffling noises of apology for the intrusion, Slater backed away and pretended to have business at the other end of the room.

Clay finished his drink and then fished out the slice of orange, chewing rind and pulp thoughtfully.

"Are you, sir," he asked, "John Spain?"

The question seemed to halt every movement in the tavern and quiet each sound. The imperious head with its heavy, massed, black

151

hair curling luxuriantly just above the stock swiveled slowly. Dark eyes flecked with odd golden lights regarded Clay without interest. Almost imperceptibly the man nodded.

Clay was not disconcerted by the reception his question had received. "In my bags I have a letter that I shall deliver in the morning. It was addressed to you by my grandfather, Clayfield Hammond. The name was unusual and when I heard it I presumed to speak to you." The speech pleased Clay immensely. It was, he thought, pretty close to being splendid, well-rounded, and firm. How in hell, he asked himself, did I ever learn to talk that way?

Much the same thought must have occurred to John Spain, and for a moment he almost seemed to be on the point of smiling.

"Your servant, sir," he said. The acknowledgment was aloof but there was a friendly interest in his gaze.

Suddenly Clay was struck by the ridiculousness of his pompous introduction. He laughed. "I guess," he confessed, "I could have just said I'm Clayfield Hammond an' let it go at that."

John Spain did smile then. At least, the delicate, bloodless lips quivered and he made a motion toward the vacant space at his side.

"I shall be happy if you will join me, sir." As Clay moved along the bar, Spain's hand was extended. "It is a pleasure to welcome you to St. Augustine."

As though the words were a signal, talk in the room again flowed normally. Slater, beaming and with a new and sudden respect in his approach, bowed and scraped from behind the bar in Clay's presence.

"Your slightest whim, sir?" He looked at Clay almost appealingly.

"I guess I'll have the same." I wonder, he thought, who the hell John Spain is.

The man snapped a fingernail against the stem of his brandy glass and sent it sliding across the bar. Slater reached for it eagerly, hastily tucked it out of sight, and placed a clean one before his customer.

"And," Spain spoke with detached interest, "how is your grandfather? It has been some time since I have seen him, although we correspond." He appeared to derive a certain humor from the statement.

"He doesn't change much." Clay lifted his mug. "Your health, sir."

Spain only moistened his lips with the brandy. "That," he said, "is a comforting thought."

Slater's "boon to the weary" was having its effect. Clay was imbued with a magnificent feeling of well-being. The weariness had slipped from his shoulders and he felt himself ready of tongue and keen of

152

wit. His eyes brightened as he glanced over the room. It was, he decided, a pleasant thing to be Clayfield Hammond.

"Will you be with us for some time?" Spain somehow managed to convey the idea that the tenure of the visitor's residence in St. Augustine was a matter of extreme importance.

Clay was flattered and made no effort to disguise his pleasure. "I don't know, sir. I just set out to see some of the world."

"A pleasant occupation." Spain examined his watch. "I regret," he continued, "a previous engagement prevents our dining together. Perhaps," he bowed graciously, "tomorrow evening? I shall send my carriage for you."

Clay grinned. These gravely elegant gestures struck him as just short of ridiculous. He scrubbed the knuckles of one hand into the bristles on chin and cheeks and glanced down at the dirty buckskins.

He met the quiet amusement in Spain's eyes. "A friend of mine advised me not to try to see the world in these. I guess he was right. Maybe I better find a tailor tomorrow."

"As you wish." Spain held out his hand. "Call upon me should you need anything. I am completely at your service." He smiled. "Also, it will not be necessary for you to present the letter of introduction. I can see the resemblance." He turned and addressed the other occupants. "Gentlemen."

Without appearing to hear the quick chorus of good nights he bowed stiffly again to Clay, wheeled, and marched with a slow and deliberate tread to the door.

Clay waited until the portals swung shut and then pushed his mug in Slater's direction.

"I'll have another of these," he commanded.

"But of course, sir." Slater seemed to dance on his toes behind the bar. "Ah," he coughed apologetically, "may I also suggest some supper? These, ah," he held the mug nervously, "have a certain potency. Minor pitfalls lurk within their fragrant depths. A good cut from the joint?" He waited expectantly.

Clay looked about the room. Many of the tables were already filled. Others, apparently, were reserved. His eyes fell upon the young man addressed by Slater as Beulow. The fellow still rested with indolent superciliousness, pre-empting the large table, feet outstretched on a second chair.

"I'll sit here," Clay said over his shoulder. Before Slater could object he moved quickly and with a sweep of his leg kicked the chair out from beneath Beulow's boots. Only by frantically clawing at the edge of the heavy table did the man save himself from being pitched to the floor. While he was scrambling to regain his balance Clay seated himself, arms outstretched on the table, waiting.

"My natural inclination, sir," Beulow was breathing heavily and the sound was distinct in the hushed room, "my natural inclination is to kill you for that."

Clay waited. He knew now he was more than a little drunk and looking for trouble. Over the world by tooth and claw with Clay Hammond, he thought.

Beulow touched at his lips with a handkerchief, heavily bordered with lace. "Your action was not entirely unprovoked, although I should not allow that to influence my desire to blow out your addled brains. I hesitate because, for all your shaggy appearance, I recognize an affinity. We may become friends, and I have too few to lose one by hasty decision."

"Whatever you say." Clay relaxed, and at his back he could hear the audible sigh of relief as it was passed around the room. The two slaves at the spit made a great rustling of platters and the voices of the men when they spoke again seemed unnaturally loud. "Take it or leave it."

"For the moment," Beulow tapped on the table with his fingers, "I prefer to leave it. Should subsequent events prove my judgment wrong I shall kill you in the bloodiest and most painful manner I can devise." He rose, bowed from the waist, and extended his hand. Clay stood up, feeling slightly foolish over the whole thing. It was all play acting and he suddenly felt loutish before this undeniably graceful and composed figure.

"I guess it was a fool thing to do," he mumbled.

"No apologies, sir, or you will completely destroy a delightfully favorable first impression. James Beulow, at your service."

Clay couldn't contain his laughter. The hand in his was firm and strong. He liked the feel of it. "I'll be damned if I don't think you are as drunk as I am. My name's Clay Hammond."

"Landlord!" Beulow shouted. "Mr. Hammond and I will sup together. Be seated, sir." He waited until Clay had resumed his place. "We shall dine and drink together. Later you will accompany me to the establishment of Madame Pelican, where we shall engage in a base orgy of the flesh with her accomplished bawds. We shall bay at the moon and reel through the streets until the watch sets up a terrified alarm. A bottle, Slater, and quickly. You," he turned his eyes again to Clay, "you, my unkempt and shaggy savage, will be a sensation among the madame's sprightly whores. I can hear their delighted screams at this moment. We are well met, Mr. Hammond."

Far too early in the evening Clay lost track of the number of drinks he consumed. Whether eating, walking, drinking, or talking, he moved and acted without effort. Getting and staying drunk was a wonderful thing, and he floated out of the public house and was borne aloft on the deep cushions of Beulow's carriage.

"God's silver buttons," Beulow remarked admiringly, "but we make a splendid pair, Hammond. You shall come and live with me. We are to be, henceforth, inseparable. The river will ring with our carousing, we shall strike terror into the hearts of the mothers of virgins. You are a monumental and primal figure." In their rounds he introduced Clay to acquaintance and stranger alike with the pride of a man who was leading about a captive bear.

"Aren't we goin' to fight?" Clay hung to the side of the carriage, trying desperately to focus on his companion.

"Never. Cut out my heart if you will. Toss it into the street to be trampled upon. It will still quiver for you."

"How the hell am I goin' to see the world, ridin' around in a carriage with you?" Clay was experiencing a great difficulty with his tongue, as it displayed an alarming tendency to curl into the back of his mouth.

"We shall make our own world, and a far better one than is now known."

Clay nodded agreeably. The idea sounded pretty good.

Until dawn their roistering formed a series of never too clear pictures. He could remember a fierce but short-lived brawl in a smoky dive and their triumphant but battered withdrawal; a peaceful and refreshing interlude outside a tavern as drink and food were brought to their carriage. They consumed vast amounts of freshly boiled shrimp and baked crab, washing down the provender with sharp wine that came foaming from the bottle as the tops were exploded outward. Their entry into Madame Pelican's was a sweeping triumph, exceeded only by the assault of Caesar's legions on a stricken city. They routed customers from their beds, chasing them half naked into the streets, and assuaged the anguish of Madame herself with wads of crumpled bills and scattered gold pieces. From time to time Clay untangled himself from a shrieking bevy of delighted young women, whose clothing seemed to slip from them at the merest touch of a finger, to call loudly for more wine, and he was dimly conscious of crawling in and out of beds in a naked tangle.

"Never, my heart's blood," Beulow assured him, "has there been such devastation since the first Spaniards arrived to lay about them

155

with fire and sword. History has been made and tomorrow the citizens will undoubtedly propose the raising of a memorial to us in the plaza. Either that or we will be confined in the fort's deepest and foulest dungeon, there to rot and wither. I care not which if we be not parted."

Sometime near morning a great weariness crept upon the pair. There was no flavor in the wine and the girls mere lumps of perfumed suet.

"We are sated, my friend," Beulow exclaimed dramatically, "and it is time we took our leave."

With weariness their only prop, they stumbled and lurched through the doorway and stood for a moment in the refreshing coolness of the dawn. Behind them the madame and her young ladies crowded at the open portal, their excited chatter ringing as so many silver coins cast upon the bricks. With the assistance of the coachman they made their uncertain way into the depths of the carriage, and the vehicle rattled noisily through the graying streets.

"It has been a night of great moment." Beulow lay back against the cushions and sighed blissfully. "Your entry into St. Augustine will not, believe me, go unnoticed. Tonight, or today if you insist on hair-splitting, I shall sleep at your side in one of Slater's beds. Tomorrow we will go down the river to my ancestral plantation until the hue and cry has become but a troubled echo."

Clay's head bobbled against the cushion as the carriage bounced over the uneven and badly paved street and he sucked in great draughts of the fresh, sweet air. Beulow might talk like a burbling idiot but he was a handy man in a fight or with a bottle. He couldn't remember when he'd had as much fun.

"Let us sleep, sweet friend," Beulow sang noisily, "and husband our strength against tomorrow's unknown rigors. Cleave to my side, place your trusting hand in mine, let your innocence be a shining mirror into which all men may peer with envy."

"You're crazy as hell," Clay mumbled drowsily.

"Aye! I am a poor mad thing, but your friend."

Clay snored with the sharp sound of tearing linen, an expression of childish happiness on his face.

13

Beulow sat on the edge of the tumbled bed they had shared at Slater's and nursed a splitting head. Now and then he glanced across at Clay as though to reassure himself that this bearded stranger was actually in the same room.

"We must," the young man said shakily, "retreat momentarily and repair the ravages incurred by our enthusiasm. At my place we shall make time stand still while our strength is renewed. Besides," he looked with distaste at the pile of buckskins on the floor, "I cannot much longer endure those hides with which you dress yourself. We are of a size and I shall see to your outfitting until proper clothing can be made to cover your brawny carcass."

"It was sure one hell of a night." Clay opened the hot kiln of his mouth.

"I was not wrong." Beulow looked at him. "We have an affinity. We shall be friends. Come." He rose and teetered toward pitcher and basin. "Let us be about the business of girding ourselves."

Although he made a determined effort to appear unconcerned, Clay was all wide-eyed wonder as they started down the river for Beulow's plantation. They made the trip in a gleaming canopied barge with eight half-naked slaves at the long sweeps. Forward, lolling on the cushioned seats, they ate from a huge hamper packed with crisped quail, juicy breasts of duck, meat pastries, and sweets. A second basket, containing a dozen bottles of French wines, provided a soothing liquid refreshment. Beulow lay back among the brightly colored pillows, tossing bits of meat and crust into the air for the small cloud of screaming, diving gulls following their progress. Now and then, behind the straining backs of the slaves, Clay could catch a glimpse of Santee, seated aft on the barge's bottom, and he grinned, wondering at the thoughts that must be gathering behind the impassive face. Nothing along the Apalachicola had prepared either of them for this magnificent display, but of the two the black seemed less impressed. The barge danced and skipped across the choppy expanse of Matanzas Inlet and slid into the calmer water where the heavy tropical growth crowded the banks and was mirrored in the unruffled stream. From his seat Clay caught a glimpse of the rearing, charging sea beyond the inlet and of white shimmering beach.

"By God," he said with unconscious wonder, "it sure is big."

The Beulow plantation was also of a size to evoke comment and respect with its enormous fields and groves. Scoffing dandy though he might appear, young Beulow managed his affairs with a tight grip.

"My late and unlamented father," he explained to Clay, "would have been happier in his grave had he another heir. He condemned me to hell as a wastrel rake and I live to make him a lying fool."

Clay thought he had never seen so many house servants on one place. There seemed to be at least four blacks to do each small chore. Beulow was delighted with Santee and spent several minutes poking, pinching, and drubbing the enormous slave's muscles and back and urging Clay to sell him.

"Old Clay would sure rear up if I came back without Santee." Clay shook his head to all of Beulow's offers. "But if you want to we can let him run loose in the quarters. That usually produces some pretty good results."

Life at the Beulow plantation was a pleasant and familiar interlude. The two men rode, hunted, and fished, and through the long evenings Clay learned to hold his bottle. They made periodic trips to St. Augustine, journeying by water or on horse along the King's Road. Here, on the accessible east coast, he discovered activity undreamed of in the more remote sections of the Territory. A chain of vast sugar plantations stretched themselves on the branches of the Matanzas and Halifax Rivers. Coastal steamers working their way from Boston, New York, Charleston, and Savannah had their cabins packed with immigrants, all eager for a place in this fabled land of riches and perpetual sunshine. In and out of St. Augustine there flowed a constant stream of traffic that trickled off into a hundred small channels to seep through the unsettled acres. For these newcomers young Beulow, Clay discovered, shared Old Clay's contempt. They formed a penniless rabble, intruding into the domain of their betters. They were, he insisted, without background or competence, and the Territory had been rendered a service every time one fell to an angry Seminole or had his cabin burned above his head.

"We're trying to get rid of the wrong people," he asserted. "It's the white trash we ought to dispose of first. Later we can find a place in the swamps for the Indians."

158

They sat before the dying fire, feet outstretched toward the heat, glasses and decanter close at hand. Beulow yawned.

"Bedtime," he said, "with an early trip to St. Augustine. Tomorrow we shall discover if, in truth, fine feathers make a fine bird."

Clay nodded wearily and rose from the shielding depths of the chair. "I'm asleep on my feet," he mumbled. " 'Night."

"I shall rouse you on the morrow with cup and horn." Beulow poured himself another drink. "Until the cock crows."

With eyes half shut Clay found his way to his room and waited with numb obedience while a slave undressed and prepared him for bed. He was almost snoring as the black guided him to the covers and tucked them about him.

His legs spraddling a chair, arms resting on its back, the gold knob of a cane tapping reflectively at his even white teeth, James Beulow watched as the fat little tailor danced nimbly about Clay's unhappy figure and tapped affectionately at the shoulders of the new plum-colored coat.

"You're a fine figure of a man, old cock," he remarked with pleasure, "a thing to delight the eye and flutter a susceptible heart. God's buckles, but you'll cut a swath."

Clay shifted uncomfortably. "I'm afraid to move," he objected, "for fear the whole thing will come apart and I'll peel out of it, jay naked, like a banana. How the hell can a man get any peace in something like this?"

"Hah! You spark my pretty wit, sir." The elegant figure astride the chair leaned back, his features screwed into a thoughtful expression. "I shall now make a pun and suggest that such tailoring will get you many a piece." He snorted with admiration. "Gad! I am the sheer essence of repartee."

The tailor cackled delightedly and held himself off from Clay at arm's length while surveying Beulow with rapt astonishment.

"If I may say so, Mr. Beulow, sir, that was well put. Peace and a piece." He spoke almost reverently.

"You may say so, Linkler," Beulow accepted the tribute unconcernedly, "and damned to you if you didn't." He sucked at the cane's top as though it held some secret and exotic sweet.

"You're a loony." Clay stretched his shoulders tentatively.

Turning before the long mirror, doing his best to offer nothing more than a bored expression to the reflection, Clay was secretly delighted by what he saw. The clothing ordered four weeks ago was, he thought, little short of a miracle in cut and line. I wonder, he thought as a grin escaped him, what Clayport would say if I walked into McCollum's dressed like this.

"God's waistcoat," Beulow muttered, "don't smirk about in such a silly fashion."

Clay's grin broadened as he pivoted before the glass. There was nothing in the figure to remind him of the buckskin-clad stranger who had walked into St. Augustine from the backwoods. At Beulow's arrogant command the fussed tailor had put aside his waiting orders and devoted his entire time and that of his assistants to outfitting Clay with a complete wardrobe in the shortest possible time. Patiently Clay had submitted to innumerable tedious fittings and discussions of materials. In the end, however, it had been Beulow who selected the cloth and dictated the cutting, and after the first couple of mild remonstrances Clay accepted the autocratic management of his personal life with wry humor.

"Cock," Beulow had exclaimed, "I can't be seen in public with a manure-scented peasant. Your idea of elegance is homespun jeans and a butternut shirt. Let us have no more feeble arguments about what you will or will not wear."

Surveying the finished product now, Clay could not deny the improvement. This new friend might act and talk as an extravagant ass at times, but he knew what he was about. I wish, he thought, Old Clay could get a look at me. I figure he'd think he was getting his money's worth.

Arm in arm, their sticks swinging lightly in the fashionable half circle, conscious of the impression they were making, the pair strolled toward the plaza, past a seated row of squalid Indians who stuffed their mouths with pastries or chunks of freshly fried fish and passed bottles of raw whisky from hand to hand. Each morning the citizens were greeted by the spectacle of this disreputable roadside gathering as the Indians came in from the woods bearing legs of venison, tanned hides, wild turkeys, braces of duck, beadwork, and carved ornaments for barter. Little money changed hands, the Seminoles being eager only for whisky and the sweet delicacies of the town. The trading finished, they squatted in the dirt beside the road, drinking themselves into a stupor, staring with blank contempt at the whites as they passed, and then rolling over to sleep off the effects of the scorching liquor in the hot sun. Outside the town their squaws, sad-eyed, barefooted, their long skirts dirty and patched, waited with the dumb misery of weary pack animals for the staggering return of their men.

As Beulow chattered aimlessly Clay's eyes swept along the wavering line and he knew a sudden compassion. Here and there he encountered a glance of flashing spirit, but for the most part there was nothing but defeat written on the faces. Their greasy hair decorated with turkey feathers, long daubs of black paint smeared over their eyebrows, heavy rings of copper and silver suspended in ears and noses, they were filthy scarecrows, mocking travesties on the Indians he had known along the Apalachicola. Here there was neither honor nor dignity but merely a desperate search for oblivion in the white man's whisky.

"Gad, cock," Beulow was watching him with amusement, "you eye that Indian rabble as though you hoped to find a handsome savage wench tucked away."

Clay shook his head quickly. "No. I was just feeling sorry for them, I guess."

Beulow was incredulous and his expression was that of one who plainly expected to discover a jest in the statement. When he was convinced his companion was serious he laughed uproariously.

"You are," he said finally, "a pigeon of great innocence. Save your tender emotions, or, if you must, display them in the practical form of a piece of silver. The brutes will understand that."

Clay nodded. "I guess you're right. That's what Old Clay would say. As a matter of fact," he glanced at Beulow's handsome profile, "the two of you sound mighty much alike at times."

Beulow accepted the comparison lightly, as a compliment. "Your grandfather must be a wise old cock. I begin to understand why he bundled you off to see the world."

Clay shrugged and forced his attention from the miserable row of Indians. "I don't seem to be making much progress," he confessed. "Up to now the trail doesn't run anywhere except to taverns and women."

"What happier road to travel?" Beulow's raised eyebrows punctuated the question.

There was, Clay had to admit, a certain amount of truth in the flippant remark. The hours had fallen into a pleasant and effortless routine. The tempo of the old town was of easy grace, and the long sun-washed days and perfumed nights lent themselves to idle pastimes. In the late afternoons there was much talk in the public houses, where men sat to drink, gossip, or play at cards and dice. An occasional horse race or a cockfight satisfied their competitive spirits, and such establishments as Madame Pelican's provided make-believe games of love without the usual complications. As his list of acquaintances among the more rakish elements of the town broadened, Clay was astonished to discover that many of the men actually had homes and families. Most of their time, it seemed, was spent at drinking and wenching, and he wondered what portion of their lives was allotted to the domestic scene. Soldiers from the fort in the town's streets, the padding figures of Indians, carefully turned-out ladies and gentlemen in their carriages, and the banks of brilliant flowers and rustling palms gave an air of carnival to the settlement. If, now and then, there came ominous rumblings from the wild interior of the Territory, then there were few ears attuned to catch the unpleasant sound. It almost seemed to Clay that he had never known any other life.

Absently nodding agreement to Beulow's monologue of trivialities without actually hearing what was said, Clay found time to wonder at the quirk of circumstance that had led him to this friendship. There was a bond between them, although Clay could not name it or tell its strength. They responded to each other's heavy humor or found much pleasure in long but companionable silences. He is a friend, Clay sometimes thought, but I'm damned if I know why. With his own hard logic, Beulow once said, "Since there is nothing you can possibly want from me, old cock, I can afford to be your friend."

Clay had laughed at the brutality of the admission. "Old Clay wouldn't think so," he retorted. "He says it's your equals you have to look out for."

They crossed the plaza, following a narrow path between crimson poinsettia and neat triangles of flower beds, past the pillared and arched slave market to the battery. Here, at a coquina trough, Beulow took a small silver cup and with a delicate shudder drank a thimbleful of the spouting sulphur water.

"Gad, but it stinks. However, they say it is good for the liver." He replaced the tiny vessel in the tail pocket of his coat. "Let us repair to Slater's, where I can get the damned taste of the stuff out of my mouth."

"It's too early," Clay objected.

"Of course it is." Beulow nodded approvingly. "It is also too early for wenching, too warm for exercise, too light for a brawl. We could hire a boatman and go to the beach or sit here on the wall and dangle our feet over the side like a couple of waifs. The possibilities for amusement are limitless."

"All right," Clay laughed, "let's go to Slater's, but I'll be a poor drinking companion. I would like a passably clear head for this evening."

"Ah! I had forgotten. Tonight you bend a knee to the beautiful Lechane and her guardian."

Clay glanced at him, wondering if he was mistaken in thinking that the word guardian had been unduly accented, but his companion's face was turned toward the bright sky as he sniffed with evident pleasure at the fresh sea wind.

"As you know," Beulow rambled on, "I have little countenance in the eyes of Mr. John Spain. He considers me an impudent rakehell and a surly tosspot. For your benefit, though, I may say that Mr. Spain's dislike does not stem from an aversion to either my habits or my disposition. Once," he continued dreamily, "I stared at Mistress Lechane with what may best be described as lechery. Mr. Spain, himself no mean authority on the subject, took offense. As a result I have been forever banished from the doubtful privileges of his acquaintance. He ignores me in the tavern and on the street, while I in turn contrive to make myself odious whenever chance places us in the same room."

"I'll take that as good advice." Clay was amused.

Beulow halted and regarded him unhappily. "My bucolic friend," he said slowly, "you must recover from an unfortunate disposition to go through life wagging your tail like an eager puppy. Why should you care for Mr. Spain? Ogle Mistress Lechane. Lay hot hands upon her if possible, and shrink not beneath the beetling brows of one who would stay a natural instinct. I am pained by you. Be damned to John Spain and fie upon you for a quaking varlet if you covet not the damsel. Come." He linked his arm with Clay's. "Slater's is our goal, and tonight, after you have minced and simpered your fill, I shall await you there for a report, and afterward we shall entertain ourselves with some attractive bawds of my selection."

The room was heavily ornate and through the half-drawn latticed blinds slender blades of sunlight pricked with futile effort at the gloom. High walls of intricately scrolled and carved mahogany panels, deep red carpet, and tall, cumbersome Spanish chairs and chests lent it the somber air of a papal chamber. The great four-posted bed with arching canopy of tasseled crimson silk was awesomely regal in its proportions and brocaded spread. It was a room in which to die with hushed dignity.

Against the massed pillows the girl's dark hair flowed out in a waterfall of midnight, inky black and vaporous, upon which floated the chaste petal of her camellia-white face. A slight reflection from drapes and rug imparted a shell-pink coloring to her breasts as she lay nakedly unconcerned on the deeply cushioned square. Now and then she wriggled her small toes, her eyes traveling to them down the length of slender legs with the bright attention of a kitten engrossed in its own pretending.

Framed in an open doorway, small flecks of lather still clinging to his lean cheeks, John Spain wiped at his face with a towel and a quietly amused smile rested briefly on his mouth.

"There is something of the doxie about you, Mistress Lechane," he spoke thoughtfully, "a congenital whorishness, at once appealing and disconcerting."

The girl yawned indifferently, pressing her red lips with gracefully trailing fingers. Her eyes were wide with assumed innocence.

"Would you have me otherwise, sir?"

Spain advanced to the bed and stood looking down at her. Almost absently he touched the full, ripe swell of her breasts. She stirred and the mockery died on her face.

"At times," he continued, "I find your abandon a challenge to my years."

The long, silky lashes fluttered. "I have no cause for complaint, sir, as to the difference in our ages. You deal with me fairly and at great length."

His laughter exploded and filled the room. The girl stared at him with spurious astonishment, implying that no words of hers could possibly account for his mirth. After a moment he rose and walked to the windows, throwing open the shutters and drawing aside the floor-length drapes. Bright sunlight flooded the chamber and the girl tossed a shielding forearm across her eyes. Borne on the soft river wind were the sounds of the ocean, the muffled clopping of horses' hoofs, the slurring liquid call of a peddler, the creaking rattle of a raised sail on a fisherman's boat, and the thin cries of excited gulls on the water front. St. Augustine was a town of sleepy movement with a gentle, lulling rhythm. In character it was still Spanish. The tongue persisted, and in the afternoons and evenings around the plaza the olive complexions of Spaniard and Minorcan outnumbered the fairer-skinned foreigners a dozen to one. Only the flag flying from the fort's coquina walls gave testimony to ownership by the United States. Spain's eyes rested with pleasure on the scene outside the window and he turned from it reluctantly.

"You will remember, Claire," he said as he pulled out the drawer of a linen chest, "we have a guest at dinner tonight?"

"I know. Your savage friend from the swamps."

Spain drew a fine shirt over his head. "He is neither a savage nor my friend, merely the grandson of a man with whom I find it expedient to do business."

He dressed quickly but carefully and the girl followed his movements with mild interest.

"What," he adjusted a scarf at his throat, "will you do today?"

"The same as yesterday." She was bored. "The seamstress at three, and at five o'clock I shall drive in the carriage and flirt over the top of my fan with the young officers from the fort."

Spain turned carefully before the mirror, examining himself from several angles. He was a handsome and distinguished figure. Satisfied with his appearance, he selected a thin black cigar from a leather case and bit the end with sharp precision.

"As my ward," he said conversationally, "the privilege of a light and harmless flirtation can hardly be denied you. As my mistress there are certain limitations to such a pastime."

"I am not unaware of my position, sir." The words were almost whispered.

He smiled and bent down to kiss her lightly. For a moment her arms seemed to be on the point of encircling his neck and then fell back limply.

"Until this evening, then." His hands lingered affectionately on her body and she stared up at him with an animal hunger until he withdrew. "*Adios*." He spoke gently.

"Go with God." She was breathing heavily and the words were all but inaudible.

For a minute or so after the door had closed behind him she lay quietly, arms and legs outstretched in a consciously wanton position of surrender; then, with a fluttering sigh, she reached upward for the fringed knob of a bell pull. There was exhaustion in the movement.

It was a large but narrow house, fronting on the river, and to it, at John Spain's invitation or command, came many men. Visiting senators and representatives from Washington, judges, Territorial officials, Florida's governor, merchants, and wealthy planters sat at his table, drank his fine wines and brandy, ate his food, and talked. Out of these conversations certain things occurred to the benefit of John Spain. Legislation was instigated or withheld, trades were made, advantages swapped, small but necessary pressures were exerted at strategic points. Florida was a new and fruitful acquisition and devil take the laggard.

At these dinners, almost wholly masculine in character, Claire

Lechane took her position as John Spain's ward and hostess. The young woman, but turned twenty, was, Spain sometimes casually explained to a stranger within the circle, the orphaned daughter of an old friend. If men looked at her with greedy eyes she seemed unaware of the attention. Always she was serenely reserved, aloof, and unapproachable, the dark crystal of her beauty unflawed. Abroad, in the town, at the markets and shops, or riding in her carriage, she was accompanied by a leathery and forbidding hag who, for convenience's sake, was designated as Tía María. The more suspicious who put a tongue in cheek at the mention of ward and aunt were careful to voice such skepticisms behind locked doors, for John Spain was a man of evil, flaming temper whose steady hand could hold a deadly pistol. If gossip rippled here and there over the quiet pools of the settlement's society, it was no more than a breath, elusive and difficult to detect. The couple made only infrequent public appearances at the theater or concerts in the plaza, and nothing in the grave courtesy displayed by the man toward the young woman upon such occasions indicated their relationship was other than that proclaimed.

To John Spain's house, also, came other men, neither so well dressed nor so sure in manner and speech as the officials and politicians. These visitors arrived and departed at unconventional hours, and what they reported to Spain behind drawn shutters remained locked within the silent walls. They were men of rude habits whose feet were more accustomed to the unplotted trails of the back country than to the drawing room and whose furtive trading with the Seminoles in whisky and guns took them to the fringes of every Indian settlement in the Territory. The overly curious might have drawn some connection between their movements and the sporadic Indian raids; the killings in thinly populated districts where undisciplined bands of warriors, inflamed and made reckless by illicit whisky, murdered and pillaged as the cry for federal intervention became louder and more persistent. The Indians, it was pointed out, could no longer be controlled. The alternatives were either their extermination or mass and forced migration west of the Mississippi. Once either of these had been accomplished, uncounted fertile acres would be thrown open to safe and profitable exploitation by a few men. If the whisky that found its way into the interior was John Spain's, then the casks were not so marked. If the guns, powder, and bullet metals falling so easily into the hands of renegade Seminoles came from John Spain's warehouses, such a thing could not be proved. If the men who came to Spain's house in the light of day or behind the cloak of darkness were, at someone's orders, deliberately and recklessly fomenting an Indian war, then such a charge could find no public supporter; there was no man brave enough to say openly this was true. If across the Territory the rotting bones of a lone trader or the black ashes of an isolated settler's cabin were victims to a carefully executed plan to force a reluctant government to action against the Seminoles, no one could say whose hand had shaped the bloody design.

As he stepped into the warm and gently stirring sunlight John Spain looked about him with a proprietary pleasure. The river sparkled in the fresh morning air and the scrubby hillocks of Anastasia Island were green and white against the sky's unclouded blue. Behind the rearing walls of the fort the power and protection of the United States dressed and polished itself. The highly varnished barouche waiting for him at the curb, its top thrown back, was the perfection of fine craftsmen. He entered and settled himself against the cushions. It was good to be John Spain. Everything he owned, from the vividly beautiful girl in the house to the blooded team and glittering carriage, represented the best his money could buy. If to preserve them or add to their luster a great many men might die, then, he felt, their sacrifices would be proper and not in vain.

14

THEY stood within the shadowy oblong of a narrow balcony overlooking the river. Below, and at a short distance, the riding lights of small craft tipped and winked on the swelling tide and were answered at regular intervals by the red glow at the end of John Spain's cigar. Over the railing and slender pillars the white massed fragrance of the Cherokee rose twined and reached upward in a persistent effort to enclose the space. So quiet was the night that the dry creak of a swinging boom was distinct and the splashing plop of a leaping mullet far off shore sounded as a sharp report.

Unconsciously Clay sighed, regretting that the evening was at an end, and the girl at his side turned her face toward him, the smile on her lips hidden in the darkness.

"Do you succumb so completely to the charm of our city, Mr. Hammond?"

"I guess so." He laughed softly, embarrassed by his transparency, acutely aware of her presence and the light touch of a wispy scarf against his arm. "It sort of gnaws at you until, after a while, it almost hurts."

"A danger inherent in all beauty, sir," John Spain reflected absently. "Yet man persists in seeking it out, intent upon self-destruction."

"You have a grim fancy, sir." Claire Lechane lifted a quick, bantering glance in his direction.

"Perhaps." His eyes met hers for a moment and then shifted with a slow deliberateness to search along the dark outline of the distant shore.

The light exchange of words was innocent enough, but Clay could not rid himself of the uneasy feeling that they were edged. The notion troubled him. This evening, for the third time within a month, he was John Spain's guest. The invitation had been ceremoniously delivered by the hand of a slave to his lodgings at Slater's Tavern and came almost in the form of a royal command, assuming acceptance. The Negro hadn't waited for a reply, and as he shaved and dressed Clay found himself a little amused by Spain's cavalier attitude even as he wondered why he should extend the hospitality of his home beyond the dictates of simple courtesy. The man's reserve was carried to the point where it was almost indistinguishable from disinterest. He encouraged no intimacies, sought no friendship. Talk at the table was confined to impersonal generalities and his bearing in the presence of his guest was one of complete detachment. After his second visit to the house on the water front Clay was puzzled that Spain should bother with the grandson of a man he hadn't seen in years and with whom, apparently, he had the most tenuous of business connections. Under ordinary circumstances he would have refused this third invitation, for the small dinners were without gaiety, being conducted with somber perfection. What drew him to the house was Claire Lechane's smoldering beauty. It was a thing to haunt a man, walking beside him in the bright light of day and crowding in upon his tortured dreams at night, the succubus of tormented fancy.

By chance, at first, he had encountered her on the streets following his initial visit to the house. Later the meetings were the result of patient design. He made a point of strolling past the open market at the time of the morning when many ladies waited in their shaded carriages while their slaves brought baskets of fresh fruits and vegetables to the curb for inspection. Always the girl was accompanied by Tía María, who sat in stolid suspicion on the seat facing her niece and whose presence was calculated to discourage anything more than the most commonplace exchange of courtesies. Again they had met when her carriage was drawn into the line on the south side of the plaza, where a band from the fort played lustily, if not well, in an afternoon concert. At other times he strolled too casually along the sea wall, hoping desperately for a sight of her or an opportunity to bow and lift his hat as she drove past. In these contrivings he received no whispered word or furtive sign of encouragement. Her attitude was graciously correct, but behind her oddly flecked eyes there lurked the faintest suggestion of amusement, as though she were well aware of his clumsy overtures and was not displeased. There had been nights when he turned abruptly from drinking or gaming with Beulow in Slater's to prowl with lonely restlessness, invariably halting before Spain's darkened house to peer helplessly up at the blank windows, trying to fix in his imagination the location of her room.

"What is it you do abroad at night, my melancholy friend?" Beulow was mockingly curious following one of these excursions. "Whose company do you seek more beguiling than mine? Do you find some occult wisdom in the stars or engage in nocturnal perversions with the watch?"

"I'm just restless, I guess," Clay replied lamely.

His friend fingered his lip skeptically. "Could it be," he asked, "that your rural heart has been touched by the sweet, sad agony of love? Do you awaken in sweaty trembling? Do your limbs become things of vapor in her presence? Are you tied of tongue and large of hands and feet when you stand before her? Confide in me. My ageless wisdom is yours to command."

Clay had shrugged off Beulow's curiosity, fearing his scornful laughter. How could a man be in love with a girl he had seen no more than half a dozen times or with whom he had exchanged little more than the barest civilities?

A small scratching sound and the whispered, apologetic words of a slave at the screen door caused John Spain to turn from his silent contemplation of the river.

"A gen'mum to see yo', Mastah." The black's words were almost indistinct.

Spain nodded. "I'll be down," he said, and turned to Clay. "It is a visitor I have been expecting," he explained. "Your indulgence for a few minutes."

Close upon his exit the door was reopened and the heavy figure of Tía María bulked within the narrow space. Without a word the woman waddled to the far corner of the balcony and settled herself with a wheezing sound in a broad wicker chair. From where they stood Clay could hear the reedy crackle of her placid, gentle rocking and understood that in the darkness the hag's eyes were fixed stonily upon him. For a moment Spain's caution fired a quick anger within him. The man took no chances with his ward and a comparative stranger even when they stood on an open balcony. His resentment died. By God, he thought ruefully, I wouldn't either. If he knew what I've been thinking he'd snatch her into a room and lock the door.

"You are amused, sir?"

He looked down into her upturned face. "A little, I guess," he admitted, "but I didn't think it showed."

Almost accidentally, it seemed, her fingers rested for a fluttering moment upon his sleeve and dropped away. In the grave and solemn setting of her face her eyes were laughing.

"The custom has its advantages, sir," she said, "if the duenna be discreet."

"Is she?" The words came automatically.

"I have had neither the desire nor the occasion to inquire, Mr. Hammond." There was an unmistakable rebuff in the reply, yet, without seeming to move, she somehow leaned lightly against him and their elbows touched and held with the slightest of pressures.

Clay could feel the quick leaping of his pulse and was certain the thunderous pounding of his heart must be audible in the street below. This is a hell of a note, he thought helplessly. What do I say now? Unable to turn away, he let his glance travel with slow hunger from the full curve of her lips past the delicate throat line and linger on the fruit of her small breasts as they thrust against the silk. For the briefest moment the girl submitted to this undisguised inspection, then, coolly and with the unmistakable intention of telling him she was well aware of what was happening, she made a small gesture of drawing the scarf about her bare shoulders.

"You unfrock me, sir," she whispered huskily and turned her face away.

"I—I—" he stammered, "I'm sorry."

Teeth pressed into a lower lip and then released it. "I did not say I found it offensive, Mr. Hammond."

He wheeled, his back to the river, to confront her. "By God," the words were muted, "you're laughing at me." He made the accusation angrily.

"Is it, then, a thing to be taken seriously, sir?"

"I don't know," he confessed miserably. His resentment drained away as quickly as it had come, but he found speech difficult. Her directness confused him and he searched his wits for a suitable apology. That was a hell of a way to talk to a girl, a nice girl and Spain's ward.

Her lips slightly parted, she continued to stare up into his face. With the cold, speculative gaze of a shopper trying to decide for one garment against another, she regarded him. Sometime during the evening of his second visit, a couple of weeks ago, she had glanced at him across the table and made up her mind to take him as a lover. It had been a completely dispassionate decision in which sentiment or tenderness had no part. Later, in her bed, she lingered over the idea, drawing upon a vivid imagination for intimate details of the experience until her breath quickened and the little nipples of her breasts became hard, pain-filled nubs. As she stood now at his side, the wanton strain in her blood was fired by his obvious inexperience. He would, she thought with a pleasant shiver, take her with the brutal heedlessness of a charging bull in contrast to John Spain's refined and languid eroticisms. It would be an exciting ex-

171

perience to guide him along the paths she had learned so well. Now she must consider the risk, the danger involved, and arrange the opportunity. For three years she had been John Spain's mistress and she understood his violence and dark furies. Carelessly played, the game would not be worth its cost.

At the age of twenty Claire Lechane had packed the evil wisdom of the ages in her lovely head. Her background was cloudy, her future uncertain. The bastard daughter of an Alabama planter and his octoroon mistress, she had cut the pattern of her life at an early age. She was untroubled over her doubtful parentage, feeling that this unknown father had done well enough by her. She felt no resentment for the sire she had never seen and whose name was never mentioned. It had been his money, delivered each month by a lawyer's clerk in cash, that had provided the prettiest of clothes, able tutors, and good schools. She had been reared and educated as a lady, but found no pleasure in the role. At the age of twelve she deliberately gave herself to a riding master. At fifteen she seduced one of her mother's elderly lovers, driving the man to such a point of distraction that he eagerly gave up his home, family, and business to run away with her to New York, where they established themselves as father and daughter. Wearying eventually of his fatuous protestations, she wheedled additional funds and jewels from the hapless man and promptly left him to remorse and solitude. Journeying westward to Cincinnati, she took passage on a river boat to New Orleans. There, for the sheer excitement of a succession of strange men, she entered a glitteringly expensive and fashionable bordello, where she met John Spain.

Now, after three years of this murky respectability and pretense of ward and guardian, she was bored with her protector. Her restlessness had not reached the point where she was willing to forgo completely the things that Spain made possible. Life was easy if dull. Clayfield Hammond, if it could be discreetly arranged, promised a diversion, spiced with sufficient danger to make it inviting. She sighed, a small, whispering sound of satisfaction, at the prospect.

"Will you remain in St. Augustine, Mr. Hammond?" She turned the conversation deftly into less personal channels.

He shook his head. "I don't know. In the beginning I had an idea of traveling north, but now there doesn't seem much point in it."

"The city is not without its attractions for a young man, I hear." She rested her finger tips on the flower-covered railing, turning her face away to gaze out over the river.

"I guess most of them are already spoken for." Clay grinned

down at the back of her head with impudent assurance. "There wasn't a lot to do in Clayport, but there wasn't much competition, either."

As if by random chance his hand dropped limply to cover hers and he felt her fingers curl up through his with quick ardor and then fall away. In the moment he was aware that the rhythmic creaking of Tía María's rocker seemed to halt in mid-swing.

"Claire!" The old woman's voice was a harsh breath of warning as though she sensed rather than saw what was happening.

"I am much alone, Mr. Hammond." She stood motionless but he could feel her trembling.

"This doesn't make much sense." Unconsciously he whispered the words. "I'll speak to Mr. Spain and ask his permission to call upon you."

Her face lifted quickly and her eyes searched his for a sign of laughter or mockery. What she saw frightened her momentarily and she moved as if to turn away.

"You are very young, Mr. Hammond," she said almost regretfully, "very young or a complete scoundrel. It is difficult to tell in the dark."

Before he could frame the puzzled reply there was a sound at the door. A moment later John Spain joined them and they turned to greet him.

"We were coming in, sir." She lifted the scarf at her throat. "There is a sudden chill in the air."

"I was overly long." Spain's glance lingered upon her and then traveled to Clay. "My apologies."

Nothing in his speech or deportment indicated how well aware he was of the small comedy played during his absence or that he found a certain sardonic humor in the situation created. Although he would have laughed at the suggestion, he experienced a momentary twinge of pity, tempered by amusement, for his visitor's apparent state of confusion. In the amorous fencing that he was certain had taken place, the body of Hammond must have yielded several wounds. Claire was too skillful with the weapons nature had placed in her hands and she used them without mercy. As she stood now in the presence of the two men, her attitude was one of demure innocence. Spain smiled to himself. It was in the nature of things that men should desire this girl, and, being a man of logic, he harbored no resentment in the face of Clay's naïve eagerness. It would have been a simple matter to take the young man aside and explain the situation to him; possible complications could be avoided with a few well-chosen words. For the moment, however, he preferred to let his visitor dangle with his tortured writhings. Spain did not delude himself. He understood that this girl, young enough to be his daughter, was not bound to him by ties of loyalty or devotion. Fear rather than affection, the contentment of a well-fed cat, kept her from straying into indiscretions. He elected to keep their relationship on this foundation, well understanding how much more secure it was than the quicksands of sentiment. He was properly appreciative of her body and cared for it with the attention of a connoisseur. It was something for friends and acquaintances to admire in its proper setting. If desire and envy frequently made them reach out to touch this treasure, then there were ways of delivering a sharp rap to the greedy knuckles. It might be amusing to watch this little drama played through a second act.

As they strolled through the upper floor toward the staircase John Spain mentioned his caller.

"My visitor," he said over the girl to Clay, "but recently passed through your part of the Territory from Pensacola, coming by way of Fort King. He brought me news of a change in the management of Indian affairs. It seems Colonel Humphreys has been removed from his post by the Secretary of War and a Major Phagan installed as Indian agent."

Clay halted. There was no mistaking the concern on his face. This was what Gad Humphreys had expected. He had said as much at Fort King.

"Colonel Humphreys," he said slowly, "has been a guest at our place on the Apalachicola. I don't know Major Phagan, but I'd make a guess at the reason for his appointment. The government is looking for trouble."

Spain nodded. "There has been an unseemly delay in the decision to take a firmer stand. It is inconceivable, sir," Spain continued as they descended the stairs, "that such a vast and potentially wealthy territory as Florida should be bottled up because of a savage whim."

Clay made no effort to choke off his laughter, impertinent though Spain might consider it to be. The sound was harsh and unpleasant.

"I don't think anyone could convince the Seminoles that wanting to live at peace on their own land is exactly a whim. Washington's hell-bent for a war, sir."

"Exactly, Mr. Hammond." There was a thin smile of satisfaction on Spain's mouth. "We have sought a solution through other channels. Now, it appears, we must use force." They paused in the brilliantly lighted hallway. "You will find most of the large plantation operators and landholders of the same persuasion. On that list I include your grandfather, myself, and," he hesitated for emphasis, "even such a profligate rascal as your friend James Beulow. The stately march of progress, Mr. Hammond, will not be halted by a few bands of thieving Indians."

Clay took his hat from the hand of a waiting slave. A quick and angry retort was on his tongue, but he held it back. If he wanted to see Claire Lechane again it would be pretty silly to get into an argument with her guardian. His smile was one of amiable agreement.

"I guess you're right, sir," he said gravely. "The march of progress won't be halted, but," an unexpected grin twisted his mouth, "don't be too surprised if it bogs down in some bloody swamps and scrub along the way."

Spain's eyebrows lifted. "You speak as though you doubted the justice or wisdom of the cause. As Clayfield Hammond's grandson you have much to lose."

Clay smoothed the glistening nap of the silvery beaver against his elbow. There was a disturbing and familiar ring in his host's words, almost a quotation of Old Clay's angry ravings.

"I suppose you're right, sir," he said innocently. "I have much to lose, including the few principles I call my own."

Spain's frown was impatient. "As you grow older you will find them an unnecessary burden."

"Gentlemen." The girl's tone held a gentle reproof.

Clay smiled quickly down at her and then glanced back at Spain. "You're probably right. Where progress is concerned, the lives of a couple of thousand Indians count for little. This," he added, "must be so, since so many white people share the same opinion."

Spain extended his slender white hand with reserved cordiality. "At the moment," a flicker of amusement lighted his eyes, "your humor escapes me. We must continue this discussion at another meeting. Consider yourself welcome in my house at any time."

Walking toward his lodgings through the dark streets, Clay tried to shake off the troubled uneasiness that had settled upon him with the news of Humphreys' replacement. I ought to go back to Clayport, he thought unhappily, instead of hanging around here for the sight of a girl's face. If there's goin' to be trouble I expect I'll have to take my share along with Old Clay and the others whether I want to or not. I sure as hell can't hide under the bed at Slater's until it's all over.

He lingered by the sea wall. The town was silent and asleep, the streets deserted. A fresh, damp breeze whipped in from the ocean and he was reluctant to turn away from it. Spain had offered his carriage but Clay refused. The short walk was pleasant and he found a rare beauty in the solitude. He didn't want to think about Spain, Old Clay, Gad Humphreys, or the Seminoles. More pleasant to dwell upon was the memory of the caressing warmth of Claire Lechane's hand as she placed it in his with her good night. He wondered at her reply to the suggestion he speak to her guardian. "You are very young or a great scoundrel." Those were her words, but what the hell did they mean? Something he did not understand lay between them. I guess I'm just a stupid yokel from the backwoods, he thought wryly. Maybe I should go home, where everything is a little less complicated.

Crossing the narrow road from the abutment on the river he suddenly found himself thinking of Sue Rogers, and with a guilty start realized that the memory of her hadn't crossed his mind in weeks. That's a hell of a thing, he mused. How can you like a girl so much one day and forget her the next? Beulow must be right. I go chasing after people and things like an eager, sniffing puppy and I better get over it. Nearing Slater's warmly lighted tavern he wondered if Sue Rogers had expected him to write. Maybe not; she wouldn't have time for much outside of getting settled in the cabin. He smiled in the darkness, recalling their first meeting in McCollum's. In many ways, it occurred to him, Sue and Claire Lechane were alike. They both displayed a cool directness, a deceptive simplicity that disconcerted a man and threw him off balance. "I wonder," he said aloud to the moonless sky, "if she really liked me, or was I just imagining things?" Then there was Claire. "I am much alone, sir." The words carried any number of exciting possibilities if they meant what he thought they did. The notion brought a jaunty whistle to his lips that trailed away on a single doleful note. Probably she hadn't meant anything. A girl could say something like that without expecting a man to climb the trellis to her balcony and crawl in bed. He continued to whistle with a sour lack of conviction. Beulow had the right idea. "Confine your love-making to Madame Pelican's little whores," he counseled. "The complications, if any, are likely to be only physical. Believe me, my downy-cheeked friend, they are less painful than the agonies of the soul."

At Beulow's suggestion they had engaged the two additional rooms adjoining Clay's and threw them together to form a corner suite on the tavern's second floor. The lodgings became a noisy retreat for the town's gay bloods, a rendezvous for gaming and wenching. Clay and Beulow entertained with late suppers and riotous bouts with the bottle, their female guests arriving and departing discreetly by way of the back stairs. Now and then they engaged barges, loading their friends and girls into the crafts for a bonfire picnic on the beach across the river, where the opportunities for love-making were limited only by the number of concealing sand dunes. It was a lazy, spirit-dulling life ideally suited to the gentle, languorous climate, and Clay found himself thinking less and less about leaving it. During those rare intervals when Beulow returned for a brief visit to his plantation, Clay, to his surprise, found himself lonely and disconsolate. The town was without flavor and he waited with impatient boredom for his friend's return. The social life of the newly arrived Americans in St. Augustine was loosely knit. The old Spanish families remaining in the settlement kept to themselves, scorning the newcomers as uncouth barbarians. Despite its age, the town assumed the character of a frontier post, filled with such gaudy establishments as Madame Pelican's and less decorous bordellos, better suited for the crews of coastal ships, traders, hunters, and soldiers from the fort. The community bore itself with a rowdy air and looked with tolerance upon the street fights, water-front brawls, and murders that were commonplace. With an easy acceptance that sometimes astonished him Clay found his proper place in the town as a young man of fortune and unlimited leisure, and in this role he was handsomely seconded by James Beulow, who had appointed himself as guide and mentor.

The hour was late and Slater's all but empty. Two men sat near the fireplace, hunched over a chessboard, and Beulow nodded in a great chair, a heavy coat tossed carelessly across his outstretched legs. At Clay's entrance he roused himself and squinted sleepily at his friend.

"I have," he said accusingly, "spent a dull and unprofitable evening. How much longer must I endure this calflike mooning?"

From beneath lowered lids he watched as Clay slumped in the chair. Wisely or not, he had decided to hold his tongue in the matter of Claire Lechane. He sighed a little unhappily, knowing that sooner or later someone within Clay's hearing would whisper of the lady's character. At which time, he thought, this amiable oaf of whom he had become inordinately fond would invite a killing. The prospect did not amuse him.

"That black expression," Beulow chided, "sits upon your countenance as a scraggly raven. Is life so completely without hope, or did the lady resist your clumsy advances?"

"I think I ought to go home." Clay did not respond to the gibe.

"I've a feeling Old Clay is going to need me. Anyhow," he waved at the room to include it and all of St. Augustine, "this seems pretty silly after a while, sitting on my tail all day and," he grinned suddenly, "humping it at night."

"Is it possible you have abandoned the idea of becoming a backwoods Marco Polo? Is the Alexander from the Apalachicola already wearied of the world he was to conquer?"

"You're crazy as hell." Clay absently tossed the dice from a leather cup.

"My friend," Beulow sat up, "mock me not. It is my insanity that may save your own poor wits. Slater," he called to the innkeeper drowsing behind the bar, "fetch us some bowls of grog. We seek relief from the business of living."

Clay rose and shook his head. "I'm going to bed." He spoke with unnecessary curtness.

Wearing an expression of weariness, Beulow untangled his legs, stood up, and yawned. Playfully he poked at his friend's ribs.

"You are an ungracious dog, sir," he said, "but I shall accompany you. Tomorrow there is a fete with the racing of horses, the pitting of cocks, roasting beef and swine for the peasantry, dancing in the plaza, and the tumbling of wenches in the bushes. All of this merrymaking I look forward to with unutterable disgust, but since I know there is no escape, I shall fortify myself against it with a good night's sleep. Let us seek our couches together, and quickly, before someone is witness to our shame. I find you a dull fellow."

With hands locked behind his head Clay lay in the darkness. When he closed his eyes the misty vision of Claire Lechane's face hovered above his bed, haunting him with a mocking smile. When he opened them to stare at the ceiling he found himself thinking of Old Clay, of Gad Humphreys' unhappy predictions, of Asseola, Sue Rogers, and her brothers. They merged and separated, whirling as small leaves in a spinning wind, and the images filled him with a frightening uneasiness.

"I'm a damn fool." Without thinking he spoke aloud.

There was a rustling in the adjoining room. "I am asleep," Beulow's voice came through the open door, "but I awaken for the brief moment it will take to agree with you."

Clay laughed, somehow feeling better. "What will you do," he called, "if there is an Indian war?"

Beulow snorted. "I shall buckle on saber and pistols. For a while I shall fight with our gallant troops, killing and scalping Seminoles with bloody enthusiasm. Then," he laughed happily, "I shall become

178

a renegade and join the Indians, assisting them in the extermination of the whites. In such a manner I shall become a hero on both sides and the name of James Beulow will go down in history in glorious infamy. Put your toy soldiers away now and sleep, sweet prince. Tomorrow we shall wrestle with the devil for your soul."

15

WITH the first gray pearling of dawn over the dark and scalloped ridge of Anastasia Island the earliest arrivals of the throng that was to crowd in upon the city for the fete of San Marco were already in the streets. They made small camps on the grassy plots of the parade ground, munching a cold breakfast of side meat and corn bread, or stamped against the chill by the sea wall, straining their eyes for a first sight of the laggard sun. In couples and small groups they stood within the fort's shadow, whispering timidly in the presence of its grim majesty and waiting for the sunrise gun in a state of excited apprehension. Along the shallows of the river boatmen were netting tubs full of blue crabs and buckets of shrimp, to be sold by the pennyworth as they were ladled out of the scalding caldrons set up on the shore. To the men, women, and children who had traveled from inland points these salt-water delicacies were rare and unforgettable treats. Later in the day they would flock to a shaded grove beside the narrow San Sebastian River for the picnic and games. Here, in the deep and narrow pits, sides of beef, pig, and venison would be roasted, small mountains of freshly caught fish fried, kegs and jugs of whisky and pale wine of the scuppernong grape set out on the long pine tables beneath the trees. Beyond the west bank of the little river a crude track for the racing of horses had been marked out in the flats. Here the animals entered by the large plantation owners of the Territory vied for local honors and ran against the best from stables as far away as Savannah. There would be cockfights, foot races, wrestling and shooting matches, dancing in the streets, and gambling. At night the poorer element would have an opportunity to gather at the sides of the Government House and strain on tiptoes for a glimpse, through the cloudy windowpanes, of the fashionably attired gentry at their brilliant ball.

From estates to the north and south brightly painted carryalls, heavy coaches, light rigs, and prancing horses charged along the King's Road, bringing the landed aristocracy and the guests of St. Augustine's leading families. Out of sandy trails to the highway came the people of the backwoods, the small farmers and the Territory's poor whites, the curiosity-impelled Indians. For these the fete with its free barbecue and entertainment had an ironic history. In the old days their share in the day had been a device to spare the ladies and gentlemen from their unwelcome stares and uninvited interest. Exasperated by the intrusion of the rabble, who crowded the streets by day and pressed into the doorways and halls of Government House on the night of the ball, the governor had caused to be set aside a certain small sum each year to provide food and entertainment for them at a distance. This, it was felt, would keep the unwashed at more than an arm's length, and the perfumed gaiety of the evening would not be spoiled by their presence. Over the years, though, the character of the fete day changed. Although the climaxing ball was strictly limited to the first families, their guests, and officers from the fort, there was a democratic mingling during the day as the town turned itself over to sport and merrymaking. Privileged slaves were permitted within a special enclosure at the races. Indians and white immigrants rubbed shoulders with banker, merchant, and planter in the crowded and noisy streets. Madame Pelican and her sisters of joy brazenly displayed their girls in open carriages. From behind half-opened shutters of second-story windows the town's well-bred young ladies and their giggling and excited guests tossed flowers and an occasional handkerchief to admiring swains who waited in attitudes of humble supplication below.

Now, in the early hours, the city was but half awake. Within the fort's walls the clear notes of the bugle sounded reveille, hawkers began setting up their small stands where their wares would be displayed, silvery wisps of smoke curled upward from kitchen chimneys as the cooks set their fires for the morning, and slaves appeared with buckets, mops, and brushes to wash down doorsteps and shutters. Out of the woods came the first of the Indians, their women bringing up the rear and carrying the small packs of alligator hides, egret plumes, baskets, and beaded novelties that could be traded or sold. At the city gates and within the fort the guard changed with a clashing of arms and barked commands as the sun moved higher in the sky, driving the night's chill before it and encrusting the palms and dew-laden grass with fiery brilliants.

On the stroke of noon an especially selected slave, seriously proud of the honor and magnificent in purple livery with its silver buttons, white stockings, and buckled shoes, would begin his rounds of the important residences. To the top of a long pole was affixed a wooden bird, the "patgoe," and as the Negro halted before each house and

181

lifted the symbol to balconies crowded with twittering girls dressed in their most elaborate daytime frocks, he was greeted with delighted screams as the young women leaned forward to tie lengths of brightly colored silk ribbons to the shaft. By afternoon the pole was all but hidden beneath a cascade of dazzling streamers as the slave marched with slow dignity beside the sea wall. Along the roadway the carriages and coaches of the elect formed an unbroken line, and behind them were pressed the less fortunate spectators. With rifle and pistol the dashing blades from town and plantation gave demonstrations of their skill or lack of it as they tried to shoot down the patgoe bird while their admiring ladies squealed or sighed with uncontrollable rapture at the spectacle. To the marksman who succeeded in hitting the bird went the honor of leading the first dance at the ball with the girl of his choice, to whom he presented the beribboned trophy as a token of his true love.

Clay thrust his head deeper into the yielding depths of the large feather pillow and tried to shut out the sounds of Santee's guardedly clumsy movements. Adaptable as the Negro might be, he seemed unable to find room enough to move about quietly. Behind tightly drawn eyelids Clay could feel the strong sunshine as the slave threw open the shutters. From the street below came the incoherent babble of many voices. The excitement of fete day was gathering. Reluctantly Clay rolled over.

"What the hell are you doing up in the middle of the night?" he asked.

"Hit's ten o'clock, Marstah." Santee brought a tray with coffee, hot milk, fresh rolls, and stewed guavas with slices of sour orange in the syrup and placed it on a small table beside the bed.

"Mr. Beulow awake?"

Santee smiled warily. "No, Marstah. Aftah he throw dat pitcha at me I'm scared to move aroun' his room."

"Hey, Jamie. Time to get up."

A weary grunt from the other room was the only response.

"Mr. Beulow, sir," Clay shouted, "it is the day of fiesta and time to be up and about. Want some breakfast?"

"God's sunrise," the growl was smothered, "don't be so eager to display your virility. Only the drunk and homeless are abroad at such an hour."

The long nightshirt trailing and flapping about his ankles, Beulow wandered with a sleepy lack of purpose into Clay's room and stood, rumpling his already disordered hair, as he watched his friend attack the breakfast.

"You are a revoltingly healthy clod," he muttered, and padded to the open windows, from where he could stare down at the crowd milling along the river street.

"Marstah Beulow, kin Ah git yo' some brekfus?" Santee waited by the doorway.

"A bottle of wine, and mind it is cool." Beulow didn't turn from the windows. Intercst flickered in his eyes as he noted the number of girls who strolled arm in arm, flirting their small backsides with exaggerated movements as they glanced covertly up at the tavern's second story.

Clay crunched happily on the crisp rolls dripping with sweet butter. Although he was careful to guard against a betrayal of his feelings, he was a little excited over the prospect of the fete day and the ball, where, he was certain, he would see Claire and perhaps even dance with her.

From his post Beulow whistled and flipped his hand at a young woman below, who promptly giggled to her companion and made a pretense of hiding an embarrassed face in her hands.

"Simper, you silly bitch," Beulow snorted. "Before the day is done the shattering of hymens will sound as so many Chinese firecrackers." He turned, seated himself on the ledge, and regarded Clay with a mournful expression. "Why," he asked in a voice from the tomb, "is it foreordained that I spend my beautiful life in pursuit of the drab and inconsequential?"

"You need a drink." Clay drained the last of the coffee from his cup.

"Your debut into this fair city's social whirl," Beulow continued morosely, "is being made under doubtful auspices. I am, as you have perhaps noticed, *persona non grata* to the best families. They are polite but fearful. Because my unpleasant parent elected to die a wealthy man, I am accorded a certain knavish courtesy. Because I am honest I am distrusted. Were I honorable, with a proposal of marriage lurking on my tongue, the doors of every house in the Territory would be thrown open to me with a torchlight procession of slaves lighting my way. As it is, the doting mothers timidly permit me to glance at their stupid daughters only after they have thrice turned the keys in their chastity belts. I fear my friendship has done you a grievous wrong. You are tainted now beyond all sweetening; one who in innocence has touched the hand of a leper."

Clay shouted with laughter and hurled a remaining roll at his friend's head. This surprising man of many but always diverting moods had elected, for the moment, to see himself in the role of a gentle and misunderstood soul.

"The only thing wrong with you is too much of Slater's brandy last night."

"I am of a humor," Beulow ignored him, "to enter a monastery or to return with you to the backwoods and spend my remaining years among the savages." His expression changed as Santee brought a bottle and glass on a tray. "First," he amended, "I will fortify myself."

"You'll be drunk as a goat on rabbit tobacco by the time you finish that," Clay warned.

"You select oranges and guavas for your morning fruit. I prefer grapes. That they come without skins or pulp, unencumbered with seeds or stems, is but a happy accident."

Clay swung his long legs over the side of the bed. "You know," he said abruptly, "I think I'll get married." An expression of amazement rested on his face as he heard his own words. What was he talking about? Yet, somehow, the declaration having been made, it no longer sounded as fantastic as he first imagined. "Yes, by God, I think I'll get married." He repeated the words as though to convince himself he had spoken them originally. They sounded better the second time.

Beulow halted in the act of lifting the glass to his lips and stared over the rim at the figure on the bed. A jest of monumental proportions was in the making, and as his quick mind explored its possibilities an almost satanic gleam of pleasure was in his eyes. If it could be carried off, if this simple fellow could disrupt John Spain's ménage, unseat him from the saddle as it were, what a sport to witness or have a share in!

"The lovely Lechane?" he asked quietly.

"I don't know what made me say that," Clay confessed. "I guess maybe I've been thinking a lot about her ever since the first night I went to Spain's house. Now that it's out, it doesn't seem such a foolish idea. Why not? Here I've been walking around like a sick calf, and maybe all I have to do is ask. I guess she likes me. Sometimes I think so, anyhow."

"What about your grandfather?"

Clay hesitated for a moment. "Old Clay? I hadn't thought much about him." He grinned. "I didn't even think of getting married until a minute ago. I guess," he pondered, "he might like it. There are only the two of us. Maybe he'd like a daughter-in-law and some grandchildren."

Beulow's conscience, usually safely throttled, was whispering. If, he thought, I try to tell him the truth, then I shall probably have to fight him. He was momentarily appalled by the spectacle of shining virtue seated in a nightshirt on the edge of a bed. God deliver me, he mused unhappily, from the pure in heart. Perhaps, though, he thought in an attempt to assuage his conscience, nothing will come of it. The Lechane, likely enough, was too comfortable and secure where she was to exchange a bird in the hand for this one, who most certainly belonged in the bush. It would be a thing of high humor, though. The chilly and inflexible Mr. Spain made the butt of a joke, his doxie installed as the mistress of the Hammond acres. It was worth a try.

"I will aid you." Beulow made the announcement with a proper dramatic emphasis. "I, the master of intrigue, will stand at your side in the darkness. Together we will execute a flanking attack upon John Spain's citadel. Seek the lady alone and touch her heart. Stand not upon foolish ceremony and breathe no word to her guardian. Speak to the lady and, if she be willing, fly with her in the swashbuckling tradition. My plantation will be your refuge until his impotent anger cools." With swinging arms he paced the room, improvising as he walked.

"No," Clay was doubtful, "I think I ought to ask Spain's permission."

"Fie upon you, an unweaned ninny. The situation requires a veritable gascon of a fellow." He fixed Clay with a threatening eye. "Suppose he refuses?"

"Well," Clay paused, "I don't know. Why should he refuse? I am not unknown to him."

"My comrade, this Mr. Spain is an evil and selfish man. Perhaps," his fancy rapidly stroked in the colors of the argument, "he dreads the loneliness of his dotage, the miserable silence of an empty house in which the beautiful music of a woman's gay laughter no longer sounds. Would you willingly relinquish the company of one such as Mistress Lechane to a comparative stranger?"

"But," Clay had to laugh at the extravagance of his friend's words, "I'm not her guardian."

"Ah!" Beulow shouted, fixing an index finger to the side of his nose and regarding Clay with an expression of impish glee. "Exactly!"

The innuendo escaped Clay, intent as he was upon this bewildering decision he had made. Watching him, Beulow shrugged his shoulders, ashamed of his own weakness. For a moment he had almost hoped Clay would rise to the implication or that it would at least set him to thinking. Allow me, he breathed a silent prayer to himself, to be a complete knave. Iago I would be. That Clay did not understand the true relationship between Spain and his ward was not surprising. He was a newcomer to the city. His list of acquaintances was limited, and he was not on sufficiently intimate terms with any of the local families to be privy to their hushed and guarded gossip. Beulow sighed. He had tossed his conscience a sop. Now there remained nothing but to play out his part in the approaching comedy to the confusion of John Spain. He was immensely cheered by the decision. There were still diversions in this life of dullness if a man were fortunate enough to find them. It would be far better, of course, if Clay could contrive for the sly use of Mistress Lechane's undeniably beautiful body and return her, slightly soiled, to be sure, to her unsuspecting protector. To put horns upon the devil would be a feat indeed. Regretfully he dismissed the notion. This Hammond would insist upon the book and ring and wear his honor as a scapular for all to see.

"You have given me new hope." Beulow finished his wine. "We shall plot together and I shall be at your side to the very moment of the lady's couching, and for this you may name your first-born after me. Now," he slapped his hands smartly together, "let us be shaved and laved and go out into the streets to mingle with the rabble."

With a sense of frustration and growing disappointment Clay turned his back on the brilliance of Government House, pushing rudely and with only a mumbled apology through the crowd blocking the entrance. Once in the darkness he walked slowly and without purpose, kicking with the aimless petulance of a child at the loose surface of the palm-bordered path. From open doors and windows the vivacious swing of the orchestra rollicked on the soft night air. Inside, beneath the dazzling lights of heavy chandeliers, the dancers formed swirling patterns of bright color as fingers touched and hands rested on slender waists in the long, free glide of the Spanish dance. Melting eyes and parted lips silently invited intimate whispers and promises under the very eyes of matrons and chaperons, drawn into a forbidding line at the side of the hall. It was a night for youth and love-making.

On King Street he paused irresolutely for a moment, half tempted to return to the ball. Then, with a shrug of defeat, he set his course in the direction of Slater's Tavern. The day that had seemed so promising had ended dismally. Throughout the evening he had waited, eagerly at first, then impatiently, and finally with the dull ache of frustration. Claire and John Spain did not appear. Dutifully he had made his bows to the few families he knew, carefully avoiding the more unattractive daughters. When he danced it was with his eyes fixed on the entrance, his attention wandering from the small talk and flirtatious pleasantries expected. There was no humor in him and he plodded through the measures with dogged determination, returning his partners with an almost audible sigh of relief. Once he had caught sight of Beulow, framed for a moment in the doorway, but by the time the dance was over and he had an opportunity to seek him out his friend had disappeared. With derisive laughter he had brushed aside Clay's earlier suggestion that they attend the ball together.

"A weasel in a chicken yard would cause no more consternation than my appearance in Government House this night," he said. "There would be such a clacking and efforts by the old hens to secrete their pullets beneath their wings as to disrupt the entire evening. You go, my fine cock, in the role of a hero, for did you not shoot down the patgoe bird? Bask in your glory, enjoy this moment of triumph, and when you weary of it all seek me out at Madame Pelican's. I shall be very drunk and in an amorous tangle."

Now the city's streets were all but emptied of the revelers and Clay found comfort in his solitude. The hour was well past midnight and the shuttered windows of the darkened houses were tightly drawn and locked. His footsteps in the white and powdery surface of the street awoke no answering echo. He fancied himself as a wronged and melancholy figure, his moment of triumph dissolved to a hollow mockery. Desperately he wished he could awaken in the morning and find himself back on the Apalachicola. Love was a jade, a careless strumpet, and a man was well off without her.

He and Jamie had driven back from the races with a snapping of whip and a fine flourish as Beulow handled the reins of the dancing, spirited pair, weaving in and out between the slower-moving vehicles choking the narrow road, spinning the flashing runabout between scattering groups on foot. They had eaten and drunk well from the hamper prepared by Slater, wagered successfully on three of the runnings, and as they sauntered through the excited and fashionably dressed crowd within the reserved enclosure Clay knew many a pretty head was turned and whispered comments dropped as they passed. His pleasure at the attention was so evident that Beulow was forced to sarcastic comment.

"Vanity leers upon your peasant features. May I remind you, the coy glances dropped our way may be inspired by Linkler's faultless tailoring and not, as you so fatuously suppose, your rare beauty."

Clay had only laughed at him, his eyes roaming over the throng. It was more than possible that Claire and Spain were at the races. What more natural than for him to stop by and exchange a few words, perhaps stand at her side and watch the remaining heats?

"If you seek your heart's sweet agony," Beulow tapped his shoulder for attention, "it is a waste of time. I have already assured myself she is not here."

Only when he had satisfied himself that neither Spain nor the girl was hidden within the crowd did Clay consent to their leaving, consoling himself with the thought that he must certainly see her later.

At the sea wall the crowd had already gathered for the shooting of the patgoe bird. Coach and carriage stood wheel to wheel, their occupants standing, braced against the sudden lurches and jolts as the nervous and suspicious horses fretted and tossed their heads against the restraining hands of the slaves. Behind the vehicles the less favored spectators strained and took turns at boosting each other on their shoulders for a fleeting glimpse of the resplendent Negro who waited with the long staff and bird, his woolly head hidden under the trailing ribbons. With a complete disregard for the cramped space and danger to those who would not move quickly enough, Beulow maneuvered the light rig into a narrow opening in the front row. Clay waited for an angry bellow of protest from someone in the standing ranks, but no protest was uttered. At first he had thought that Beulow's scornful indifference and supercilious attitude toward his fellow men was a pose, a gesture of contemptuous defiance. As he learned to know the man better he revised this notion. James Beulow just didn't gave a damn. He was without conscience or kindness save when it pleased him. His manner was a continual challenge, and so serene was his confidence that the rest of the world was beneath his notice that few, if any, dared dispute the regal assumption of superiority. Secretly Clay envied this dashing figure and he sometimes wondered at the lavish gift of friendship Beulow had given so casually. He had few companions, no intimates in the city, or, as far as Clay could learn, among the neighboring plantation owners. With such companionship as Clay could offer Beulow seemed content.

"You are a simple fellow," Beulow had once assured him. "There is no guile in your heart. You listen to one side and nod, saying yes, that is so. To the other argument you shake an agreeable head and admit that it, also, has reason. I am possessed of strong and, perhaps, unreasonable convictions. We balance each other and I love you with a deep and unshakable confidence. That you are not cast in a heroic mold should not disturb you."

There was a sudden spattering of applause from the far end of the line and almost immediately the shrill notes of a trumpet. With measured step the Negro began his stately march. A pistol shot sounded to the accompaniment of shrill screams of delight. The ball whistled harmlessly past the wavering bird and the would-be marksman sank disconsolately back, eying his firearm accusingly as though it had betrayed him. As the slave moved slowly other shots from pistol and rifle were loosed at intervals as eager swains sought to capture the coveted trophy for their ladies. Slaves struggled with the horses as they reared in panic, wheels became locked, and the entire assembly seemed to be on the point of degenerating into a wild scramble.

With strong hands and easy words Beulow quieted his pair, holding them with confidence until they stood trembling but subdued. His elbow touched Clay's side.

"Your patience is rewarded." He nodded to the left. "There is the sultry beauty of your torment."

Clay's glance followed Beulow's nod. A half-dozen carriages away, her eyes bright and cheeks flushed with excitement, Claire Lechane was standing in John Spain's landau. The top had been laid back and with one hand resting on her escort's shoulder the girl strained upward to watch the approaching slave. As though he had called her name she turned, looked squarely in Clay's direction, and then waved a gay and happy salute. Bending over, she said something to Spain, and the man, leaning slightly forward, lifted his hat and nodded gravely in recognition. Several persons near the landau searched with frank curiosity among the spectators for the object of the pair's attention. Conscious of the fact that many eyes were turned his way, Clay rose from the narrow seat and bowed. The gesture was almost spoiled by an unexpected jerking of the horses and he was forced to clutch wildly at Beulow's neck to save himself from being catapulted into the air.

"You are going to appear exceedingly foolish, lying on your

face in the dirt," Beulow warned. "Save your embraces for the Lechane."

The slave, bearing the still unmarked patgoe bird, was drawing abreast. The firing was spasmodic and from along the line there sounded short cheers of encouragement and groans of disappointment as gallant after gallant took aim and fired, missed, and hurriedly reloaded for a second try. The bullets sang harmlessly through the air or clipped futilely at the fluttering ribbons and the marksmen turned shamefacedly to their ladies, clinging with assumed fright to their arms.

Without thinking, Clay took the rifle as it was thrust into his hands, and then, realizing what had happened, he turned quickly and glanced down into the upturned and unsmiling face of Asseola. The Indian was impressive in creamy buckskin leggings and brilliantly designed long shirt of many colors, drawn at the waist with a beaded sash. A silver chain glinted over the scarves at his throat and the purple-tipped egret plume curled in a graceful sweep over his black hair.

"Shoot, child." The Indian's eyes were alight with subdued pleasure. "It is an easier target than a gray squirrel in the trees along the Apalachicola."

The long rifle, in perfect balance, came easily to Clay's shoulder. For a second he led the unsteady bird as it was silhouetted against the cloudless sky. Then, as it lay full on his sight, his finger tightened on the trigger. The crashing report threw the horses into a frenzy. Asseola and several men jumped forward to snatch at their heads as Beulow cursingly braced himself against their plunging. Clay grasped at the back of the seat to save himself from being pitched out of the rig. As the team reluctantly responded to the restraining hands and the runabout was backed into place Clay became aware of the applause and enthusiastic shouting. The shot had been clean and the patgoe hung limply on its support, all but buried in the nest of color. In every carriage faces were turned for a glimpse of the tall young stranger who had made the kill. Handkerchiefs were fluttered in his direction, and in the packed rows of those standing, hoarse cries of delight were raised in recognition of the well-placed shot. Clay made a desperate and completely unsuccessful effort to appear unconcerned, but a grin of satisfaction spread itself across his features. By God, he thought exultantly, I did it. I knocked it right on its ass.

"Straighten your hat, you drooling booby," Beulow growled, but it was evident he was pleased. "In addition to having almost upset us, you have just won the dubious honor of paying for next year's ball."

With an assumption of dignity that did not quite come off, Clay adjusted his headpiece from a rakish angle over one eye. He looked about, uncertain as to what was expected of him now, and embarrassed by the field of upturned faces. The crowd was in a holiday mood and their admiration spontaneous as they waited for his next move.

The slave, bearing the staff before him, crossed the road and stood waiting a few feet beyond the heads of Beulow's trembling horses. The volume of applause increased and Clay looked pleadingly at Beulow for some clue. I wonder, he thought unhappily, what they expect now? Am I supposed to eat the damned thing?

Beulow nudged him. "Go and claim your trophy, simpleton."

Handing the rifle to Asseola, who again stood by the wheel, he leaped lightly to the ground. The Indian regarded him unblinkingly.

"I thought I had taught you well, child," he whispered.

"Wait for me." Clay's hand rested on the Indian's arm as he edged past. "I want to see you."

Bent into an attitude of exaggerated obeisance, the liveried black lowered the slender pole and extended it toward Clay. The carved bird was secured by a single ribbon and it came away at a touch. For a moment he stood, holding the patgoe and its mass of silken streamers in both hands, then turned with a quick decision and strode down the line in the direction of John Spain's landau. So intent was he upon his purpose that he failed to hear the startled gasp rising from the incredulous spectators as his destination became apparent. It sounded as a single intake of breath and rose sharply, sibilant and apprehensive. Heads turned as though pulled by a mysterious power and the scattered handclapping died as if on signal, many persons arresting their palms scant inches apart and holding them there in a frozen gesture.

Still standing, Claire Lechane waited; concern and a helpless expression of consternation had replaced her smile. Still oblivious to the warning hush and the girl's fright, which was clouding her eyes, Clay halted beside the carriage. For a moment he looked up at her and then, removing his hat and inclining his head, he extended the colorful trophy.

"Would you do me the great honor of accepting this?" The grin hovering about his mouth broke into the open and then died as he became aware of her hesitation and half-concealed panic. She stood immobile, appearing not to see the patgoe. Questioningly Clay shifted his glance to John Spain.

The man's face was cold and darkly furious. "You presume, sir." The words, spoken softly, carried a sharp rebuke, and they struck Clay as a blow across the mouth.

Involuntarily he stepped back, surprise and bewilderment stamped clearly on his features. What have I done now? He stared at the patgoe as though to reassure himself it hadn't changed into some obscene figure. What the hell, he asked himself dazedly, is happening? There was something so completely helpless in his attitude, a silent appeal for enlightenment in his eyes, that those persons who witnessed it were moved to pity. Claire's hand touched at her breast with an unconscious gesture of compassion.

"I repeat, sir, you are presumptuous." Spain was unrelenting and his voice was raised for everyone to hear.

"But I am not. I'm sorry if I have offended." Clay sought frantically for words.

With complete self-assurance the girl extended her hands and gently lifted the bird from Clay's nerveless fingers, indifferent to the rippling whispers of astonishment, which ran as a bright flame among the spectators, and to John Spain's sudden stiffening of protest.

"You are thoughtful, sir," she said gently, "and perhaps unaware of the significance custom has given the presentation of the patgoe. I accept it as a token of friendship and I am certain," she half turned to the man beside her, "Mr. Spain regrets his words."

"I didn't know." Clay was grateful but still mystified.

"It is traditional," she smiled tremulously, "for the trophy to be presented by a gentleman to—to his sweetheart. You could not be expected to know of this."

"I was hasty, sir." John Spain spoke crisply and without a suggestion of kindness. The thing was done and it had better be carried off as an unthinking and harmless blunder by a young cub who knew no better. It was either this or set the tongues to wagging. He forced a chilly smile for all to see and then touched the girl's arm to move her to seat herself beside him. "I regret my unfortunate display of temper."

"Permit me," Clay's face was crimson, "permit me to take it back." He made a movement to remove the figure from the girl's lap but Spain's hand restrained him.

"That would serve no purpose, sir," the man's words could not be heard beyond the carriage, "other than to stimulate speculation and idle gossip." He raised his hat and nodded pleasantly in Clay's direction, certain that his amiability was carefully observed. With a word to the coachman he settled back as the carriage pulled away, his eyes fixed stonily on a distant point.

The return to Beulow's runabout was sheer torture and Clay had an almost overpowering desire to break into a run, dodging through the crowd and escaping from the curious stares that beat upon him as staves as he walked slowly through the gantlet. The distance seemed interminable and by the time he reached Beulow he was sweating.

They spoke no word until Beulow had threaded his way through the departing crowd and they were out in the open road again.

"You should have warned me," Clay said accusingly.

"How did I know you were going to make a blithering idiot of yourself?" Beulow was intent upon his driving and appeared indifferent to his glowering companion.

"Was it that bad?"

Beulow chuckled. "Probably not, old cock. In any event, it has given John Spain something to think about. As for others, they don't matter. You are but a country lad, gauche and impetuous."

Clay gnawed thoughtfully at his lower lip. Perhaps, he clutched at any hope, it wasn't as serious as he imagined. No one could expect him to know of the silly custom, and Spain, when he drove away, seemed willing enough to dismiss the episode.

"Tonight, at the ball," Beulow continued, "you may have an opportunity to set things right. Be properly contrite and humble in the gentleman's presence and I fancy he will forgive and forget."

Clay brightened. He would seek John Spain out at the ball and offer further apologies. These being accepted, he would possibly be permitted one dance with the girl. Anyhow, he thought as his mood lifted, it was damn fine shooting.

"I knocked it over, didn't I?" He grinned at Beulow.

His companion tossed back his head and roared. "Like a pot beneath a bed, cock robin. Like a pot beneath a bed."

Clay waited until the noisy mirth subsided. "What became of Asseola?" So engrossed had he been in his efforts to escape from the crowd that he completely forgot to look for the Indian.

"Who?" The name was unfamiliar to Beulow.

"The Seminole who lent me the rifle. He's a friend of mine. I told him to wait, but I guess he didn't."

Beulow whistled tunelessly. "Having a Seminole for an intimate

193

is hardly calculated to improve your already precarious social position in St. Augustine, my buck."

"Don't be a fool." Clay was short. "We grew up together."

Throughout the afternoon and early evening, up until the moment when he left for the ball at Government House, he had hoped Asseola would seek him out. Now, walking homeward through the dark and silent streets, he wondered what had brought his friend to St. Augustine and why he had disappeared without a word.

As he entered the tavern Slater came bustling to his side with whispered words and the air of dark conspiracy.

"I have a message for you, sir." He glanced about to assure himself they were unobserved. "It was delivered shortly after nine o'clock." He pressed a sealed and folded note into Clay's hand and stepped back with the attitude of having performed a feat of legerdemain. "Also," he shook his head sadly but with a certain grudging admiration, "Mr. Beulow sent word he was awaiting you at the establishment of Madame Pelican."

Brushing off the landlord with a brief word of thanks, Clay sought out an unoccupied table near the fireplace and opened the letter. It bore no salutation or signature.

"I shall be riding Thursday afternoon at three o'clock near the south boundary of the town on the river trail."

With an effort Clay controlled a desire to leap into the air and shout his happiness, and he stared at the undeniably feminine handwriting as if he intended to memorize every slanting line and gracefully formed character. To hell with John Spain, he thought exultantly. She wants to see me. Thursday? This was Monday, almost three days to wait. He leaned back in the heavy chair and stretched his boots toward the fire. How would he pass the time until Thursday?

Slater approached. "Will you have something to drink, sir, or a bite of supper?"

"Drink?" Clay stared at him. "Man, I am drunk already. Can't you see for yourself? I am reeling with such heady stuff as to make your puny cups a tipple for babies. Leave me with my intoxication of the moment. I would wallow in it."

He refolded the note, creasing its edges carefully, and started to slip it in a pocket. Then, with methodical regret, he tore the paper into small pieces and, leaning forward, dropped them carefully into the flames.

16

As SHE had for the past five days, Claire Lechane awoke with a frightened and guilty start, her eyes snapping open out of a deep sleep and sweeping rapidly about the still unfamiliar room. Slowly the small feeling of panic clutching at her heart ebbed and she laughed with nervous irritation at her fears. Clay's place beside her in the massive bed still bore the deep indentation of his heavy frame, and she raised herself on one elbow to stare pensively at the crumpled pillows and rumpled sheets. There was no warmth or pleasure in her studied contemplation of the spot where her husband had rested.

The thing was done. She had married Clayfield Hammond, the hasty, matter-of-fact ceremony performed in the small chapel on James Beulow's plantation by a circuit-riding preacher who mouthed the words through a tobacco-stained mustache, pocketed his fee, swallowed a pint or so of whisky, and rode away on his dreary rounds.

At the wedding breakfast, Beulow lifted his glass of champagne, eyed the pair with quiet amusement, and bowed with sardonic humility to the bride and groom.

"For the respectability that has been visited upon my home, even though it be by proxy, I am grateful. I am honored and hard pressed to meet the occasion." His gaze rested upon the girl for a moment. "Time was too short to purchase a suitable wedding gift, but if you like I will have John's head delivered to you on a silver platter."

Punching the pillows into a mound for a prop at her back, she called to the slave girl who waited outside the door. When her breakfast had been brought in and the broad windows thrown open to the morning sun she ate slowly and without interest in the food, thinking uneasily about John Spain and secretly suspecting she had been betrayed by her body.

From the beginning, on the first day of her clandestine meeting with Clay along the little-used river trail, she had known what the inevitable consequences of this recklessness must be. St. Augustine was too small, John Spain too important a figure, for her movements not to be under constant scrutiny. They would be discovered, someone would stumble across them, a voice would whisper in choice gossip, and the word would reach John Spain. If the word was not spoken, then he would somehow know. He was too well attuned to the constant demands of her nature not to sense the change when she took a lover. Yet she had persisted in the folly, giving herself to Clay on the ground and behind the bushes like any common street slut.

John Spain had not been deceived. Leaving her bed one night, he paused at the doorway, turned, and regarded her with chilling speculation.

"I find you annoyingly distrait of late." He spoke softly while she watched him through half-closed eyes. "I dislike to have your attention wander at such moments. It should be unnecessary for me to warn you against attempting a thoughtless diversion outside this house. If you persist in such a heedless course I shall beat you severely and turn you out as I would any paid strumpet. Good night, my dear." He closed the door behind him.

Now, she thought a little grimly, she was married and bound for a remote plantation in the interior of a wild and turbulent territory. It wasn't at all what she wanted. Materially, her position had been greatly improved. At the moment, though, this didn't seem particularly desirable. Spain had been more than generous, and she was accustomed to him. This eager, fumbling man she had married was a stranger who made love with the rough and tumbling antics of a bear cub and took her as a peasant would tumble his wench in a hayloft. She smiled at her reflection in a mirror opposite the bed. He had been so humble, transfigured at the moment of her eager surrender. Later, lying with her head in his lap, her body enveloped in a warm and satisfying lassitude, she listened to his faltering speech. With the vanity of a male he was certain he had seduced her. Tilting her face back to watch him, she made a gesture of shy modesty, crossing her arms across her breasts.

"You overwhelmed me, sir." She permitted her voice to break on a note of breathlessness.

"I want you to marry me, Claire. More than anything I want that. Maybe," he hesitated, "you won't like the Hammond plantation. It's pretty wild out there and not much of a place for a girl like you. We'd have to go back to see Old Clay, but afterward, well, we wouldn't have to stay. I was going to see the world and," he drew a deep breath, "by God, now we can do it together. We'll go to Charleston, New York, Boston, and even to Europe if you like."

"It is a pleasant dream, sir." She pulled his head down and kissed

196

him, her mouth lingering upon his as she stirred in quick awakening.

"It doesn't have to be a dream." He held her with a tight possessiveness. "I'll speak to Mr. Spain. Tonight."

She straightened up, alarmed at the earnestness in his voice. Of all things, this stubborn honor must be circumvented. If she were to speak, now was the time. Why, she thought desperately, can't I bring myself to utter a simple truth? I am John Spain's mistress. That is all I have to say and have an end to this rashness. Instead, she shook her head.

"You must not speak to Mr. Spain. Believe me." She covered his hands with hers. "It will serve no purpose."

"But why?" he protested. "I don't understand. Is there something shameful in asking for your hand, speaking to your guardian since you have no father?"

She put him off, extracting a reluctant promise to avoid a meeting with Spain, quieting his objections with a kiss.

It was not a simple matter to arrange a rendezvous. John Spain was not a man of fixed habit. There were days when he would be away, out of the city on business or at his office from early morning until night. Again, he would not leave the house. His movements were unpredictable. There was no time she could safely call her own, no one she could trust. She was tormented by the idea that Spain was having her watched until it became an obsession and she fancied spies and informers at every turning. To make the situation doubly difficult, Clay was becoming more and more stubborn.

"I don't want this," he objected. "It is making you cheap. I'm in love with you and I want more than a meeting in the scrub."

The margin of time was wearing dangerously thin while she tried to make up her mind. The decision must be hers and not John Spain's. Either she must give up Clay, tell him the truth, and return to Spain's bed, or break with Spain. With a flash of honesty she admitted to herself that she wanted to do neither.

She was not permitted to make a choice. It was forced upon her with frightening abruptness, leaving her without an alternative. One of John Spain's men found them in the woods together. He had waited until they parted at a fork in the river path before he rode into the narrow trail, blocking Claire's passage.

"Why," she had no need to pretend surprise, "what are you doing out here, Barton?" She knew the man; he came frequently to Spain's office and to their home. His being out here could be without significance, yet she knew this was not so.

The man was respectful, holding his hat on his saddle and acting as though he didn't realize he was blocking her way. He worked a quid of tobacco around to the back of his mouth, and when he spoke, embarrassment shaded his words.

"I guess there ain't any use in lyin', miss," he said, almost regretfully, "since you're bound to know sooner or later. I been watchin' you at Mr. Spain's orders."

"How dare you!" She tried to summon an attitude of outraged imperiousness but failed. Her momentary and trivial concern was whether he had stood in a place of concealment and watched her being taken in the bushes. "How dare you." She repeated the words with faltering conviction.

"Well, miss," Barton plainly had no stomach for the job, "I just couldn't dare not to. It was by Mr. Spain's orders and he hires me. He's mighty peculiar about havin' such things carried out."

"You ought to be ashamed of yourself, a sneaking spy." She felt a desire to cut him across the face with her crop.

"Well, miss," he actually grinned at her fury, "I wouldn't say this is any time to talk about shame."

"I'll have you flogged." She fought to keep from screaming in her helplessness and then quickly changed her tactics. "I'll pay you, Barton," she pleaded. "I'll pay you well to forget you saw me. It will be a lot of money, more money than you've ever had."

Barton shook his head regretfully. "I'd sure like to, miss," he said, "but I can't. Pretty girls come an' go but Mr. Spain has a way of goin' on forever. He'd be bound to find out an' then where would I be?" He laughed shortly. "About where you are now, I reckon."

In desperation, hardly realizing what she was doing, she spurred her horse, lashing out at the man with her crop as she raced past. It was as though in leaving him behind she were somehow escaping from Spain's wrath. She rode with reckless abandon, indifferent to the low branches and scrub that clung and tore at her clothing.

Clay was riding into Slater's stable yard when she charged up. He took one look at her wild and disheveled appearance and hurried to her side.

"For God's sake," he stared at her incredulously, "what's happened?"

"Nothing." She had difficulty in speaking as the breath was pumped in and out of her lungs. "I've made up my mind, Clay. I—I wanted to see you. If—if you want to marry me, then come now. We'll run away without saying anything to anyone."

Under other circumstances his bewilderment would have been funny. At the moment, though, she wanted to shout with impatience.

It was either now or never. By nightfall John Spain would make good his word. He would throw her and her belongings into the street for all to see and the story would be on everyone's lips. If that happened she would have neither Spain nor Clay.

"Of course," desperately she strove for a semblance of dignity, "if you didn't mean what you said ... If your words were idle conversation, sir ..."

"You know better," he interrupted, and came to her side. A young Negro hostler peeked curiously around the corner of the barn, staring at them with furtive wonder. Clay reached up and swung the girl down from the saddle. "You shouldn't be seen out here this way."

"What difference does it make?"

He took her elbow. "Come in through the back, upstairs to my rooms. I'll find Jamie. You can't stand here."

Beulow suffered the intrusion upon his afternoon's drinking with exaggerated grace. He ordered his carriage, personally brought brandy and glasses to the rooms where Claire waited with almost hysterical apprehension, and entered into the adventure of an elopement with more enthusiasm than might ordinarily be expected. He passed lightly over Clay's stubborn objections and lavished a sarcastic gallantry upon the girl.

"We shall flee to my home and bar ourselves against intrusion." He struck a pose. "Tomorrow I will scour the woods for a man of God and see you bound in holy wedlock. Until then," he spoke in a whisper, "I trust your impetuous natures will remain under control and you will spend the night in decent restraint."

Not until they had crossed into the Beulow acres did Claire feel safe, and only when Beulow's itinerant preacher pronounced the final words did she experience a return of confidence. It was one thing to be a homeless piece of baggage and quite another to be Mrs. Clayfield Hammond.

"You have been generous, sir," she thanked Beulow, her eyes wide and youthfully appealing.

The man chuckled. "No more so than you, madame." He didn't attempt to hide the mockery in his voice.

Now, pushing aside the breakfast tray, Claire stared up at the bars of light slanting across the ceiling and wondered what John Spain was doing at the moment. Three days ago one of his slaves had ridden to the plantation bearing a note for Clay. There had been no mention of her in the letter, nor had Spain wasted time with preliminary courtesies.

"At our first meeting," he had written, "I shall shoot you down without further warning. Under the circumstances I feel that a punctilious observation of the code would be wasted upon you. I shall kill you, sir, not because of any loss sustained or outrage suffered, but because I find your insolence unbearable."

Clay read the letter aloud to Beulow and Claire, his features drawn in anger and his voice shaking. It took the combined efforts of the girl and Jamie to keep him from riding into the city and seeking out the man. With a hand on his shoulder Beulow guided him to a chair.

"No purpose will be served by bloodletting, although I must admit the letter is provocative. Either you will kill Mr. Spain, who, you must admit, has been shabbily treated, or he will kill you. In either case a lady will be left desolate."

Clay scowled at him from the depths of a chair. Claire, surprised at the fury mustered in this large and almost timidly gentle man, thought he acted a little like a small boy who had suffered a dare.

"Am I supposed to hide from him?" He chewed with bitter emphasis on the thought. "I'm not afraid of John Spain, and the sooner he knows it, the better for everyone concerned. If there was a spark of decency in him he'd wish us well. If he wants a duel he can have it."

Beulow poured himself a small glass of brandy. "Cock," he held the glass to the light, peering through the yellow liquid, "if Mr. Spain can curb his impatience for your gore I suggest you do likewise. I cannot help but feel he is the injured party. You did, and without so much as a by-your-leave, make off with his ward. Is that not so, madame?" His glance lingered with bright interest on the girl and she colored slightly beneath the deliberate irony.

"You are familiar enough with the circumstances, sir," she said gently.

Beulow smiled. He was beginning to admire this trollop, who apparently had the moral conscience of a cat in heat. They struck a spark when their eyes met and he understood well enough that she was not unaware of the attraction. We are much alike, madame, he thought. Sometime, somewhere, you lusty wench, I shall bed with you.

He returned his attention to the still glowering Clay. "Instead of brawling with Mr. Spain," he drawled, "I suggest you enjoy the carnal interlude so conveniently sanctified by the Reverend Whitewater. We shall drink and make merry. When the sport begins to pall, my coach, horses, and servants are at your disposal for a return to the Apalachicola."

Claire cried an immediate protest, touching at the heavy skirt of her riding habit, which had also served as a wedding gown.

"I must have clothes," she wailed miserably. "How can I travel for days in this?"

"Doubtless Mr. Spain has already placed your things on the curb." Beulow laughed at her consternation. "I doubt he will permit us to recover them. However, I am not completely unfamiliar with the garments a lady requires. I shall shop for you, purchasing such ready-made silks and laces as I can find."

Claire called for the Negro girl and stood by the window while she carried in the buckets of hot and cold water for her bath. They would leave for the Hammond plantation this morning. Clay and Beulow were probably down at the stables now, selecting horses, coach, and equipment for the trip. Her shoulders compressed with a gesture of helpless submission. A journey of a week or ten days through the wilderness was a frightening prospect and she had not been reassured by Clay's enthusiasm. When he spoke of the country through which they must travel he became as eager as a boy getting ready to start on a hunting trip. He rebelled stubbornly against her suggestion that they go north by schooner, stopping at Savannah or perhaps going on to Charleston, where she could be outfitted with a complete wardrobe.

"You look fine in what Jamie bought for you in St. Augustine. Besides, you won't see anyone much except Indians between here and the Apalachicola. We'll lay over in Tallahassi and take a seamstress and whatever you need back to Clayport with us." He grinned. "It isn't exactly a fashion center. Anyhow," he became serious, "I think we ought to see Old Clay. After that, if you like, we'll go to Pensacola and New Orleans, and maybe even Paris. I guess we ought to get around some before we settle down and start raising a family."

Seated in the tub while the girl bathed her back, Claire dabbled her fingers in the warm and scented water and tried to imagine what the Hammond plantation was like. The old man, she knew from the few things Spain had said, was a powerful and formidable figure whose great wealth was drawn from many sources. But the Apalachicola? She had traced its course across the Territory's heavy shoulder. On the map the section looked desolate and terrifyingly remote. She smiled with a certain grim amusement at her position and wondered why she hadn't been able to see this far ahead. A pleasant hour of love-making with Clayfield Hammond was one thing. It was quite another to strike out into a wild and turbulent country, tracked only by the Indians, as Clayfield Hammond's wife. A small sigh of regret escaped her as she thought of the completely ordered, if unexciting, life within John Spain's walls.

She was dressed when Clay returned from the stables and he carried her downstairs for a second breakfast. Beulow was at the table and he rose as they entered, waiting while Clay, with rough affection, placed his wife in a chair.

"You are only supposed to carry a bride across the doorstep, cock," he said. "Don't make a silly habit of it by loading her in your arms every time you go from room to room."

"She likes it," Clay proclaimed happily. "Don't you, Mrs. Hammond?"

"I'm not certain, sir." She smiled at him. "It is probably an acquired taste." She shook her head as the slaves brought in the hot platters of eggs, bacon, crisp fried fish, hot breads, and cold ham, taking only coffee. Sipping the strong black brew, she glanced about the bright and gracious dining room with its exquisitely carved paneling and delicate mantels. It would be much pleasanter to remain here, pleasanter and, she thought as she glanced down the length of the table at Beulow, a little dangerous.

"You'd better eat something," Clay interrupted her entertaining speculations. "From now on the food won't be so good, although Santee is mighty handy around a fire."

Her eyes widened with surprise. Such commonplace things as eating and sleeping hadn't occurred to her. "Do you mean there are no inns, we'll have to eat and sleep in the open?"

"I guess so." Clay was actually pleased by her expression of troubled astonishment. "We'll take the Bellamy Road out of St Augustine. It's traveled some between here and Tallahassi but not enough, I don't expect, to provide a string of inns. What I came through was a damn sight worse. There wasn't even a road, only a few Indian trails. Oh!" He beamed at her. "You're going to see some wonderful country, Mrs. Hammond."

"But," she stared at him in an effort to discover if he was joking, "how will I dress and bathe and—well—just and?"

The humor on Clay's face died quickly. He hadn't given much thought to the complications of travel with a bride. The problems began to mount.

"I don't know," he pondered. "I guess I'm not quite used to having a wife yet." He brightened. Other women had crossed the Territory with less. "We'll have a tent. You'll sleep and dress in it. When you want a bath I'll get a pole, stand on the bank, and keep the alligators and moccasins away while you splash around."

"I am enchanted, sir."

Beulow roared at the spectacle of her frightened and immediate confusion. Deliberately she stuck her tongue out at him.

"I'll send a girl with you, if you like, madame," he offered between gasps. "You can let her step into the river first as a sort of test."

"Thank you, sir. I shall forgo the baths and permit a relentless nature to take its course."

The heavy coach was in the driveway. Two of Beulow's Negroes, a coachman and a groom, rode on the front seat. Santee, solemn and unblinking, was perched uncomfortably on the rear box. Trailing on lead ropes were the mounts Clay had brought from the plantation. The gear, provisions, and equipment they would need for the journey had been tightly stowed and lashed down. As he assisted Claire into the deeply cushioned compartment Clay turned and grinned at Beulow.

"I can't help but think that Santee and I came down and across the whole Territory with nothing much but a couple of saddlebags and a gun. I wish you were coming along," he added impulsively.

"Some other time." Beulow took his hand. "I dislike the idea of being a specter at your nuptial cavortings."

Claire's head and shoulders were framed in the narrow window as she leaned forward. The luxurious appointments of the coach reassured her. There were freshly cut flowers in the small crystal vases. The compartment was padded with quilted silk, the curtains neatly tied back with tasseled cords. In a little drawer she found eau de cologne and smelling salts in gold-mounted bottles. Somehow, these adjuncts of civilization made her feel better. She was not being hurled unceremoniously into a strange new world. At her feet on the floor was an impressive-looking wicker hamper, packed with wine, smoked doves' breasts, pastries, and sweetmeats.

"When that is exhausted," Beulow remarked as a slave stowed the basket inside, "you will probably have to chew on the dried jawbone of an ass. Until then, *à bonne bouche*."

With a cracking of the long whip the coachman guided the heavy vehicle down the oak-shaded driveway. Clay and Claire turned to look back at the figure of Beulow as he stood before the house, hands locked behind him, feet planted firmly in a widespread stance.

"I'm going to miss that fellow." Clay spoke with regret.

Claire removed her bonnet and settled herself in the corner. The horses were trotting with steady rhythm and the coach, on its thick springs of cradling leather, swayed with the easy motion of a boat.

"It is curious you should select such a man for a friend," she said.

203

"I thought so in the beginning," he confessed. "We were at each other's throat the first time we met. Then I learned to know him better."

She smiled at his seriousness and then impulsively slipped her hand beneath his arm.

"Such is the task I have set for myself," she spoke gravely, "my husband is a stranger. I do not know you at all, Clay."

He drew her to him. "It won't take you long to learn all there is to know about me. Sometimes, when I listen to other people, I don't think I am too bright." He laughed without affectation. "Anyhow, Old Clay says so, and I expect Jamie felt the same way. He had an idea he had to sort of look out for me. I wonder," he turned the thought over slowly in his mind, "I wonder what Old Clay is going to say when I turn up with a wife." He squeezed her arm against his side with a reassuring gesture. "He's the one who takes some knowing. Don't let him scare you."

"I am not frightened easily by men," she said. Her glance lingered on the heavy woods bordering the highway. "Is it dangerous the way we travel, where we go?"

"A little, I guess." He leaned back against the cushions. "There is a lot of talk and some trouble here and there that breaks out like a rash. It all depends on how much pushing the Indians will take, and," the lines about his jaw tightened, "from what Mr. Spain said the government is getting ready to do a lot of shoving. It looks as though the white people aren't going to be satisfied until the Seminoles are herded into the swamps or pushed right out of the Territory. When the fighting starts in earnest it will be the damnedest killing you ever saw." He leaned forward and touched her shoulder with his chin, nuzzling her affectionately. "When it happens we had better be someplace else."

Idly he glanced out of the window. On either side of the King's Road the tangled forest of oak, magnolia, bay, and spiny bootjack palmettos pressed relentlessly against the avenue that had been so painfully hacked, yard by yard, through the green barrier. It was good to be going home. This was not the Florida of his childhood. He had missed the broad sweep of rolling countryside, the dusky pink of the clayey earth at sunset, the sharp chill of mornings along the river.

"You'll never recognize where we're going as part of Florida," he said. "People who know say it looks more like Virginia or even Ohio. A palmetto tree is almost a novelty."

"You've missed it, haven't you? I could see it in your eyes and hear it in your voice when you spoke to Mr. Spain at the dinner table. I used to wonder why you ever left."

"It was Old Clay's idea, and," he chuckled, "when Old Clay gets an idea most people don't argue with him." Impulsively he straightened up, reached for the small sliding panel in the dome of the coach, and pulled it open. A square patch of blue sky met his eyes. "Santee," he called. "Santee?"

The opening was blotted out as the face of the slave appeared in the opening. He leaned forward from his perch on the heaving seat, staring into the depths of the compartment.

"Yes, Marstah?"

"How does it feel to be going home?"

The slave's face broke into a wide, shy smile. "Hit feel good, Marstah." He laughed and the deep, rich sound filled the coach. "Ah'm strainin' mah eye foah a sight o' d' rivah. We bin gone a long, long time."

Clay closed the trap and sighed contentedly. They had been gone a long time, not in weeks or months, but so long that things would never again be the same. He was going home a man, a man with a wife and a feeling of responsibility. It amazed him to think how quickly everything had changed. A man with a wife was getting old and it was time he began giving some thought to the things that mattered. Secretly he was a little troubled by his inability to define these desirable objectives, but he supposed they included the plantation, more land, more money in the bank, the raising of a family.

"I guess I could do that, all right," he said.

"What?" Claire glanced up at him.

A slow grin broke at his mouth. "Raise a family. I was just thinking aloud, trying to figure out how a married man should act. I thought I'd better get it straight in my mind before I meet Old Clay, otherwise he'll be telling me."

17

SHE stood before Old Clay, waiting for him to speak, understanding that his silent malevolence was deliberately calculated to strip her of confidence and poise. With an unwavering stare he held her attention, his bright eyes probing with an alert curiosity for a betraying flutter of nervousness or fear.

He had sent for her, summoning her through a slave to the sparsely furnished, high-ceilinged room he called "the office" where he received his overseer, the white hired hands, and the foremen. The insult was undisguised, the implication unmistakable. Intuitively she had known what he wanted, what he was going to say, and this knowledge somehow gave her confidence.

"You are a whore, madame."

The tone of accusation was level and without malice. He would have used the same inflection to say, You are young or dark or fair.

"I know who you are, where you came from, what you were. What I don't know is why you married Clay."

"Why don't you ask me in the presence of my husband?"

"Because," he bent his shoulders forward, "I want a straight answer."

"Then, sir, I'll have to tell you that I do not know. No choice was given me."

"By God, I'd have had you peeled and whipped if you told me you were in love with him." He relaxed slightly, but the ferocity in his eyes was undimmed. "Did you think I wouldn't know or find out who you were?"

She smiled for the first time since entering the room. "I regret, sir, that at the moment you didn't enter my mind."

"I suppose you think I'm goin' to pay you off an' send you packing like they do in storybooks." He leaned back in his chair. "Well, I'm not." His eyes narrowed. "What do you think of that?"

"It arouses my curiosity."

"I ain't goin' to say a word. For all of me Clay can find out about you for himself or never know. When he left here I never figured he'd diddle a man like John Spain out of his trull. He's got what he deserves."

"You flatter me, sir."

"I ain't meanin' to. I'm goin' to leave things as they are because I don't figure that a spell with a fancy woman will do Clay any harm. Also, you ain't goin' to be able to take much of the life out here an' you'll go of your own accord. That way I'll save myself a considerable sum. You look expensive."

"Not unreasonably so."

He reached behind him and took a letter from the cluttered desk. For a moment he held it in his hand and then deliberately tore it into small pieces, which he crumpled into a loose ball.

"John Spain has the idea I'll throw you out. I ain't goin' to do it, just for spite. Also, Clay won't ever hear anything about you from me. No one gets thanked for that kind of information. Right now he'd probably be fool enough to call me a liar an' go away with you. I'm goin' to need him here."

"And," she said meditatively, "all of this leaves me in what position?"

"Why," he shifted his body to a more comfortable angle, "whatever you want to make it. We ain't exactly hemmed in by convention or society out here along the Apalachicola. The few Indians, traders, an' white trash don't give a damn what you are or where you came from. If you don't make Clay a good wife while you're here he'll likely enough throw you out himself an' save me the trouble." He squinted up at her. "There ain't nothin' more I've got to say."

"Thank you."

She turned slowly and walked away, head high, back erect. Along the seemingly interminable length of the corridor she was conscious of the fact that his eyes followed her steps. The silence of the great house weighted her down and she wished desperately Clay would come back or that she had gone riding with him when he suggested it. Now she would go to her room feeling a little like a child who has been chastised and sent from the company of her elders. Actually, she thought as she ascended the staircase, the old man had been more tolerant than she had a right to expect.

The day was oppressively warm and she stripped away her clothing, tossing the garments into an untidy heap on the floor. Stretched out on the bed she listened to the drowsy murmur of the afternoon and tried desperately to see her life from this point on.

"You need a crystal ball, my girl," she said aloud, "and even that must be cloudy."

The journey from St. Augustine to the interior had been far more difficult than anything she could imagine. The road that Clay had spoken of so confidently proved to be little more than a single set of deeply rutted tracks gouged into the earth. It wandered and curled, taking advantage of every small clearing without regard for distance or direction. Mosquitoes, fiery gnats, and savage black flies plagued them by day and night. With the windows drawn against the insects the interior of the coach became a steamy and oppressive box that jolted and lunged forward in sickening heaves until her stomach revolted with a churning nausea. The nights were filled with strange and terrifying sounds, and when Clay grew lyrical over the star-filled sky she could think only of the tormenting redbugs burrowed beneath her itching skin.

Tallahassi, which Clay had pictured as a metropolis, a second Paris, with modish shops on each corner, turned out to be a dirty, hot, and crudely violent settlement where the trading posts stocked bolts of coarse calico and sunbonnets fit only for the fields. Grimly she had clung to her senses through the nightmarish trip, sustained by the knowledge that at the end lay the plantation. She pictured it as shining white with high, gleaming pillars, set in cool and shaded groves. There would be long, flower-bordered walks, boxwood hedges, magnificent sweeping verandas overlooking terraced gardens. When she saw the huge and rambling structure, almost indistinguishable from the sprawling barns and warehouses, a cry of pain escaped her trembling lips.

"You mean," she turned with helpless dismay to Clay, "this is it? Is this where we are going to live?"

Her disappointment was unmistakable and his concern immediate. Some of the pleasure and excitement at being home again died in his eyes.

"Well, honey," he tried to soothe her, "it isn't exactly like a picture book, I guess. It always seemed good enough for just Old Clay and me."

"But," she had a hunted look, "it is so enormously ugly."

The interior of the plantation house had reassured her somewhat. Here, at least, was evidence of wealth and a certain taste, but when she looked from her windows across miles of rolling woods beyond the cultivated fields she felt they had come to the end of the earth.

Clay had prepared her in a measure for the old man, but his words had been woefully inadequate. He was seated on the porch when they drove up and made no gesture of recognition or welcome as they climbed the broad flight of steps. When they stood before him he grunted, an impatient, animal sound, and stared at Clay, ignoring her completely.

"You didn't stay very long," he said.

"Long enough to get what I wanted." Clay smiled encouragingly down at Claire.

"Who's this?" The old man jerked his head in the girl's direction.

"My wife." The pride was evident in the two words.

Old Clay grunted and his eyes shifted. Beneath his penetrating stare she was first uneasy and then indignant. Her head lifted and she traded cold insolence with him.

"This is a hell of a place to bring a white girl, madame," he rumbled, "and Hammond marriages have had a way of turnin' out unlucky."

"I'll do my best to make this an exception, sir," she replied.

Old Clay turned his gaze to the coach. "I see you brought Santee back, anyhow," he said sourly. "Whose coach is that?"

"Belongs to a friend in St. Augustine." Clay's anger at his grandfather's deliberate rudeness crackled in his voice.

"That as far as you got?"

"Yes, by God," Clay shouted, "that's as far as I got, and you know better than to act this way." His voice was trembling and he took a step forward. For a moment Claire thought he was going to strike the seated figure.

"Don't raise your voice to me." Old Clay's words were whispered with disarming gentleness. "I ain't used to it."

Clay shook his head with a slow movement of disbelief and wonder. Then he laughed shortly but without mirth and took Claire's hand in his.

"I've been away so long I'd almost forgotten folks say you're the meanest bastard on the Apalachicola," he said.

For a moment Old Clay seemed to be on the point of smiling. "It takes in a lot of territory," he said judiciously, "an' don't never think I got this way without tryin'."

"Come on, Claire." Clay took her arm, turning her toward the doorway.

"You just wander around, madame," Old Clay called, and she somehow understood the words were now meant as a welcome, "an' pick out whatever rooms you want. I'll see you at supper."

This first meeting with the old man had occurred three weeks ago, but time had lost its meaning. She was still a stranger within this house. Until today Old Clay's manner toward her had been roughly polite; he made no obvious distinction between her and his grandson in speech or attitude. The letter from John Spain that he had so pointedly torn up a few minutes ago must have been delivered yesterday by the post rider from Tallahassi. She wondered why he had allowed a full twenty-four hours to elapse before confronting her with his knowledge of the fact that she had been John Spain's mistress.

She closed her eyes, hoping to find in sleep a brief release from the overpowering sensation of desperate loneliness. During the uncomfortable journey from St. Augustine she had amused herself by trying to imagine what her life as Mrs. Clayfield Hammond was to be. Her fancy had colored the picture until it emerged in vivid and exciting hues. First, she would have the dignity of being mistress of her own home. There would be parties, balls, gay picnics, and excursions, with continual visiting between the great estates. She would have friends, young women of her own age, and they would spend hours in gossip and chatter of clothes and beaux. The men would all be dashingly handsome and gallant, stimulatingly aware of her beauty, and not too secretly envious of Clay. She would move through the brilliant assemblies with confidence and charm, serenely aware of her unassailable position.

Now, although she was reluctant to admit the truth, she was frightened by her isolation. There were no neighboring plantations, no social intercourse between the Hammonds and the few white families in near-by Clayport. They were marooned in a vast sea of wilderness. Life on the plantation apparently moved in relentless cycles with the seasons. It was geared to the plantings, the harvests, the baling and processing, carting and shipping. Everything on the land was caught between the stones of a gigantic mill, the wheels of which turned with ordered perfection. In St. Augustine her life had been restricted. She had been permitted no intimates and John Spain had few, if any, friends. Her life had been tightly bound to his, but somehow she hadn't felt so alone. At least there were people to be seen in the streets, markets, and shops; the sensation of being part of an organized community broke the monotony. Here they were people set apart from the world and she lived among strangers, married to a man whose habits and emotions she had not even begun to understand.

At night, lying within the circle of Clay's arm, she felt secure, but this security was the safety of a jail cell. Nothing could touch her, but neither could she escape.

"What do we do, Clay?" In the darkness she had brushed his ear with her lips, whispering the question and knowing in advance he would have no answer. "What shall we do with the mornings and days stretching ahead? I have no place here."

He had moved uneasily at her side, made uncomfortable by the question. It was difficult, he thought, to understand people who didn't know what to do with themselves. What did anyone do anywhere? A man didn't always have to be at something. Sometimes it was enough just to lie on the bank of a river, listening to the sound, following the whirling pools of sunlight, tossing an occasional twig into the current and watching it float away. He could get on a horse if he felt like riding or take a gun into the woods, not really caring much whether he shot anything. A man felt good doing such things, but if he wanted to talk there were plenty of people on the plantation who were glad enough to stop what they were at and exchange a word or so. Women, he supposed, were different, and he was a little irritated by the suspicion that she expected him to fill her days.

"I don't know," he mumbled vaguely. "I never had much trouble before finding things to do. You get used to the place and the slack takes itself up naturally."

His indifference jolted her. "You said we would go away," she persisted, "that we could travel. When are we going to leave, Clay?"

"But," he protested, "we just got here, honey. This is my home. We ought to get settled." He made an attempt at lightness. "I'm an old married man now, with you and maybe a family to think about. Old Clay can't run things forever. He's breaking up a little. I figure I ought to dig in here for a while and get to know more about the plantation than I do if I don't want it stolen out from underneath my feet. Don't you really like it here?"

"I think," she spoke with resignation, "I can learn to despise it with unlimited enthusiasm."

"Oh, it's just strange to you." He was soothing a pouting child. "You probably need something to occupy your time. A woman ought to have babies."

"How do you know?" She could not help smiling, amused by his innocent assumption of wisdom.

"Well, that's what people say."

"You have been listening, sir, to a particularly vicious form of male gossip."

"We ought to try it, anyhow." He laughed softly and his arm tightened about her.

"I will not be cozened, sir." She made a halfhearted attempt to wriggle away. "We were talking of serious things. I want to know about my husband."

"There's no better place than a bedroom."

"Well," she sat up quickly, her dark hair making a filmy shawl over her bare shoulders, "tell me about yourself. What did you do before we were married? Didn't you have a girl here, someone? A white girl, I mean?"

"You say the damnedest things." He was embarrassed. "I don't know where you ever learned to talk like that. It doesn't sound decent. A respectable girl wouldn't have such thoughts."

"Sir," she purred, "my respectability became doubtful one afternoon in your company."

"By God," he was laughing with her, "and I was scared as a rabbit. I don't mind telling you so now." He drew her back to his side and they were warm and happy in the knowledge of an intimate secret. "I had sort of a girl once." He was in a reminiscent mood. "Anyhow, I thought so for a couple of weeks, but I don't suppose she really knew it. Her name was Sue Rogers. They're newcomers here from someplace up north."

"Did you make love to her?"

"No," he said slowly, "I went looking for you."

"You say pretty things sometimes."

"She and her brothers," he appeared not to have heard, "live up the river a couple of miles. I've been intending to ride over and see them. Maybe we ought to go together. You and Sue might like each other."

"And use you as a subject of mutual interest?" she asked.

"You talk like a woman."

"Have you had any reason to question my sex?"

Lying alone now in the silent room she thought wistfully of how rarely they shared such a moment of easy understanding and the pleasure of small talk. In the presence of his grandfather Clay was restrained, almost self-conscious in his attention to her. It was as though he were avoiding a display of unmanly weakness. Away from Old Clay he was a different person.

The thatched roof of the lodge was bleached to pale yellow, chewed at by time and the wind. Where the once tight sheathing had fallen away no hand had repaired the damage, and so when it rained the rotting floor became as damp and cold as stone. Spiders, small lizards, and chameleons hunted for insects along the supporting poles, and thick black roaches fed upon ragged and filthy matting.

Near the edge of the platform Clay sat cross-legged on the sagging and broken boards. His limply clasped hands dangled with knuckles down in the triangular space between jutting knees. Beside him Tommie Macon, he who had been the greatest hunter of all the Red Stick tribe, rested on his bony buttocks and trembled with the ague of his years. His thin lips moved with soundless twitchings as though he would speak but could not form the words. When he tried to draw on the cheroot Clay had given him, his mouth, no longer braced by teeth, caved inward with a moist, sucking sound. An infection in one eye spilled a thin trickle of slimy lymph down his withered cheek and he lifted a hand now and then to brush away the hungry flies.

Clay waited for him to speak and his eyes roamed over what remained of the *istihapo*. Only the skeletons of lodges ringed the compound; boards and thatching had been stripped away and fed to the untidy fire by men who could no longer go into the woods for the great logs. Old fish heads and whitened, spiny lengths of bones rotted on the ground and the ants fed upon carcasses of small birds that had been stripped of their flesh and tossed carelessly aside. Only the old remained, and Clay thought there must be not more than a dozen of them. They sat motionless in patches of sunshine, warming their marrowless bones, picking at their lice, and scratching at scabs and sores while they waited stolidly for death and its release. Their eyes, without light or understanding, peered vacantly at nothing. Even the dogs had left, slinking away to run wild in scrawny, savage packs.

"They went," the old man was mumbling, and Clay bent his head to catch the words. "The young and the strong. By twos and threes they disappeared, carrying with them only the few things that could be put upon their backs. In Washington, we were told, the White Father said it must be so. The Seminoles were to have a new home and could no longer live here by the great river. This earth in which the bones of the old ones lie no longer belonged to us. Go now, they said, or we will send soldiers, but first we will let you starve for a while. At first we did not believe this and remained within our town. Then came the word we could no longer trade at the posts of the settlement. When a bad year came we could get no corn for planting and we hungered. When our cattle sickened and died we had none to replace them. Although the kegs of the traders were filled we were not permitted to barter for a few grains of powder and no one would trade our skins and feathers for a piece of bullet metal. Go to this new land, they said again, and the Father in Washington will take care of you as his children. Many left, as I have said, and the old stayed behind. The words that have been spoken I do not believe.

It will be the same again wherever they are. What we will settle the white men will want and they will come among us as before. Now, they will say, you go to another place, and in this new place we have found for you it will be good. Each time it will be the same. Always they will have to move and each time there will be those who are left behind to die. Then the white men will come once more. We have found a new place for you, they will repeat. Now you go there to this big swamp. No one will want it, for no man can live there long. Here you may stay in peace. The Great Father in Washington makes his promise this will be so." The old man sucked on the tobacco, licking at it with his tongue. "I am," he continued, "too old to listen to more lies. Of my life there is but a little blackened dust, which waits only for the wind to blow it away. I would have it scattered here. This is so."

Clay bent his head, eyes fastened upon locked fingers. The old man did not speak accusingly, but Clay could feel the chilling hand of guilt at his heart. In this town, he thought, I walked as a child and these people gave me their friendship. The misery and degradation he now looked upon had been planted by the hands of his people and he was ashamed.

Tommie Macon lifted a lusterless glance. The skin on his face was as hard and wrinkled as a dried peach pit. "Is it so," he asked, "the white men lie to each other as they do to the Indian?"

"I do not know," Clay replied almost humbly. "But I suspect it is so."

The old man pondered. "There must be great evil among them," he said after a moment. "Yet," he studied Clay, "there is none in your speech or bearing. Although you have grown to manhood you remember the tongue and come as a friend among those of us who are left. The memory of things is all I have and I think clearly of you as a child and also the son of my people who called you brother. At our fires you were warmed, from our food you ate. In the lodge of Asseola you slept, and together on the ridge at the first light of day we three watched the great turkey cocks as they strutted and made love and the doe lie beside her young. We have seen the moon rise above the cypress and the sun rest upon the world's edge. Among men such things are not easily forgotten. It was I who taught you to hold the long rifle and shoot with skill and truth. We were pleased when your tongue mastered the speech of our people, and although we laughed sometimes as you formed the sounds, it was the laughter of understanding among friends. Why were these things so with you and not with the others of your people? The land is fair and large enough for all. Why do the white men make it small with their greed?"

"I have no answer," Clay replied faintly.

Tommie Macon nodded, satisfied with the reply. "I have found none either." He swiped at his eye with the back of his hand. "You have traveled," he continued, "in this new place where my people have gone. Do they live as a nation or are they scattered?"

"They have been sown in many places and the yield is discontent. Asseola, my brother, I have seen twice. Once we met upon the trail and again in the town of St. Augustine. He feeds upon hatred."

The old man's head bobbed slowly. "It sustains a man when his belly is empty."

Clay slid his legs out from beneath him, dropped to the ground, and stood before the Indian. Impulsively he dug into his pocket and then laid a handful of coins and paper money on the platform.

Tommie Macon regarded the little pile and the shade of a smile hovered at his bloodless lips. After a moment he pushed the offering aside.

"With it," he said, "I could buy nothing, and if I tried the white men at the trading post would say only that a thieving Indian had killed and robbed a traveler."

"I'll have food brought to you, a sow and a boar, some chickens and a cow," Clay said hopefully. "I'll have rice and corn for planting sent."

Tommie Macon shook his head. "Who is there left with the will for planting? In whose arm is there strength enough to drive a cow or slaughter a pig? No, it is better we die as we do, quietly and without hope. I cling to the great tree of life as a dead leaf. Let me fall quickly. Go now and you will not come again." He lifted his skinny hand and the gesture was one of absolution.

Clay rode slowly back along the ridge. The trail, once marked clearly by the passage of many feet, had yielded to the woods again and the scrub brushed against his stirrups. Melancholy was astride the saddle with him and he could not rid himself of its unwelcome presence.

Earlier in the afternoon he had made a wide circle from the plantation up-river, intending to surprise the Rogers men and their sister in their new home. Instead of the cabin and cultivated fields he expected there was only a scattered heap of charred and half-burned logs. The scrub had reclaimed the clearing. For several minutes he surveyed the tract from the back of his horse and then dismounted, leaving the animal to graze as he walked thoughtfully over the ground, pausing beside the blackened square of earth where the Rogers brothers had laid the timbers for their house. The ruins were months old, and as he kicked along their edge he wondered what had happened and why no attempt to rebuild had been made. He studied the earth carefully and was certain no other feet had trod it for a long time.

He puzzled over the mysterious disappearance of Sue and her brothers on his way to the Seminole town, and now, as he rode away after his meeting with Tommie Macon, he thought again of the family and wished he had spoken of them to the Indian. It would have taken more than a fire to drive Will and Hadley Rogers from their land. On a sudden impulse he turned his horse's head in the direction of Clayport.

Old Andrew McCollum thrust his spectacles up on his forehead and came around from behind the counter to greet him.

" 'Tis the young Muster Hammond," he exclaimed, "though not so young any more, pairhaps. The look of the traveler you bear upon your face, and I hear a pretty wife you have brought back with you."

Clay grinned with pleasure as the trader pumped his hand. "I don't know where people ever got the idea that the Scots were a grave and silent tribe," he said. "You chatter like an Irish biddy on washday."

"The traditional dourness," the old man twinkled, "I resairve for my recalcitrant debtors. 'Tis a sheepshead I put on to frighten them out o' their wits an' pennies." He stood off and examined Clay. " 'Tis good to see you back, lad."

"I'm glad to be back."

"An' how's your grandfather, God forgive me for askin'?" McCollum lifted his eyes piously to the ceiling.

Clay laughed. "I guess he doesn't change much."

"Aye!" McCollum nodded. "The settlement does, have you noticed? Trade is brisk with new people arrivin' every day. As you may have seen, the Indians are gone, good riddance, an' there is even talk of a new road that will one day pass this way an' link Tallahassi with Fort Brooke." He jerked his head in the direction of the counters, where three assistants waited on the customers. "I have had to engage clerks, who spend their days tryin' to figure out ways of cheatin' me."

Clay wanted to ask him about the Rogerses but hesitated. McCollum sensed his indecision and cocked his head to one side.

"If your travels have given you a taste for good whisky, pairhaps

216

you will join me in a drop behind the partition. I keep a jug handy for special customers an' friends an' the back of my hand to the others."

He led Clay into a dim and cluttered cubbyhole and filled two cups from an earthenware bottle.

" 'Tis the dew of Scotland's glens an' my only extravagance in this God-forsaken but profitable Territory. Good health, young Hammond."

Clay drank and placed his cup on McCollum's untidy desk. The old man was waiting for him to speak.

"I was wondering," he said finally, "what happened to the Rogers men and their sister. I rode up to their place today."

"Then you know, lad," the Scotsman answered gravely.

"I only know their cabin must have burned. What happened?"

The old man scratched at his head. "Some have said the Indians set fire to the place." He glanced keenly at Clay and the tip of his tongue tapped at his upper teeth.

"Why would the Indians want to burn them out? There's been no trouble here, has there?"

"No-o-o-o." McCollum drawled the reply.

"Well, then," Clay continued, "I don't believe it."

"Aye!" The trader winked elaborately. "Neither did they."

The man's attitude was one of sly skepticism and Clay bridled.

"What are you trying to say?" he demanded shortly. "What am I supposed to know?"

McCollum's expression changed. "I should have known better, lad," he apologized. "The thoughts were those of an old man steeped in guile. Of course you wouldn't know."

"Well, if the Indians didn't burn them out, who did?" Clay was beginning to feel uneasy. A suspicion took shape in the back of his mind and he almost dreaded the answer McCollum would make.

"For a straight answer," the Scot said quietly, "there might be no better man to ask in the whole Territory than the master of the Hammond acres."

Clay could only stare at him. "I don't believe it," he finally said.

McCollum tapped gently at the cork in the whisky jug. "There was no proof," he admitted, "an' there may be naught to it but the clackin' of envious an' idle tongues," he said, and then added significantly, " 'Tis strange, though, the Indians should pick a half-finished cabin. Stranger still that the cabin should be rising on land once claimed within the Hammond grant."

Clay nodded dumbly. Of course it didn't make any sense. Seminoles out looking for trouble wouldn't have started and ended with such a small place.

"Where did they go, the Rogers men and the girl?"

"But two went, lad." McCollum sighed heavily. "The one called Hadley and his sister. The brother Will was found a week after the fire with a bullet hole in the back of his head. He was murdered on the river road leading into the settlement. It would be a careless Indian who would shoot down a white man there. The brother an' sister, I have heard, are living in Pensacola."

"I think I'd like another drink." Clay's voice was unsteady with suppressed anger and the hand holding out the cup trembled. "Make it a big one."

"Aye." McCollum poured liquor for them both. " 'Tis a fecky business. They were good people an' the Territory could use more like them. It could be seen," he ventured a brief smile, "the lass had an eye for you."

Clay gulped the whisky and shook his head. "I can't walk around believing this," he said miserably.

The graying Scot laid a gentle hand on his arm. "Then don't, lad. Put it from your mind. 'Twas a drunken Indian, let us say. Who knows?"

Clay's shoulders dropped with a gesture of resigned assent. With a brief nod he turned and walked slowly from the post. On the shallow boardwalk he paused. The pleasure at being home was gone. What McCollum had told him must be on the mind of every settler in Clayport. His mouth twisted in a bitter grimace. Clayport. The word mocked him. Clayfield Hammond had forced his name on the community and then contemptuously turned his back on the town. He felt no pride in having established this small, determined settlement on the frontier. He had stamped it with his name and thereafter ignored it. Glancing down the warm length of the unpaved street, noting the new buildings and evidences of industry in the face of danger and continual hardships, Clay felt he was a stranger. There was no place for him here. He belonged on the Hammond plantation. Walking to McCollum's hitching rail he was tormented by the unfriendly pressure of many eyes. Silent hatred followed him as he rode with hasty recklessness out of sight.

As he galloped across the plantation's boundaries he wondered what he should say to his grandfather. This thing that the old man had done was so monstrous, so unnecessarily brutal, that to accuse him of it would be nothing more than a futile protest, a confession of weakness. Old Clay would snort and ignore him as a weakling fool who wouldn't protect his own property.

Dismounting at the side of the house he went up to the second floor. Claire was asleep on the bed, sprawled naked on the counterpane with the awkward innocence of a child. He looked tenderly down at her, listening to her gentle, untroubled breathing, and then tiptoed into the adjoining room to wash away the dust of the ride and change into fresh clothes. He wondered what had been left to Sue and her brother. Probably their horses had been shot, also. The old man would have done a thorough job. I'll find them, he thought as he pulled a fresh shirt over his damp hair. I'll find them and do what's right. He knew this was but an empty promise. Neither Sue nor Hadley would accept help from Clayfield Hammond's grandson. He could try, though. He halted in the act of fastening a button at the collar. What am I going to try with? he asked himself. For the first time he realized how dependent he was upon Old Clay. Save for the substantial sum and the letters of credit his grandfather had given him when he and Santee left months ago, he had never had a dollar of his own. That he had no need for money on the plantation or in Clayport didn't alter the startling fact that he was as fully bound to the old man's whims as any of the plantation's white employees. I'll be damned. He whistled a low note of astonishment.

Old Clay was deep in his chair on the shady side of the porch. He looked up at the sound of Clay's step, nodded, and watched as his grandson took a place on the railing before him.

"If you'll stop bouncin' out of the house like a jack rabbit in the mornings," he said, "I'd like a word or two with you. I been figurin' on some things."

"So have I." Clay waited.

"Now that you're back an' likely to stay, it might be a good idea if you began to get an idea how things are run. There's more to keepin' this place goin' than fishin' on a riverbank or warmin' your tail in a soft bed. Startin' tomorrow you can take over some of the books, an' when Salano comes in at the end of the month you sit down with me an' him."

Clay nodded. "That's all right with me. I was just thinking upstairs I'm a grown man with a wife. If I was to need money I'd have to come to you for it."

"What do you need money for?" Old Clay shot the question suspiciously.

"How the hell do I know?" Clay could feel his anger mounting.

"I just said it didn't seem right for me to be a man and still have to come to you."

Hammond pursed his thick lips and eyed the younger man with undisguised curiosity. "You can have all the money you want," he said agreeably, "when you earn it. Anyhow," he chuckled with malicious satisfaction, "this is a different tune than you were singin' a few months back. Then, if I recollect, you were ready to turn your pockets inside out an' whack the plantation up into plots for every raggedy immigrant who came along. I'm glad to see you're gettin' some sense."

"Call it whatever you like." Clay was controlling his temper. "If you want me to take hold of things here, then I'll do it as good as anyone, but I want to see a fair share of the profits in my own name. I don't trust you."

Old Clay grinned approvingly. "You'd be a fool if you did."

"All right then." Clay planted his feet on the porch. "I'll work at it and get paid."

"That's fair enough." Hammond relaxed. "Takin' out board an' room for you an' your wife, I figure your contribution to the place right now would come to about ten cents a day. I'll toss in a little more on account of you bein' my only kin. You want it by the day, month, or year?"

"Who killed the Rogers man?" Clay hadn't meant to drag the question into the open this way. The words were spoken before he actually realized what he was saying.

"Somebody get killed?"

"Who burned the Rogers cabin at the bend?" he persisted foolishly.

"I heard some squatters got fired out," Hammond replied mildly. "Indians, more'n likely. They been causin' trouble here an' there."

"I don't believe it and neither does anyone in Clayport. People in the settlement think you did it."

Old Clay's eyes widened. He was beginning to enjoy the conversation. "Now," he said with assumed innocence, "how could an old man like me, with a bad leg an' all, get around to settin' fire to a cabin? That's just plain foolishness."

"You know damn well what I mean," Clay protested with exasperated weariness. Had he really expected Old Clay would admit anything? "I think you had Salano or Jake Cutler and some of the men do it."

Old Clay sighed with hypocritical regret. "I still figure it was the Indians. They're always up to somethin'."

"All right. I just wanted you to know I knew, and right this minute I'm not very proud of being your grandson."

"Who the hell asked you to be?" Old Clay spat the question.

Clay laughed in the old man's spiteful face. He never changed. "Speaking of Indians," he said conversationally, "we're shaping up for a real war. Did you know that Colonel Humphreys isn't acting as agent for the Seminoles any more? There's a new man, Major Phagan, at Fort King."

"Know it?" Old Clay was gleeful. "It was me who got Gad Humphreys tossed out. Now, by God, we'll see somethin'. This Phagan will steal an' cheat the Indians until they'll have to start shootin' an' the government'll have an excuse to cut 'em right down to the last squaw. That's what I been waitin' for."

18

THE long blue and orange flames strained upward, swaying on the crimson base of the huge council fire. Weaving and twisting with the frantic movements of tormented serpents they licked with a soft rushing sound at the sky's black hole high above the pines.

Drawn into a wide circle along the shifting perimeter of light the men waited, their eyes staring at a point midway in the whirling ribbons of fire. There was no sound save that created by the furiously burning logs. Speech would come at the proper time, prompted by the inner voice that would not be hurried. All night they had been sitting this way and in each man the small seed of conscience had been warmed and nurtured. They broke slowly as do the kernels of corn when dampened by the rains and touched by the sun's heat. Given time, the truth would flower, and when each man present could see it for himself he would speak of his convictions. The moment for talk was drawing near. How they all knew this none could have said. There had been no movement, no shifting of eyes, no motion, no exchange of glances. Yet the words were to be spoken soon and each man listened.

Micanopy, he who was called the Pond Governor, lifted his face to the starless sky, and then his eyes dropped to move slowly about the circle. He was old and with the fat layers of many good years upon his great belly. So cumbersome had he grown that he walked rarely now but was carried from place to place on a litter borne by slaves. The acres of Micanopy were rich and profitable. In his fields the black men toiled from sunup until dark, harvesting his crops and tending the heads of sleek cattle grazing on the broad pasture lands. These things he was reluctant to disturb; yet, as his glance traveled, it encountered lean and hungry faces and the features of men drawn and made ugly by anger. A great wrong had been done, a lie told, and a trick played. He stared unhappily across the fire. Throughout the long hours these many men and their chiefs had waited for him to speak.

Patiently they held their peace, for these things could not be hurried. As they had sat this night, so, if necessary, would they wait throughout the day and another time of darkness. Micanopy made a silent count of their names. Holati Emathlar, Jumper, Cat-sha Tustenuggee, Alligator, John Hicks, Sam Jones, and Black Dirt. As was proper, these men of authority had restrained their voices until the Pond Governor should speak, but fury smoldered in their eyes. There were others, younger men, whose impatience was mounting. Contempt was darkening their faces as the aging Micanopy hesitated. The old one knew them also. Wildcat, Little Cloud, Tigertail, Nethlocke-mathlar, and the man of strange tongue, Chekika, chief of the Spanish Indians far to the south in the great swamp of Okeechobee. They stirred and a ripple moved through the council. It was time for the great talk.

Micanopy sighed, a small, whistling sound. Pudgy hands rested on the swell of his belly. He moved slightly, his arm brushing the shoulder of the younger man who sat at his side. For a moment his troubled eyes were held by those of Asseola and he shivered although it was not cold.

"It is the time now," Asseola whispered.

The sagging lips of Micanopy formed for a protest but the words were not uttered. There was a day, he could remember, when swift punishment would have countered the impudence. Now he only nodded, for this Indian seated at his side had become both his conscience and his scourge. Why this was so he could not say. The relentless will of the younger man had entered his body and spoke through him. This strange Seminole who could not wear the authority of a chief yet who walked and spoke as one had cast a spell upon him. His words were persuasive, his knowledge of the white men and their ways infallible. When he sat in the lodge of Micanopy his attitude was that of a respectful son who would lend his support to an aging parent and shoulder some of the burden. At first Micanopy had brushed aside his counsel. The white men will do this, Asseola warned. The things they tell you now are lies, he cautioned. Their word in this matter cannot be trusted. Each time he had been right and Micanopy saw his prophecies come true. No longer did he trust his own judgment. He made timid decisions and hastily withdrew them as Asseola placed his fingers on the spot of folly. The younger man had become a flame, melting his will, and the Pond Governor would cast out the evil magic but lacked the courage. His breath sang gently.

This thing that each man in the council looked at within the fire tonight was war. It bubbled slowly and was rising to overflow. No longer would it be a matter of an Indian against a white man but nation against nation.

At Fort King, Major John Phagan, his beefy red face smirking and satisfied, was congratulating himself. The job had been well done. It mattered little to him that his office as Indian agent was without dignity or significance. He could sneer at the report of James Westcott, Jr., secretary and acting governor of the Territory, who charged him with malfeasance and wrote to the Commissioner of Indian Affairs at Washington:

> On my visit to the agency, I regret to state, I discovered evidence of fraud and improper conduct on the part of Major Phagan. I discovered that in regard to the employees of the agency, he had subcontracts with them for much less than the amount they receipted for to the Government, and that even for the amount of these subcontracts he was in debt to several Indians and to Abraham, one of the Seminole interpreters; to the contractor, for beef at the agency, for provisions at the payment of the annuity, and Col. Blount, an Indian chief has a claim of fifty dollars for arrears of his annuity receipted for to him.

In his name at Charleston there had been deposited a considerable sum of money and before him on the desk of the agency lay copies of the treaties, signed by President Andrew Jackson. What did it matter that the treaties had been born of deceit, written in trickery, and sealed in fraud? They were signed by the Indians and the government could force their fulfillment without fear of censure by the country or the world.

At Payne's Landing, on the Ocklawaha River, it had been written:

> The Seminole Indians, regarding with just respect the solicitude manifested by the President of the United States for the improvement of their conditions, by recommending a removal to a country more suitable to their wants and habits than the one they now occupy at present in the Territory of Florida, are willing that their confidential chiefs, Jumper, Fuch-a-lus-to-had-jo, Charley Emathlar, Coi-had-jo, Holati Emathlar, Ya-ha-had-jo, Sam Jones, accompanied by their agent, Major Phagan, and their faithful interpreter, Abraham, should be sent, at the expense of the United States, to examine the country assigned to the Creeks west of the Mississippi River, and should they be satisfied with the character of that country and the favorable disposition of the Creeks to reunite with the Seminoles as one people, the articles in this treaty shall be binding.

The articles had been well drawn. The Seminoles should relinquish all claims to property within the Territory of Florida. A sum of $15,400 was to be divided among the chiefs and warriors of several towns. Arriving in the Creek country, each Seminole should receive a blanket and a homespun frock for his woman. An annuity of $3,000 a year was to be paid for fifteen years. The Seminoles would be reimbursed for their cattle at a figure agreed upon by an impartial arbiter.

Through the blizzard-swept months of January, February, and March the Indian delegation, accompanied by Major Phagan, plodded through the desolation of Arkansas. The fury of the icy winds and whirling snowstorms wracked their bodies and beat at their faces. Accustomed to the gentle warmth of their homeland, they regarded with terror this that they were asked to accept. Terrible, devouring, implacable evil spirits rode on the rushing winds and screamed in their ears. Cold the like of which they had never known gnawed at them and gripped their hearts. Where were the sun, the high pines, the green and white beauty of the magnolia, the scent of warm grass, the perfume of flowers, the placid mystery of their lakes and rivers? Fear pinched their features and made them speechless. They stared at Phagan. Could this be the land that the Great Father in Washington, with "solicitude for the improvement of their conditions," was offering? Dumbly, huddling together for the warmth of their bodies and spirits, they waited like bewildered sheep for the answer.

It was given to them at Fort Gibson, Arkansas, on a blustery, ringing wet day in March that drove the cold of death into a man.

Timid, uncertain, anxious to return home, the Seminole delegation stood in confused silence. Herded into a small room, they wanted only to escape. Behind a table stood the three commissioners appointed by President Jackson. In their hands they held a second treaty. The contract drawn at Payne's Landing was too conditional, for it bound this Indian delegation merely to examine the land and report to their people. If they, meaning the Seminole nation, were satisfied with the findings of the ambassadors, the Indians would migrate. Here, in this cheerless box of a room in a strange country, the Seminoles were given a second treaty. Surrounded by armed troops—listening to words they did not wholly understand even when translated by the Negro Abraham—the chiefs Jumper, Sam Jones, Charley Emathlar, and the others eyed each other uncertainly. When they protested that they were without authority to bind the Seminole nation to a contract their objections were swept aside.

The weather was unpleasant. The commissioners, Montfort Stokes, Henry Ellsworth, and John Schermerhorn, were anxious to finish their business and get out of this God-forsaken waste of dreariness and return to the comforts of home. The room was cold and Phagan suggested they have a drink as the talks went on. Bottles were opened. The Indians drank with their friends and protectors. After a while the room was no longer so unpleasantly chilly. The words of the commissioners and Phagan took on a new note of solicitude. More wood was thrown into the stove and a new bottle passed from Seminole hand to Seminole mouth. With a flourish the commissioners signed their names to the paper. Who could doubt their sincerity and good will? To the brief treaty that for the most part restated the conditions of the one drawn at Payne's Landing, there was attached an additional clause:

> The undersigned Seminole chiefs, delegated on behalf of their nation, hereby declare themselves well satisfied with the location provided for them by the commissioners, and agree that their nation shall commence the removal to their new home as soon as the Government will make arrangements for their emigration satisfactory to the Seminole nation. The Seminoles also have expressed their high confidence in Major Phagan and desire that he may be permitted to remove with them to their new homes west of the Mississippi.

These were the words that the chiefs had brought back to their nation.

Micanopy began to speak, and at the sound of his voice Seminoles, Tallahassees, Creeks, Mickasukies, Cherokees, and the curiously featured men from the Big Swamp leaned forward, firelight catching at their faces, touching the dyed tips of turkey feathers, glinting on silver ornaments and the bright steel of knives.

"I am old," the Pond Governor's words came slowly and on a high note of protest, "and I wish my bones to lie here in the soil of my people. The white men declare this cannot be so and hold before them a piece of paper saying: 'Here are the marks of your chiefs. By them it was agreed you and your people would move to the land of Ar-kan-sas beyond the great river.' Those chiefs have now told us this land is barren, the days and nights so cold a Seminole cannot breathe the air, for it shrivels his lungs. He sickens and dies. How is it, then, that they signed this paper?"

Small, sucking sounds of approval raced about the ring of seated figures. Here was truth and the question each man had asked himself.

"They have said," Micanopy continued, his voice quavering with anger, "that they were not dealt with in honesty. The meaning of the words was not understood. They were given whisky and made stupid by the drink so that when the time came to make their marks they were not aware of what they were doing. If this be so, then fools sleep in the lodges of our towns at night and men with the wisdom of children are called chiefs.

"I am old," the Pond Governor repeated, "and would have peace with the white men. They will not have it so. As agent they have sent this Major Phagan who robs us of our annuity, takes our cattle as a fine, levies tribute on every town, and mocks at our protests. He will go with us, he says, to this land of Ar-kan-sas, where he may cheat and steal as before. When I have said the Seminoles will not leave the land of their fathers he shows me the paper, signed by our chiefs, which says we must. Time presses upon us. Soon more white men will invade our land, taking what is ours. If we complain, asking the White Father in Washington for justice, he will point to the paper. See, he will say, it was so agreed by your chiefs. What shall we do then?" His voice was shrilly accusing.

Each man now must say what was in his mind. A great mistake had been made. To take those responsible, beat and drive them from the lodges, would not repair the damage. The truth must be examined.

As they talked and the intervals of silence between the speeches grew longer, Asseola listened and his anger mounted. What was being said was without meaning. It was Indian talk. The white men spoke better. They drove at a point, fixing their attention upon it, refusing to be led astray by the empty sound of words. Here was the ancient mummery, the timid hopes, the talk of spells and incantations, the passive fatalism of his people that sucked the strength from their arms and the will to act from their brains. He bowed his head.

Charley Emathlar, he whose name was with those of the others on the fraudulent pact made at Fort Gibson, spoke from beyond the sagging fire.

"It is true," he said, "we were tricked and so made our marks. Yet we are not fools. I too am old and wish to lie with the bones of our people, but this cannot be so. The power of the white men is greater than ours. Each day the strength of their soldiers increases. If we resist they will sweep over us as a great wave of fire. Our towns will be burned, our cattle destroyed. Those who are left will be forced to hide in the swamps, where they will die.

227

I have seen much bloodshed and wish for peace. Let us have no more talk of what is right and who was wrong. I will take the white man's blanket and seek a home in this new land. It is written so in the treaty."

A confused murmur rose from the council. It was made of many sounds. Some of the old men nodded. Little time was left to them anyhow. It was better that it be spent in peace. Soon they would die and this fair land would not even be a memory. The younger men chirruped rasping barks of scorn and disapproval. The noise was that of angry foxes.

Asseola listened, and as he waited for the confusion to subside he thought of the man Powell and of his words. "They'll drive you out, lad, or reduce you to a pitiful handful of basket weavers and cattle tenders."

Without fear he stood within a broad fan of light so all might see. This thing I am going to do, he thought, will cause much misery, yet a man must speak what is in his heart. He must tread carefully, though, taking one step at a time. He had no right to raise his voice and the privilege was jealously guarded. Even the younger men, with whom he had held secret talks, might look upon his intrusion with suspicion. Since I cannot speak for myself, he thought, I must seek the aid of another. I shall be a chief in all things but name. He would capture their attention; make them angry, if necessary, but they would listen.

"What is being spoken here tonight," he said boldly, "is but the nervous and frightened cries of black carrion birds, satisfied to live upon the rotten leavings of the hunter. With this I am not content."

A startled and angry buzz arose from the assembly and above it was lifted the waspish voice of Charley Emathlar.

"Who is this," the man called, "who dares to speak at the council as a chief yet does not wear the mark of authority and wisdom? Be silent or be punished."

"I am no chief," Asseola turned quickly to confront him, "yet I am a man and will be heard, for this land is as much a part of me as it is of you. For my home I am willing to die. Will you say as much? Can you say more?"

He advanced a few paces toward the fire. Naked to the waist, his only ornament the curling, bright feather of the egret at his head, he was a figure of rebellious strength.

"With talk and chants and the crawling sounds of empty words you think to dispose of this evil as though it were a sickness of the body. The medicine you seek to make lies within the barrels of your rifles. It is hidden in the steel of your knives and waits to be called forth from warrior hearts. Do you think it hides beneath the drumheads and can be summoned by childish thumpings?"

There was a quick rustle of approval in the assembly and many men leaned forward. Excitement was gathering in their eyes.

"You talk of the white man's treaty. Has he not broken all we have made? Who among you is so foolish as to believe that if this land beyond the Mississippi is made good and fruitful by our settling he will not come again and take it? Has one word been spoken of this? I will have no more of the lying or listen to the empty promises. Let the paper be torn and scattered, for it has no meaning." He whipped the broad-bladed knife from its sheath and with a swift movement of his arm sent it flying across the fire to bury itself in the side of a pine. "This is the only treaty I will make with the white men."

The singing blade sounded the pitch for a murmur that grew in volume, punctuated by the sharp, furious barks of approval. The sound was angry and shrill on the night and echoed in the deep woods. These were the words the younger men had been waiting for. They too were wearied of tradition and the laws that bound them to the ineffectual counsel of their elders. From the circle a figure rose and stepped into the light, lithe and eager, his eyes snapping with pleasure at the uproar.

"I am Coacoochee, called Wildcat by the whites, son of King Phillip. This is known to you. I speak as a chief and will be heard. What my brother has said is the truth. I have been driven like an animal from place to place. Today I stand upon a piece of land and say it is mine. Tomorrow a white man comes with soldiers and says, 'Go away, Indian. You no longer live here.' I have moved for the last time. Now I will fight, for it is better that I die here as a man than be stoned and beaten as a dog."

A movement gathered along the edge of the circle as man after man left his place to stand and by this act signified that the traditional ceremony that bound them to a solemn etiquette was broken. The cautious reign of the old ones was at an end. One by one the bold and adventurous allied themselves. Ta-ho-loo-chee, called Little Cloud; Halpatter-Tustenuggee, known as Alligator; Otee Emathlar, sense-bearer to Micanopy and called Jumper; Holartoochee, who bore his fifty years as a youth; Tigertail, Fish King, and Sam Jones, chief of the Mickasukies; here was the gathering power of the nation. The age-old ritual of the council was being flaunted and was one, now, with the blackening ashes of the fire. The old men

229

murmured weak protests. Here was the dissolution of authority, yet even as they whimpered objections, they were caught in the drama of the moment. Out of their misery and degradation a spirit was rising to shape itself. It was a thing to be regarded with awe.

"As a chief," Wildcat's voice sharpened, "I say my brother Asseola will be heard." He glanced defiantly at Micanopy, and after a moment the Pond Governor nodded and shrugged helplessly. Wildcat smiled triumphantly at Asseola and then he and the other chiefs slipped back into their places.

"For this moment," Asseola was more confident now, "we stand as free men, but this night alone will not save our people. Let the sticks in every town be counted, for if we are to fight we must have all our strength. There can be no holding back. It must be agreed that the first among us to take the white man's blanket and move westward at his orders will be killed swiftly and by our hands. Let it be a warning to the timid and faltering. If the whites wish to practice deceit and cunning we will meet it. This treaty that they hold says we will move beyond the Mississippi within three years. This time we will take, not in preparation for abandoning our homes, but to make ready for war. We cannot resist with knives and clubs. We will be quiet and obedient. We will take the annuity and with it we will buy their powder, a keg here, a pound there. We will sell our cattle and trade our skins. For these things we shall receive guns and knives, bullet metal and corn to be put aside. Our bellies may grow lean and hungry but in secret places our weapons will be fat."

At Fort King the sun burned a hole into the sky and the settlement sweltered. Sentries at the garrison gates stood listlessly at their posts, sweating and cursing in heavy uniform, staring hopefully at the mountainous piles of white clouds in the west for a sign of rain. Waves of heat rippled and raced over the sandy hillocks and drew the pitch in liquid seams from pine boards and logs.

In his office at the Indian Agency, Major John Phagan rested his booted feet on a scarred table and wiped at the sweat that trickled down his jowls and ran in sticky rivulets across his chest. He gestured with a nod of his head toward the half bottle of whisky.

"Help yourself," he offered. "It isn't cooling but after a while you forget the sun."

His visitor rejected the invitation and rose listlessly to stand by the open window. He stared thoughtfully down the deserted road and then turned to the agent.

"Where the hell are all the Indians?" he asked.

Phagan laughed with a horse croak of amusement. "They've been gone for five days now. Usually my office is stunk up with them. Right now they're probably out in the woods burning owl feathers or some other damn foolishness." He chuckled and held up thumb and forefinger, pressing them together. "We've got them like this and they know it. With the Fort Gibson treaty the government can send the whole United States Army down here to clean them out and there wouldn't be a single protest. If there's one thing the American people like it's a good treaty, particularly when it favors their side." He laughed and dropped his feet, leaning forward to reach the bottle.

When the news of the signing of a Seminole treaty at Fort Gibson was made public, land speculation in the Florida Territory spiraled to heights of frenzy. Over a period of years shrewd traders had bought up vast sections. From the timid, disgruntled, and perpetually harassed settlers they made purchases at fifty and seventy-five cents an acre. While the threat of Indian occupation hung as a dark cloud over the Territory the land had a dubious value. No man felt secure. His home, crops, and stock were at the mercy of any roving and angry group of Indians who might decide to raid him. The tide of immigration turned or halted at the border. Now a boom was on. The Seminoles were to be cleared out and the vast resources of this fertile peninsula thrown open. A man could build and plan with confidence, and the sections that had been so carelessly abandoned for a few dollars were again eagerly sought. A vast fortune was being reaped.

Phagan drank heavily and unbuttoned his shirt below the navel. He blew softly at the pink skin in an effort to cool it and cocked an eye at his companion.

"Mr. Spain," the visitor said, "wants to know what he should do. If this is the end he wants to unload."

"I wrote him," Major Phagan whined irritably.

The second man smiled. "Mr. Spain likes to get things firsthand. That's why he sent me over here. He wants to know if the Seminoles are goin' to get out without a fight. If so, this land market is at its top."

The Indian agent grinned craftily. "Some of them will leave, but," he pursed his lips thoughtfully, "there'll be enough who'll stay and make trouble. Some hell, maybe not much, no one can say for sure, is going to break out. When it does the price of land will drop right

231

through the bottom again. I'd sell now an' then buy it all back again."

The man nodded. "That's what Mr. Spain figures. He doesn't want any mistakes, though. There's got to be some shootin'."

"It'll get hot," Phagan said.

"How do you know?" the man persisted, and Phagan squirmed beneath his gaze.

"I know because I know," the agent said. "I haven't made any mistakes so far, have I?"

The agent's visitor seemed satisfied. "Mr. Spain," he said, "doesn't like men who make mistakes. He'll pay for what he gets, but he wants to be sure he's gettin' it."

"Well," Phagan took another drink, "you tell him for me the Indians will fight. We're gettin' their slaves stirred up now. They think Arkansas is somewhere deep in hell. When the time comes they are going to refuse to go and the Seminoles, the wealthy ones like Micanopy, aren't going to leave without them. They won't be able to stay without taking on the United States Army, and if that doesn't mean shooting I don't know what will."

"All right." The visitor picked up his hat. "I'll tell Mr. Spain what you said."

For several minutes after his visitor had left, the agent rocked back and forth on the hind legs of his chair. His face was creased in a smile of satisfaction. By God, if a man knew the right people, he thought, he could eat high on the hog. Yes, sir, real high, and as much as he wanted any time of day or night.

19

THROUGHOUT the long, hot days of summer, and into an October whipped by the streaking rains of a changing season, the Territory was held beneath the spell of an uneasy complacency. Why men felt insecure or shared a strange and restless foreboding none could say. It was a year of bounty. Crops had been good. Cotton was bringing twenty cents a pound in the sheds at Mobile and New Orleans. Bank balances were swollen to more than comfortable proportions and the Indians neatly caught in a treaty that would clear the peninsula of their unwelcome and disturbing presence. Andrew Jackson was firmly seated in the White House and no gathering opened or concluded without several toasts to the fiery soldier who could be counted on to deal vigorously with the stubborn Seminoles. New settlers poured across the border and there was talk of slashing a canal through the throat of Florida to link the Atlantic Ocean with the Gulf of Mexico.

On the great plantations of middle Florida, Waukeenah, Belmont, Whitehaven, El Destino, and Casa Bianca, the Territorial barons embarked on a season of lavish and glittering hospitality with costume balls, picnics, hunting parties, and horse racing. At Lipona, Achille Murat, Prince of Naples, nephew of Napoleon, lived a solitary but exuberant life in a log cabin, talked of democracy with his pet owl, and vainly tried to interest friends and visitors in the flesh of roasted buzzards as a substitute for chicken and turkey. A new spirit of decorum and gentility was abroad. In the theater at Pensacola traveling players presented *The Tragedy of Douglas, A Wife's First Lesson*, and *Fortune's Frolic* to packed houses. Literary discussions and reading societies occupied the time of the more serious-minded ladies while their husbands drank heavily and talked of crops and a growing sentiment in the North against slaveholding. During the meet the grandstands at the race track at Tallahassee, the spelling of which had been changed, were crowded with fashionably dressed ladies and gentlemen who wagered, gossiped, and flirted. Yet behind this façade of careless merriment there lurked a disquieting shade that slipped abroad at night to trouble

233

a man's slumber. Hidden deep within the swamps and tangled forests ominous shadows moved, gathered, and dissolved, and the sound of drums rose faintly. If fewer Indians were seen on the streets of St. Augustine, St. Marks, Fort King, Tallahassee, and Pensacola, the absence of the Seminoles wasn't particularly noticed. The red-skinned men were unpredictable savages, anyhow, and were undoubtedly up to some mysterious mumbo-jumbo of their own. If traders noted that their stocks of powder, caps, knives, and bullet metals were depleted by an unusually large number of small purchases, they chose to ignore the significance of the trade. The garrisons at Fort Brooke and Fort King were at full strength, and when the time came Jackson would see that sufficient troops were on hand to force an orderly evacuation.

On the plantation, Clay Hammond was in the saddle from early in the morning until late afternoon, covering the boundaries of the many acres, poking into the management of every phase of life from rice, cotton, and cane fields to the sawmill, turpentine stills, grazing cattle, warehouses, and repair depots. Often he rode with Salano, asking innumerable questions, gathering facts on production—the number of acres under cultivation, the yield of bales of cotton, hogsheads of sugar, casks of molasses, the number of board feet sawed and shipped. Slowly he began to understand something of the complex nature of the wilderness empire Old Clay had created, and the knowledge that he now had a working part in it filled him with a gratifying sense of importance. It was a good thing he had something to do. A man couldn't chase rabbits all of his life. He had to grow up sometime.

In the beginning Claire had ridden with him. Together they galloped and raced with reckless enthusiasm in the sharp morning air. She rode well, driving her mount over fence and ditch with superb handling, laughing at his caution. Sometimes they took a small lunch and picnicked along the river or deep within the cathedral-like hush of the pine forests. They idled along the edge of the rice fields, where the slaves worked in water above their ankles, walked their horses between the hills of cotton, or paused in the slave quarters to talk with the women. Once in a while they stopped by the barracks, where Old Clay's guard loafed and chafed beneath the never ending monotony and followed the eager figure of the new Mrs. Hammond with hot and covetous eyes. The presence of so many men had a stimulating effect upon the girl. Consciously she posed, lifting her head or throwing back a shoulder to accent the curve of her breasts, and her breath quickened as she sensed the feral hunger reaching out to envelop her. With maddening insolence her glance traveled over the shaggy, restless band and she wondered what it would be like to be taken by them, fought over and brutally handled, passed from man to man until exhausted. The fancy left her weak and trembling. Once, as she and Clay reined up in the compound and he lounged in the saddle talking to one of the men, she caught Jake Cutler's eyes upon her. The guard's captain was leaning against the building in a patch of sun, hands thrust into his pockets, head tilted to one side, indifferent to the honor of the visit. For a moment she imperiously tried to outstare him, but his gaze did not falter and she saw the suggestion of a crooked smile on his mouth as though he were well aware of what she had been thinking. He looked at her as he would at a desirable tavern slut and she flushed, not uncomfortably, beneath the confident swagger in his eyes. Later she caught herself wondering about him and secretly envying the young Negro wenches who came to the barracks at night.

Of late, Clay had ridden alone or with the overseer, Claire protesting drowsily when he tried to awaken her in the gray light of morning and wriggling down beneath the fluffy warmth of feather comforters.

"I've seen it all, Clay," she objected. "It isn't going to look any different today than it did last week. If it does," she smiled appealingly up at him, "you can tell me about it later."

At first he had been a little hurt, disappointed by her lack of enthusiasm. This was home and they were building a life together. He wanted her to be a part of the plantation, to see it as he did. The mornings had seemed to draw them closer together. Sometimes he worried about her, realizing how restricted her life had become. She was without companionship. Their meals with Old Clay were silent gatherings into which a social exchange of small talk did not intrude. Only when Claire had a tray sent to their rooms and he was left with his grandfather did the old man relax and drop his mask of cold indifference.

"What's the matter with you?" Clay asked once. "Don't you like Claire?"

The old man grunted. "Hell, am I supposed to like someone just because you do?"

"It isn't that," Clay protested. "You could loosen up a little, though, and open your mouth now and then for something besides a forkful of food. After all, Claire's my wife and the only grand-daughter-in-law you're likely to get."

"Maybe." Old Clay sucked at his teeth and stared at the ceiling.

The girl's presence was a constant challenge. She had spirit and intelligence. Grudgingly the old man admitted this. She hadn't knuckled down. In a way he liked her you-can-go-to-hell attitude in the face of his stubborn refusal to accept her on an equal footing. He didn't think she was any good, not good the way a woman and the wife of this grandson should be, but she wouldn't cringe. By God, if things had been different they would get on together. His leg was getting worse and shot his body with excruciating agony. Because of the pain he rarely left the house. Clay and Salano were running the plantation. It would have been pleasant to have someone to talk with, but this girl was another man's woman. She had married Clay only because the change looked like a better deal. If she had been honest with the boy he could have excused a lot, but she had tricked him. One fool in the family was more than enough. He waited grimly for some overt act, a display of authority over the household slaves, an assumption of position, that would give him an opportunity to humiliate and crush her for all time. She left no opening. Toward him her manner was coolly civil, nothing more. She ignored him. In the evenings she and Clay would play at a two-handed game of cards or she would read aloud from the stack of papers that came from New Orleans once a month. Dozing in his deep wing chair in the library he would pretend not to listen, but her voice was pleasant, and unconsciously he found himself looking forward to the arrival of the post.

"What do you mean, maybe?" Clay's words interrupted his moody speculations.

"I just mean maybe. What the hell else does it mean?"

Clay took a cigar from the box and lighted it carefully at a candle's flame. He knew his grandfather too well to pursue such a fruitless exchange.

"The next time Bartlett comes up with the sloop," he said, "I think we'll go back down the river with him. There's something I want to do in Pensacola. Maybe Claire and I'll go on to New Orleans and look around." He smiled. "I've been promising her a trip and I think she ought to get away for a while."

Old Clay nodded indifferently. "Go ahead. You've been doin' all right here. Maybe you've earned some fun."

The younger man looked up, surprised by the note of mellowness in his grandfather's voice. If he felt this way about things, this was probably as good a time as any to broach an idea he had been turning over in his mind for several weeks.

"When we get back," he said slowly, approaching the subject as warily as he would advance upon a skittish colt, "how would you feel about inviting some people over? I don't mean anyone from around Clayport," he added hastily as a scowl gathered upon the face at the end of the table. "I thought we could ask the Campbells, the Beekmans, and some others from the plantations over near Tallahassee. I don't know them but you do even if we never see them. We could have a shoot, get in some music for a ball. I guess something like that would make Claire happy, and," he grinned confidently, "it sure as hell would liven things up and not do either of us any harm. We ought to have some friends."

"I been gettin' along fine without 'em for eighty years," Old Clay snorted.

"Well, I haven't. It was all right when I was a youngster. Then it didn't make any difference. We could live like we were the only people in the Territory. Things are changing. One of these days I may have children of my own. There isn't any reason why they should grow up like wood's colts. Besides, Claire has a right to expect more than just me and this plantation. A woman isn't like a man. She needs people of her own kind around."

"Seems to me you're gettin' mighty knowledgeable about women all of a sudden." The old man smirked at his joke.

"It isn't only women," Clay pressed the discussion. "I'm beginning to find out about people, too. There's no reason for us to hole up here like a mean wolf."

Old Clay spat into his napkin. "You'll be puttin' water in your likker next," he said.

Clay grinned at him. "I discovered that isn't such a bad idea, either." Maybe the old man wasn't going to be so hard to handle after all. He was softening up a little.

"When do you figure on givin' this garden party?"

"There's no use in your pretending you don't know what I'm talking about," Clay insisted. "It isn't just a party. We're going to change things all around and stop acting as though this were a closed fortress with no one getting in or out."

Old Clay closed his eyes, feigning a sudden drowsiness. The zest for argument had left him. He was getting old, he guessed.

"Another thing," the younger man continued, and to Old Clay the words seemed to come from far away, "I figure it's about time we got rid of Jake Cutler and that gang in the barracks."

Old Clay's eyes snapped open. Having a silly party was one thing. Interfering with the plantation was another.

237

"They're always in trouble at Clayport these days," Clay continued, "fighting with the townspeople, giving us all a bad name, drawing wages every month, getting drunk and rowing among themselves. The place is running over with their yellow bastards and the Negrah stock is getting watered down."

"No one's goin' to meddle with my men," Old Clay said flatly. "For all of Andrew Jackson and the rest, we're goin' to have trouble. When it comes I don't want to have to depend on no one else."

Clay shook his head. "You can't depend on them. If there was fighting to be done they'd be the first to take to the woods, or maybe turn on you, burn and loot the place and hang you to an oak tree. I'd take Santee and half a dozen like him and lick the whole bunch before breakfast."

"Them men stay where they are. They come in handy."

"Like burning out the Rogers family?" Clay couldn't resist the opportunity.

"Yes, by God," Old Clay's angry bellow filled the house, "if that's the way you want it. Like burnin' out any damned squatter who thinks he can put his feet on my land, Indian or white. If they was to offer me the whole United States Army I'd tell 'em to go to hell. I can take care of what's mine in my own way."

Clay stubbed out the cigar, dropped it in a saucer, and rose wearily from the table. I don't guess I'll ever learn, he thought. I was easing him into the stall without so much as a nervous twitch, then I had to keep flapping my big mouth and spoil everything.

"I'm tired," he said simply.

"We got one thing in common, anyhow," the old man muttered.

"I'm going to walk around a little and then go to bed."

"You do that," Old Clay nodded, "and sleep real good, knowin' everything'll be in its place when mornin' comes."

The night air was heavy with the persistent, clinging dampness of the equinox that muffled all sound. It seemed to drip from the trees, although the rains had stopped at midday. The ground was soft beneath his feet. Next to full summer, Clay thought, he liked October and November best of all the year, and as he walked along familiar paths in the darkness he wondered how many times he had said this to himself. He could remember, as a youngster, standing beneath these same oaks, huddling against the old gray trunks for shelter from the pelting storms and listening to the low moaning of the wind as it came down from the north. Always he had been filled with a strange feeling of excitement. Up there, high among the black, racing clouds, something was happening. In the scudding smokiness of dawn, long flights of geese and ducks drove southward, and along the river there were daubs of color, bright reds of holly and Christmas berries and crisp browns in the reedy grass. It was a time for hunting, when the new cold nibbled at your cheeks like an affectionate raccoon and coveys of quail rose and sailed away like flat stones hurled from a sling. It was a season to watch at the smokehouses while the slaves hung fresh hams and long sides of bacon on heavy cords in the curling, hazy warmth of smoldering hickory. Always, it seemed, the words and subdued laughter of the black men were pitched on a different note at slaughtering, pickling, and smoking time. There was something about the sight and smell of blood and the pink-white skin of hogs when the bristles had been scalded and scraped away that agitated them. When you grew up, Clay thought, things were a little different. A man couldn't just sit on the tail of a wagon or a stump and watch Negrahs working. He had to give orders or say how something should be done; that, or go back to the house. A man didn't have half so much fun. He had to think about things and, when he had a wife, he had to think twice as hard. This business with Old Clay was an example of how complicated simple things could become. He hadn't meant to irritate the old bastard, but one thing led to another, just because he wanted to do something that would make Claire happy, and they were snarling at each other. It was a crazy thing, anyhow, to mention Sue Rogers and her brothers, because any damn fool would know it couldn't do any good now. Up until then Old Clay had acted as though he weren't going to make any trouble. They could have gone ahead, made preparations for a party, sent a couple of the boys out with invitations, and the fiddles would have been playing before his grandfather had realized what was happening. After that, little by little, he and Claire would change things. They'd visit and see people and act civilized the way other families did. Dammit, the Hammonds were one of the first white American families in the Territory. They shouldn't live like backwoods trappers.

He turned at the edge of the big road that wound across the plantation. The upper rooms of the house were dark. Claire must have gone to sleep early and the old man was either in bed or still sitting at the table. Retracing his steps, he began to wonder about Claire. They'd been married a year now. He grinned. More than a year if you took into account the few times they met on the riverbank at St. Augustine. She ought to be showing some signs of a baby. Maybe, though, it didn't always go that way. It was only when you didn't want it to happen that a girl got caught. Then all you had to do was loosen your belt buckle and somebody's belly would begin to swell. He whistled, forcing an uncertain melody between his teeth. It would be something to have a son, now while the country was pretty wild, before it was tamed. It would be like being able to do over again all of the things a kid can do. He recalled the pony Old Clay had given him and the first time he had pulled the trigger on a musket and felt it slam into his shoulder with a terrible roar. He could remember the first time he had seen the big-breasted, wild tom turkeys, scraping, bowing, and strutting before the hens on a pine ridge, and a pet squirrel he kept in his pocket with only its beady eyes and quivering tail showing. There was the first time he had entered the Seminole town with Asseola and the fright that lay in his throat. Afterward he felt as a man, confident and set apart from the other white people. The first deer you shot, the first girl you handled were things a man couldn't forget and they never were the same again, but you could take a second look through the eyes of a son.

He looked up at the house again and chuckled. "I sure can't do anything about it," he said aloud, "out here by myself."

Claire stood at the open window, the sheer linen of a nightdress molded to her by the moist wind. With a gesture of weariness she laid her forehead against the cold frame and stared helplessly out into the night. Far away a single light made a small yellow patch on the darkness. It came from the barracks and she trembled suddenly, caught in the torture of her fancy. The thing was happening as it always did and the knowledge of her weakness caused her to raise her arms, pressing her hands to the wall in an attitude of crucifixion. She squirmed in agony, thinking of Jake Cutler.

It had occurred, as she knew it must from the first moment the lazy insolence in his eyes met hers; thereafter, only time and the opportunity were needed. He had not moved from his place against the barracks walls, holding himself with a studied negligence, his glance moving over her with shrewd calculation. Without speaking he told her that he had seen the hunger on her face many times before with other women and would not be hurried.

It was strange, she thought, that she had never noticed him before. Suddenly he was there, and afterward she seemed to be encountering him constantly about the plantation. There was an ugly formality about the chance meetings that, she began to understand, was contrived. He was whipping her into submission, watching the supplication gather in her eyes. Every move he made, the effortless shifting of the lean toughness as he walked or swung from the saddle, the half-defined twist of his lips, were devices aimed at her complete surrender. If he had been eager, groping, and uncertain she would have laughed in his face. Alone, she told herself he was unkempt and common, probably unwashed and with the sharp stink of a Negro wench on his body. She was a fool; her position was precarious enough with the old man hoping for something like this to happen. The arguments were futile. Cutler was waiting. There would be no flirtation, no dignity, no pretense that she was anything but what they both knew her to be. He would not permit her the small, grace-saving sham of the plantation's mistress dallying with a hired hand. She would lie like a bawd and be grateful that the torment was stilled.

She had ridden into Clayport alone, more to escape from the house than because she needed any of the small purchases made at McCollum's. Clay was away, up the river where a gang was preparing to cut an old stand of pine, and would not be back until early evening. She had called for her horse and dressed hurriedly, a curious breathlessness catching at her, her heart pounding unaccountably.

He had been waiting, drawn to the side of the road as she came back from Clayport. She knew he would be there and understood he expected her to know it. He rested in the saddle, watching her approach, making no motion of greeting, and confidently seeing her pull out of the canter to a slow walk. When their horses were abreast he kicked his mount out into the road and dropped it into step with hers.

They rode without speaking. Now and then his leg would touch the toe of her boot at the edge of her heavy riding skirt. This, she understood, was accidental. He was not pressing her. She stared straight ahead, experiencing a gathering sensation of suffocation, and then her eyes darted wildly to either side as though she would escape. She didn't want to run. She only wanted him to say something. The brutality of his indifference was dreadful and she felt stripped of all dignity as though she were being exhibited naked on a block. With an effort she forced her eyes back to the road, lowering her head into an attitude of defeat.

A narrow footpath branched from the sandy ruts and wandered off into the dense scrub. Cutler checked his horse, forcing the animal against hers, nudging it into the path, and they rode into the concealing brush, single file, she leading the way.

He made no move to assist her to dismount but stood leaning

241

against his horse's rump, watching through slitted eyes, his face impassive. There was no strength in her. She was conscious of the warm sun and enveloping quiet. Her mouth twitched and she slid limply to the ground, waiting, now, unashamed, and his hands moved over her with rough certainty.

"Say something," she pleaded. "Speak to me. Don't you understand?"

Later, exhausted and submissive, she watched him draw away and stub with his boot toe at the loose earth, impatient to be gone. He ignored her and made no move to help her from the ground, indifferent to her crimsoning awkwardness as she adjusted her clothing. There were small bits of twigs and fragments of leaves in her hair and on her dress. She ignored them, understanding that he was grimly pleased by her confusion and delighting in her uncertainty. Now, the fury of her desire spent, she was no longer so completely at his mercy. Her oddly flecked eyes measured him. He was no different from any other man and she had been a fool to permit him to dominate the situation. She had drawn his strength and in that moment he had been as helpless as she.

Intuitively he felt her self-assurance collect and his face sharpened, a coarse laugh springing to his lips as he took a step toward her, his hand dropping with familiar presumption to her half-covered breast. She didn't pull away but a suggestion of scorn met the advance.

"I've heard about women like you," he said with a shrewd freedom. "You like to say those things, don't you? It gets you crazy to say words like that when it's happening, doesn't it? What does your husband think when you scream out those things, or can't he make you want to?"

The palm of her hand caught him full in the mouth and the shock of the blow numbed her wrist. He didn't move or raise a finger to the spot, but stood looking down into her flushed and angry face. Then he spat at her, the tobacco-stained saliva striking her cheek and stringing to the point of her lifted chin. Without a word he snatched at the bridle of his horse and mounted. Not until he was out of sight did she dare to touch a handkerchief to the indignity.

Now, as her eyes searched the night, returning over and over to the single square of illumination in the barracks, she knew she would meet Cutler again. The creeping hunger left her without pride. She wondered what he was doing and which of the black girls was sharing his sweaty pallet, and she wanted to scream, not out of anger but from frustration. The idea that she was unfaithful never entered

242

her mind. This was a thing apart. It had nothing to do with a husband or being a wife. The sickness must be assuaged.

The sound of heavy footsteps in the hall caused her to start and turn quickly from the window. She didn't want to talk with Clay at the moment. Hurriedly she re-entered her bed, sliding beneath the covers, turning her face away from the door.

She heard him enter and sensed that he paused on the threshold, his eyes adjusting themselves to the dark room. Then the door was gently closed.

"Claire?" The whispered inquiry came faintly. "Claire, are you awake?" There was an eagerness in his voice that trailed away in disappointment.

Without moving she listened as he went into the adjoining room, heard him fumbling in the bureau as he searched for a nightshirt. One by one the sounds of his undressing reached her; the dropping of a shoe, the creak of a chair as he settled himself to remove his socks, a muttered exclamation at a stubborn button. When he returned she could feel his presence in the room, knew he was standing and looking down at her. Cautiously he lowered himself to the bed and wormed himself beneath the covers. He lay with his hands locked beneath his head. The sound of his breathing was heavily regular. He was thinking about something, slowly and methodically. She could almost feel the question gathering in his mind. He moved a little, twisting his head to one side. He wanted to awaken her but hesitated.

Through half-opened eyes she stared from her burrow at the blank wall, wondering with twisted sorrow why she felt that this man beside her was a stranger. The warmth of his body reached out to her but there was no response. It's because I'm no good, she told herself. He's decent, thoughtful, and kind, and wants only to be a husband. I'm dirt for the feet of men like Cutler and belong in a Mobile crib or on the Natchez water front. She shifted uneasily.

"Are you awake, honey?" Clay bent over hopefully and then sank back into the pillows when she didn't reply. One arm reached out carefully, gathering her to him, and she murmured a sleepy protest.

In the silence, his face pressed lightly in the dark fragrance of her hair, it was easy for him to shape into unuttered words all the things he wanted to say to this girl, who, by a still bright miracle, was his wife. He wanted to lie this way and talk about children, their life together; planning for a future they would share. If she would only awaken, he thought, he would be able to speak of them aloud. In the light of day the things that would sound all right now had a foolish ring that embarrassed him into a stumbling and awkward silence. A man, he mused, ought to have had a lot of women before he married one. It took practice to be natural in their company. Either you were hot to crawl into bed with them or you were standing around, wondering what to say. There didn't seem to be any neutral ground. If you didn't secretly want to tumble a girl, then it was hard to pretend to be interested. You just couldn't be friends the way you could with a man. It had to be one thing or another.

Tomorrow he'd tell her about going to Pensacola. Planning a trip would give her something to do. After they came back he'd see about inviting some people to a party and to hell with Old Clay if he didn't like it. He wondered if he'd be able to find Sue Rogers and her brother and if they blamed him for what had happened. McCollum, at first, seemed to think he must have known about it all, known what was going to happen before he went to St. Augustine. Maybe Sue also suspected he had left for that reason. Well, she ought to know better, and if she didn't he'd tell her so. If they wanted to come back he'd stand up to Old Clay and make him let them alone. At least, he grinned in the darkness thinking of what a knockout battle it would be, he'd try.

For no particular reason he suddenly found himself thinking of Asseola. Perhaps it was the season; the melancholy hunting of the wind outside, the memory of other years shared and spent. You couldn't grow up with someone and have him drop out of your life without leaving a vacancy. I wonder, he pondered, where that child is. Save for the moment over a year ago when he had handed his rifle to Clay at the patgoe shooting there had been no word or sight of him. Maybe, and the idea amused him, the Indian had married the girl he had spoken about and disappeared with her into the woods. It was funny to think about Asseola having a wife and perhaps children who tagged along behind, clinging to his leggings. Indians always seemed to have children right away. At their wedding ceremonies the bride handed her groom a small cake of baked corn meal. "I," she said solemnly, "will furnish the bread." The man then gave his woman a strip of venison or a piece of rabbit flesh. "I," he declared, "will furnish the meat." After that they settled down to the business of having kids and they popped out the way a melon seed would that you'd squeezed between your fingers.

Just before he dropped off to sleep he decided to write a letter to Colonel Humphreys. Maybe he was still living at Fort King even though they had booted him out as agent. He might know what had happened to Asseola. It was a good idea, anyhow.

20

Pensacola was flung like a soiled and rumpled cloth at the edge of a shining bay. It was an unlovely town, bleached and weathered, backed by stretches of glaring white sand in which the scraggly oaks, clumps of sea myrtle, and twisted pines struggled for existence. Flanked by ancient buildings, its narrow streets were contested for daily by pedestrians, carts, horsemen, and a roving assortment of amiable pigs, goats, chickens, and dogs. In its inhabitants the blood of Spaniard and Frenchman, Negro and Indian, Creole and Englishman was brewed into a scummy broth. The town had withstood war, hurricanes, and pestilence. Through its crowded lanes the yellow fever had burned, withering the population to less than a hundred persons who sweated in steaming terror. The years, though, had buried the misery and the stench had long since been blown away by the sea's fresh winds. New blood was pumped into the community. Congress established a navy yard on the sun-swept point. Seamen and carpenters, shipwrights and metal workers, adventurers and thugs moved upon the old town. Coastal maritime commerce boomed the port, and the harbor was studded with the masts of many nations. It was a wild and open community, made dangerous and noisy by tavern and street fighting. Painted strumpets sat on small stools before their narrow cribs or leaned across the half doors of the establishments, their naked breasts exposed invitingly. Gamblers flourished on every corner and a hand could be turned to murder for a trifling piece of silver. Alternately wracked by the storms of winter and seared by the almost intolerable heat of summer, Pensacola was a shrill and raucous dive of many tongues and passions.

From the balconied windows of their rooms at the Collins House, Clay looked down upon the leaden waters of the bay and beyond, past the broken line of Santa Rosa Island, to the blue freshness of the Gulf. He moved restlessly from the opening, stalking about the parlor, halting to flip absently through a stack of newspapers and periodicals they had brought back with them from New Orleans. From a wicker chaise longue Claire glanced up now and then, following his prowling with an understanding smile. He was as unhappy as a cat in strange surroundings, anxious to be home.

The room was cluttered with boxes and small bales from which colored paper ribbons, silks, and laces foamed. Gay slippers rested in pairs on tables and chairs. New frocks hung stiffly from supports on walls and doors. Claire was reluctant to repack her extravagant purchases and send them to the dark hold of the sloop. Not without argument had Clay consented to go on to New Orleans. After a long trip down the Apalachicola and a rough voyage along the Gulf shore to Pensacola he was ready to turn around and go home. Only after a well-timed and tearful exhibition had Claire won his grudging consent. He had booked passage for them aboard a coastal vessel, arranging to rejoin Bartlett and the sloop at Pensacola in a month. Now they were back from the Louisiana metropolis and he could barely contain his impatience for the sailing hour tomorrow. Claire thought of the plantation and Clayport, sighing regretfully over the memory of New Orleans. The time had been too short and she had wanted to gather the frothy gaiety of the Creole city in her hands, to be held and treasured. Her eyes sparkled as she thought of the cafés, music halls, restaurants, and theaters. They had laughed, danced, and made love, borne aloft by sparkling champagne bubbles. They had eaten strange foods, sampled shrimps, crabs, and gumboes at the market stalls and breakfasted in an open carriage on coffee and flaky brioches, their eyes and ears enchanted by the colorful scene. Clay had been more than generous and she had shopped and made purchases with prodigal disregard for expense. Once again she had known the excitement of having men look upon her with smoldering eyes and caught the frankly envious glances of their women. In this carefully tended hothouse of dazzling artificiality she had bloomed as a rare and exotic flower. The days and nights had brought a fresh breath of life, and she wondered helplessly if and when she should ever enjoy their like again. She awaited their return to the plantation with the despairing resignation of a condemned person.

Clay stood irresolutely in the middle of the room, staring down at the floor, and he kicked lightly at the carpet's flowered design as though he would eventually uncover what his mind was seeking.

"Why don't you go and see her?" Claire asked with lazy good humor.

He looked up quickly and assumed the innocent surprise of a boy caught among the jam pots. She dangled a slipper from a bare toe, turning deliberately so that the sheer and daring negligee she wore dropped away, exposing the white nakedness of one leg.

"Who?" He flushed and pretended not to know what she was talking about.

"It is fortunate, sir," she laughed at him, "that you do not earn our living as an actor. You pretend so badly. Why don't you go and see this girl, Rogers, or whatever her name is? Isn't that what troubles you?"

He was unprepared for this direct assault upon his secret thoughts and for a moment seemed to be on the point of denying her light challenge.

"Certainly," Claire continued with a smile, "you must think me a dolt indeed, if after all the talking you have done about this Miss Rogers and her brother I shouldn't expect you to call upon them or her."

"Oh!" Clay grinned. "It was just an idea I had. I sort of felt I ought to try to do something. After all, Old Clay had them run out. Anyhow, I don't know where they live."

Claire yawned prettily. "I should imagine you could find her by exercising a certain amount of diligence. Pensacola," her nose wrinkled, "isn't so large that one could easily become lost."

"Well, maybe." He seemed to agree reluctantly. "You're sure you wouldn't mind? I mean," he suggested reluctantly, "would you like to come along?"

"Thank you, sir." She was amused. "I prefer not to see you smothering in the faded rose petals of an adolescent passion."

"You know it isn't anything like that." He was sheepishly pleased by the suggestion.

"Whatever the reason," Claire was graciously indulgent, "your devotion to a childhood sweetheart is a personal matter. Let us leave it so. I anticipate nothing more than a light mental infidelity." Her smile faded and she stretched out her fingers, taking his with a quick gesture of tenderness. "I'm only joking. Do whatever you think you should."

"Well," he hesitated, "I ought to see Captain Bartlett about to-morrow. Besides," he twisted his shoulders, "I get all cramped up in these hotel rooms."

Claire nodded understandingly. "And after you see Bartlett, what should be more natural than for you to stroll about the town? If, by the merest chance, of course, you should pass the home of Miss Rogers . . ." She lifted her hands, accepting the mysterious workings of fate.

"You know," his hand touched the side of her face, "I have an idea you'd like to have me get tangled up with another woman just to see me come running back."

Her teeth nipped at his fingers. "Somehow, I just don't see you in the role of a philandering husband."

Impulsively he bent down and kissed her, marveling as ever that this warm beauty was his. She moved with the soft ripple of a sunning animal.

"You make it sound like you'd like to have me try." He spoke with difficulty.

"You'd better go now," her mouth was on his ear, "or I'll change my mind."

"Hell," he drew away, "I don't want to now and you know it."

"I'll take a nap and be here when you come back. Get on with your intrigue."

He found the Rogers house without difficulty. It was a small frame cottage in the town's newer section and set back from the road at the end of a phlox-bordered path. As he touched the gate latch Clay glanced along the low, neat picket fence. Yankees, he thought, couldn't be happy unless they brought something of their native states with them. A white picket fence in Pensacola was as startling as a palm tree would be in Maine. In a town where all the new buildings carried balconies and small porches to catch the sea breezes the Rogers house was foreign. It looked like something out of the pictures he had seen of the northern countryside. Walking slowly up the path of crushed shell he noted the stiff white curtains in the trim windows. Unhappily he caught himself wondering what had happened to the red and white checked material she had bought for the cabin on the Apalachicola.

Almost as his hand reached out for the knocker the door was opened. Sue stood in the opening, the cool dimness of the hall a deep shadow behind her. With an unconscious and involuntary motion she touched at her throat with her fingers, as though to stifle an exclamation of surprise. For a moment they stared at each other.

"I saw you from the window." Her voice was shaky and she needlessly explained her presence at the door. "It had to be you, and yet I couldn't believe it."

"Hello, Sue." It was a hell of a stupid thing to say. He was ill at ease, suddenly made uncomfortable by the moment and the knowledge of what lay between them.

She smiled understandingly. "Hello, Clay."

"I was in Pensacola." He stated the obvious and she didn't laugh.

"Come in, Clay." She moved to one side, holding the door as he entered. "I used to wonder if I'd ever see you again." The door closed behind them. "Come into the sitting room. I'm glad you came." She was talking rapidly, trying to cover her nervousness.

The room into which she led him was small and almost primly furnished. Its spindly, uncomfortable-appearing chairs looked as though they were not meant for use. Crisp hand-worked doilies were exactly centered on small tables. From the walls a series of forbidding family portraits stared down coldly from heavy mahogany frames. Window shades were drawn to keep out the sun and the room was hushed and cool. On a mantel a squat clock counted off the seconds with austere regularity. Clay looked around; he had never seen a room like this before. It was chilling and he felt that when he spoke he should lower his voice to a hushed and respectful whisper. Gingerly he sat at the end of a curving sofa, the black walnut frame slickly upholstered in shining horsehair fabric.

Sue caught his glance of inspection and smiled easily for the first time. "New Englanders use the parlor only for special occasions. It's ugly, I know, but Hadley likes it this way. It reminds him of Providence. Would you rather sit in the kitchen?"

"This is fine." Clay dropped one arm over the sofa's back, feeling the spiny prickles of the hair with his fingers. He was wishing he hadn't come. Now that he was here there didn't seem to be much to say.

Sue took a place at the opposite end of the sofa. Her eyes were on her hands, resting in her lap. She sighed.

"I'm glad you came, Clay. It isn't easy, is it?"

"No," he replied slowly. "I don't suppose I thought it would be."

"It all seems so long ago." Her eyes lifted to meet his.

"When I got back," he forced the words, "McCollum told me where you had gone, what had happened. I went up to the bend and saw for myself." He moved uncomfortably.

Her eyes softened. "If you're trying to tell me that you didn't know what was going to happen," she paused, "you don't have to."

"I hoped you would believe that." He was grateful. "I wanted to be sure. Somehow, it was important. It's really the reason I came down here to Pensacola."

"Mr. McCollum—" She hesitated and the sound of the clock was crisp and hard. "He—he told you about Will?"

"Old Clay had him killed." It was easier to say right out what they were thinking. "I didn't believe it at first but I guess it's so."

"That's the part I don't understand." Her fingers picked at her dress. "It wasn't necessary. We were going. The three of us talked

249

it over. Hadley wanted to take the matter to a court. There wasn't much fight left in us. All of that work for nothing, and then Will."

"Would you come back?" He had to say something, afraid she was going to cry. Even as he spoke he wondered what he could do if she said yes.

She shook her head with a wistful smile. "No, Clay. I know what you mean. I don't think Hadley or I would want to start over again without Will. We're settled here. Hadley has a good position in the navy yard. He has even stopped talking about home. I don't think he could bring himself to leave Will here alone."

"Does Hadley think . . ." He couldn't finish the question.

"He never said anything about it, Clay."

"I'd do anything I could, Sue." He was miserably conscious of his inadequacy. "You know—well, you know how I feel about you."

She laughed then, the clear beauty of her features lighting unexpectedly. This, he thought, was the way she had looked and acted when they first met.

"No," she said, and amusement danced along her lips, "I never did know how you felt. You went away without making your intentions clear, sir."

"You don't," he said gravely, "always have to say those things." Even as he spoke it occurred to him that this wasn't the way a married man should talk to a girl.

"I suppose not," Sue agreed softly. Her glance lingered on his face. There was a new maturity in it. "You've changed, Clay," she finally said. "It isn't just the difference of a year or so. It's something inside. You're a great deal older than when you went away. Tell me," she leaned back, "did you see the world?" She made it sound as though it were an intimate joke that they alone shared.

"No." He laughed with her. "I guess I sort of ran into the end of it at St. Augustine. That's as far as I got."

"Hardly a Gulliver, were you?" She met his eyes, smiling companionably. "What made you call off your travels?"

"St. Augustine took me far enough. I . . ." He paused and wondered at his reluctance to tell her about Claire. "I met a girl there."

"Oh?" She waited.

"I—we—I'm married." He rushed the statement.

The clock made the only sound in the room. Sue laced her fingers together, studying the pattern, unwilling to trust her voice for a moment. How close, she thought miserably, she had come to a complete betrayal of her feelings as he stood in the doorway a few minutes ago! Even so, had he cared to look or had he been wiser he might have seen what was in her face.

"I hope you are happy, Clay." She would not say she was glad.

"Why do you suppose," he was honestly puzzled, "I didn't want to tell you?"

"I'm not certain," she made no attempt to hold back a smile, "but I would like to think I know. The vanity of a woman, Clay, is a strange and incorrigible trait."

"It happened sort of suddenly," he said thoughtfully, as though he felt it his duty to offer an explanation.

"Not entirely without precedent, however." She had to laugh at his seriousness. "Tell me," leading away from the subject, "when do you return to Clayport?"

"Tomorrow."

She rose. "Can I fix you something? I'll make some tea, or would you rather have a drink? Hadley is partial to Medford rum."

"No." He stood beside her. They were strangers or, at the most, casual acquaintances. "No," he repeated, "I guess I had better be going."

Without a word she waited as he took his hat and then led the way to the front door. There should have been so much to say, yet the words dribbled away without substance.

"I'm glad you came." She held the door open. "I'll tell Hadley. He liked you."

"This is a hell of a way to say good-by to you, Sue." He was angry with himself. "Maybe I shouldn't have come."

"I'm glad you did." Swiftly she rose on tiptoes and her lips brushed his cheek as he bent toward her. For a moment her hands rested on his arms and then she drew away with a nervous laugh. "I might have picked a less conspicuous place for that," she said, "but then, I didn't know it was going to happen. Good-by, Clay."

The door closed behind her and he stood for a moment staring at the gleaming brass knocker, tempted to seize it and call her back. Then he turned and faced down the path. She probably wouldn't have answered.

Along the water front the sun was as sharp and bright as a hot new penny. He walked without purpose, delaying his return to the Collins House. Gulls screamed and fought over small fish, and on rotted pilings the solemn pelicans nodded and blinked at this display of energy. Nets dried on heavy racks and there was the sharp scent of salty muck in the air. Clay found himself thinking of St. Au-

251

gustine, wondering what might have happened if he had gone on north instead of tarrying.

Without actually wanting a drink, he turned into a dingy tavern. The short bar was crowded. Swarthy, gesturing seamen from Cuba and Spain stood shoulder to shoulder with American and English sailors. Here and there a fringed buckskin jacket and flapping soiled leggings marked the wearer as an outlander who had strayed into the port town. The air was foul and filled with the sound of many tongues. As Clay searched for a place among the standing men an old crone hobbled to his side, fingering the cloth of his suit with an appreciative touch.

"Meester want a nice little girl?" she wheedled. "Young, clean, smart?" She nodded toward the back of the room where a half-dozen skinny, unwashed, sad-eyed whores huddled like wet chicks.

He shook his head and stilled the imprecations springing to her lips with a coin. Mumbling her disappointment the hag backed away and spat in the direction of her unenthusiastic charges. They regarded her without a change of expression, too weary to care that their appearance did not please.

Clay found an opening and ordered. He watered the heavy Barbados rum and swallowed slowly, tasting the thick, biting flavor of molasses in the heady liquor. As his eyes became accustomed to the half-light he began picking out individual faces among his companions at the bar. They were acid-etched in villainy, scarred and pocked with sly brutality. Clay wondered idly what uneasy bunks the masters of their ships must occupy with this scum in the forecastles.

He ordered another drink, already feeling better. Now and then he caught a glance of speculative cunning turned his way and understood that the contents of his pockets were being silently appraised. One voice, louder than the others, lifted above the senseless babble of the gutter. Its owner, one of the buckskin-clad men, thumped a cup on the bar.

"I'll tell you," he said to the man at his side, "there ain't no use goin' in to trade with the Indians no more unless you carry powder an' shot. It ain't like it used to be when you could pick up a bale of skins or plumes for a few yards of calico or a sack of beads. They'll trade, if you can find 'em," he added significantly, "but only for powder, guns, knives, or bullet metal. You ask me what's happenin' an' that's what I tell you." He buried his face into the replenished mug.

"When do you figure to pack in again?"

252

The first speaker wiped at his mouth with the back of a hand and then drew a finger across his throat.

"When I want to get this cut," he said. "It used to be that the Seminoles only killed when you stole somethin' from them or rutted in among their women. Now, by God," and there was outraged virtue in his voice, "they just cut you down for the hell of it. They're stirred up like smoked-out bees. It ain't the old ones who are makin' the trouble but the young ones led by niggers like Wildcat an' Osceola—Powell, some call him. I heard he's half white, but by God, he looks an' acts like pure Indian and thinks like a white man. I hear, an' more'n likely it's true, they got an underground storehouse stocked to the ceiling with powder an' shot."

"Well," his companion nodded sagely, "it ain't no skin offen my ass."

The other man laughed heartily. "It sure as hell will be if you get caught out there with your pants down." He breathed a gusty sigh of regret. "If I could lay my hands on a wagonload of powder I could do enough trade to make myself a rich man. Every dollar of bounty the government gives them red bastards they spend for powder. I'll leave it to you to guess what they're storin' it up for."

Clay leaned over the bar to catch the speaker's attention. "Did you see this Asseola?" he asked.

The backwoodsman glanced up, his eyes traveling shrewdly over Clay. There was a suggestion of suspicion on his features as though he wondered what had brought him into this water-front dive.

"Yep," he said after a moment, "I saw him. Friend of yours?" He added sarcastically and nudged his companion.

"Matter of fact," Clay replied evenly, "he is."

The trader whistled skeptically. "You're likely to lose a friend then, mister. The army's about ready to hang him." He chuckled. "Course, they got to catch him first."

"Have a drink with me?" Clay jerked his head in the direction of the bartender and moved down to wedge himself in alongside the pair.

The men gulped their raw whisky and were silent, waiting for him to speak. After their mugs had been refilled Clay took a full swallow of his rum.

"Where did you see him?" he asked.

"Fort King. They had him in jail for a couple of days, said he'd shot another Indian down in cold blood. Fellow by the name of Charley Emathlar. It seems like this Emathlar sold his cattle an' was gettin' ready to move out to Arkansas. Funny thing, too. I heard

253

that Emathlar had a lot of money in his pockets, what he got for his cattle. Not a penny of it was touched. They never could prove this Osceola done the shootin' an' finally let him go."

"What happened then?" Clay finished his rum.

The man brushed the palms of his hands together. "Gone like that," he said, and eyed Clay with awakening interest. "You were jokin', weren't you, when you said he was a friend?"

"No," Clay replied. "We grew up together on the Apalachicola. Drink up."

"Well," the woodsman said, "you'll find him some changed. From what I hear there ain't nothin' this Osceola hates so much right now as a white man."

"What's happening in the interior?"

The two men laughed simultaneously and without mirth. "It's stewin'," one replied, "like a kettle about to boil over. I wouldn't set a foot below the Suwannee unless I wanted it chopped off."

Clay paid his bill. "Thanks," he said shortly, and turned away. The men looked after him as he walked toward the open doorway.

Outside, he strolled leisurely in the direction of the Collins House. That child Asseola, he thought, must be getting himself pretty well known if his name was being passed about way down here in Pensacola. He shook his head. It was still hard for him to think of him as a bad Indian. They'd get him at the end of a rope sure as hell.

He chuckled suddenly and for no particular reason. The idea of that grave-eyed Indian twisting the tail of the United States Army somehow seemed funny. He began to feel better. Maybe it was the rum. He cocked an eye at the high blue sky and began to whistle.

Moored in close to shore he found Bartlett's sloop. The craft was trim and sturdy. More than that, it represented the link with home. Bartlett came out on deck and Clay hailed him.

"Will we get away in the morning, Captain?"

Bartlett glanced across the brief span of water, shading his eyes with both hands. "Oh, Mr. Hammond," he replied. "Yep, if the weather holds. Anxious to leave?"

Clay nodded and laughed. "I've been ready to go back ever since we started."

"I don't blame you." Bartlett pinched his nose with an expressive gesture. "It's a stinkin' hole for fair."

"We'll be on hand in the morning. If you change your mind about sailing, send someone to the hotel and let us know."

Bartlett tossed a brief salute. "Want to come aboard now?"

Clay hesitated and then shook his head. "Not now." He moved along the sandy street. Then he laughed. A block or so away was the Collins House. A man with a pretty wife who was waiting for him in black lace French underwear had something better to do than sit on the deck of a boat.

21

FROM a corner of the porch Claire Hammond saw the first of the carriages they were expecting this day as it turned in at the far end of the plantation road. Excitedly she called the news to Clay and then turned to fix shining eyes upon the swaying dot and the small dusty cloud rising from its wheels.

All morning she had been in a state of nervous, dancing apprehension for fear something would happen to mar the event. A half-dozen times she had raced upstairs to change her frock or re-examine her hair, twirling before the mirror, pouting at her reflection, reducing the hapless slave girl to a twitching state of nerves. Now, as she saw the approaching coach with the first of their guests, she experienced a moment of panic.

Without consulting the old man Clay had sent a white foreman and two of the Negro boys on a round of the plantations beyond Clayport as far west as Tallahassee. He knew the families by name only and addressed them on behalf of Old Clay, inviting them to the gathering. For weeks the preparations had gone steadily ahead. Rooms long dark and unused had been thrown open and subjected to frenzied scrubbing and polishing. In an oak grove the barbecue pits were deep and waiting. Two coaches had been sent to St. Augustine to fetch the musicians. Floors were waxed and ready for dancing. The house sparkled, gay with flowers and greenery. The kitchen was a confused scene of hushed activity, the household slaves white-eyed and proudly self-conscious in their new livery, cut and sewn by two tailors and their assistants who had been brought up the river.

Old Clay was indifferent to the charged air of excitement that hung over the plantation. At first he pretended not to notice anything unusual. Then, after Clay had told him about the party, he bluntly announced his intention of ignoring the affair and such damn fools as elected to come. To these rumblings of dissatisfaction Clay was serenely indifferent. They would have a party and the old man could come or stay away, whichever he preferred.

Joining Claire on the porch now, Clay took her arm and smiled at her straining excitement. By God, he thought proudly, there isn't a prettier woman in the Territory. It made him feel good just to stand by her side this way.

"See." She pointed at the approaching vehicle. "Oh, Clay!" She clung to him. "I'm frightened."

"Honey," he tried to quiet her, "they're only people. They're just coming for some fun."

She looked up at him, her eyes troubled and deeply shadowed. "I know," she said, "I know they're only people, but their being here is important to—to me. To Mrs. Clayfield Hammond."

He understood what she meant. Old Clay had not yielded her an inch. She meant to show him, standing before their guests as mistress of the Hammond plantation, that he had lost.

"I'll tell you a secret." He bent down confidentially. "I think you're the most beautiful woman in Florida today."

"And how was I yesterday, sir?"

"Passable." His arm encircled her slim waist. "There's an almost daily improvement."

He was proud of her, proud and happy in the reflection of her beauty. The past year and a half hadn't been easy for either of them. He had had to fight his way slowly past Old Clay's will to achieve an identity of his own. In this small world that for so long had revolved around his grandfather, he had been forced to grow up quickly or not at all. He had come home not as a man with a wife but as a boy leading a new and timid playmate by the hand. Had he not rebelled against the plantation's resistance to change, both it and Old Clay would have absorbed him. He had asserted authority and saw the old ways yield slowly. Standing beside his wife now, he felt somehow that this day marked their independence and the beginning of a new, full life. Unconsciously his arm tightened. He wanted to draw her close, sharing the moment.

As the approaching coach swung into the oak-bordered drive the bright yellow and crimson paint glittered with a magnificent display of pomp and the coachman's long whip snaked out with a lashing report.

"That's Jamie," Clay shouted. Actually, he hadn't expected his friend to make the long journey overland. "No one but James Beulow would ride in a rig like that."

The coach whirled up before the house and two stableboys sprang out to reach for the tossing heads of the lathered horses. A household Negro hurried down the steps to open the door. Before his hand could touch the handle Beulow's handsome head was thrust out of the window.

"Let the minstrels sound in the galleries," he called. "Smite the lyre. I have arrived."

With an impudent grin and superior self-assurance he mounted the broad steps and swept an exaggeratedly low bow to Claire, bending over her hand to touch it with his lips.

"Madame, you are far too cozy a lass for this peasant hind. I have come to relieve the tedium of your backwoods penance. Where," he glanced about, "are our companions in merriment?"

"You're the first." Clay clapped his shoulder affectionately.

"Then," Beulow linked his arms with theirs, "we shall bar the doors and force the tardy to press their noses against the panes while we cavort." He dropped a keen glance upon Claire. "There is a milkmaid's flush upon your cheeks, madame. The country air does you good."

"I am surprised, sir," she said, "that you recognize a blush, since you must encounter one so rarely."

Beulow laughed. "Exile has sharpened both your wit and your tongue, madame. I am mortally wounded yet suffer not."

Arm in arm they mounted the steps, swept along by the flood of nonsensical chatter. Beulow was as effervescent as an exploded bottle of champagne. Words, meaningless but gay, flowed from him in an effortless torrent. Neither Clay nor Claire had an opportunity to interrupt; their guest was blandly unconscious of his almost overpowering personality. With an inward grin Clay wondered what the old man would think of him at their first meeting.

They halted on the porch and Beulow turned to look out over the plantation. "It has," he admitted, "a rugged charm, although the spectacle of armed lackeys on towers and at the gates must disconcert the casual visitor."

"I didn't think you would come," Clay admitted.

Beulow dusted at his sleeve. "I was bored, old cock. St. Augustine grew pallid following your departure. I bring you both," he continued happily, "the ill wishes of John Spain, Esquire. A surly fellow who stews in his bile."

Claire flushed. The sarcasm was unnecessary. As always, she found herself uncomfortable in Beulow's presence, and yet, perversely enough, she was stirred and stimulated by the touch of his fingers as they rested lightly on her arm.

"Your manners, Mr. Beulow," she looked squarely at him, "wear well, losing none of their insolence." Curiously enough, there was no sting in her words, and she smiled.

What reply the visitor might have made was interrupted as the central doors were swung open and Old Clay, his chair supported by Santee and two other slaves, was brought out. The old man hadn't been moved by the occasion to change his habitual attire. He was coatless, the shirt open low at the throat. His gray hair was, Clay was certain, in a deliberately tousled state and he was unshaven. He ignored the group before him, holding firmly to the chair's sides as he was carried past and to his customary place.

Beulow's eyes lighted at the spectacle. "Gad," he said audibly, "a Nero not yet come to the baths." He whistled a long note of appreciation.

They could hear Old Clay grunt as his chair was lightly settled, but whether the sound came from the discomfort of his leg or Beulow's words they could not tell. Clay nudged his guest.

"Come along. We'd better get this over with."

The old man didn't look up until they stood before him, and then his eyes moved slowly from the tip of Beulow's boots to the top of his head. The thick underlip jutted in an expression of annoyance.

"I want to present my friend James Beulow." Clay performed the introduction.

"Charmed, sir, and your servant." Beulow was enjoying himself. His eyes sparkled and he seemed to be balancing lightly on the balls of his feet as a boxer.

Old Clay blew soundlessly over his projecting lips. "Heard about you," he finally said, "from Clay. Met your father once, years ago, and didn't like him worth a damn." His ungraciousness was heavily calculated.

Beulow appeared to find nothing offensive in the words. Instead, he seemed pleased. He bowed and there was restrained amusement in his manner.

"I am enchanted, sir," he replied. "Unintentionally, you have endeared yourself to me beyond all measure. I, also, found my parent's sanctimonious penury abhorrent and have done my best to erase the memory of it."

Old Clay grunted but somewhere within the sagging folds of his face a smile formed and vanished. He relaxed visibly. This swaggering coxcomb pleased and amused him.

"If it ain't too early for a drink?" He made the suggestion to Beulow alone.

"Sir," the guest answered quickly, "that hour has not yet been calculated."

Claire excused herself. She wanted another look in the mirror. Beulow's arrival lent a piquancy to the morning. She could feel his magnetism touching them all. For the twentieth time she changed her mind over what she would wear that night. Before the long mirror she touched at her hair with perfume and smoothed the bodice of her dress, pressing the fabric around her breasts until they were in bold and provocative relief. She found pleasure in the sensation of her body beneath her hands and there was a sensual caress in her fingers as they lingered over the firm mounds. Her eyes closed and she drew a single sharp and almost painful breath. Through the open window from below came the sound of Beulow's mocking laughter and she caught herself listening intently. He was a twisting, beckoning flame, touching her as no other man ever had. In his presence she knew a strange and exciting fear; she tried to hide it from herself and others by a pretense of indifference, but the deception was shallow. Yet he remained banteringly aloof, examining her from a distance as a particularly interesting specimen that, at his leisure, he might someday add to an already large collection.

When she rejoined the three men they were already mellowing under the influence of several drinks. Clay lounged on the porch, his back against a pillar. The old man had thawed, Beulow having achieved this major miracle through a lazy impudence that ignored his host's initial testiness.

"So you see, sir," he said, rising at Claire's approach, "we must share the distinction. While you may justly lay claim to being the most heartily disliked man in middle Florida, I am equally loathed on the east coast. In a measure my triumph is greater since the population there is larger."

Clay sprang up at the sight of Claire and took her hand.

"I've ordered a rig," he said. "I thought we might drive Jamie over the plantation. It's still early." He answered her hesitation. "We'll be back before any of the others arrive. Come along."

Old Clay emitted a series of half-intelligible grunts, the gist of which seemed to be an announcement that he was considering the advisability of changing into a more suitable costume for the reception of their guests. Clay exchanged a quick wink with Beulow, wondering if he realized the magnitude of the concession.

In the open phaeton, Claire seated between them, they drove over the plantation. Now that he took an active part in the direction of the vast establishment Clay couldn't keep a note of pride from his voice as he pointed out various sections and activities to the visitor. Claire secretly considered the ride a dull but unavoidable interlude. However, the narrow seat wedged her against the thighs of both men and she leaned back, a small parasol shading her face, and felt herself pleasantly suffocated in maleness. Oddly enough, and she was a little surprised by the discovery, Beulow dropped his studied attitude of foppish negligence. His questions concerning various workings of the estate were incisive, interested, and intelligent. He spent several minutes inspecting a new set of flood-control gates for the rice fields, oblivious of the mud that smeared his varnished boots and stained the gray fabric of his elegant trousers. This was a new facet of a complex character she made no attempt to understand.

They stopped at the barracks, driving into the hard-packed compound, and Beulow listened incredulously to Clay's explanation, his eyes traveling over half a dozen of the men, who drew themselves up in attitudes of uneasy attention.

"Do you mean to say, cock," he asked, "that your saintly grandparent keeps this vulture offal around solely for the purpose of potting stray and belligerent Indians?"

Clay answered with a short, mirthless laugh. "That and whatever else bothers him. He weeds them out when they get too old and finds new ones."

Beulow whistled. "I should hate to have them at my back in the event of trouble."

"I've tried to tell Old Clay that," Clay agreed, "but he won't listen."

As the coachman turned the light rig a horseman trotted into the square, the horse's hoofs striking sharply on the sun-baked earth.

"Mornin', Mr. Hammond." Jake Cutler touched at the splintered edge of a palm-leaf hat. The gesture was without deference; the man somehow managed to shade it precariously close to burlesque. "Mornin', Mrs. Hammond."

Claire didn't dare ignore the greeting. Reluctantly she tilted back the parasol and nodded. Cutler's eyes lingered on her for a moment and in his glance there was the silent intensity of a summer lightning flash.

"Morning, Cutler." Clay's reply was short. He could not say why he disliked this man.

Cutler leaned forward, resting crossed arms on the pommel of his saddle. "Anything I can do for you?" he asked.

261

Clay shook his head and spoke to the coachman. "No, thanks."

As they rolled away Claire could feel Cutler's taunting gaze following them. He had good reason to be smugly amused. She felt her cheeks burning and lowered her head to hide the flush. An uncomfortable silence settled upon them and she sensed, rather than saw, Beulow's lightly quizzical alertness.

"Never could bring myself to like that fellow." Clay seemed to be speaking to himself and neither Claire nor Beulow made reply.

Clay left them alone in the phaeton for a moment as he went into the overseer's house to speak with Salano. Beulow's fingers tapped lightly on his knee. She could feel his thoughts gathering.

"You amuse yourself with the hired hands, madame?" he reflected.

She could not dismiss the words. "I don't understand you, sir."

He was humming softly. "I think you do, madame. Having played many times at the game of cuckolding, I am sensitive to its design."

She could not force herself to meet his eyes. A helpless anger tore at her but her lips were dumb. A protestation of innocence would only amuse him and that satisfaction he should not have.

"I am no champion of virtue, madame," he continued almost absently, "nor would I ordinarily spring to the defense of a friend's honor, having sufficient difficulty with my own. I suggest, however, that you take immediate steps to extricate yourself from this situation. I am fond of Clay, and while I would not hesitate to use you for my own purposes, I will not stand by and see him soiled by such a mangy dog."

She turned her eyes toward his face. "Your scruples, sir, are as difficult to understand as your words."

He shook his head. "Do not attempt to match wits with me, Mrs. Hammond. I outreach you."

Clay's return put an end to the sparring. He took his place beside Claire. He was cheerfully ebullient again.

"That Spaniard," he jerked his head in the direction of Salano's house, "doesn't like the idea of coming to heel. I think he had an idea he would take over things as Old Clay grew older. I'll surprise the hell out of him one of these days by booting him off the plantation. Now," he turned to Beulow, "let's take up that drinking we interrupted."

The morning wore slowly to noon and yet there were no other guests. As the day lengthened Clay no longer made an attempt to hide his concern. He sent for the white foreman who had accompanied the two slaves on their rounds of the plantations, pressing him for details. The invitations had been delivered. There had been no mistakes, the missives having been handed at the front doors. The man was certain of this. Clay shook his head.

"I can't figure it out," he muttered, sick with a gnawing feeling of helpless disappointment. "Maybe some couldn't get here, but that wouldn't happen to them all." He turned to stare hopefully at the long and empty road.

Old Clay brooded silently in his chair. He understood. With malicious satisfaction he chewed on the sour cud of knowledge and a bitter fury took root and flowered. No one had come, save this popinjay from St. Augustine. No one had come and they could wait a hundred years without seeing the wheel of a guest's carriage turning on the highway. Ever since Clay told him about the invitations he had been waiting for this day. No decent family would set foot in the house where John Spain's trull had the effrontery to call herself mistress. Call her Mrs. Clayfield Hammond! Call her whore! Her flight from John Spain's bed would have been common knowledge, a subject for titillating gossip on every plantation in the Territory, a week after it had happened. He felt no pity for his grandson. If the young fool didn't begin to understand now what he had done, then he never would until his face was rubbed in the dirt. His mouth twisted into a snarling, mirthless grin. This would be something to watch. She'd have to crawl a little now. He finished the drink in his glass and lowered his eyelids against the afternoon's sun.

A feeling of uneasy constraint crept through the big house. The two young stableboys crouched in the bushes on either side of the steps, waiting like peeping monkeys for a coach or carriage. The early, cheerful bustle in the kitchen had died and the women moved from block and table with silent perplexity. When they spoke they dropped their voices to a troubled whisper. The other servants shuffled unhappily, their air of expectancy changing to a curious listlessness. Something had happened. They didn't exactly understand what had gone wrong, but their uneasiness communicated itself. A pall settled over the halls and the black men and women darted quick and perplexed glances at each other. The days of preparation and steadily mounting excitement, the food that had been taken in hot perfection from oven and spit, the carefully polished crystal and silver, all became as depressingly meaningless as the massed flowers and wreaths at a funeral. Although none could have said why, they began to experience a collective feeling of shame.

In her room Claire lay face down on the bed, her hands clenched into small fists, her eyes aching with a dry feverishness. She would not cry and no longer did she bother to go to the window, nursing a forelorn hope. The shadows lengthened, reaching out beyond the house and surrounding trees. The first evening call of a whippoorwill sounded a clear and distant lament. Bitterly she told herself she should have known this would happen. Yet she hadn't expected such complete and devastating ostracism. Living on this wilderness island, isolated from everything she had ever known, she had found it easy to imagine that the past was of no consequence and her identity was unknown in other sections of the Territory, as it was in Clayport. She had forgotten or ignored John Spain's long arm and the effortless power of gossip. What a stupid fool! She was angry, raging silently against the feeling of being trapped. Clay's solicitude, his bumbling attempts to pretend that the fiasco was of no consequence, only irritated her. She listened halfheartedly to his explanations and then became unreasonably infuriated by his lack of perception. Confused at first, and then angry himself, he left her and went to seek comfort in a bottle.

With an effort she rose from the bed, uncorked a flask of eau de cologne, and dabbed at her face. For a long time she studied herself in a mirror and then came to a decision. With a slap of her hands she summoned the slave girl and stood rigidly defiant as the black fingers worked hurriedly with button and fastening and the clothing dropped in folds about her feet.

In every room light poured from chandeliers and candelabra, spilling through the windows and thrusting back the darkness. Half concealed within a flowered alcove, the sextette of musicians worked doggedly at their instruments as though by volume alone they could evoke a hidden spirit of merriment. At the long dining-room table, Claire, Beulow, and Clay touched at their food and made no effort at conversation. Clay was getting drunk with sullen determination. Only Beulow made an attempt at casual gaiety, but even his light sallies were hollow and he frequently gagged on them, the words dropping away into abrupt silences. At the head of the table Old Clay deliberately indulged himself in a display of exaggerated grossness. He shoveled food into his mouth, allowing sauce and gravy to collect on his chin. When he wiped at the unsightly stains he scorned the use of a napkin, swabbing at his lips with the palm of one hand and then smearing the collection upon the tablecloth. He belched frequently with sickening explosions.

"Gad, sir," Beulow remarked once, "it is a pity such power is wasted. A man with your capacity should be able to fill the sails of a merchant ship."

Claire sat stiffly in her chair. She would not yield to this deliberate torment, and when, now and then, her eyes lifted, they stared coldly down the table and past Old Clay as though he were not there. She well understood that this revolting exhibition was solely for her humiliation and not by any sign did she intend to give him the satisfaction of seeing her flinch. The mellow candlelight accented her beauty, touching the dusky radiance of her hair and falling with the dusting of roses on her cheeks and throat. She had dressed as carefully as though the great house were filled with guests. Earlier in the evening, as she swept gracefully down the staircase, she saw the admiration flicker suddenly in Beulow's eyes. He was moved by this unexpected display of spirit and came forward to take her finger tips at the last step.

"You delight me, madame," he said approvingly. "At this moment you deserve no less than a roomful of dazzled gallants." He pressed her hand, not flirtatiously but with a warm understanding of a defiant gesture.

Even Clay had responded. He brightened visibly at the sight of her, the cloudy disappointment in his eyes vanishing before her radiance.

"We'll make a night of it," he said stoutly, "the three of us. We'll have our party and to hell with the others." His words echoed through the hall and they pretended not to notice the empty sound.

Beulow took his arm affectionately. "Let us don our gaudiest plumage. It is not in my nature to present such a drab contrast. Remember, it is the peacock and not the hen that excites cries of admiration."

Later, when they rejoined her, Claire took a glass of sherry in their company as they fortified themselves with stronger drink. The musicians, who had been pressed together into a small, uncertain group, settled in their places at a command from Clay. For a moment, as the dancing strains filled the lower floor, it was almost possible to believe that the rooms and dressing chambers above were filled with the light gaiety of their guests, who, any minute now, would be trooping downstairs to join them. As the minutes lengthened, though, it became apparent that the veil of pretense was too sheer. It parted and left them self-conscious and miserably uncomfortable, seeking words with which to cover their nakedness.

"I can't figure this out," Clay repeated for at least a tenth time. "It seems funny that out of all those people no one would show up."

He regarded Beulow hopefully as though expecting a simple explanation.

"Perhaps they are victims of a wholesale massacre." Beulow made the suggestion and then shook his head. "No. That is too much to hope for."

For all the attempt at lightness the words dropped soggily. No one was of a mood to pursue humor at the moment. The strains from the musicians' alcove became a threnody. They shut their ears to the sound, welcoming, finally, a call to the dining room.

The seemingly endless courses of the meal dragged to an end, and although she had barely touched her food, Claire thought she should never be hungry again. Always the specter of this meal would haunt her.

Old Clay sucked noisily at his teeth and then thrust a finger inside his mouth, poking and hunting down stray fragments of food, which he carefully laid on the cloth beside his plate. Claire tightened herself against the spectacle.

"Are you planning a journey, sir?" Beulow asked with artless interest.

Old Clay grunted, leaned back, and nudged a brandy glass for a slave's attention.

"I thought," the guest continued, nodding innocently at the dirty smear, "that perhaps you were husbanding provisions against a day of want."

The old man looked sleepily at him. "You know," he said, "I'm beginning to think I don't like you any better than I did your father."

"I shall add you to the list, sir." Beulow was unperturbed.

"Even if I don't like you," Old Clay added, "you're a damn sight better company than my grandson and," he paused, "Mrs. Hammond." For the first time during the meal he addressed Claire. "Why do you suppose your guests didn't show up, madame?"

Claire pushed back in her chair. She had no intention of feeding the old man's wolfish desire to glut himself upon their disappointment.

"I have no idea." She rose quickly and stood looking down at him. "I suspect, though, that your imagination is not quite so barren." The challenge was unmistakable. She was past caring. If he wanted it so, then let the truth be flung across the table. "Perhaps you would like to venture an opinion?"

Clay splintered a glass on the table's edge. "I'm sick of the whole business," he said thickly, "and it doesn't get any better by the two

266

of you slashing at each other. What's done is done, and if they didn't want to come it's their business."

Old Clay sniffed. "I could hold my likker better than that when I was five years old. You been drinkin' too much an' you ain't got the head for it."

Beulow left the table and stood beside Claire, offering his arm. She hesitated for a moment and then laid her hand upon it.

"I grow weary of this domestic exchange," he said. "Have the musicians play. Let it not be said they are unworthy of their hire. Let us dance. I have an agile calf." He glanced at Clay. "With your permission, cock?"

Clay struggled with the liquor he had drunk. "Sure, Jamie," he said. "I'm sorry. I'll come with you."

Beulow sighed with counterfeit regret. "If you must, although," he added, "I have no intention of leading you in a measure."

With grim concentration the musicians worked determinedly through their repertoire. They had been engaged to play, and play they would. If the members of this incomprehensible household had elected to transport them from St. Augustine for the purpose of furnishing music for a single couple, the extravagance was their affair. As they played their heads were turned to watch the gliding rhythm of Beulow and Claire as they twirled and sped on the impressive emptiness of the polished floor.

Her fingers were firm in Beulow's hand and she clung to him. To twirl and balance, across the floor, out of the door and away. Out of sight of this desolation, away from the hateful presence of an evil old man. This was what she wanted. She was only half aware of the music and completely indifferent to the ridiculous spectacle of the two of them, dwarfed into spinning marionettes, moving across the smooth surface with perfect accord. I should like to get drunk, she thought. Perhaps I shall.

"These new steps," Beulow said, "give to the dance an intimacy I didn't suspect existed outside a bedroom."

Oh, the relief of being with a man who could remember to laugh! She turned her face toward him and smiled. Tomorrow or the next day, she thought desperately, he will be gone and nothing will remain but the seeping bitterness of an old man, a husband I do not love, and the degradation of Jake Cutler. Suicide had been born of less.

"The allusion does not capture your fancy, madame?" He adopted an attitude of concern.

Her eyes widened. "Your allusions, sir," she replied softly, "are as subtle as a blunderbuss."

The music of the violins trailed away on a lacy figure, and once again the depressing silence of the all but empty house closed about them. They stood at the center of the floor. At the far end of the room four slaves waited with unblinking solemnity behind the punch bowls and heavily laden plates and platters.

"Some refreshment?" Beulow nodded toward the buffet.

Claire could not control the nervousness in her laughter. They were engaged in a ridiculous charade. She looked about for Clay. He had left them.

"A breath of air?" Beulow suggested.

She took his arm and the sound of their footsteps was unnaturally loud as they crossed toward the long windows opening upon the porch. The sharp clicking of her heels caused Claire to turn and cast a hasty glance over her shoulder.

"I thought someone was following us," she said.

"Only your conscience, my dear. A poor companion and easily lost. We shall elude the unpleasant fellow."

They strolled the length of the darkened porch. halting at the end where it swung in a shallow curve at a corner of the house. Beulow stood, hands locked behind his back, peering out into the limitless blackness. Surreptitiously Claire studied his face and wondered what manner of man he was beneath the conscious flippancy.

"Take me with you when you go," she whispered.

He was not surprised. "The idea had occurred to me, madame."

"I can't stay here any longer. Something dreadful will happen if I do. I can feel it. It's like a gathering sickness." She implored him with her eyes.

"You should have taken the pulse of your desires before committing yourself so completely, Mrs. Hammond." He was unimpressed by her urgency.

"I want to go with you," she pleaded. "You know that."

He laughed in gentle reproof and took a slender cigar from a case. "You miss the point, madame," he said thoughtfully. "I rarely concern myself with the desires of others unless they happen to coincide with my own."

She sagged inwardly. "Don't you see that sooner or later Clay must find out? The longer I stay the greater damage I do."

"Ah!" Beulow regarded her with delight and simulated astonishment. "You make an appeal to my better nature? In a fashion I shall be doing my friend a favor by carrying off his wife?" He shook his head with an expression of sadness. "You underestimate my intelligence. I will not debase myself with such spurious nobility of character."

She shrugged. The attempt had been clumsy but her desperation great. She took his arm, a most casual gesture.

"Shall we return to the ball?" Her glance held him for a moment. "I should dislike to give our guests additional tidbits for gossip. I am already suspect, sir."

"Now," he turned with her, "you interest me again, madame. For a moment I was nauseated by your kittenish mewling. The possibility of flight with you becomes an entertaining notion despite the difficulties involved."

Her laughter was spontaneous and pleased. "If you thought to have me without inconvenience to yourself, sir," she mocked him, "you were in error."

"Ah!" he exclaimed happily. "We are *en rapport*. You are not at your best, Mrs. Hammond, in an attitude of supplication. I shall take you with me and use you for the hot-blooded wench you are."

"You mean that?" She halted, searching his face for a sign that he no longer toyed with words.

"No more scoundrelly declaration was ever uttered," he assured her. "I shall violate the confidence of a friend, abuse the hospitality of his home, and take his wife in adultery. Why all of this should amuse me I cannot say."

They approached the doors and the muted strains of the orchestra crept out upon the porch.

"You are a swine, Mr. Beulow." Claire laid her hand upon his wrist.

"As yet, Mrs. Hammond," he held the door for her, "you have that only on hearsay."

Clay was waiting for them. Beside him a slave stood, bearing glasses and champagne on a tray.

"I've been looking for you," he called. All trace of his earlier ill humor had vanished. "This stuff," he nodded at the wine, "isn't cold the way it should be. We don't have any ice but it's been in buckets under a well."

"It will do well enough." Beulow accepted a glass.

"Where have you been?" Clay took Claire's arm. "The old man went to bed, sore as a stuck pig. Now let's have some fun. I wondered where you were."

"We were conniving, old cock." Beulow looked at him with pleased approval. "I was arranging a rendezvous with your wife.

We are going to flee your roof and live a while in sin. A delightful, though slightly hazardous, prospect."

Clay put his arms about the shoulders of his wife and their guest. They would have fun after all, and to hell with those who didn't come.

"Well," he said happily, "you couldn't run away with a prettier girl."

22

THROUGH an open window the gray of early morning trailed across the bare room and the mist hung like a swamp fog above the carpetless floor. Sprawled on the damp and filthy ticking of a straw mattress Clay Hammond twisted uncomfortably in sleep and tried to draw his body into a knot against the creeping chill. A beard of weeks was matted on his face and tiny globules of moisture gathered in the course hair. The cotton shirt he wore was soiled and rank. It was his only covering. Beneath his head a wadded pair of buckskins served as a meager pillow. In his troubled sleep he breathed with the heavy, labored effort of a man long in drink, expelling the used air over parted lips with a sticky, burbling sound.

On a torn piece of grass matting beside the pallet an Indian girl had spun herself into a coccoon of faded blanket. Only the tip of her head with its snarled, lank, and greasy hair was exposed. She also felt the cold and shivered against it, wriggling deeper into the blanket's folds.

The room was without furniture but McSwain, the landlord, considered it to be something in the nature of a choice accommodation. If he had been pressed for a bridal chamber this would have served. The guest fortunate enough to occupy it could close and bolt the door against the boisterous, drunken wanderings of the tavern's less select clientele, who were forced to bed down in communal squalor, sharing bugs and vomit and the overpowering stench of unwashed bodies.

The girl twisted unhappily and awoke slowly, her head emerging from the blanket with the cautious movement of a turtle. Black, expressionless eyes fixed themselves on the sleeping man and then shifted to a gutted candle, an overturned wicker jug, and the scattered butts of half-smoked cigars. For a long time she stared at the jug and then writhed out from her cover. Without bothering to look for her rumpled dress of cotton she slipped across the room and lifted the jug, shaking it for a sound, and finally tilting it up to pour the few remaining drops in the palm of her hand. She licked greedily at the small pool and then wiped soiled fingers on her buttocks.

271

She was still young, her body firm and her small breasts hard and high. She, also, needed a bath. McSwain, in a moment of generosity, had made Clay a present of her for as long as he cared to remain beneath the tavern's roof.

"I don't know what the hell her name is. I call her Tangerine. If you want to hose her off she'll probably smell better, but you can never really wash away that Indian stink. I'd let her be an' get used to the smell. It's easier, an' anyhow, when you're real drunk you don't mind it so much."

The girl replaced the empty jug on the floor and shuffled silently to her mat. After a quick glance at the sleeping man she slid into her dress, unlatched the door, and closed it softly behind her. Clay mumbled and thrust his face into the moldy straw of the bedding, pressing his eyes down against the gathering light.

When Tangerine returned she carried a tin bucket in which circular rows of jagged holes had been punched. The vessel was filled with red-hot embers. In the other hand she held a steaming metal pitcher. Black coffee, into which she had poured a pint of whisky, slopped from the rim of the container when she moved. To remedy this she drank from the pitcher's hot mouth until the level of the liquid had been reduced by a full inch. She settled the bucket a couple of feet away from Clay's side and placed the coffee on the coals. This done, she rummaged through the cigar ends until she found the longest. Lighting the tobacco at the makeshift stove, she settled herself cross-legged on the matting and waited, drawing contentedly on the cigar and inclining her body toward the spreading heat.

Clay struggled from the dead hands of sleep. The sharp odor of smoldering oak and pine coals nibbled at his senses, and for a moment he thought he must be in the woods, bedded down beside a campfire. When he took a deep breath, though, he could feel his throat and lungs stabbed at by dull knives and his eyes, as they were forced open, saw only the bare and cheerless walls of the room. Painfully he turned over and looked at the girl beside the brazier. His tongue, a sodden and nerveless thing, circled the noisome cavern of his mouth.

Without a word the girl rose and picked up a tin cup from the floor. She filled it from the pitcher and handed it to Clay. He drank slowly; the scalding liquid, trickling down his throat, formed a warm and comforting puddle in his stomach.

"Jesus Christ!" He spoke with an accent of wonder and rubbed his mouth against a forearm.

The girl waited until he had emptied the cup and then replenished it, holding it in both hands with the handle extended for his shaking fingers. She dropped easily to the floor again, feet tucked beneath her, catlike, her eyes fixed upon Clay's face with a dull passiveness.

He rested the cup on the boards between his spraddled knees and stared at the black and oily liquid. He revived slowly as he had each morning for the past three weeks, dragging himself back to reality, reluctant to face another day, nursing a persistent and numbing ache that yielded only temporarily to whisky. Time, as such, had lost its significance. He no longer cared how it passed.

How long ago had it been since he awoke on the plantation to find the place in the bed beside him empty? It didn't matter. What was the name of the day when he had walked from room to room and discovered Claire and Beulow gone? What was the hour when he questioned the slaves and listened to their timid and uneasy replies? No, d' Mistress an' Marstah Beulow ain' eaten breakfus. No, Marstah, d' Mistress ain' ridin'. Yes, Marstah (this slowly and with downcast eyes and a shuffling of feet), d' Mistress an' Marstah Beulow they come together to the stables 'fore sunup an' have d' coach hitched to Marstah Beulow's double team.

What moment was it when Old Clay, who seemed to have known what had happened before he was told, had cackled with the sound of dried bones rattling?

"So they've run off, hey? Your friend an' John Spain's slut. Good riddance."

What morning was it when he had struck the gloating old man savagely across the face, again and again, with the flat of his hand?

"Shut your God-damned filthy mouth!" He had screamed the words into the evil, grinning mask.

What was the afternoon when he had ridden from the plantation, charging wildly through the scrub, losing himself in the deep woods, not caring where he was bound? How many days and nights had passed while he wandered like an injured animal, nursing the festering sore of hatred? How had he lived on the broken trail through that first period of agony? When had he come, finally, to Tallahassee and McSwain's Tavern? Who cared?

He finished the coffee and rested, elbows on naked thighs, turning the cup senselessly over and over in his hands. Finally he passed the can to the girl, who returned it, filled for the third time.

"You will eat now?" She spoke haltingly and without any particular interest in his reply.

"Later."

He drank, feeling the pleasant anesthetic of the hot whisky envelop him. With an effort he rose, steadying himself on outspread legs against the sudden whirling of the room. The cup clattered from his fingers and rolled across the floor. The girl did not move and he kept his eyes fixed on her face.

"I don't know how the hell you can look so good to me at night," he said wonderingly. Then he touched his chin and cheeks and fingered the dirty shirt. "Maybe," he grinned, "it seems the same way to you."

He spoke in English and the girl could not follow the words. She was Cherokee, from Alabama, and her mother had traded her to McSwain for a quart of whisky and a dollar. Clay was the second man to take her and she was not completely familiar with the male vagaries. She watched and listened, trying to puzzle out the meaning of a still strange tongue.

Carefully he reached down for the buckskins and drew them on, balancing unsteadily as he thrust in each leg. How long could a man stay drunk, he wondered, before he began to see things and go crazy? What good did it do if, when he sobered up, he began to remember and the hurt inside was like a maddened scorpion?

On bare feet he walked from the room and down a long, dark, musty hall to the back of the tavern. Outside, the sun was eating slowly at the mist, clearing it from the sky. Beyond the outhouses a sulphur-water well boiled noisily out of a four-inch iron pipe. The clear, cold stream thudded on a board platform and splashed over the broad green leaves of an elephant-ear plant.

Clay undressed and with the timid and fearful step of a man going to the rack he bent beneath the cascade, dropping with a yelp face down on the boards, the water drumming over his spine. When the shock had softened he turned over on his back and the stream spilled over face and chest. Half turning his head, he opened his mouth and allowed a small torrent to flood in and overflow. There was no soap and he scrubbed at his hands and feet with coarse sand.

Regretfully he crawled from beneath the spring and slapped his body partly dry. I guess, he thought, I'm caught up with my drinking. Maybe just one or two this afternoon. He was feeling better and he thumped and pinched at his muscles with satisfaction. I can't keep running away. He dressed slowly. I'll do what I set out to do. For the first time he found himself thinking of Claire and Beulow with an almost impersonal detachment. The fury no longer burned at him. His anger was a cold and dangerous companion and to-

274

gether they were self-sufficient. He would walk alone, taking no man's hand again.

He ate a Gargantuan breakfast: ham and gravy, grits and eggs, corn bread, sorghum, and black coffee. He was alone in the vast room, still unswept and reeking of the night. When the last bit of food on the platters had been consumed he walked out into the street.

The town had grown since he and Santee had first passed this way. It began to look like a territorial capital. New boardwalks had been laid on each side of the main street and a moderately successful effort had been made to surface the thoroughfare. Recently erected buildings proudly displayed their painted surfaces instead of the gleaming yellow nakedness of freshly cut pine boards. The people abroad at this early hour moved with a brisk and purposeful stride as though they were aware of their importance as members of the legislative seat.

Clay walked slowly across the street to the barbershop and waited his turn at the chair.

"Get into all of it," he directed, touching his hair and whiskers.

He lay back while the barber busied himself with soap and strop, fussing over his face with lather and kneading vigorously at the wiry growth.

"Got the beginnin' of a fine beard there." He poised the blade over Clay's cheek. "Many a man would think twice before havin' it cut away. Of course, I'm jus' talkin' myself out of trade because gents with beards don't get shaved. Jus' the same, they come in for a trim, so it evens out. I always say everything gets into balance somehow if you give it a chance. Stranger in town?" He prattled happily at the job.

"Just give me a shave and a haircut," Clay snapped. "If I wanted conversation I'd go to a bar."

"Well, yes, sir." The barber was offended. "No need to get mad."

"I'm not mad. I just want a shave and a haircut."

Clay drew his lips into a tight line. Maybe it was the liquor. He was angry for no reason. The words sounded strange coming from Clay Hammond. I never used to talk that way to people, he assured himself. I'm getting mean inside. Somehow, he didn't care.

As he walked from the shop he was conscious of the slowly turning heads as the loungers, in their chairs against the wall, swiveled about to stare after him. To hell with them. When a man wanted a shave he wanted a shave and not a lot of woman's cackle. He explored the smoothness of his face and the closely cropped hair.

275

By God, Tangerine wouldn't recognize him. He experienced a feeling of revulsion and the rank odor of the girl seemed to pinch at his nostrils here in the street. I'm getting out, he told himself, this afternoon. If I don't, and keep drinking, I'll end up in a lean-to with a squaw.

McSwain was at his place at the corner of the bar. Already the room was filling as the customers dragged in to fortify themselves against another day. Drovers and salesmen, small-caliber politicians, land speculators, and slave hunters fed noisily at the long tables. The landlord crossed his fat arms on the counter and eyed Clay with the sleepy interest of a sow.

"I almost didn't recognize you." He jerked his chin upward to indicate Clay's face. "You look twenty years younger."

"I don't feel it." Clay looked around the room.

"Want a drink?" McSwain reached beneath the bar and brought out a demijohn of rum. "I ain't washed my mouth out yet so I'll join you." He filled two glasses and slid one across to his guest.

Clay swallowed half a tumblerful and gagged back the impulse to spray it out between his teeth. He waited until the nausea subsided.

"I'm leaving today."

"Well," McSwain shook his head, "I'm real sorry to hear that. I was beginnin' to take a likin' to you. You're a nice quiet drunk an' the kind that don't give a place a bad name."

Clay finished his drink. "Is there any of my money left?"

"I ain't totted up the account." McSwain was affable. "You didn't leave much with me when you started drinkin'. Figurin' everythin' an' a little wear an' tear on Tangerine, I'd say you were about even."

"I need some cash."

The tavern keeper shook his head sadly. "Most people do at one time or another. How much?"

"I don't know." Clay was honestly confused. He had never asked a man for a loan before. Where was he going? What did he need money for?

McSwain whistled soundlessly and his blue eyes were vacant. "How can I say no till I know how much you want?"

"A couple of hundred dollars, I guess." The sum had a nice round sound.

McSwain rubbed at his lips. "I reckon," he finally said, "the Hammond plantation ought to be good for it if you wanted to sign a note at fifteen-per-cent interest."

"The Hammond plantation isn't borrowing. I am."

The tavern keeper grinned. "Just the same, I figure the plantation is a good risk." He brought out ink, paper, and a quill from behind the counter.

Angrily Clay scrawled his name at the bottom of the note. Borrowing anything, even this way, made him feel furtive and dishonest.

"Don't get fired up about it." McSwain eyed him curiously.

"God damn it," Clay snarled, "I'm not fired up. What the hell is wrong with everyone? All I heard so far today is don't get sore. What am I supposed to do, kiss everybody's ass?"

McSwain scratched thoughtfully at the back of his neck. "You could get elected to the Legislature that way," he commented gravely, "but outside of that there don't seem to be no practical advantage in it."

"All right, then, just let me have the money."

McSwain slowly counted out the bills and laid them before him. As he wet his fingers to separate the notes he glanced up now and then into Clay's scowling face.

"What's chewin' at you, Mr. Hammond? You ain't like the fella who come in here a couple of years ago for the first time. A maggot's got you. It ain't pretty to see."

Clay finished the rum. "I'm going to kill a man," he said flatly.

McSwain pushed the loan toward him. "You could hire it done for less than is here."

Clay thrust the wad of notes into the pocket of his shirt. "This is something I've got to do for myself." He rested his hands on the bar's edge. "You have my rifle and gear?"

McSwain nodded. "Be sure you shoot first," he cautioned. "I got what they call an equity in you now. Good luck."

Clay took his rifle and small pack. "I'd leave some money for Tangerine," he said, "but I don't figure she'd ever see it."

McSwain chortled. "That's right," he agreed. "An Indian girl ain't got no use for money."

"Well," Clay hesitated, "so long. I want to get my horse an' some clean stuff."

"Hell," McSwain replied, "you don't have to get dressed up to kill a man. If he sees you first it'll just be money throwed away."

The sun was high when he rode out of Tallahassee. The mare, after almost a month's idleness, was skittish and eager, whirling and dancing to the side, pretending alarm at every leaf and branch. Finally he gave the animal her head and she raced up and over the long hills until the wind sang and whipped at his face.

In the high-ceilinged room of their hotel on St. Charles Street, James Beulow flicked at a nonexistent speck of dust on the velvet collar of his coat and made a final examination of himself in the mirror. From below the morning noises of New Orleans were blended into a confused murmur.

"You are leaving me, sir?" Claire Hammond, clad only in a sheer negligee, her head resting on the stacked pillows of the bed, glanced up from a thoughtful inspection of her fingernails.

Beulow nodded into the looking glass and smiled. "Not," he said pleasantly, "without regret, madame."

"I am touched." She dangled a feathered slipper from the tips of her toes.

"Come, my dear." He swung about. "That is unworthy of you."

"Are you returning home?"

"Naturally." He tugged gently at the ends of his waistcoat.

"Clay will seek you out." She leaned into the cushions and the dark hair fell in a rippling swirl about her shoulders.

"Unfortunately," Beulow replied, "I have had to consider that possibility. My impulses have generally been expensive."

"What is to become of me?" Her large eyes held him.

"Please." He held up an admonishing hand. "Let us not wallow in bathos. It does not become the hour or the circumstances."

"You have no feeling for me, no qualms?"

"Tch-tch." He shook his head regretfully. "You know better. I have found you a sportive bed companion. The interlude we shared will always remain a pleasant memory. Now, however, I must make my adieu."

"How shall I survive?" Her question was exaggeratedly plaintive. She mocked him with a quick smile.

"Ah!" He was pleased. "That is better." He reached for his tall hat of dove-breast gray. "I shall leave you amply provided for. There will be an envelope awaiting you at the desk downstairs. Also," his glance lingered over her, "New Orleans is a city particularly suited to your undeniable talents. I have no fear for your overwhelming success."

"Spoken like a cad, sir." Her laughter filled the room.

He came to the bedside and stood looking down at her. "I am filled with a regrettable tenderness," he admitted. "Of all the women I have known you are the best suited to my nature. It is not easy to leave you."

"Why, then, do you go?"

"Ah!" He touched a finger to his cheek and struck the pose of a

278

player. "In such a fashion do I smother the small voice of conscience. To keep you would be an unconscionable act of baseness. I should be perpetually haunted by the knowledge of your husband's melancholy. To have loved you and, in this noble fashion, turn away is a gesture of renunciation that all must admire. I sacrifice myself. What could be more generous?"

"Kiss me again before you go." Her arms stretched up to him and the fragile silken garment fell away from her shoulders and breasts.

"That was my intention." He bent toward her.

She giggled with a sudden throaty pleasure. "You might at least remove your hat, sir."

23

For dragging minutes Clay stood within the darkness of the porch. There was no longer any hurry; the sense of desperate urgency had left him. He had come upon the Beulow plantation from a little-used trail along the river, skirting the main entrance, the overseer's house, and the slave quarters. His horse had been left tied within a concealing thicket and he had made his way on silent feet over the acorn-strewn slope. Once a dog had barked—a high, nervous challenge that died away on a note of doubt as though the animal were questioning its instinct. Clay waited and then moved upward toward the manor. A northeast wind, booming in from the distant ocean, drove black herds of heavy clouds over the moon and strained at the long gray clusters of Spanish moss in the high trees. When he reached the house he was breathing heavily although the way had not been difficult.

From his place of concealment he could look through the lightly curtained French windows and into the warm depths of the book-lined room. A fire tossed curiously shaped figures of light on the dark paneling of the walls and reflected the high polish of the boots on Beulow's outstretched legs. The spreading wings of a chair, upholstered in red leather, almost hid his face, but now and then the head emerged in full profile as the man leaned forward to lift a drink from a small table at his side. Once he laid aside the book he was reading and bent down to touch the head of a drowsing setter. He remained this way for several moments, staring thoughtfully into the fireplace as though he would find an answer to a problem in the flames. Clay fancied he could hear him sigh as he straightened up and slid back into the enveloping comfort of the chair.

The wind brought a quick scattering of raindrops and he moved toward the window. Although he had made no sound, the setter's muzzle came up from the floor and its fine head turned, alert and questioning. Beulow placed the open book, pages down, on his leg and spoke to the animal. He did not look toward the porch but seemed to be waiting in an attitude of resigned patience.

The metal handle of the long window turned beneath Clay's **hand**

and as he swung the glassed frame open the wind snatched at the curtains, throwing them straight out into the room. The setter was on its feet, a heavy, menacing growl rumbling in its throat. Clay thrust his back against the window, closing it to the night. The curtains dropped into place with a silken whisper.

Beulow's fingers were linked with the chain collar on the dog's neck, holding him.

"I've been expecting you, cock." He did not shift his position and spoke to a point straight ahead. "That's why I didn't have the windows or doors locked. You could have come in the front way."

Clay felt the weight of the pistol in his hand. He couldn't remember drawing it from his waistband. It dangled, now, in his fingers, heavy and ugly.

"Get out of that chair." His voice was strangled. The setter, recognizing the threat, growled again and darted a quick, worried glance at its master. "I've come to kill you," Clay continued, "and I want you on your feet."

"I suppose so," Beulow said regretfully. "There are certain amenities to be observed." He drew the setter closer to his side. "I wonder," his eyes met Clay's for the first time, "if you would mind my closing the dog in another room first. You see," he explained agreeably, "when you fire that particularly unpleasant thing you are holding I shall undoubtedly be forced to release my hold on Bruce's collar. With commendable loyalty the animal will go for you and in the resulting confusion one or the other is bound to be hurt. I would not like to have that happen."

Without waiting for Clay's reply he rose from the chair and in a stooping position crossed the room, tugging at the reluctant setter. When the door closed behind the animal Beulow turned again to Clay.

"Under the circumstances I don't suppose I could offer you a drink?" He examined Clay critically. "Gad, cock, but you look a filthy menace." He moved without haste to the fireplace and stood before it facing Clay. "Now?" he asked gently. "Here?"

The weapon in Clay's hand straightened and the hammer came back beneath a thumb.

"Slightly on the theatrical side, aren't we?" Beulow rested outspread arms on the mantelpiece. "Oh," he continued hastily, "don't think I view the situation with complete indifference. I haven't the slightest desire to die. Yet," he added sadly, "I cannot cringe. There is that in my nature which forbids me to crawl. Fire, you idiot!"

The pistol did not waver. Clay seemed not to have heard the

words. His eyes were on Beulow's face. He felt nothing. All of the humiliation, the raging anger, the sickening knowledge of betrayal had long since been washed away. Standing here in this room he could remember crying, sobbing in the woods alone. Strangely enough, those tears had sprung from the knowledge that he had lost Jamie Beulow. He was empty and dead. The man across the room was a stranger, an interloper, occupying a friend's place. Toward him he experienced a cold and terrible remorselessness.

"Where's Claire?" The words were without emotion, almost without interest.

"In New Orleans, I fancy. That is where I left her."

"Alone?"

Beulow's shoulders were lightly shrugged. "Perhaps." Compassion rested for a moment upon the handsome face. "She would have gone anyhow, cock," he said gently.

"You're a liar." The accusation was toneless.

Beulow shook his head. "Tactless, perhaps, but not a liar. She wasn't for you, cock. Not for you or me or any one man."

"She was my wife."

"She would have broken your heart," Beulow's words were soft, "because she couldn't help herself."

"We were happy."

"You were fooling yourself." Beulow regarded him pensively. "She was diddling you with one of your grandfather's hired hands, that fellow Cutler."

"You're a lying son of a bitch." The pistol roared, the angry crimson flame spurting from the long barrel.

Beulow seemed to snap in at the waist and he sagged as his head jerked once or twice with a nervous twitch. The outflung arms on the mantel supported his weight and he forced his eyes to Clay's face.

"You fool," he whispered, "you hulking, innocent fool. I was fond of you, cock."

As Clay watched he was conscious of the setter's hysterical clamor and the sound of his weight being thrown frenziedly against the door. Beulow's fingers trailed from the mantel's edge. He crumpled slowly and, for an instant, stood in a limp half crouch before toppling forward to fall face down before the fireplace.

Clay stood looking at the sprawled body and the pistol dropped with a muffled thud on the carpet. Unconsciously he drew his fingers across the smoke-blackened jacket as though to cleanse them. Then he turned and walked unhurriedly from the room.

Far down by the river's edge he untied his horse. It was raining now, driving through the trees in whirling, fitful gusts. In the distance a lantern winked as someone ran and he thought he could hear confused shouts.

He rode away without haste, leaning forward in the saddle, his head bowed in an attitude of weariness. He felt no regret; no sustained fury held him. An ineffable sadness drifted with the wind. At the edge of the King's Road he checked his tired horse. Now that it was done he was without purpose or destination. Which way, or did it matter how he turned? Leaning forward he ran a soothing and understanding hand over the wet and glistening neck of the mare and the animal twisted her head back to look at him with sorrowful and patient eyes.

"There's no help for it," he explained, "we can't stay here and it's going to be just as wet moving as it is standing still."

He touched the mount with his heel and guided her to the left, southward. It wasn't important. All roads now would end in the same way.

From behind his desk in the Indian Agency at Fort King, Wiley Thompson studied the tall, bearded stranger who stood before him.

"No," he said reflectively, "I don't know where Colonel Humphreys moved to. He left Fort King before I succeeded Major Phagan here as agent."

Clay nodded. "Thank you," he said. "It wasn't important. He was an old friend. I just thought I'd look him up while I was in town."

Thompson was curious. His visitor spoke in cultivated accents, yet he bore the fierce imprint of a backwoodsman. The buckskins and moccasins he wore were weathered and smoked to a shining hardness. Hair, long untrimmed, reached almost to his shoulders, and the beard was heavy and uncared for. Here in the small room he loomed unusually large and savage. The rifle within the crook of one arm was a fine and expensive piece and he bore it with the air of a man whose weapon was as much a part of him as his hands or eyes.

"You look like you've been in the woods for a long time." Thompson leaned back in his chair.

"I have."

"You didn't say your name?" The agent drummed his fingers together.

"Hammond." The word came without hesitation. "Clayfield Hammond."

Wiley Thompson's eyes widened. "I thought," he said after a moment, "he was a much older man."

"My grandfather." There was no resentment in the tone. If the visitor was annoyed by this mild inquisition he concealed the fact.

Thompson's tilted chair dropped to the floor and he drew a bottle of whisky from a desk drawer and with it two cups.

"Drink?" he asked, and shoved the liquor across to his visitor.

Clay drank slowly and then wiped at his beard with a sleeve. He shook his head when the agent offered a box of slender black cigars.

"Sort of got out of the habit," he explained.

"You come in from the Apalachicola?" Thompson said conversationally.

"No. From the east, down from St. Augustine, and then in and across from the Tomoka River."

Thompson whistled softly. "That's a long haul. Any trouble?"

Without waiting for an invitation Clay refilled his cup from the bottle and drank soberly. Thompson thought there was something close to a smile hidden within the beard but he couldn't be sure.

"If you mean Indians," Clay said, "I got along all right, but I passed a lot of places where those who lived there didn't. It looked to me," he hesitated, "like there was killing going on just for the fun of killing. Indians and whites."

"You were lucky."

Clay shook his head. "No, just careful." He touched his hair. "I figure to keep this, all but what I let a barber take."

Thompson nodded. He was new in this post as Indian agent, harassed and made uncertain by conflicting policies and confusing directives out of Washington. The agency no longer commanded respect from the Seminoles, who ignored its existence. Day and night, Thompson was troubled by the suspicion that he occupied an uneasy seat on the cellar door to hell. It swelled and buckled beneath him, threatening to erupt.

"I'd like to hear something." The agent looked up at his visitor.

Clay shrugged. How could this man be expected to know about or understand some of the things he had seen? How to tell him what the blackened and smoking timbers of a settler's cabin looked like at dawn; the desolation of the small plot; the strange, heartbreaking silence of what was once a home? How does a woman appear after she has been scalped and staked out in the sun for the ants and buzzards to work over? Could you tell of the terrible fascination catching in your throat at the sight of a pointed stick driven into a young woman's private parts so that even in another life she would be unable to bear the hated offspring? Was it possible to picture a man, stripped and strung by his heels to a branch, his belly slit open and

284

his hacked genitals stuffed into a gaping mouth? Could you tell how a little girl looked after her head had been clubbed to a flat and pulpy cake? Could you speak of the small boy, his eyes burned out, left to run in screaming agony until he beat himself to death by slamming, head first, into the trees he couldn't see? Clay didn't think so.

"It'd be hard to know where to begin," he said. "One thing, though, don't think it is only the white people who are being killed. I saw a lot of dead Indians, and from the looks of things they weren't doing anything more dangerous than hunkering around a fire and eating when someone lit into them."

"We're doing everything we can." Wiley felt uncomfortably on the defensive. "I just hope to God we can get 'em out and into Arkansas without any more trouble."

"You don't believe that, do you?" Clay asked slowly.

The agent's face sagged and his eyes were fastened on the desk. "No," he finally said, "I don't guess I do, Mr. Hammond. That," he nudged the bottle toward his guest, "that's why I keep this around. It helps sometimes."

Clay didn't accept the offer of a third drink. He had been too long without whisky. It bothered him now, making his tongue heavy, singing in his head.

"Anything I can do for you?" Thompson suggested.

"No, I don't guess there is." He hitched the rifle in his arm. "I'll find a barber and get cleaned up some." He grinned warmly. "Later I might look around for a woman. You begin to talk to yourself in the woods after a while and whisky sort of gives a fellow ideas."

"Well," the agent rose, "let me know." They walked to the door together.

"I wonder," Clay hesitated, "if you know where I might locate an Indian. His name's Asseola."

Thompson halted. "If I did," he said bitterly, "I'd have him in jail. How," his curiosity was evident, "does it happen you know him?"

Clay couldn't hide the smile. Always the same question, as though there were something a little queer about a white man who knew an Indian.

"We were kids together on the Apalachicola. He came from a Seminole town down the river from our place."

"Well," Thompson bit the word, "it's too damn bad he didn't stay there. Half the Indian trouble in the Territory now can be traced to him. He's called Powell around here. We would have had the

Seminoles across the Mississippi by now if it wasn't for him. No," he repeated, "I don't know where he is."

They stood on the doorstep. Across the road, huddled miserably near a hitching rail before a tavern, were a dozen or so ragged and beaten figures. A guard on horseback, one hand trailing a long black whip, watched over them. With a start Clay noticed that the men and women were chained together and, although they wore Indian dress, were Negroes.

He turned to Thompson. "What the hell is that?"

Thompson spat into the dirt and eyed Clay morosely. "Runaway slaves," he said. "Hunting parties are in and out of here every day, running the poor bastards down and taking them back into Georgia that way." He bridled beneath his visitor's sarcastic glance. "What the hell can I do?" He spread his hands. "They come into the Territory with dogs and guns, holding a whip in one hand and a federal writ in the other. Everything's properly signed, they're looking for runaway slaves. They comb the woods and brush, raid an Indian settlement, and capture a few blacks. 'What's your name, nigger?' they ask. The ignorant maroon, if he knows, mumbles something about Marten or Jones. 'That's right,' the captain tells him, 'your grandfather ran away from Marten's plantation in Alabama seventy-five years ago. Come on, nigger, we're takin' you back.' That's the way it goes, and they round them up in bunches and drive them over the border. The Indian Agency," he spat again to emphasize the point, "meanin' Wiley Thompson right now, gets blamed by the Seminoles for what is going on. No wonder they stay away from Fort King. Right there, across the road, is the beginning of another Seminole war."

Clay studied the pitifully stricken band, herded in the bright sunshine, moving with small, shuffling motions in the hot sand beneath the eyes of their guard and captor.

"I don't see," he said thoughtfully, "how anyone can figure they're slaves after all these years."

Thompson's laugh was without mirth. "A federal judge says they are. He ought to know."

"Well," Clay thrust out his hand, "thanks for your time and whisky. I think I'll move along."

He walked across the road and his stride shortened as he neared the miserable group. At the approach of a white man they seemed to bunch together, bound in bewilderment and silent dread. Their chains tinkled with a small musical sound as they shifted their positions. Already, Clay noticed, the heavy iron gyves were wearing the flesh at their ankles raw and bleeding. He halted and counted their number.

"You want something, mister?" The guard edged his horse toward Clay and the metal tip of the lash wriggled suggestively in the dust.

Clay glanced up at the man, staring at him with cold and deliberate insult. Without replying he turned again to the prisoners. On the edge of the tight circle a young girl was shackled between two men. She wore a loose buckskin garment and the fringed hem hung over the dirty bare toes. Her face was averted but not concealed and Clay's eyes sharpened as he noted the cast of her features. That's no Negrah, he thought. She's pure Seminole if I ever knew one.

Impulsively, he spoke to her in the dialect. "You are not black, girl. How are you called?"

At the sound of his voice her head lifted with a startled motion and her eyes, heavy with fear, met his. She looked fearfully in the guard's direction.

"Che-cho-ter," she whispered.

"What is your town?" Clay persisted.

"All right, mister." The guard's eyes were hard with anger. "I said once that if you had some business you'd better git on with it." He maneuvered his horse, crowding Clay backward. "Git the hell away from them niggers."

"That girl's no Negrah," Clay flared and stepped away from the animal's circling rump.

"She's nigger to me now." The hand holding the heavy whip stock tightened. "Git movin' now or I'll lay this 'cross you."

Clay ignored the threat. Che-cho-ter. He spoke the name again to himself. Morning Dew. It had a pleasant sound. He looked her over carefully. She wasn't much more than a youngster, seventeen, maybe. He stepped again toward her. A quick intake of breath rising as a sound of warning from the captives caused him to whirl about. The long, snaking lash of the whip sang through the air and he felt the savage bite of the oiled leather through his light jacket. The sensation was that of a hot iron drawn across bare flesh.

The guard was screaming, his face mottled with rage. "You nosy bastard," he yelled furiously, "didn't you heah me tell you to git goin'?" The lash snaked out again, curling viciously at Clay's face.

As the ugly length of the weapon whistled out a blind and terrible fury enveloped Clay. He pivoted and spun away, his hand closing on the plaited thongs. With a sudden heave he jerked the man halfway out of the saddle and as the contorted face bent low Clay's fist smashed full into his mouth. Beneath his knuckles he could feel the yellow teeth give way in a spongy quiver. Before the man could recover Clay hit him again, a short, punishing jab that broke and flattened the sharp nose. He reached for the man's coat, eager to drag him from the rearing horse. A shout caused him to half turn and then his head exploded as a heavy club thudded on his skull. He pitched forward and lay still.

When he came to he was lying on the floor of Wiley Thompson's office, a rolled piece of matting beneath his neck. The agent bent above him.

"You all right now?" he asked worriedly as Clay's eyes stared without recognition.

After a moment Clay nodded painfully. "I guess so." He forced himself into a sitting position and allowed his head to dangle listlessly between hunched shoulders. He thought he was going to vomit.

"Who got me?" he asked. "I sure as hell didn't see anyone."

Thompson relaxed. "One of the guard's friends. The rest of them were coming out of Qualter's saloon when the trouble started. He took a rifle butt to you. Feel better?"

"I guess so." Clay lifted his head, managing an uncertain smile. "I'll take that third drink now," he added.

Thompson helped him from the floor to a chair and uncorked the whisky. Clay drank from the bottle, a full swallow.

"I guess," he admitted ruefully, "I went looking for it. But I'm not used to having a man put a whip on me."

"You're lucky they didn't stomp you to death. I guess they wanted to get out of town; otherwise they'd have kicked you to pieces."

Clay touched lightly at the swollen knob at the back of his head. Beneath the tender skin he could feel a throbbing pulse.

"That girl isn't colored. She's Indian." He wondered why it should make any difference to him now.

Thompson made a gesture of resignation with his hands. "They claim her grandmother was a nigger. According to the law that makes her a runaway slave. What can you do? I don't write the laws."

Clay stood up. He was feeling better and began to realize how lucky he had been to get out with nothing more than a sore head.

"I'll try going out again." He grinned. "If I want a haircut and a shave I'd better get it while I've still got something for the barber to work on."

Thompson accompanied him to the door. "You ought to look in on a doctor. That fellow really bore down on you. There might be a fracture. I could hear the sound clear across the street."

"Maybe. I'll see how it feels. Thanks again."

Clay walked slowly down the main street. Fort King hadn't changed much. Maybe it was spread out a little more and additional troops had been moved into the garrison. They stood in bored and silent groups, staring listlessly at the civilian population, or leaned against the shaded walls of buildings. Uncommunicative, clannish, they chewed and smoked, eying the scene with the aloof indifference of soldiers away from their barracks and wondering what to do with the liberty. As he trudged through the sand Clay thought he had been a damn sight safer in the woods. At least, no one slipped up from behind there and tried to beat his head in with a rifle butt.

He found a barbershop and submitted to a hair trim and a shave, offering no encouragement to the barber, who wanted to discuss the cause of the lump on his head. He was restless and uneasy in the chair. People, so many of them at one time, made him uncomfortable. In their presence he felt crowded, hemmed in. The protective cloth fastened about his neck gave him a feeling of suffocation. All he wanted now was to make a few small purchases: grits, salt, corn meal, and maybe a slab of bacon. A man didn't need to carry much in the woods if he knew his way. He also wanted powder and a chance to run some bullets.

He escaped from the chair with a sigh of relief. It was hell to be tied down that way, trapped so you couldn't move and with a stranger working around your throat with a sharp blade. For almost a year he had moved alone, drifting along ridge and through swamp and hummock with no more purpose than a wind-swept cloud. He had known the passing of that first winter deep within the woods where no white man's foot had trod. April had broken slowly and then the fragile and elusive spring melted into the long days of summer when the sun was fiercely hot, the air stifling and without breeze enough to shake a leaf. Now it was October again. The months had folded into each other and disappeared. He had forgotten the sensation of being alone and felt no need of companionship. He had lost his horse, the animal succumbing to an unfamiliar malady that he had been unable to treat. For the past four months he had traveled without haste, moving on foot, a solitary figure against the sky at evening or merging unobtrusively with the dusty green of the scrub. When he chanced upon a spot to his liking beside a stream or among the tall pines he settled down, fashioning a lean-to and amusing himself with a small routine of domesticity and a pleasant feeling of permanency. Then, and for no reason he could name, he would awake one morning with the urge to be moving again and stride away, leaving behind the marks of his passing in the burned circle of a stamped-out fire and the curled and yellow palmetto fans of a hut. Once in a while he came upon a small settlement, four or five spindly houses or a solid cabin springing suddenly out of the brush. Now and then he stopped to exchange a word or to buy a few supplies, but always he plunged back into the forest with a feeling of relief. Being alone, he discovered, played curious tricks with his memory. Often he caught himself thinking in detail of the things that had happened when he was a boy. He wasn't much concerned with the man. The present was too filled with immediate problems. The boy interested him. Sometimes, at night, when he lay snug and warm, his face turned toward the dying fire, he traced back over his childhood, filling in the years, arranging events into an unbroken continuity. Rarely, if at all, did he ponder on this strange, nomadic existence he now led. Old Clay and everything he represented seemed remote and almost unreal. It was as though he were part of a story once told and listened to. He felt no regret, no yearning for half-remembered things. This was a good life and a man needed only to trust himself. At times he felt the soaring freedom of an eagle pinpointed in the sky above. Never, from the moment he had ridden from the Beulow plantation, had he considered himself a fugitive. Perhaps the authorities knew or guessed who had shot and killed Jamie Beulow. The chances were, though, that they didn't. No one had seen him enter upon the Beulow land and no one had been near to watch him ride away. Anyhow, he wasn't running off to escape. When Wiley Thompson had asked his name he had given it freely. If anyone was looking for him it was just as well to know it. He kept to the woods now not because they offered a haven but because he had found a great wild and satisfying beauty in them. He was happy and his soul had been cleansed of any lingering bitterness. He could think of Claire without pain or anger. Only the memory of James Beulow haunted him. He sat many nights by his fire, dry-eyed but heartsick, speaking the man's name softly.

With a start he realized he had stopped walking and was standing in the road, staring straight ahead, lost in thought. He grinned as he caught the worried glance of a passing woman. I'd better get back into the woods before someone tries to toss me into a cage. That woman acted as though she thought that was where I belonged. He hitched at his rifle and pressed on. Maybe, he told himself, I'm going a little loony and don't know it.

THIS was the wide and open country of dark, unruffled lakes, hard sunlight, and distances so vast that the eyes ached in measuring them. It was a land of many colors where, for hours at a time, not even the small cry of a bird intruded and the hush of eternity was held beneath the sky's great bell. Here the enormous red pines towered straight and motionless and in their shadows a man hesitated to breathe for fear of disturbing the enchanted solitude.

Clay rested on a low ridge, staring out across the lake's black mirror. Long ago the sea had rolled here. The ledge supporting his back was formed by countless millions of tiny shells and there was a pattern over the earth not unlike the markings left upon a beach by the flow and ebb of tides. Men, also, had paused here, raising their camps and villages, and had been absorbed by the centuries. Of them nothing remained but ancient arrowheads and an occasional broken implement or utensil. Scratching across the mounds Clay had dug them out just below the surface; more, and the bones of those who had fashioned them, were deeply buried. At his feet the lake and behind him a tangled wall of scrub with stunted clumps of sour wild oranges. A hundred feet or so from the shore a buck lay on its side, legs stiff and straight in the air, its gas-filled belly high and tight. Another day in the sun and the bag would explode with a horrible stench. Then the buzzards would come down from where they rode the upper winds in sweeping circles and soon nothing but the whitening skeleton would be left.

The ground was covered with hundreds of thousands of bleached and meatless snail shells. How or why the things had come here to crawl and die he did not know. In a cleared space between his outspread feet Clay had pressed some of them into the black dirt, forming the word and numerals "December 1835." Dusting off the grains of coarse earth he surveyed the legend and wondered if the rains would wash it away. It stood out boldly now, white and sharp.

Here, by the lake, he had fashioned his shelter, thinking, perhaps, to spend the winter. Woven fish traps dried on the water's edge and deerskins were stretched on crudely wrought frames. To pass away the time he had made bowls and small vessels from the heavy shells of lumbering gopher turtles. Racks of smoked fish hung suspended from an oaken branch and a heavy spit on forked limbs spanned the smoldering fire. His lean-to was tight and roomy. Now, strangely enough, he felt the desire to move on. There was no reason for abandoning the camp. He had been comfortable and contented here. Perhaps, he thought, it was the season. December meant Christmas, and no matter where a man was he felt the tug at his memory. Suddenly he knew he was tired of being alone. The time had come to seek out his people, to talk and drink, laugh and sing if he felt like it. God rest ye merrie, gentlemen.

On a worn and faded tracing he tried to fix his position. There were many lakes in this section of the Territory. On the bank of which one had he rested? Well, it didn't make much difference. In the morning he would push westward. There lay the Gulf and settlements strung along its shore. He'd find people to be with on Christmas. It was funny how a man could get sentimental all of a sudden and begin missing things. He thought about his grandfather and wondered if the old bastard was still alive. On a stick where he notched a calendar of sorts he counted the days. It was December and the nineteenth day. If there was a chance he could cover the distance he'd try going home. It would be kind of nice to wake up in a bed on Christmas morning. He thrust the piece of wood back in his pocket. It was too far away; too far and, he mused, too long ago for a man to catch up with in a hurry.

The thin column sweated and moved forward slowly. It wound through the clinging scrub, circling small ponds and the deep cool swamps. The sun followed relentlessly and the men cursed and itched, sweltering beneath their heavy uniforms. Mounted, with his officers, Major Francis Dade rode near the head of the plodding file. Behind him stretched the bobbing, weaving line; detachments from the Fourth Infantry and the Second and Third Artillery. Their marching feet made almost no sound in the deep and clinging sand but the screams of wheels turning on the dry axles of supply carts and the snorting of weary horses could be heard for miles.

Major Dade turned in his saddle and spoke to a young lieutenant.

"See that those wagons are greased. Every Indian in the Territory must know by now we are on the march."

Secretly the Major thought this hurried move from Fort Brooke, at Tampa, to Fort King was a monumental piece of nonsense. It was also a hell of a way to spend Christmas. Of all the God-forsaken sections of the country he had soldiered in, this was the worst. Unshaded, save for an occasional stand of pine or a treacherous swamp, the miles of sand threw back the sun's heat, catching men and beasts in the middle and frying them slowly. He thought wistfully of the shaded porch of his quarters at Fort Brooke and the breeze that sprang out over the bay at this time of day. His eyes roamed behind, over the exhausted troops. They were good men, tough and disciplined. He could count on them. He eased his seat back into the saddle and wished he could be as sure of their guide, a half-breed by the name of Pacheo. Maybe this Pacheo knew what he was about, but there were times when he damn well didn't act like it. The Major spoke through dried and cracked lips to Captain Frazer.

"Where's that fellow Pacheo? I haven't seen him since we broke for noon mess."

"He's up ahead, sir."

"I don't trust him, Captain." Major Dade squinted and tried to ease the burning of his eyes. "I wish to God we were in Fort King." He smiled grimly. "Have a nice Christmas?"

"Thank you, sir. The iced punch was delicious, the cool mint juleps frosted in the glass." The young captain sighed happily.

Major Dade winced. They had all dined on field rations and the beans were heavy in his belly. "I could have you dismissed from the service for that, Captain." He consulted his watch. "We'll break for the night at five o'clock. I'd give the men a breather now save for the fact that I don't think the effort to get going again would be worth the rest." He wheeled his horse and rode back along the column. He was a good officer and he liked to see for himself how his men fared.

Clay picked up the advance patrol about an hour before sunset. For a full ten minutes before the six mounted men and a sergeant broke out of the scrub he could hear their approach. Puzzled, he backed into the bushes and waited. When he saw the horses and the uniforms he chuckled and stepped from his hiding place.

The sergeant held a pistol on him and the patrol edged their sweating horses into a tight circle, cutting off any possible retreat. Clay watched these precautionary maneuvers with quiet amusement.

"He's white, sergeant," one of the men called.

The hard-bitten trooper kept the ugly muzzle of his weapon on a line with the chest of this shaggy and indifferent figure that had appeared so mysteriously from the thicket. Maybe he was white. Maybe he was Indian. How the hell could anyone tell what color was beneath those buckskins?

"What are you doing out here?" he demanded sharply. Civilians, particularly those who were not impressed by uniforms, always irritated him.

"Walking," Clay replied easily, and glanced around the circle. The faces of the men displayed their interest and they hunched forward, intent upon the exchange of words. Clay thought amusedly that this wasn't exactly what he had in mind when he set out to find company for Christmas.

Slightly reassured by the unmistakable accent of a white man, the sergeant lowered the barrel of his pistol an inch or so. He was still suspicious and regarded the stranger with frank curiosity.

"This is a hell of a part of the country to take a stroll in." The trooper mentally thumbed through the regulations, seeking a paragraph to cover the situation.

Clay nodded agreeably. "I was thinking the same thing."

"Where're you bound?"

"No place in particular." Clay found himself sniffing hungrily at the smell of steaming horses and damp leather. It was a good mixture and made him think of home.

"Don't you know that this part of the country is filled with hostile Indians?" The sergeant wasn't quite satisfied. No man in his right mind would be abroad alone.

Clay laughed softly. "I do," he answered, "but I sure didn't think you did from all the noise you were making. You didn't figure on surprising anyone, did you?"

"Never mind that." The reprimand was curt. The sergeant didn't like the implied criticism. He looked Clay over carefully. "I guess I ought to take you in. The Major will want to ask you a few questions."

"All right. Where's the Major?"

"A couple of miles back." The trooper extended his hand. "You'd better give me the rifle until we find out more about you."

Clay shook his head amiably. "No," his words were quietly firm, "I guess I'll keep it, Sergeant. I'm sort of used to the feel of it."

The trooper scowled. That was the trouble with a God-damned civilian, he always refused to admit the etiquette of a situation. He was half tempted to have the fellow disarmed by force and was on the point of issuing the order when something in the steady eyes made him hesitate.

"All right," he said gruffly, "I guess you can't make any trouble."

"I wasn't figuring on it, Sergeant," Clay replied.

Camp had been made quickly, set up with a minimum of confusion; guards were posted, fires laid, horses watered and fed, wagons and field pieces drawn into an orderly line. While he waited Clay looked about, absorbing every detail. He had never seen troops on the march before.

"This the fellow, Sergeant?" Lieutenant Bassinger, one year out of West Point, strode up and halted before Clay.

"Yes, sir." The sergeant saluted and stepped back.

"What's your name?" The officer snapped the question.

Clay was faintly irritated by the tone. Lazily he allowed his glance to drift over the lieutenant and then he smiled to himself. What the hell? They probably taught them to talk that way in the Army.

"Hammond," he said after a moment.

"What are you doing out here? Where did you come from? Where are you going?" The questions were crisp and businesslike.

Clay eyed the bristling officer indifferently. "I guess," he said thoughtfully, "there's some sort of mistake, Lieutenant."

"What do you mean?" Lieutenant Bassinger demanded.

"Well, you see, Lieutenant," he said quietly, "I'm just a lousy civilian and," his voice hardened, "I don't have to answer any of your God-damned questions. As a matter of fact, I don't think I will."

Bassinger flushed and he wondered a little painfully what the sergeant was thinking.

"You'd better come with me and see the Major," he said. That was a good thing about the Army. You could always pass on any unexpected difficulty, either up or down.

"That'll be all right with me, Lieutenant." Clay made a concession. "If," he added innocently, "you think it is the thing to do."

Major Dade took the young officer's salute casually. He was seated in a folding chair before his tent, boots off, collar open. Formality didn't belong out here in the field. He looked at the tall and rangy figure before him and nodded to the officer.

"The patrol picked this man up, sir." Bassinger's words suggested that he had chanced upon something important and sinister. He was disappointed when his superior didn't share the notion.

"All right, Lieutenant." Major Dade nodded a dismissal. "Thank you." He waited until his officer had left. "Were you alone?" he asked Clay. The tone was impersonal but not rude.

"Yes." Clay didn't unbend.

"What's your name?" Dade tilted his head back.

"Hammond. Clayfield Hammond."

The officer's interest was apparent. His eyes took in every item from Clay's worn and patched moccasins to his matted hair. The name of Hammond was too well known in the Territory for him to have missed it, even within the closed Army circle at Fort Brooke.

"You're a long way from the Apalachicola, Mr. Hammond," he said and then smiled. "Forgive my curiosity, but you must admit," he gestured with one hand, sweeping over Clay from head to foot, "your appearance is a little unconventional under the circumstances."

Clay loosened perceptibly. "I suppose so," he said. "I've been in the woods for quite a while."

Major Dade nodded as though the explanation was completely satisfactory. If he wondered why Clayfield Hammond was here on the lonely trail to Fort King, as dirty and dark as a savage, he kept the question to himself. He turned and called to an orderly, requesting a second chair.

"Sit down, Mr. Hammond. Have a cigar?" He waited until his guest was seated. "I imagine," he added pleasantly, "Johnson can find us a drink if you'd care for one."

"Thank you, sir. Not now." Clay took the chair and sank into it with a grateful sigh. He had covered a lot of ground. He wondered what the young lieutenant must think, seeing him seated here this way with the Major. He was probably ready to resign from the Army.

"This is a strange place in which to spend Christmas," Major Dade said conversationally.

"Do you mean for you or for me, sir?"

Major Dade tossed up his head and laughed wholeheartedly. "That wasn't exactly subtle, was it, Mr. Hammond?" He examined his cigar. "Frankly, I am curious as to why a man of your position should be here as you are."

Clay didn't reply immediately. He owed Major Dade nothing, certainly not an explanation.

"I'm not running away from anything, Major," he finally said, "if that is what you are thinking. I just happen to like it this way."

Major Dade lifted a hand in protestation. "My apologies, sir," he said. "I am too inquisitive. You are quite right. It is none of my business."

The officers' mess was laid on a table of loose boards spread over sawhorses. Clay sat near Major Dade. The orderly, Johnson, had worked well with razor and scissors. He was clean-shaven, his hair neatly trimmed. Over hot whisky toddies he met Dade's staff: Captain Gardner, Lieutenant Henderson, Captain Frazer, Lieutenant Mudge, Lieutenant Keais, and Assistant Surgeon Gatlin. As they talked the officers made no attempt to hide their interest in the stranger. Where had he been? How had he traveled? What was the nature of the country deep within the interior? More important, how had he managed to keep his scalp? Clay replied to their questions easily and without embarrassment or restraint. He was flattered by the attention and secretly amused by their ignorance of actual conditions. It was pleasant to sit among men again, to exchange courtesies with his equals.

The table was cleared, cigars and brandy passed about. Darkness fell quickly and the only light was shed by four candles spaced along the boards and small fires dotting the encampment. The officers leaned back on their canvas stools, comfortably weary, warm, and well fed. There was a reassuring feeling of tight order and smoothly functioning discipline in the camp.

"That fellow Pacheo hasn't returned, sir." Lieutenant Henderson leaned forward and addressed Major Dade. "I checked with Sergeant Phillips."

"I don't know whether that is good or bad," the commander mused behind his cigar. "Pacheo," he said to Clay, "is a guide assigned to us at Tampa. I never trusted him. I have a feeling he has been in communication with the Seminoles ever since we left Fort Brooke." He turned to Henderson. "Tell Phillips to have the man confined if he comes back tonight. I'll have a talk with him."

"Has there been trouble, sir?" Clay nodded to indicate the camp. "I've sort of been out of touch with things. This movement of troops to Fort King?"

"No-ooo." Major Dade lingered over the word. "We're simply taking one hundred men and their officers to bring Fort King's garrison up to full strength—routine precaution."

"The Indians won't fight." Captain Gardner tapped the ash from his cigar. "They may jump a man alone or burn a cabin, but they'll never move into the field in strength where we can get at them."

"I don't know, Captain." Major Dade was quietly serious. "It is difficult to tell what desperate men will do. Mr. Hammond?"

Clay watched the slender flame from the candlewick before him. It rose without a flutter in the still air, yet he had an uneasy feeling that the night was filled with movement.

"They fought once before, sir." He spoke unhurriedly and without any particular emphasis. "They stood up to General Jackson and

297

a lot of Creeks. This time they would have a better reason. Now they are being forced from their homes and into an alien country. I think they'll make a stand before they accept that."

"You don't suggest, sir," Lieutenant Keais was young enough to be eager, ignorant enough to be scornful, "that a pack of untrained savages would be foolish enough to tackle the government of the United States. Why," he rested his arms on the table, "a dozen pieces of artillery will blow them out of the Territory."

The words, Clay thought, were a part of a ritual. They must be included in the curriculum at West Point. Every soldier he had ever spoken to had said the same thing.

"The trouble is, Lieutenant," he said patiently, "you will first have to find a place to set up your artillery, and if the Seminoles fight they will not permit you to select the time or situation. You'll have to go after them and that will be like crawling into a hole to look for a bear." He glanced about the encampment and grinned. "If I was a Seminole I'd jump this place right now before you had a chance to finish that cigar."

There was a moment of silence and Clay wondered if his words had been offensive. He looked across at Major Dade.

"If you have no objections, sir," he added, "I'd sort of like to tag along with you to Fort King. I wasn't bound for any place in particular and," he smiled warmly, "I like your cook."

The officer made a gesture of assent. "I think we can circumvent the regulations, sir," he said good-naturedly. He addressed Captain Henderson. "We'll place Mr. Hammond's name on the roles as a guide, Captain." To Clay he continued, "Loose ends confuse the military mind, Mr. Hammond. Fifty years from now a clerk in the War Department will grow haggard trying to explain your presence with the detachment. We'll make it all correct and formal for him by listing you as a civilian guide."

"I'll try not to get you lost, sir."

There was an abrupt movement along the table as the officers rose to Major Dade's signal. Clay stood with them and wondered, a little foolishly, if he was supposed to snap to attention.

"Gentlemen." Major Dade bowed formally and then extended his hand to Clay. "Good night, Mr. Hammond. Johnson will have prepared quarters for you." He nodded pleasantly. "We'll move at daybreak, Captain Henderson. Good night."

The group broke apart slowly, drifting away from the table and disappearing into the darkness. Small cherry-colored mounds of fire

298

were dying reluctantly. Sentries at their posts were stiffly correct, their eyes and ears searching the darkness. Clay stood before his small tent and listened, wondering why he, alone, seemed to hear the sound of muffled drums.

25

CLAY rolled out of his blankets at the first sharp challenge of the bugle and was on his feet, dressing hurriedly while the notes still hung in the cold, damp air. It was dark within the tent, and when he tossed back the flaps and looked outside the movements of the men already about their duties were formless and indistinct. Through the low trees to the east he could see the thin, faint cracks in the shell of night. As he was slipping into his jacket Major Dade's orderly brought him a can of coffee.

"Morning, Johnson." He warmed his hands on the metal.

"Morning, sir." The orderly moved on, carrying a long stick from which small buckets were suspended by their handles. A fragrant and steaming cloud trailed in his path.

Clay drank with grateful swallows. This was his third day with the detachment and he marveled at the ease with which he had adapted himself to the unvarying routine. He was a little surprised to find himself enjoying the experience. There was a good feeling in the company of men. He liked the talk, the easy exchange of tobacco and friendship, the sharing of food, weariness, and the knowledge of an ever present danger. He could understand why soldiers set themselves apart from civilians. As the encampment stirred and more and more figures were drawn out of the darkness he sensed the kinship binding them here in this harsh pine barren. It occurred to him that he had been long alone and he felt a timid gratitude for the easy hospitality granted a stranger.

Major Dade and his officers messed at the bare table, standing about the board in the chilly dawn, stamping their feet lightly to drive the prickling numbness from their toes. They helped themselves from the platters stacked with hot corn bread, fried ham, and grits, eating determinedly but without haste. They buried their faces in the curling vapor from the mugs of coffee and silently stared up at the sky, each occupied with his own particular problem that would develop with the day.

"December twenty-eighth, gentlemen." Major Dade glanced down the length of the table. "With good fortune we should make Fort King by tomorrow."

Camp was broken quickly. It still astonished Clay to witness order emerge from what, to his untrained eyes, seemed a senseless and cursing confusion. It took a mighty lot of profanity to get troops on the march. Each morning he had confidently expected to see men and animals, wagons and the pieces of light field artillery irretrievably tangled while corporals and sergeants clubbed their shouting subordinates to death in a fit of profane exasperation. By some miracle, though, this disaster was always averted at the last minute. The camp cleared, the column formed into a whole. The twisting pieces of the serpent were once more joined with the brisk slap of hands on metal and leather. With a rolling clash of arms and the musical tinkle of trace chains the detachment moved forward to the measured slogging of booted feet.

At the end of the first day's march Clay had turned his horse in to the remount sergeant. He had spent too many months out of a saddle.

The sergeant was surprised. "You sit a horse well, sir. Anything wrong with him?"

Clay rubbed at his sore tail and felt tenderly of the chafed sections along his thighs. It would take a day of walking to work out the stiffness.

"The horse is all right," he explained ruefully. "He's tougher than I am. That's the trouble."

He liked being afoot better. That way he could drop back along the length of the column, talking with the troops, sharing the small conversations that lightened packs and made marching easier. There were men from as far west as Ohio; boys from Pennsylvania, New Jersey, Georgia, and Tennessee. Few, if any, were quite sure why they were trudging through this wilderness. It was all part of a plan arrived at by God and the Secretary of War. They had had no experience in Indian fighting and the only Seminoles they had seen were those who came regularly to Fort Brooke to sell baskets, tanned alligator hides, beadwork, and moccasins. From what they knew of these Indians they didn't think much of them as fighting men.

Clay formed the habit of marching with a downy-faced private, George Lasker, who came from Nashville. The youngster regarded this big stranger as a combination of Daniel Boone and Florida's original settler. His curiosity about the Territory, how the people far in the interior and along the eastern seaboard lived, was insatiable. Now and then Clay found himself inventing things to satisfy his interest.

"Hit's a funny thing," Lasker had said after he had cautiously accepted Clay's unspoken offer of companionship, "my daddy fought down heah 'longside Andrew Jackson. Naow," he squirted a fine stream of tobacco juice from between broken teeth, "heah Ah'm at hit, packin' a gun with one hand an holdin' onto my scalp with the othah. Looks to me like they shoulda done the job right at fust so's theah'd be no need foah us all to do hit again."

On his way to the head of the column this morning Clay passed Lasker and gave him a friendly nod. The mountain boy grinned back. He wasn't, Clay thought, accustomed to having a fight end indecisively. When men lit into each other they kept at it until one or the other was licked.

The column moved slowly, its pace measured to the creeping oxcarts supplementing the horse-drawn wagons. That, Clay reflected, was a hell of a way to send a detachment through hostile territory. If the government was going to fight Indians they'd have to lean heavily on mobility, otherwise they were dead roosters.

Major Dade glanced down from his horse. "Still walking, Mr. Hammond?"

"It's harder on my legs, sir," Clay replied, "but easier on my rear end."

"Soak it in brine, sir," the Major laughed. "You want to sit in a pickling vat for a few days. Stick pins in yourself after that."

"That's a hell of a pastime, Major." He chuckled and dropped back a few paces. The officer was a fine man, he thought. All soldier, hard and strict, he softened his discipline, however, with understanding and solicitude for the welfare of his men.

The guide Pacheo never returned. Either he had been picked off by a roving band of Seminoles or he had run away from an unpleasant and hazardous job. Clay thought the latter was more likely. Actually, there had been small need for a guide. The trail between Tampa and Fort King was marked well enough. In volunteering his services Clay had little to offer save his general knowledge of the terrain and suggestions for scouting parties and the selection of camp sites. A patrol was already out, half an hour ahead of the column, fanning away from the trail and gathering at agreed-upon intervals. Clay privately considered these sorties foolish. If the Indians intended to attack they would have been scouting the detachment from the moment it marched away from Fort Brooke. They had by this time roughly calculated the number of miles the column would average each day and had settled upon the point where a battle could be joined. Major Dade's noisy and inexperienced patrol could serve only to keep the warriors alerted.

This was a thinly wooded section of stunted, spindly trees, palmetto scrub, and high grass. The trail was little more than a faint thinning out of the bush and the old marks of wagon wheels in the yielding sand. During the summer months the country hereabouts was almost unbearably hot, storing up the sun, rarely touched by a cooling breeze. Now it was locked in the chill of midwinter. In the east the sun was breaking out of the early-morning clouds and the light glistened on the moisture-laden scrub, turning the wet grass into rainbow spinnings. Clay slowed his pace and allowed the column to inch past. He'd walk with young Lasker for a while. The men, accustomed to the sight of him, no longer turned their heads to stare. One or two called a greeting, but for the most part they were settling their shoulders to the weight of rifles and packs, adjusting themselves to the grinding monotony of a full day's march. That was soldiering, marching and waiting. From their warming bodies and those of the horses and sad-eyed oxen a cloudy barnyard odor rose and hung like a scarf of fog along the trail.

Clay dropped in beside the boy from Tennessee.

"How you, suh?" Lasker pushed the peak of his cap back. "Hit's a suah enough good day foah walkin'." He dug in his blouse and handed Clay a plug of tobacco.

Although the sun had not risen high enough to warm the air, the soldier, like his companions, was already sweating. Clay bit off a chew, and as he worked the tobacco into a soft ball he wondered what boys and men like Lasker here would do when they had to campaign in Florida during the summer months. They'd sag and drop beneath a sun that could curl the hide from a snake, suffocating in the shoddy woolen uniforms. In July and August the heat here developed with the intensity of a desert oven. The small and fitful winds carried no relief but licked hotly at a man until he gasped for breath and his tongue lolled out like a dog's. There was no escape, not even in the dark of the swamps. There the heat lay sluggish and evil. Swarms of savage mosquitoes moved in ravenous clouds bringing sickness and torture. Everyone in the government couldn't be a fool, although that seemed to be the general opinion. Sending troops into the Territory with equipment that would have been fine for exploring the Northwest was a hell of a mistake on someone's part. He had read how the British tried to fight the Indians wearing red coats and fur hats and with white cross-belts marking the target. This was the same stupidity.

"What are you going to do when you get out of the Army?" Clay made idle conversation.

"Ah'm goin' to build me a still in th' mountain an' lay beside hit foah th' rest of my life, lettin' th' run trickle into my open mouth." The boy's eyes grew dreamy over the prospect.

Clay hitched his rifle to a more comfortable position. The muffled sloughing of many feet in the loose earth was the sound of heavy breathing against the morning's silence. The column snaked jerkily forward, topping a gentle rise, and the trail led down beside a broad pond, dark as the polished surface of mahogany, unwrinkled in the calm of daybreak. The thick pads of lilies floated without motion and the marshy grass was stiff and yellow along the path's edge. To the left the high scrub and scattered trees showed no sign of living things. Unconsciously Clay checked his easy stride and his forehead wrinkled as he attempted to define a vague apprehension. Something, he could give it no name, was wrong; something was missing, and his inability to name it filled him with an uneasy caution.

Young Lasker cast a quick glance out of the corners of his eyes and noted the expression of puzzled concern on the face of his companion. Clay's head turned slowly from the pond to the scrub, his inspection moving rapidly in a wide arc.

"Somethin' botherin' you, suh?" Lasker was curious.

Clay nodded. What, he experienced a momentary irritation at his stupidity, what was it that his eyes were failing to see? Something should be here, and yet it was not. Instinct nagged and warned. His searching glance swept back from the bush and lingered on the water.

"If I was an Indian," he spoke to himself but the words were loud enough to carry the short distance separating him from Lasker, "if I was an Indian," he repeated, "and wanted to whack into this column, here's where I'd do it, where the pond on one side would bog down a maneuver and cut off a retreat."

The detachment leveled out on the slightly ridged trail. Over the weaving heads of the men Clay caught a glimpse of Major Dade and his staff, riding slowly and unconcerned. His gaze went back to the pond and suddenly he knew what it was that had troubled him. Here was a natural resting and feeding place for the wild fowl. Ducks straying from southbound flocks would light and perhaps winter here. The slate-gray, long-legged cranes would feed within the reedy brakes and coots dive and fish beneath the green pads. Now nothing moved on the placid surface of the water, nor was there a circling of startled fowl frightened into the air by the noise and movement of the troops. Something had already sent them winging away. Something, crowding into the scrub before the arrival of the column, had hurled the birds aloft and out of sight. His eyes went again to the scrub and he knew a sudden breathlessness.

The long rifle came up quickly and he held it across his chest. Beneath his thumb the hammer rose and clicked sharply. The sound was crisp, decisive. Young Lasker regarded him with amazement and in his hurried glance there was a shadow of surprise.

"Watch yourself," Clay whispered, his eyes intent upon the motionless scrub. "I've got a funny feeling."

The entire column was strung out now within the narrow defile, its bobbing reflection drawn upon the pond's mirrored surface. Clay swallowed at the lump that refused to be dislodged from his throat. This had to be it. The whole God-damned detachment backed against the pond. The scrub out there crawling with Seminoles, concealed in the thick palmetto clumps. So certain was he of the ambush that when the frenzied, piercing cry shrilled to the sky he was not surprised.

"Yo-ho-e-hee." There was a terrible, raging insanity in the shriek.

The scrub boiled with the eruption of dark figures, rising from each gray-green tangle of spreading fans. Half naked, smeared with red and blue splashes of color, their mouths stretching with hideous screams, they turned a sheet of roaring fire on the detachment and the entire forward section of the column withered and curled beneath the fury. As he dropped to his belly Clay saw Major Dade pitch from his horse and fall heavily. With him crumpled his staff. Captain Gardner, Lieutenant Keais, Surgeon Gatlin, and Captain Frazer bent forward slowly, as though possessed by an uncontrollable weariness, and were tossed roughly to the ground by their crazed and rearing mounts. One horse plunged madly across the scrub, straight in the direction of the Indians. Its rider's foot was caught in the stirrup and the lifeless body flipped and bounced with idiotic gymnastics. Even as the thunder of this first volley roared in his ears Clay could distinguish the agonized screams of wounded men lay in death or convulsed in agony, their blood staining the piping whinny of horses. As the heavy, searing powder smoke blotted out the scrub, fully seventy-five of the column's one hundred men lay in death or convulsed in agony, their blood staining the sand. The Dade massacre had begun.

Out of the confusion the hoarse shouts of the noncommissioned officers tried, with futile blasphemy, to call some sort of order from the demoralized survivors, who were scattering like hysterical chickens, sloshing through the pond's shallow waters, crawling backward on their hands and knees, scuttling forward and then back in panic-stricken feints and sallies. A field piece was swung out in the direction of the invisible enemy and fired, but the shot whistled high above the trembling scrub, and as the men worked to reload three Seminoles stepped coolly from behind protecting trees and shot them dead.

Clay moved back with deliberate caution, sliding on the loose earth and trying to keep his body within the rutted trough. He reached for Lasker, tapping him gently on the shoulder as a signal to follow. When the boy didn't move Clay rolled him over and stared at the bloody mask of his face. No more than twenty men attempted the slow retreat. Only a brief interval was allowed them as the Seminoles scattered to reload. A hundred yards or so back there was a thick stand of saplings. Clay tossed a quick glance over his shoulder, estimating the distance, and then turned to face the enemy. A faint twitching movement in the scrub brought the rifle to his shoulder and for a second the object lay on his sight. He fired and through the smoke saw the Indian's arms flung high toward the sky and the figure topple forward across the palmettos.

The Seminoles were yelling from their places of concealment and firing spasmodically. The bullets whacked into the sand, kicking the dirt into little showers. A couple of soldiers who had sloshed in panic-stricken haste to the middle of the pond stood waist deep in the water and screamed their helpless terror as they found themselves trapped. The reports of two Seminole rifles sounded almost simultaneously and the men spun awkwardly and dropped with heavy splashes.

"We better get the hell out of here and fast." Clay, busy reloading, spoke hastily to a grizzled corporal at his side.

The man was cursing, slowly and methodically—terrible, deep-throated words—firing as fast as he could load and sight his piece.

"Flies on a wall," he muttered, "Christ-bitten flies on a wall. That's what we are."

The fifteen or so survivors were scattered about the trail. They were leaderless, demoralized, and only the will for self-preservation made them load and fire at unseen targets; they held death at an arm's length.

"Maybe we can make those trees." Clay gestured with his head. The corporal twisted about, looked behind him, and nodded.

"Let 'em have it all at once," he shouted to the men, "an' then run like hell for them trees. Now!"

The pitifully few rifles spoke in unison and as the belching smoke formed an uncertain screen the men rose and fled back along the trail toward the dubious shelter. Three were caught at the edge of the woods. Clay could hear the soggy thump of the balls as they ripped into their unprotected backs. They fell as they ran and then heads dug short channels into the earth.

Behind the thin barrier of trees they could look far down the trail where the sprawled and twisted bodies of Dade's command were dark humps on the short, yellowed grass. Wounded horses and men screamed in their fear and pain, thrashing helplessly. Clay wiped at the sweat pouring over his face. This was bad enough, to lie here and watch the dead and dying. What would come next would be worse. Somehow he had dug his open mouth into the sand and he spat the gritty mess from tongue and lips.

The corporal stormed among the men, kicking and cursing, rousing them to action. With hatchets they felled the slender pines and stacked them into a triangular breastworks. The Indians were out of range. They moved with darting wariness at first, sliding from one cover to the next, but when their movements drew no fire they abandoned all caution and raged among the dead and stricken. The triumphant gibberish of their frenzy was thin and distant. They bent, leaping from body to body. Knives and ax blades rose and fell as they hacked and mutilated the hated foe. Clay watched with helpless fascination as one warrior raised a dripping scalp and with a yell rubbed the streaming thing over his chest. The blood was bright and red against the dark skin. Their fury unslaked, the Indians raced among their victims, beating heads into sticky pulp with the butts of captured rifles.

"God A'mighty." The corporal licked at his lips, his eyes wide with incredulous horror. "God A'mighty."

A young private, not more than seventeen, began to laugh with uncontrollable hysteria and then fell forward, burying his contorted face in the dirt, his body twitching with a terrible and consuming fear.

"We ain't goin' to get out of this." The corporal spoke to Clay. "A hundred men an' some good officers. A hundred men," he repeated wonderingly, and wiped his hand across the loose pine needles with a motion of erasure.

While the main body of the Seminoles raced among the fallen, stabbing and scalping, looting the wagons and dragging the field pieces from the tangle, a small group broke away and began a wide circle that would bring them to the flank of the survivors among the pines.

The cornered men watched, their heads turning slowly to follow

307

the movement. They were silent spectators at a macabre dance, and their rifles swung about, tracing the fantastic measures.

"Hold your fire," the corporal said wearily. "It won't do no good from here." His short laugh was bitter. "It won't do no good at all, no time." He scrubbed at his mouth with the back of a hairy wrist.

Clay squinted through the chinks in the barricade. The Indians were stripped down for the grim business of war. They had not come into the field bedecked with feathers or traditional finery. Short breechclouts or loose, seatless leggings and moccasins were their only garments. Unencumbered, intent upon the business at hand as a stalking lynx, each warrior made his moves with deadly certainty.

"How do they fight?" Without realizing it the corporal lowered his voice to a husky whisper. "I mean, do they come with a yell and a charge?"

"Not now." Clay drew a plug of tobacco from his shirt, bit off a piece, and passed it over. "They'll just pin us down here. When the rest get finished they'll move around and begin picking us off."

The corporal returned the plug. "The recruiting sergeant didn't say nothin' about this when I joined up. He just said the food was good an' the pay steady." His jaws worked silently for a moment. "What the hell you doin' here?" He cocked an eye at Clay.

"I'm damned if I know," Clay replied thoughtfully. "I wanted company."

The corporal grunted. "Then you sure an' hell got it."

Clay looked up through the trees to the sky. Already there were black dots high in the blue dome. Tonight or tomorrow they would come down, slowly at first and then with an evil rush, to seize the choice bits, the staring eyes and the soft meat of swelling guts. His mouth was suddenly dry, the tobacco without juice. What the hell am I doing here? he asked himself. I was just an easygoing sort of fellow, and look at all the things that began happening to me. I shot and killed a friend and now I'm stretched out here in this God-neglected scrub waiting for an Indian to lift my hair. How the hell did all of this get tacked onto me? I sure didn't go looking for it. First one little thing and then another. How the hell can a man get so tangled? All I had to do was take things easy back there with Old Clay. After he got used to the idea, I could maybe have married Sue Rogers and raised a fine family. No, by God, that wasn't enough, and so here I am and the chances are a thousand to one that the buzzards will be working on me by sunset. If that isn't a hell of a prospect I don't know what is.

The corporal, who had moved away, crawling among the men,

talking with them, checking their rifles and ammunition, returned and dropped down again beside Clay. The bodies of the crouching Indians to their left were all but concealed by the high grass and palmetto scrub and the clamor down the trail was dying as the bloody excitement cooled and the stored fury spent itself. They were looting now, carefully and with a purpose, stripping the wagons of the supplies they could carry away and use. From a distance their movements seemed not quite real, part of a demoniac pantomime. As he watched Clay couldn't stifle a reluctant feeling of admiration. This was it. Damned if the Indians weren't taking on the whole United States government.

The warrior party on their left had crept within range and they fired, scattered shooting that sent balls nicking across the pine logs or sinking with vicious thuds into the soft wood. When the Seminoles down the trail were ready they'd move up and the dozen or so men within the stockade would be trapped.

"You suppose we could run for it?" The corporal's eyes were trained on the scrub.

"Where?" Clay's rifle followed the distant tip of a blue turkey feather as it rose behind a clump of palmettos. When the jerky movement halted for a second he fired. The mark vanished but he couldn't be certain of a hit. He reloaded. "Where do you want to run?" He didn't look at the corporal.

"By God, it'd be better than waitin' here." The soldier couldn't keep a note of panic from his voice.

"You'd be on the wrong end of a rabbit hunt." Clay drove a wad home and tapped it with the rod. "They'd chase you down, one by one, if you separated. If you tried to keep together they'd drive you to the edge of a swamp like tame chickens."

The firing from the left had increased and there was a shrill, fluting scream of pain as a random ball found one of the men. His hands pawed at his face and the crimson stain spread through the fingers. The remaining men drew away from him as though the horror could contaminate them all. With convulsive jerkings the stricken man dropped to his knees, fell forward, and lay still. A boy still in his teens began to retch. He crawled to the opposite side of the stockade and sobbed, choking on his vomit, while his companions pretended not to notice.

"Don't get the idea," Clay turned from the spectacle, "that I'm any hero. I'm as scared as you are." He ducked as a ball scarred the top of a log and sent a shower of bark into his face. "Here it comes." His head jerked quickly in the direction of the trail.

The main body of the Seminoles had begun to move around in a slow, cautious sweep. They fired as they crept through the cover, spending the captured powder recklessly out of range, blazing away with triumphant abandon as they closed in for the kill. The corporal divided his forces on each side of the barricade, and as the men took their places Clay marveled at the discipline that held them together in the face of certain annihilation.

"You could cut an' run for it." The corporal glanced at him. "After all, this ain't your fight. You've got no reason to stay. You're a civilian."

Clay nodded. "I was thinking the same thing," he admitted frankly.

"Well," the voice carried a faint note of irritation, "why the hell don't you go?"

"I'm damned if I know. I've been lying here trying to figure it out." He couldn't take his eyes from the slow, relentless movement down the trail.

There was only a short yell of warning and then it happened. The pine glade was suddenly filled with Indians. They roared out of the scrub and over the breastworks, clubbing their muskets and rifles, working frenziedly with knives and hatchets. Clay discharged his piece full into a naked belly and rolled to dodge a sweeping blow of a hatchet. On his feet he swung the long rifle in a tight arc and felt it smack into a screaming face. Then someone was on his back, and as he twisted he took a long slash in one arm. The stinking, wet-dog smell of the Indian was strong in his nostrils as he spun with his attacker, over and over. Rolling and snarling, he tried to hold off the quick death as his fingers closed over a wrist and thrust back a bloody knife. They were outside the stockade now, their heads and bodies beating into the small pines with sickening jolts. For a second a lucky shift of weight brought him astride the Indian. He thrust with all of his power on the upraised arm and the knife blade disappeared into the exposed throat. Hot blood sprayed across his face and the man died with a small gurgling sound. Gasping and spent, Clay pulled himself across the still body. A quick glance over his shoulder told him that the issue there was in no doubt. The Seminoles, three or more to a man, were killing and scalping with insensate rage, too busy to notice what went on outside the slaughtering pen of the stockade. Clay ran. He bent his body and sprinted through the trees. Behind him he could hear the exultant screaming. Only seconds were left to him before the main band would have closed the circle, shutting off the last avenue of escape. His rifle was somewhere on the ground but there was no moment to seek it. He ran bounding between the trees until he had cleared the grove and was in the open scrub. He could not take the time to look around to see if he was being pursued. All that mattered now was to get away, to lose himself in the heavy brush. As his feet raced over the uneven earth he could hear the pandemonium receding and above it the triumphant war cry was fiercely exultant.

Within the high scrub at the edge of Fort King tight and angry bellies were flattened to the lean earth and the Indians stared out through the dense tangle with unblinking patience. During the night and in the brief hours of dawn they had come to this place and now they waited. As each man arrived he laid the short stick of counting before Asseola and then moved silently to an empty patch of ground. The sticks, fifty in number, made a jackstraw pile at Asseola's hand. His fingers played among them, balancing one upon the other. The chill of evening crept upon the dying sun and in the stripped fields of corn the wind moved and the curled brown leaves whispered with a dry crackle. In the clear distance the plaintive notes of a bugle sounding retreat awoke a pensive owl.

Propped upon his elbows Asseola gazed fixedly at the barnlike structure of the sutler's warehouse and home. Soon a man, Wiley Thompson, must walk forth. Having taken his nightly meal with the merchant and his clerks, the agent would stroll through the twilight to his quarters at the fort, a mile away. This night death would be waiting to take him by the hand.

Asseola's glance swept quickly over the warriors gathered on each side and a brief smile of understanding played for a moment in his eyes. Discipline did not come easily to his people, and yet they held themselves upon his signal. Deep within him the small voice of conscience sought again to make itself heard. This day he should have moved swiftly to join Alligator and the war party assembled somewhere near the Great Wahoo Swamp. Now the hour had come and gone. The blood of Seminole and white dried upon the green shoots or made small coppers in the sand. Alligator, with over two hundred warriors, would already have struck at the soldiers marching from the west. How had this battle gone while he tarried because the man Thompson must die at his hand? An Indian of great spirit, he thought regretfully, would not have acted so. He who would be a chief in actions as in words would have thrust aside all promptings for personal vengeance and given his strength where it was needed. This I have not done. Perhaps, he mused sadly, I am no chief. While my people are ready to die, as

311

they cling helplessly to a small portion of this fair land, I remember only how the voice of a maid was gentle. This girl, Che-cho-ter, who was the dew of morning, is dead to me now. Yet there will be many deaths, and in the lodges of my people the song of lamentation will not be stilled by the years. How is it then that I dare say, Hold a while and forget this dream of freedom while I pause to kill a man? Witness how I have suffered. Is this not greater than your misery? My wife was called a slave, taken as a common black girl by the whites, and this man Thompson and his office stood idly by. When I went to him he said nothing could be done. When I protested and later raised my voice he caused me to be chained as a dog and locked within a cell. Is not this enough? It may be that I am no chief but only a man who had taken a girl as wife. A man has but his own honor and must satisfy it in his own way. There would be no heart in me for the long fight if I knew the agent Thompson went unpunished. So I have waited. He glanced up through the low-hanging branches. How, the question repeated itself over and over, had the attack been met? Where stood the results of this first battle? It had been carefully planned. Even the fat and reluctant Micanopy had been forced to it, lending authority and significance to the blow, so that all within the Seminole nation should understand the hour had struck.

The door of the sutler's house opened and men stood upon the bare porch. Two of them parted from the group and left the steps, walking without haste down the path. The waiting Indians were tense, their breathing suddenly audible and an eagerness gathered within each sprawled body.

Thompson and his companion, Lieutenant Smith, were in no hurry. They had eaten well. The flavor of tobacco was pleasant on their tongues, the evening hushed and fragrant. They moved with quiet confidence. A dispatch delivered earlier in the week had advised that a detachment under the command of Major Dade might be expected at Fort King from Tampa. The news of reinforcements had been welcome to the small garrison and the agent was certain an end could be put to this Indian nonsense. He turned to speak to the officer but a movement in the scrub ahead caused his head to jerk back with quick suspicion and he stared at the all but naked Seminole blocking the narrow lane.

In the bright twilight the shining white of the curling egret plume, full and purple tipped, rose as a tumbling crest. There was no time for the agent to cry out. The report of Asseola's rifle shattered the silence and then the bunched scrub spewed whistling flame and the heavy slugs of a dozen or more rifles tore into Thompson and Smith, beating them to the ground. The Indians swarmed from their hiding place, streaming past Asseola. One yelping warrior, the first to reach Smith, paused and stripped the scalp from the officer's head and then ran with the others as they closed upon the sutler's house.

Asseola stood above Thompson. The short, excited barks of his warriors were meaningless. Let them burn and loot. They had been patient and should have their share of the triumph, things men could hold in their hands or stuff into their bellies. At the moment he wanted none of them. He bent over Thompson and slashed at the agent's head. Never before had he scalped a man. Never, save as a youthful jest, had he made the circular motion with a knife at a man's head. As the blood started along the moving edge of the blade he knew a compelling exultation and his scream of triumph echoed back along the dark corridors of his heritage. This was truth, and only by holding it in his hands could a man know it. Let them call him Powell, as the white man had been spoken of. Let their bastard accents sound his name as Osceola. Let those of his own people whisper guardedly that perhaps he had lived too long among the whites and spoke their tongue too well. This that he now felt was Indian and would not be denied. He snatched at the grisly trophy and the small fibers parted with a dry, ripping sound. As the furiously yelling warriors raced upon the sutler's house he held the wet hair in his hand and the dripping crimson fell in vivid splotches on his moccasins.

The sutler and his assistants died quickly and the raiders looted the warehouse of its stores of powder, lead, whisky, dried beef, bacon, and corn meal. At Fort King the garrison, alerted by the distant shooting, hesitated. They were few in number and no one could say the strength of the Seminoles out there. As Asseola walked toward the buildings smoke was already twisting through the windows. Soon the flames would belch out and lick across the fat pine boards and the smudge would be a black warning on the clouds.

Weighted heavily with the spoils, chattering delightedly and barking with short, furious yaps of triumph, the Indians trotted with doglike intentness into the lowering night. They moved in a single, shortly spaced file, swinging with an easy, ground-covering stride. It was good to watch whites die. They made so much noise.

Behind them the sutler's house was a vast roaring cone of flames. At the wood's edge Asseola swung around and looked back. The fiery pillar was ugly against the sky. All men who looked upon the evil stain would know that the menace must envelop them. For the Indians there could be no retreat save to the grave.

26

In the surgeon's office at Fort Drane, Clay sat on the corner of a bare table and gritted his teeth against the pain as the officer re-bandaged his swollen and throbbing arm. The stink of pus-filled cloth in the old wrappings was sickeningly sweet and he turned his eyes from the yellowed mound of scraps and wadded cotton.

"I'd give a lot to know," the surgeon made a few quick ties, "why that arm hasn't dropped off. It was crawling like a piece of rotten cheese. Offhand," he remarked cheerfully, "I should say you ought to have died thirty-six hours ago."

Clay took a deep breath. The arm was a thing of throbbing agony from finger tips to shoulder and enlarged to almost unrecognizable proportions.

"I smeared some pitch on it," he said after a moment, "and then bound it with a strip from my shirt and green pine needles."

The officer nodded happily. "That helped," he agreed. "Of course, it would have been better if you had taken a whisker from a red cat found in a graveyard at midnight. They do say that combination is pretty good for knife wounds." He stepped back and squinted at his work. "Burning a quill from a blue-tailed frog is reputed to be equally efficacious."

Clay couldn't hold back a grin. "I'll tell you the truth," he said. "I was running too damn hard from those Seminoles to stop and hunt a blue-tailed frog. I'll remember it, though."

"Do that." The officer grunted and waved him from the table. "It seems to be draining all right, and maybe you won't lose it after all. Medical science will never understand why. I don't suppose it would do any good to suggest you go to bed for a few days?"

"I don't guess so. Too many things are happening."

The surgeon went to a small cabinet and poured two drinks of whisky. "I always take one with the patient," he said and handed Clay a glass. "Makes 'em feel better."

Clay sipped at the liquor. It was strong rye of a dark red color with a heavy, unfamiliar taste. "You sterilize the instruments in this?" He held it to the light.

"It's better than pine needles."

Clay tossed off the balance of the whisky. If it wasn't for the painful heaviness in his arm, he thought, he'd feel pretty good. Five days ago he had slumped into Fort Drane, northwest of Fort King, exhausted, half-maddened by the pain, and delirious from the mounting fever. His arm had grown to the size of his leg from the poison in the gash, which had laid it open from shoulder to elbow. In his lucid moments he told a slightly incredulous officer of the massacre near the Wahoo Swamp. Later, while a muttering surgeon worked over the arm, he repeated the story for General Clinch, filling in the gaps and adding details that swept away any doubts the post's commander might have entertained. Then he collapsed and slept for sixteen hours. Now his strength was returning, and it was possible to look back over the nightmare experience and wonder how he had survived. Those damn Indians had run him like hunters on the trail of a wounded deer and he'd beaten them, outsmarted and outthought them in their own country. It had been a hell of a chase. Of one thing he was certain: It was mighty hard to like people when they were yelling for your guts. He'd sort of look at Seminoles a little differently from now on.

The surgeon, washing his hands at a basin, tossed a question over his shoulder. "You don't think any of them got out alive?"

"I don't know, Doctor." Clay stood up. "From where I was it didn't seem likely. Maybe one or two wounded men could have crawled away in the excitement. The only reason I'm here is luck."

"It's hard to believe." The surgeon dried his hands carefully. "They were good men with competent officers. Can you imagine," there was grudging tribute in his voice, "those bastards taking on the United States Army?"

An orderly stepped in through the open doorway, saluted the surgeon, and turned to Clay. "General Clinch," he said, "would like to see you, Mr. Hammond, when you've finished here."

"Go ahead." The officer laid a hand on Clay's shoulder. "Come back in the morning and I'll put another dressing on that arm. If you can't sleep I'll send over some whisky."

As he walked across the compound toward the low building that housed headquarters Clay thought a little acidly that he might just as well join the Army and have it over with. A half-dozen times during the past days he had repeated his story from the moment he joined Dade's company until the final minutes of catastrophe. The

316

military mind's insistence on every small detail began to irritate him. It was almost as though General Clinch and his staff didn't want to believe the story. I'm damned, he thought crossly, if I don't sometimes get the idea they think I'm responsible. Why don't they shoot me as a Seminole spy or something and have it done with? He had flared once, in the face of persistent questioning, and suggested that General Clinch send out a detail from Fort Drane and satisfy himself.

As though the ambushing of Major Dade and the murder of Wiley Thompson fired a long-awaited signal, the entire Territory exploded, blazing with incredible violence. Along the east coast, from New Smyrna to St. Augustine, the Indians ranged in small, fast-moving bands. They killed and burned with bloodthirsty abandon. As the reports trickled in to Fort Drane the extent of the crimson onslaught became apparent. Not even the most complacent desk officer could delude himself any longer that these were savage, unplanned attacks by unorganized bands of Seminoles. The pattern became disconcertingly clear. The Indians were fighting as they pleased, throwing the Territory into a state of heaving panic. They struck and vanished, reappearing miles distant to hit again. A cumbersome military machine was powerless to anticipate their movements. Artillery, cavalry detachments, and infantry were useless against an enemy that would not stand and permit itself to be engaged. No less than sixteen of the largest plantations on the eastern seaboard had gone up in flames. The whites, trapped and defenseless, were slaughtered without mercy. Their homes were reduced to blackened heaps, their crops destroyed, cattle slaughtered or driven away, slaves killed or herded into Seminole camps within the dark swamps where they worked with the Indian women and children, running bullets, planting, and caring for the wounded. St. Augustine was an almost closed and besieged town. Transportation and commerce were at a standstill and the red tide of destruction spread as a creeping smear into central Florida. Pitiful bands of refugees tried to reach the safety of the larger communities or flee across the northern border into Georgia. They were trapped and cut down. The Indians spared nothing. It was as though they hoped that in one furious outbreak they could destroy the entire white population. Those who had called loudest for military intervention now screamed frantically for protection. Settlers abandoned their farms, and land values disappeared. No one could know when the terror would end. Anxiously Clay had listened to the reports as they came in to Fort Drane. He wondered what was happening along the Apalachicola and wanted to get home to see for himself. There were rumors that the Creeks in Georgia were rising to join the Seminoles. If that happened, then the entire northwest section of the Territory would be enveloped in the fury.

The orderly conducted him to General Clinch and a meeting of the staff. The officers were seated at a long table and concern was apparent on each face. Fort Drane was rapidly becoming an isolated position. The garrison could no longer count on supplies. Communication was uncertain and it had become virtually impossible to send or receive accurate information. All of the neat mechanics of operation had been disrupted.

"How are you feeling, Mr. Hammond?" General Clinch indicated a seat with a gesture.

"Better, General, thank you." Clay took the chair, wondering if this was the opening of another inquisition.

"That's fine." The officer nodded pleasantly. He hesitated briefly. "I'll come to the point, Mr. Hammond," he said decisively. "Our situation at the moment is," he sought the exact shading, "delicate; not precarious, but delicate. We are temporarily off balance because of lack of information. The two scouts and dispatch riders we depend upon have apparently been waylaid and killed. They are overdue and I can only assume they are dead. Among my own men," he stared reflectively at the ceiling, "none is familiar enough with the Territory to undertake more than the simplest of missions. For instance," his gaze returned to Clay, "I am almost certain that Fort Brooke is invested by Negroes and Indians, yet I have no way of determining the exact situation. Also, I have only fragmentary reports to the effect that General Eustis, commanding at Charleston, has been directed to proceed to the Florida Territory and open communications. To operate intelligently I must have more than rumors. From what you have told me I conclude that your knowledge of the Territory would be an invaluable asset. I ask you now if you would consider attaching yourself to my command in a civilian capacity as dispatch rider and intelligence liaison. You would, of course, be subject to orders but not the routine discipline."

Clay was aware that the head of each man at the table was turned in his direction. He delayed a reply to the unusual request, weighing the many implications. There was a fine, dashing sound to the words "dispatch rider." There was also a fine chance a man could die unpleasantly at the job.

"I never thought much about fighting Indians, General." He spoke quietly. "Actually, I don't think I like the idea."

"Good God, man!" The explosion came quickly. "We are surrounded by murdering, insane savages, and you, a white man, hesitate to ally yourself with your own people. This is war, Mr. Hammond."

Clay smiled good-humoredly. "I ought to know, General, having already seen some of it."

"Mr. Hammond." General Clinch laid emphasis on the words. "You don't entertain any doubts as to the ultimate decision in this conflict, do you?"

"No," Clay admitted, "I guess the United States can lick a few thousand Seminoles. It may take a little longer than a lot of people think, but in the end I imagine the government will do the job. It'll have to when you come right down to it."

General Clinch nodded. "That being the case, Mr. Hammond, what is the purpose of delaying the inevitable? If by any contribution, no matter how small, you could bring the conflict to a close one day or one hour sooner, wouldn't your action be justified no matter what personal feelings you may entertain as to the justice of the cause?"

That was a long speech and Clay grinned despite the gravity of the moment. The officer was right, of course. The Indians were only going to get themselves killed off. The sooner they learned it and gave in, the better for everyone in the country.

"That sounds reasonable, General," he agreed. "I guess I'd better pitch in with you. Right now, though," he touched his arm, "I'm not fit for travel. When this swelling goes down I'll do what I can, short of enlisting. First, though, I want to make a trip back home and see how things are with my grandfather."

The officers stared at him and Clay wondered what he had said to call forth such a unanimous expression of skeptical disbelief.

"Do you mean to tell me," General Clinch seemed to lean down the table, "that under the circumstances you would undertake a lone journey back to the Apalachicola? Why, man, you wouldn't get beyond the Suwannee River."

Clay couldn't control the laughter. Maybe the General didn't know what he was saying or how foolish it sounded on top of just having asked him to undertake missions of the same nature for the Army. If he couldn't make it back to Clayport for himself, then he sure as hell couldn't ride around on a horse for anyone else.

"Isn't that just what you've been asking me to do for you,

319

General?" he asked. "Or do you mean if I'm working for you the Indians won't bother me?"

The officer had the grace to smile. "Well," the explanation was halting and he knew it, "I had thought to offer you whatever protection you deemed necessary."

Clay was tired and his arm hurt. No matter what anyone wanted of him, he was going home first. The Indians would wait. After he had seen how things were back along the Apalachicola he'd lend a hand if they thought it would help.

"You'll forgive me, sir," he said, "if I point out that Major Dade and one hundred men should have guaranteed some sort of protection. I'll get around faster alone."

"Yes, of course," General Clinch agreed heavily. "I suppose if you are determined to go home you must. We certainly can't stop you. I'll be grateful for your word, however, that you'll return at the earliest opportunity."

"I'll be back if I say I will." Clay rose. "Before I go I'll need a new rifle. Mine is somewhere along the Fort Brooke trail."

"We'll arrange the proper requisition." The General's smile was wintry. "The Army has plenty of rifles. What it needs is some targets that will stand in one place long enough for us to use them. Thank you for coming in, sir."

Clay strolled back to his quarters. The brazen sunlight hurt his eyes and he wanted to lie down where it was quiet and think this over. Fighting Indians because you had to, the way it had been with Major Dade, was one thing. Going out and looking for trouble was another. Actually, he thought soberly, it wouldn't make much difference from now on. The tribes were out and raising hell, ready to jump any white they found. The only way a man could be safe, if that was what he wanted, was to lock himself away or get out of the Territory. Things had, he reflected, gone beyond the point where you could stand on the side and watch. It was shoot, get shot, or get out of the way. I'm damned, he told himself, if I'm going to hole up until it's safe to come out again. He kicked along the path. To do a real good job of fighting a man had to be angry, and the trouble was he couldn't get mad at the Indians. He'd fought the best he could out there near the Wahoo because no one had given him a choice. Even while the lead was chewing around his head he hadn't really been sore. You don't get riled up at the moment of a battle, only scared, careful, or killed. It was just bad luck to be caught in the middle of something like that. A catbird in a tree quarreled with itself and he stooped, picked up

320

a pine cone, and shied it through the branches, grinning at the angry scream of protest. That was the way things went. Suddenly something came at you and you had to duck. He followed the bird's erratic flight and then smiled to himself as he recalled General Clinch when, during an earlier conversation, he had mentioned Asseola.

"What sort of a man is this Powell, or Osceola, as you call him?"

Clay hesitated, not quite certain how to answer the simple question. Trying to frame a reply, he realized he didn't know much about Asseola. That was a funny thing. After all the years they had spent growing up together it ought to be easy.

"I don't know, General," he said. "We used to have a lot of fun deer-hunting together."

General Clinch had permitted himself the rare luxury of a smile. "That wasn't what I had in mind, Mr. Hammond."

"No, I guess not." Clay had stared at the floor. There were a lot of things he could say but they wouldn't make much sense. "He was always sort of quiet." The words came slowly. "Shy, the way an Indian is even when you know him well. He was proud of being a Seminole. I guess he was proudest of that. It meant more to him than anything else and he didn't like to be called Powell. He's smart and stubborn. I guess I licked him fifty times wrestling when we were kids, but he'd never really give in. If, as everyone says, he's out in front in this trouble, he'll be a hard man to whip because he believes in what he's fighting for."

That conversation had ended there, but many times during the days that followed Clay caught himself thinking of it and trying to answer the question. What sort of man is Asseola?

He turned into the doorway of the junior officers' quarters, a crude, unfinished pine-board structure, heated by a big iron stove, shared by half a dozen men. He had sort of liked it here, enjoyed the talk and companionship. The officers had gone out of their way to see he was comfortable. After the novelty of having a civilian around wore off they were friendly and considerate. In the evenings they talked of the war and of Dade's massacre. They knew little of this Florida to which they had been assigned and were silently interested by his accounts of the deep, wild Territory and the lonely interior. In a way he was going to miss the easy banter and conversations.

Two weeks passed before the surgeon would give Clay permission to travel. The arm had healed and the stiffness was gradually work-

321

ing itself out. The scar, a livid, serrated ridge, stood out, slick and shiny, from the rest of the skin.

The surgeon ran his finger down the welt. "This will be a fine thing to show your grandchildren when you sit around and tell how Grandpop fought the Indian war." He wondered why the harmless suggestion should cause the cheerful light within his patient's eyes to die so abruptly. For a moment he had a glimpse of a raw wound lying behind a face, drawn suddenly into a tight mask.

"Thanks, Doc." Clay unemotionally rolled down the sleeve and fastened it at the wrist. "I'm grateful for what you've done."

"Witchcraft," the surgeon scoffed. "Now you take care of yourself."

"I'll do my best. I figure to get away at daybreak."

The violence of the Seminole attack had not abated as many thought it would. The fury spread, gathering strength as it swept over indecisive countermeasures. It blazed in white-hot patches, sown in cunning rage, and left the Territory black and smoking. Here a settlement was attacked, there a cabin burned. A patrol was cut down in the scrub. A lightly held position was obliterated. There had been no formal engagement of large opposing forces. The war was being fought between detachments of fifty or sixty soldiers and small bands of well-armed Indians who lived off the land, firing it behind them. No one could be certain how many Seminoles, Tallahassees, Mickasukies, and Creeks were at large. The best guess was that they had assembled almost two thousand warriors. Fighting with them was an unknown number of Negroes, slaves of the principal chiefs and the descendants of runaway slaves. The Indian towns had been abandoned and the women and children lived and worked out of reach, within the swamps. The names of such leaders as Wildcat, Little Cloud, Alligator, Tigertail, Sam Jones, and King Phillip were sprinkled liberally in the conversation of the whites as far west as Ohio, and found prominence in the press reports. Above the confusion of rumor, hearsay, and inaccuracies there rose the bright feather of an Indian, Osceola. The name caught at the imagination and became a symbol. His likeness was sketched from a safe distance, and always the shimmering plume of the egret curled in a graceful and challenging sweep. It captured the fancy of artists and writers. He was portrayed as a renegade Scotsman named Powell who incited the Seminoles and drove them forward. He was drawn as a fierce and arrogant chief of noble Indian blood, who fought in an *opéra bouffe* costume of

322

white buckskins and a massive feathered headdress. He was described as a remorseless, murdering savage who killed for an animal's pleasure in the sight and smell of blood, and a clamor rose for his capture.

Little was said of a man untrained in war who defiantly carried the attack to a superior force because he believed the cause to be just. No words were spoken of honor, justice, liberty, and the precious right of a man to walk in freedom. It was inconceivable that a stinking Indian who painted his face and adorned his body with feathers would offer his life in defense of his land and people. Indians fought and died only because they enjoyed horrible conflict. Sometimes, as Clay listened to this Indian's name as it was handed about in conversation, he wondered if they talked of someone he had known. Could this Osceola, this Powell, be the soft-spoken, quiet-eyed child of his youth? What now drove that dark and slender boy to these desperate measures? He was, of course, a boy no longer. They two, Clayfield Hammond and this son of the Creek Amaltha, were men grown and tempered. Yet they had played and fought, eaten and slept, as children will, and had loved each other in the rough-and-tumble fashion of bear cubs. From what hidden spring of courage did this Asseola draw the will to fight so stubbornly against an enveloping tyranny of injustice? Why, out of all the Indians along the Apalachicola, had it been his shoulder the mysterious hand had touched, bidding him go forth? Many times at night, when he was alone, Clay thought of these things and felt a strange pride welling in his heart that this man had called him brother.

After the first surprising shock of assault, the Army began to draw itself together. At New Orleans, General Gaines was embarking with eleven hundred men, his destination Tampa. General Winfield Scott had been ordered to Florida, and it was expected he would march inland from the east coast, sweeping the Seminoles before him. The War Department authorized General Clinch, at Fort Drane, to call for any number of troops from South Carolina, Georgia, and Alabama. There remained only the problem of getting these additional forces into the beleaguered Territory, transporting them quickly, and maintaining the lines of communication that would keep them supplied. Once the situation was stabilized, the power of the United States would deal quickly enough with the savages. Who was there foolish enough to suggest that this war would rage for seven years, smudging the careers of good officers and sickening the nation with futile bloodshed? The wheels within the military machine turned, however, and while the massive preparations were under way the Seminoles did not rest. The dark lightning struck in many places, and the fires rolled against the sky as men died in terror and alone.

27

OLD CLAY's puffy fingers played aimlessly through the candlewicking of a spread, drawn tightly over the swelling mound of a great belly, and his eyes stared into the high murkiness of the ceiling. He was not ill, unless the suffocating weight of accumulated years could be called a sickness. He felt no pain save that which lurked constantly within the twisted leg and hip. Even this sharp and vindictive companion seemed to have mellowed with the years. He gnawed with toothless gums. They had grown old together.

A single taper floated on the liquid tallow in a ruby glass, and the small flame rose straight and smoke-tipped, tossing its uncertain illumination to the far corners of the room. The big house and the acres it commanded were silent, and the night was a frosty vacuum where nothing moved. The old man listened attentively, waiting for the brushing of a twig against the windowpane or the rolling bounce of an acorn on the roof to betray the existence of a world outside. There was no sound.

Old Clay was dying; not tonight or tomorrow, perhaps, but the hour was not far distant. He could feel the minutes running out and he no longer rebelled or sought to hold them back. Lying here alone he wondered where the years had gone. In the beginning the store had seemed inexhaustible, the credit limitless. He twisted his massive head on the pillows, finding a softer roll. An old man, he pondered, had plenty of time for such thoughts. If he wished, he could amuse himself by tracing back over his life, marking the unsuspected turnings and the small decisions that shaped everything to come. If he did that, then dying no longer seemed important. It was only the final segment that must be added to complete the design. When the time came, the piece assumed no more than its just proportions and could not dominate the whole. It was locked into the puzzle and someone could say: There, it is finished.

It was proper for a man to die alone and in his bed. Only vanity prompted him to want a pack of sniffling relatives tiptoeing through the house or standing in solemn groups about the chamber, their ears attuned to the final wheezing. Well, he had no relatives—no pious brood to wait upon his passing—no one but that son of a bitch, Young Clay. What the hell could one suppose had happened to him, anyhow? That was a fine thing—hit his grandfather in the face and ride off the plantation without even a backward look. How did he think the place was going to be run if he didn't come home? A man with any decency would have whaled his grandfather, walked away to get himself drunk, slept with some girls, and then come around in a few days or weeks and everything would have gone on as before. That damn Young Clay never did have any sense. He was probably off somewhere brooding about it as though a man didn't have a right to hit his grandfather or anyone else if he felt like it.

He pushed himself into a sitting position and reached clumsily for the decanter of whisky on the bed table. Disregarding the glass, he drank from the wide neck and the liquor sloshed in his throat. He put the bottle back and sucked at the roof of his mouth with noisy pleasure. His eyes sought the window.

"Where the hell are you, boy?" The whisper was barely audible.

For minutes he stared at the rimed panes. The frosting obscured the night. He pulled the covers up beneath his chin and held them there. If he yelled for Santee, the slave would rekindle the fire and get the room warm again. It was less trouble to take another drink.

That was another thing. He settled back. Young Clay ought to be thinking some about the plantation Negrahs. Suppose he died now; who would take care of them? That no-good Spaniard, Salano, would have the running of the place. They just couldn't dig a big hole and put everything he owned in it along with him and pat the dirt neat. If Clay didn't come home, Salano would move into the big house and settle for good. There weren't any Hammonds he knew about to make a claim. That would be a hell of a note, wouldn't it, now? The idea made him angry and when he took another drink he banged the decanter heavily on the table.

There were a lot of things to get mad about if he started thinking. There were Jake Cutler and that scum in the barracks. They just packed up, all of them, and left the minute this new trouble with the Indians began. They ran like a pack of mongrels, scared to death. When Salano came and told him what was happening, he called to be carried to the barracks and he sat there for a while, right in the middle of the compound, and watched. The men were hauling their gear out, stacking it in small piles, and they ducked their heads to avoid his eyes. When he could stand it no longer he roared in a voice that halted them in their tracks.

"What's goin' on here, Cutler?" He shouted the question. "What's the meanin' of this?"

The men pretended not to hear. They were waiting for Cutler to speak.

"Answer me, Cutler. I said, what's goin' on here?"

Jake Cutler spat into the dirt. "We're gettin' out. The men don't figure to have anythin' to do with Indian fightin', Mr. Hammond." Somehow he managed to sneer the title.

Old Clay had half risen from the chair. "Don't speak my name that way, Cutler."

Jake lifted his head. "All right, you old bastard," he snapped, "I'll call you right, then. We don't figure to stay here an' fight for you or anyone else. The Seminoles are out an' killin'. Maybe they'll come this way an' maybe they won't, but there ain't no man here fool enough to risk a hair of his head for your skin or a stick of wood on this plantation. We're leavin' an' you can't stop us. We ain't your niggers." He swung a pack across his shoulder and glared his defiance.

"You miserable whore droppings." Old Clay's voice had risen. "I fed an' kept you for years. If it wasn't for me most of you would have been hung before this. You lived easy on my place, layin' with my Negrah girls, eatin' my food, an' takin' my money. Now, when a thievin', cowardly Seminole peeks out from behind a tree, you spill your guts arunnin'. Get out. I'm glad to be rid of you, there ain't a man among the lot. Lice can always find a place to crawl. Go look for it." He had roared his curses and would not leave the place until the last of the band had shuffled down the dusty road and out of sight.

Even thinking about them now made him mad all over again. When he took another drink the glass neck of the bottle clattered against his teeth and his body trembled beneath the blankets. A man who dealt with scum was bound to stink himself up.

It was easy enough to wonder now why he had kept them around all these years. The faces had changed; they'd come and gone; tough, swaggering, and furtive men, and he'd always found new ones to take their places. Away back there, when he'd first started assembling the Hammond plantation, they'd been handy. The Indians, squatters, and title jumpers had walked softly and mighty minchin' at the sight of the Hammond men. It had sort of amused him, too, to yell and beat respect and discipline into the mongrels. Their tails were lifted high when they rode into Clayport. Well, let the bastards go. He didn't really need them. Young Clay had always said they'd run if there was any real trouble. If that was the way he felt, he should have stayed home an' taken care of things. It riled him to think of the way the boy acted.

Lying this way in the semidarkness, he wondered how much truth there was to the reports of a Seminole outbreak. The Negrahs on the plantation were scared. In the quarters you could feel the uneasiness, and at night it was a dark and formless thing prowling behind the cabins. Well. He blew between his lips with a whistling sound of satisfaction. The government and the whites had only themselves to blame. Twenty years ago, when Jackson was down this way, the nation could have rid itself once and for all of the dirty pack. No, by God, that wouldn't do. A lot of mealy-tongued folks began to feel sorry for the noble red men. They made treaties and concessions and began apologizing to each other for the way the Seminoles had been treated. It served them right, now, if the lousy brutes were loose again; pettin' a skunk on the head only makes him want to pee on you.

Thinking about the Indians made him doubly angry, and he reached again for the bottle. As he drank, it occurred to him that maybe he was getting himself drunk. He was in a rare humor, mellow one moment and snorting the next. He spoke aloud now, directing accusations at the heavy chairs and blank walls. His voice rumbled and Santee, bedded down on a pallet just outside the closed door, listened and wondered fearfully at the sound. D' ol' Marstah, he thought, suah talkin' to d' de'l.

Old Clay held the bottle to the small light, squinting at the contents. Usually he drank only enough at night to satisfy his leg and make him drowsy. Now, by God, he'd finish the bottle, and when it was empty he'd call for Santee to fetch another. The idea pleased him and he sent a fine trickle of the corn down his throat. He couldn't remember when he had felt so good. If he had Young Clay here this minute he'd flail the hell out of him. Runnin' away like some raggedy-pants squatter with no idea of responsibility.

"It's a good thing you ain't in this room," he shouted challengingly. "You know good an' well I been countin' on you to take care of things. It'd serve you right if I died this minute an' left you without a cent. I would, too," he threatened, "if I could find me someone to will it all to."

He was breathing heavily. For a moment it had almost seemed as though Clay were in the room and they were at each other again. He waited until the excitement within him flickered out. Suddenly he was chuckling. I wonder if Young Clay ever caught up with

328

that hot-eyed slut he'd married an' the fella who run off with her. That would have been a tussle to watch, all right. The world was filled with nice girls. The boy could have had himself a fine family by now an' an old man wouldn't have to lie here in bed alone without anyone to keep him company. No, sir, not Young Clay. He had to pick himself a twitchy-tailed thing who couldn't keep her back off the ground. Young Clay hadn't treated him right, by God. When he came home they'd have it out.

He had a little trouble with the bottle. When he raised his arm it seemed to sail through the air and some of the whisky splashed out over his forehead. With straining difficulty he eased the flask back in a wobbling arc. Where the hell was his mouth? He spat to fix its position and then giggled. It was a lewd and frightening sound to come from the swathed hulk.

A lot of men, when they got old, whined and explained how different they would be if they had their lives to live over again. Well, he wouldn't change a minute. He'd done what no other white man in the Territory could do. He tore this plantation out of the wilderness. He'd killed Indians, whites, and blacks alike to hold it. There wasn't anyone in the whole peninsula who didn't know the name of Hammond. When the time came to write Florida's history they'd have to put him in the story.

"Boy," he shouted furiously, "you better come back home. You hear me, Clay?"

His breath was a gusty whistle and his huge chest strained against the covers as his lungs fought to absorb the air. It was hot, too. He clawed at the blankets and ripped at the collar of his linen nightshirt. Well, whisky always made a man warm. He ought to have known that. He tossed back his head and drained the bottle, coughing with a strangling sound. There. It was better. He could feel the bed as it floated crazily. By God, it ought to, ridin' the way it was on a couple of quarts of whisky.

He leaned back into the pillows. He couldn't remember when he'd ever felt so easy in his mind about things. Tomorrow he'd take that big gray stallion and ride him; should have done it today, but a man couldn't find time for everything. His head lolled to one side and he was dimly conscious of a weight in one hand. Painfully he raised his arm and flung it across the bed. The heavy decanter twirled into the wall with a crash.

The sound woke Santee in the hall, and the Negro waited. D' ol' Marstah bin gettin' drunk laik dis foah a long time now. Hit'd be God's blessin' ef young Marstah Clay'd come home. He rose and turned gently at the knob, peering through a widening crack as the door swung. By the small light he could see the bulking shape of Old Clay. Santee waited and then closed the door. D' ol' man asleep agin. He dropped back to the lumpy ticking with the comfortable grunt of a sleepy dog. The house was quiet once more.

Outside the night was moonless and in the sky the stars were heavy with their brilliance. It was cold, almost freezing, and the stubble grass was brittle and slickly coated.

They came slowly from the woods, scarecrow figures in a loosely joined crescent, moving as a thin, dark tide. Upon their bodies the patches of tattered buckskins and filthy cloths hung in limp rags. Hunger and frustration pinched their faces and their bellies were flat and empty. For days and weeks they had been gathering in the swamp far up the river—the misfits and outcasts of the great tribes—Mickasukies, Cherokees, Creeks, Seminoles. No warrior band this. They crept and wriggled upon their stomachs, snarling and cringing. They had come from deep pockets within the scrub and from the dank and hidden swamps, gathering strength as they traveled. No resolution of high purpose drove them. They quarreled and bickered among themselves, uniting only to fall upon a solitary cabin or lone wagon. They were as leaderless as a hyena pack and as warily savage, fighting over the pitiful loot they amassed. The stronger snatched from the weaker and only the safety of their number bound them. Far to the south the men of their tribes were throwing themselves against the white soldiers. Here they could roam and kill with little fear of pursuit. They had looted and burned among the smaller farms and plantations, arming themselves as best they could with knives, axes, hatchets, and an occasional musket or rifle. The blades twinkled now and then beneath the chilled starlight. The wave of their creeping movement lapped through woods and scrub and across the open fields, flattening out and then rising to press forward again. At the tips of the wide curve those in the lead seemed to drag the others behind them as the heavy pocket of a seine. In the darkness sixty or seventy pairs of greedy eyes searched the outlines of the big house and plantation buildings. They had been told that the white men and their guns had left days before and this knowledge gave them the slinking courage to set foot upon the land. Now only the fierce old one who could not walk and the black slaves in their cabins stood to block their way. Here, unguarded, was the rich prize. In the barns and warehouses there was food enough for all. Within the great and ugly house were blankets and whisky, guns, gold and silver ornaments, and, for the bravest, the hair of the old one. To do this thing tonight they had made strong medicine in the swamps, leaping and shouting threats and defiance and boasting of the terror to be loosed. Who would be such a fool as to fight against the soldiers or attack the Clayport settlement, with its many men and guns, when this great wealth lay at hand for the taking?

There was no hurry, and sometimes the broad half circle seemed to halt of its own accord, as courage for the venture drained away. But it moved again, softly and with the ugly menace of a water moccasin in grassy shallows. Somewhere beyond the slave cabins a couple of dogs began barking with nervous and worried suspicion. The raiders had made no sound but their rancid stench upon the night alarmed the animals. Soon other plantation dogs would take up the cry and the moment for surprise would be lost. The crescent moved swiftly now, the figures bent and running, closing upon the cabins. One section broke away and bore down upon the overseer's house, where a light suddenly showed yellow in a window.

The ragged horde poured into the narrow corridor from both ends of the quarters, screaming in an insane frenzy as they broke through the unlatched and sagging doors and fell upon the terror-stricken slaves while they were struggling to rise from their straw mattresses on the floors. In the dark and narrow space the raiders killed by smell alone. Knives and hatchets slashed into the velvet black of naked bellies; as they felt the sticky warmth of fresh blood upon their hands and faces, the madness mounted. The Negroes fought as best they could but they were crowded into corners, beaten to their knees by clubs and axes. The high soprano cries of the women and the shrill screams of children died suddenly in choking bubbles. The trapped men had nothing with which to fight back and the slavering gibberish of the infuriated Indians as they pranced and mocked, driving their knives again and again into tormented bodies, filled them with helpless terror. A few broke away in the confusion, charging wildly through open doorways or diving out of paper-sealed windows. Others stood for a moment, flailing with their huge arms before an ax blade slashed into their faces or bit deeply into crinkled polls. The raiders charged in and out of the small cabins, tangling with each other in a whirling insanity. Their tongues lolled and they panted as they ran in confused circles, hunting down their victims, pursuing them across the fields, and yapping with ecstatic, maniacal idiocy.

Faggots of pitch-bound straw were thrust into the embers of banked fires and the seasoned wood of the cabins caught quickly. As

331

the flames mounted, the wounded shrieked their awful terror and tried to drag themselves across the doorsills. Those who managed to crawl through the openings had their protruding heads beaten into quivering lumps and they hung like bloody monsters over the boards. The fire swept quickly, and the ruddy glow mounted to the sky in swirling towers of smoke and flames. At the far end of the plantation a second blaze assaulted the night. Salano's house belched with crimson spewings. Salano had died quickly, and he lay sprawled across the defiled body of a mulatto wench while the fire's heat dried the bloody patch on his head. The slave quarters were blazing from one end to the other and in the light the grotesque figures of the Indians spun and twirled or charged through the hot lane, crying aloud of their feats of bravery. The heat singed their matted hair and warmed the feral stink of unwashed bodies until the odor was that of old grease scorching. Then, without command, they turned and trotted toward the big house, and their running had the unwavering intensity of a dog pack in pursuit of a ready bitch.

Santee murmured with a troubled sound in his sleep, and then suddenly he was awake. He crouched, his head upthrust, his broad black face turned questioningly toward the sound. Against the panes of the windows in the far end of the long gallery he could see the dancing reflection of the fires and his ears caught the confused murmur of distant shouts. The Negro moved with long strides until he stood at the windows, and then he began to tremble as fear tightened around his throat. In the distance he could see the billowing flames and he watched as they closed the gap between cabin rows. In the fantastic light he made out the scurrying figures as they leaped in and out of the rolling curtains of smoke. When he flung up the sash the wild and dreadful cries seemed to float lazily upon the night. He stared, unable to move, and the animal sweat of fear was strong on his body.

"Lor' God," he whispered dully, "us got t' git out heah." He backed away from the open window, his feet dragging reluctantly, and then, as the full impact of what was happening struck him, he turned with a yell and raced back along the gallery.

Old Clay was sprawled on his back, arms outflung, one hand trailing limply at the edge of the covers. His mouth hung open and in the closed and airless room the reek of whisky was strong.

"Marstah Clay, Ol' Marstah, Marstah Clay." Santee bent above the bed and repeated the call with mounting terror. There had to be someone to tell him what to do.

332

With an effort he unsnarled the bedding, and his enormous arms slid beneath the still figure of Clayfield Hammond. With a heaving grunt the slave lifted the sagging weight and steadied himself for a moment, rocking back and forth on the enormous pillars of his legs. The Indians were at the big house now. He could hear the crash of breaking windows as they poured into the lower floors. With a heave he slung the old man up and across his shoulder, carrying him as he would a heavy sack of rice. He backed through the doorway and moved toward the rear of the house, and then he heard the splintering of wood and the singing music of shattering glass as the savages swarmed in and through the rooms, tearing at drapes and at the heavy, pendant-hung chandeliers. The barbaric yelps and high notes of screaming victory filled the old house and set the echoes to rocketing deliriously. Trapped in the hallway, Santee spun from side to side. His breath came in whistling gasps and the big head seemed to sag and waggle without support. Panic sprouted and he ran clumsily from one end of the long hall to the other, the body of Old Clay swaying like an ugly growth from his back. Smoke from the ground floor swirled in a dancing eddy and as his flaring nostrils caught the dread odor Santee lost all reason and cunning. With one arm locked beneath Old Clay's legs he charged with furious disregard down the broad staircase and the Indians surged up to meet him. The blade of an ax caught the Negro full across the face and the meat parted in a terrible gap. The slave tumbled, his shoulders bent beneath him, and the keen steel of many hatchets thudded into the convulsing muscles. A dozen knives opened long and jagged wounds and the flesh peeled away in thin furrows. Old Clay bounced awkwardly, rolling halfway to the door, and as his body slowly turned a dozen snarling Indians were fighting over it, their knives driving again and again through the thin undershirt with hungry, sucking noise. One of the attackers spraddled the wide shoulders and then dropped his naked buttocks to the massive neck. Leaning forward he grasped the hair in one hand, straining to pull the head back. The wet blade circled above the ears, and when the scalp finally came away the Indian howled and smeared the dripping thing across his chest as he bounded away, leaping high with screams of demented pleasure.

The big house burned with the roar of many winds, and beyond the widening rim of fire the Indians watched. They were bent beneath their loot, and walked with awkward tripping as their feet caught in the folds of brocaded curtains, wrapped about their bodies. Around their necks they wore circlets of crystal pendants, snatched from the lighting fixtures, and tried to balance plates of silver on their heads. They clutched bottles, segments of broken mirrors, and handfuls of dining-table service, and they yapped their furious pleasure at the roaring spectacle. In the big oaks the leaves curled back from the thrusting heat and the long gray streamers of moss twisted and ignited in quick flashes. The Indians turned and ran. There were the many warehouses to plunder and fire; the barns and storerooms where cattle could be slaughtered or driven away, food could be gathered or destroyed.

In Clayport, men crept from their beds and stared with frightened wonder at the marks of the fires upon the sky. They were too far away to hear the sound of murder and the exultant howls of the victors, but in each one's mind the picture was clearly drawn. With loaded rifles they gathered in small groups along the sandy roads, their faces turned toward the east and the false and ominous dawn rising there. This was the terror they had expected, and before its menace their arms seemed woefully inadequate. Secretly, each hoped that the raiding Indians would be satisfied with the Hammond plantation and circle away from the settlement, dragging their prizes into the woods.

All night they watched from concealed positions within their cabins and stores. They were not fighting men, these farmers, homesteaders of small plots, merchants, and smiths. While their women huddled fearfully in the corners and the children whimpered, they wondered at the curious fate that had brought them to this wild and bloody Territory. Throughout the long hours they waited; their eyes grew weary, the hands wrapped about stock and barrel numb and lifeless. The red and wavering glow to the east died reluctantly and the small community was locked within itself. Beneath their breaths the men cursed a government that found itself unable to deal with a few thousand rebellious savages. At the edges of the settlement, other men lay hidden in the scrub or leaned against protecting trees. If the Indians came, they would be able to fire but once and raise the alarm before they fled. After that it would be each family for itself. They had heard of what had already happened along the east coast and in the southern central section of the country. The raids came quickly and without warning—came as they had to old Clayfield Hammond's plantation this night.

Dawn seemed to break reluctantly, and on the fresh morning winds the people of Clayport caught the odor of burning wood and the sickening smell of charred flesh. Against the shell-white color, the black smoke rose in trailing clouds that were caught and torn

334

apart by the early winds. Along the road doors opened and men stepped out, bleary-eyed and grim of countenance. They breathed deeply of the new day, and turned to peer thoughtfully overhead. They stood in silence for a few minutes and then walked slowly back to their cabins.

On the Hammond plantation the blackened shell of the big house gaped at the morning, and in the slave quarters the brick chimneys were rows of skeletons above the ashes. Wisps of smoke curled from the still hot embers and blew among the charred and twisted bodies of the murdered men and women. The long warehouses, barns, cotton gin, and sugar factory had been gutted or leveled, and the silence of death was heavy on the land. Over the desolation a shining black crow sped in startled flight, croaking with harsh sound, and high in the sky the first buzzards rode slowly, their sharp eyes fixed intently upon the ruins below.

28

CLAY stood upon the high west bank of the Apalachicola and looked back across the swirling river. The long journey was at an end. Behind him, stretching to the horizon and beyond, lay the miles. He was home, or would be in another hour, and the realization of this gave a triumphant lift to his shoulders as he turned and swung down through the light woods. He knew them well; they backed against the plantation's southern border.

He had walked the distance from Fort Drane, sleeping where the nights caught him, leaving the hidden camps at daybreak. It had been slower and harder afoot; yet, in a way, it had also been easier. A horse would have been a nuisance many times, and he felt safer alone. As he had tracked in a wide circle from Fort Drane, moving across the barren of a westerly slope, he experienced an almost overpowering feeling of loneliness. Perhaps, he thought many times, it was because he was on his way home and the memory of old and familiar things gathered strength as he walked. Prudently he had skirted the lake country around Micanopy, crossing the Suwannee south of Long Pond, where the tall grass grew higher than a man's head. As he put the miles behind him he came into remote sections where, he was certain, no man had stood before. Once over the Suwannee he left behind the feeling of a troubled and seething land. The echoes of war had not yet penetrated here, or, if the call had been heard, it went unheeded. Rarely did he come upon the tracks or signs of Indians and only twice, from a distance, had he seen a settlement. He avoided them without difficulty.

Where the woods now broke away he halted. Ahead, no more than three quarters of a mile, the plantation buildings and the house should have stood. He stared incredulously and then inched forward, as though reluctant to set foot upon the devastated acres. Nowhere could he see an indication of life. Nothing moved over the land. As he slowly closed the remaining distance he picked out the scabby-black outlines of the warehouses, jagged and forlorn. Where his grandfather's home had once raised itself so proudly there were only broken and charred walls. He bent down and studied the growth of weeds within the rubble, trying to estimate the time of the fire. Two, three weeks, maybe, he thought. He turned and gazed down over the gentle slope. There Salano's house should be and beyond it the gin and cotton storage sheds. He shook his head. It was hard to re-create the picture in his mind.

For an hour he walked over the plantation, pausing for many minutes among the strewn ashes of the slave quarters. God A'mighty, he thought, two hundred and fifty Negrahs. Do you suppose they all went up in this? Not for a moment did he question what had happened. This was no accidental destruction; fire didn't leap the great distances between the blacks' quarters and the big house, the plantation buildings and the frame structure where Salano lived. The place had been fired, structure by structure, burned by Indians, who had killed the old man and everyone else on the place.

Beyond the harness and blacksmith shops there was a small storage shed. Somehow it had escaped, although the near wall was scorched. He kicked at the door and it swung inward, scraping and crying on its hinges. It took a few moments before his eyes adjusted themselves to the dark interior and then his rifle lifted quickly.

"All right, now. Come out of there," he called at a shapeless huddle that stirred uncertainly.

"We comin', Marstah." The voice was faint.

Clay backed out of the shed and waited as uneasy, shuffling feet moved reluctantly forward. When the man appeared he lowered the gun. A younger man, a woman, and a child peered up like timid rabbits from behind the old one. Clay studied their black features hopefully. If they belonged on the plantation they must be field hands. He didn't recognize them.

"You Hammond Negrahs?" he asked.

"Yes, Marstah." The acknowledgment came in an eager chorus.

"What are your names?"

The quartet pressed splayed feet into the dirt and wriggled. "Ah'm Shem, Marstah," the old man said. "Yondah's Bessie an' Laight, an' d' little one say she Cunie."

"You know who I am?" Four expressionless faces met his gaze but there was no reply. Clay smiled suddenly. "It's all right," he said, "I guess it doesn't make any difference. Tell me what happened."

He sat on an empty nail keg as the story came in halting sentences. The old one carried the burden of the tale, but as their confidence in the white man grew the others added details, picking up the story eagerly when the words faltered. Clay grinned. They were beginning to enjoy their roles now, and embroidered the account with rolling eyes and shrill exclamations. A day after the raid, a lot of white men had come. They rode and walked all over the place, digging things from the ashes of the big house. At their approach the Negroes had fled to the fields, hiding there until they went away. Since then they had been living in the shed, foraging in the woods and trapping fish in the river for food.

Clay rose. "All right," he halted the rambling story, "I'll take care of you or find someplace to put you. You stay here and I'll have some food sent up from Clayport. The Indians won't come back. There's nothing here they want. I'll take care of you," he repeated.

"Yes, Marstah." There was a frightening simplicity in their confidence.

As Clay walked away he wondered what the hell he was going to do with four Negrahs. Maybe, he thought, McCollum could take them on his place. The young woman and the man could work and he'd pay for the keep of the old one and little girl. Stripped of the slaves' dramatics, the story of the assault was one of swift destruction. No one, save these four who managed to get away in the excitement, had survived. Old Clay must have burned with the house. Maybe, he thought hopefully, they had killed him first. It would have been easier that way.

The road into Clayport seemed unusually long this day, and as he strode along the mound between the ruts Clay made an attempt to adjust himself to this unexpected turn of affairs. Always, during the years he had been away, he kept with him the knowledge that the plantation and home would wait upon his return. Now he had no home. Old Clay was gone. He was alone, really alone. He came upon the first Clayport cabins with a feeling of relief.

Andrew McCollum, once he recognized his visitor, turned the post over to his assistants and led Clay back to the untidy office.

"I've wondered many times about you, lad." The Scotsman surveyed him with something close to affection and raised a stone jug from the floor. "Fairst, let us obsairve the amenities o' the occasion." He filled two cups with the whisky.

Clay drank slowly, savoring the light smokiness of the liquor. McCollum peered at him expectantly.

" 'Tis no joyous home-coming, lad." The old man put his cup on the desk's edge.

"They didn't come into Clayport?" Clay looked about the room.

"No, the devils murdered an' ran. We were fortunate this time."

"It's worse along the east coast and in the south. I've seen a lot of it. Maybe," he shrugged, "maybe that's why it hasn't hit me as hard as it might. You get used to seeing men die and places burn."

"Aye." McCollum sighed and his eyes traveled over Clay. "Lord," he said wonderingly, "but you've changed, man. There's a terrible quiet fierceness about you. What happened to the lad I knew?"

"He grew up, I expect." Clay shrugged. "It took a lot of time, though."

McCollum nodded. "What are your plans?"

Clay grinned. "I don't know. Right now I've four Hammond Negrahs to take care of. The Indians missed them, somehow. Can you find places for them?"

"Aye," the little man agreed instantly. "You won't stay here, then?"

"I don't think so. It wouldn't make much sense, trying to build the place again the way things are right now. Maybe," he smiled wearily, "I ought to go out and kill a few Indians to get even. The hell of it is," he scratched thoughtfully at the back of his head, "I don't feel that way. I keep saying to myself: If I was an Indian I'd have done the same thing. What do you suppose is wrong with me?"

"No more than ails any honest man." The trader tapped reflectively at his chin. "'Tis a great fortune you've come into, lad?" he asked quietly.

Clay looked up quickly. "I suppose so," he said, after a moment. "I hadn't thought much about it. Old Clay's lawyers in Mobile and the bank at New Orleans could tell me."

"See them, lad." McCollum was emphatic. "Make the trip an' get your affairs in shape. After that," he chuckled, "you can take up your savage ways again, roamin' like some wild an' homeless thing." He tilted back his head and regarded Clay speculatively. "I must say," he continued, "for a gentleman born you present a surprisin' appearance."

"That's good whisky." Clay winked companionably at the inquisitive little man. "I'd take another drink if it was offered."

McCollum poured quickly to hide his embarrassment. "You're right, lad," he apologized. "'Tis no affair o' mine or of anyone else why you choose to live as you do. Forgive my impertinence. 'Tis the gossipin' old woman in me comin' out."

Clay took up the conversation. "I guess I'll do as you suggest, find out how things stand. From what little I know, Old Clay has

339

his money scattered in banks all over the North and South. The Mobile lawyers can help me."

"Good." McCollum was emphatic. "If there is a thing to wring the soul of a Scot it is an improper regard for money. I have a boat going down the river at the end of the week an' could use another rifleman with the guard. From Pensacola you can easily get passage to Mobile or New Orleans."

Clay stood up and stretched wearily. "That's fine. I could use two or three days' sleep." He paused. "I'll need some money until everything is straightened out."

"Whatever you wish." The trader rested his hand on Clay's arm. "Now you go to my house an' tell Mrs. McCollum who you are an' that I said you were to have room an' lodging, on credit, of course," he twinkled. "She'll heat water for a bath, which, God knows, you seem to need, an' give you the loan of my favorite razor to whisk away that beard. I'll see you in the evening."

"You're a generous man, Mr. McCollum." Clay was touched and grateful. "And a good one, too."

The storekeeper trotted at his side. "No," he protested, "I'm a shrewd an' connivin' merchant. When you rebuild the Hammond plantation I shall expect a large share o' the trade from it as an expression o' your gratitude. Go along now an' stop mouthin' pretty words, which ill become your shaggy appearance."

As he walked away from the store and to the side lane where McCollum's house stood, Clay began to understand what the little Scot had done with a few words. No longer did he feel alien. This was his home and someday he would come back to it. The plantation would be rebuilt, integrated into the life of the settlement. The legacy of hatred that Old Clay had left would be buried and forgotten. He was whistling as he turned into the path leading to the McCollum house.

A light breeze from out of the Gulf caught at the frilled ruffles of Sue Rogers' bonnet, and she thrust the perky adornment back, lifting her face to smile up at Clay.

"The Spanish influence in Pensacola," she said, "is not to be disregarded. Ladies do not walk abroad with their heads uncovered."

"You're only a Yankee," he suggested, "so I guess people will understand."

"And you, sir," her hand rested confidently on his arm, "have been too long among the savages. However," she sighed regretfully, "you were never at ease with a gallant phrase."

Clay had been in Pensacola for a week, putting off from day to day the journey to New Orleans. The trip down the Apalachicola aboard McCollum's flatboat had been made without incident. No Indians lurked along the banks to pot at the crew from cover and the craft loafed along, swept toward the Gulf by the current. In Pensacola, Clay went directly to the Collins House, and not until he was in his room did it occur to him that he and Claire had once shared a bed here. It amazed him to discover that such a thing could be so easily forgotten. What name could you give to a love of short memory? He called upon Sue without hesitation, meeting Hadley this time. Neither the man nor the girl appeared to find anything unusual in the visit. Hadley actually seemed glad to see him again and the three of them talked long into the night. Since then he had been a constant visitor. If Sue's brother held any reservations about the propriety of these calls he kept them to himself. At the first opportunity Clay told Sue about Claire.

"I don't know where I stand," he made honest confession. "Legally, I suppose, I am still married."

"You've never heard from her?" Sue asked.

"No." He said nothing about Jamie Beulow. "When I get to New Orleans I'll ask the lawyers what to do. Until now," he hesitated, "it didn't seem to make any difference—being married, I mean."

Where they now walked the shore line curved abruptly, thrusting a sandy finger into the bay. At its tip they found a driftwood log to sit upon. The evening hour was early and along the water front the taverns and grogshops were crowded; snatches of songs and laughter and the throaty calls of the tall, swinging West Indian wenches, as they paraded beneath the watchful eyes of their pimps, came faintly across the night.

"How long will you be in New Orleans?" With a stick Sue traced a geometrical design on the packed sand.

"I don't know. It depends on how complicated lawyers can make things."

"And then?" She glanced up.

"I'd like to come back here." He paused and added, "To see a girl."

Her quick smile was tender and a little wistful. "You'll have to hurry, sir. The girl, I'm afraid, is dangerously close to spinsterhood. Have you thought about that?"

He looked at her with unmistakable surprise. Time had not dulled the clear beauty of her features or dimmed the inner radiance that displayed itself in the calm eyes. Yet time had worked upon them both. How, he wondered, had it left her untouched?

"No," he said honestly, "I haven't. I don't know why, exactly. It just never occurred to me that you could change."

She held the stick before her, balancing it delicately on her fingers. "I won't," she said slowly, "do your sums for you, Master Hammond. Not more than four years separate us. It is but a simple matter of subtraction."

"Well, I'll be damned." His astonishment was not an affectation. "If I'm thirty-one, then you're . . ." A firm and cautioning finger was laid across his lips, breaking the words off short.

"Spare me the oral arithmetic, sir." Her hand rested gently on his cheek for a moment and then dropped away. "I have said the figures many times to myself."

"I don't know why they should upset you," he said. "You don't look any different . . . prettier, maybe." This was the truth and he wondered why she attached such importance to the years.

"Believe me, sir," she laughed at him, "I resort to artifice. In truth, I am a crone. Oh, Clay." The eyes meeting his were shadowed in fright. "So much time, so many good years gone forever. Why have you waited so long?"

His arms were about her and she came into them with willing surrender. Beneath his hands he could feel her stir, her breath quicken as he kissed her eyes, the melting softness of her trembling mouth. There was a timid agony in her passion as she pressed against him, turning within his embrace and gasping with sharp gratification as his fingers moved across her breast.

"Don't leave me again, Clay." Her face nuzzled against his lips. "I don't even want you to go to New Orleans." Anxiously her eyes searched his.

He held her with an aching tenderness, his face pressed into her hair, wondering at the circuitous trail that had finally brought him to this spot.

"I'll come back," he said gravely. "I don't know how long this business will take. Do you know anything about building a house?"

"Only that you need nails and lumber." She was tempted to laugh.

"I meant what it should look like. Just as soon as things quiet down I want to build on the plantation."

"Will it be long? The war, I mean."

"I don't know. Unless the Army gets a hell of a lot smarter than it was the last time I looked, it could go on forever." He laughed. "As a matter of fact, I'm sort of under contract to the military."

She twisted out of his arms and regarded him with amazement. "You didn't enlist? Clay Hammond, don't tell me you're a soldier."

"No-o." He grinned at her exasperation. "I just sort of hired out to General Clinch without pay."

She folded her hands in her lap and stared at him. "You are going to New Orleans, aren't you?"

"Yes, ma'am."

"Then what?" She asked the question with quiet firmness.

"Well . . ." He made an attempt to draw her back.

"No, thank you, Mr. Hammond." She moved a few inches down the log. "I asked: Then what?"

"Well . . ." He wriggled uncomfortably. Why did a woman always want to pin a man down? "Well, I thought I might take a ship to Tampa. I'd sort of like to see what's going on."

"Stuff." She was impatient. "You want to shoot an Indian or something. What difference does it make to you what's going on?"

"Look, Sue." Why, he thought, hadn't he kept his mouth shut? "I sort of gave my word to General Clinch."

"Is it serious? Do you intend to marry him?" She was dangerously close to anger.

"Now, Sue," he argued solemnly, "General Clinch is already married."

"Well, sir, I am not."

He ignored her halfhearted struggle, locking his arms about her shoulders and kissing the protests from her lips. When she sagged submissively against his chest he held her there.

"Now, look," he whispered, "it may take some time for the lawyers to do something about Claire. We'll just have to wait. You know," his laughter was soft on her ear, "I've been alone in the woods for a long time. Well, while we're waiting you wouldn't want anything like that to happen, would you?"

She turned to look up at him. "Quite frankly, yes." She giggled. "If such an admission affronts you I am sorry. Put it down to the desperation of an old maid."

He rose. "You better come along home now. I want to have a talk with Hadley."

"Yes, of course." She rose with deceptive obedience. "We must speak to Hadley." She faced him determinedly. "And while you're about it, be sure to tell him that just as soon as you get tired of looking around and scalping Indians you want to come back and marry his sister. That is, of course, if General Clinch has no objections." She seemed to wilt and crept into his arms again. "I'm so afraid, Clay. Please don't let anything happen."

Yard by yard, mile by mile, throughout the short days of winter and into the sapping torment of summer, the Army dragged its cumbersome machine over the peninsula and cursingly sought to pin down an enemy who refused to fight, save on his own terms.

Volunteers, once wildly exuberant at the prospect of adventure, sickened of the fruitless and dreary campaign and straggled back across the border to their native states at the conclusion of their brief enlistment periods. Transportation snarled itself hopelessly within the roadless Territory. Food grew worse, and vital supplies frequently dribbled away to perilously scanty reserves. Men were ill and died of swamp fever, their bodies covered with deep and running sores. They collapsed in their heavy woolen uniforms beneath a merciless sun or plodded wretchedly through the suffocating scrub. There was bickering in the high places, and always the Seminoles raced and danced with the elusiveness of fox fire, remaining just out of reach and then turning suddenly to fall upon and destroy the incautious.

General Winfield Scott was relieved of his command of the troops within Florida and sent to Georgia to conduct operations against the Creeks. The President ordered a court of inquiry convened at Frederick, Maryland, and General Scott prepared a lengthy, and slightly petulant, explanation of "the failure of my Florida campaign." The list of the General's complaints was long. He accused General Gaines of recklessness, if not insubordination, in marching a thousand men from Fort Brooke, at Tampa, to Fort King and requisitioning supplies there that were desperately needed later. He charged that General Gaines later announced, in Tallahassee, that he had "subdued" the Seminoles and, as a result, the quartermaster failed to send supplies to the other forces operating deep within the Territory. "Insufficient means of transportation, insufficient supplies of hard bread and bacon, the heat of the climate, bad water and sickness, the lack of guides and of roads and bridges" were all set forth in the apologia.

The summer of '36 curled at the edges, falling with the leaves of a new season, and the violence did not abate. In small, fast-moving units the Seminoles ranged and harassed the invading army. Warrior groups, directed by Asseola, Wildcat, Alligator, Jumper, Tigertail, Sam Jones, Little Cloud, and even the lethargic Micanopy, led the assaults. They fought along the Ouithlacoochee, in the lake country, and on the eastern seaboard. The conflict lacked the drama of great clashes. There was nothing about it to stir the public imagination. It filtered as a plague through the Territory, eating into remote sections and leaving them blighted and seared. Good and brave men, red and white, died miserably in unspectacular engagements, and their bones were scattered and left to bleach beneath the sun. For a brief period the government's forces were commanded by Richard Keith Call, territorial governor, who yielded to Major General Thomas Jesup, hastily brought down from Georgia.

Tampa lay within the outstretched arms of two irregular peninsulas that enclosed its sheltered bay. During the months of summer it was intolerably hot, the lifeless water reflecting the sun and pouring it back over the settlement and military establishment, pressing with lifeless weight upon the sweltering inhabitants. Furious and unpredictable storms bolted out of the Gulf, battering and ripping at the community, leaving it wracked and debris-strewn. Despite its unhealthy climate the settlement clung tenaciously to the edge of the bay and expanded slowly. It drew a mixed population, Spanish and American adventurers, seamen, traders, and home-seekers who mingled in bilingual confusion.

In a water-front tavern, Las Tres Piedras, Clay sat at a low table near an open window and chewed unhappily at a pen, removing it from his mouth now and then to make an inspired, but brief, attack upon the paper. He formed the sentences of his letter to Sue Rogers with difficulty, piecing the words together with laborious concentration. Writing did not come easily and he suffered, leaning back on his stool now and then to survey the result from a distance.

I've got a bellyful of fighting [he wrote], but that seems to be a common complaint with the troops and Indians alike. It seems we are always at it and nothing is accomplished except the formation of a new burying detail. I don't think the Army can ever really lick the Seminoles, although I suppose you could get shot for saying a thing like that.

I wrote you two other letters, one from New Orleans about a year ago and another that I gave to a dispatch rider out of Fort Drane who was riding to Tallahassee. I don't guess that is the same as coming back to marry you but I got tangled up with this damn army and it is hard to shake loose. What I've been doing doesn't make a lot of sense but you'll have to admit that there is something about soldiering, even the way I've been doing it, that gets under your skin.

He canted the chair back and stared out of the window, thinking over the statement. For almost a year he had been attached to the Army as a civilian scout and guide. Day after day he had matched his acquired cunning and knowledge of the Territory with the Indians, and the game had come to have a terrible fascination. Also, there was the rough companionship of men engaged in war and the knowledge that he was liked and respected. More than anything he prized this. He smiled. What was it Jamie Beulow had said? You go through life wagging your tail like an eager puppy. Jamie Beulow. How many times and under what strange circumstances had he thought of the man, and always with an aching sense of loss? It was curious how the mind rejected that which it did not wish to nurture. He felt no guilt; murder did not weigh upon him. It was as though he had been a spectator at an unavoidable tragedy. The sigh escaping him was all but inaudible and he turned again to the letter.

I went back to Fort Drane as I promised [he wrote]. General Clinch seemed glad to have me but there wasn't much to do at first. Everyone seemed to be waiting around for the Army to untangle itself. Too many people were pulling in different directions. General Gaines set out from here with over a thousand men and marched all the way to Fort King as though he could win the war by himself. Later I heard they didn't see an Indian. Anyhow, his troops ate up everything at Fort King and then turned around and started back for Tampa, going far west of their original route. While he was trying to get across the Ouithlacoochee River the Indians jumped him and he sent a rider back to Fort Drane asking General Clinch for reinforcements. When we reached the ford on the Ouithlacoochee, General Gaines's men were down to killing and eating their horses. The Seminoles had pinned them and were sniping at the troops from good cover. When they got tired of this they would set fire to the tall grass and burn the Army out of its position. Of course, no one who hadn't seen it would believe the story but it's true just the same. While the Indians had them backed up and yelling for help I'm damned if the Army wasn't going through the regular routine. Every day they'd hold guard mounting and retreat, sort of a full parade, as though they were back home on a drill ground and no one was shooting at them. Every time they did this the Seminoles would pick off a few more. Some fine men were killed with this nonsense.

At General Clinch's orders I guided a small advance detachment to the position, and two days after we arrived things weren't getting any better. Then on the third evening a Negro began shouting from the opposite bank. He said the Indians wanted to talk and he was told to have them come in the next morning. About noon the following day the Seminoles came out of the woods on our rear. They had crossed the river upstream during the night. They carried a white flag and lined up, waiting for the talk to begin. With a Captain Hitchcock and Adjutant Barrow I went out. Well, of course I don't have to tell you who was there. I could spot him a quarter of a mile off with that fancy egret plume shining in the sunlight. It was that damn Indian from the Apalachicola, Asseola. He's the one I brought to see you when you and your brothers were building the cabin at Elbow Bend. The other Indians are satisfied to stick a few turkey feathers in their hair, but this Asseola is a dude at heart, I guess. The officers insist on calling him Powell. They put him down that way in their dispatches. I've sort of figured out why they do this. They don't like to admit an ignorant, savage Indian can hold off the Army of the United States the way he is doing. By calling him Powell and pretending he's white, or at least part white, they excuse their own blundering. Anyhow, I walked forward with Captain Hitchcock and Barrow and spoke to Asseola. Damned if he didn't just look at me as though I was a stranger.

"Child," I said, "these soldiers have been living on horsemeat and a few handfuls of corn for over a week now. They'd just as soon chew your leg off as not. You're the biggest damn fool of an Indian I've ever known and that's saying a lot. What the hell do you want?"

He chuckled at the memory of the scene and took a long swallow from the rum in a cup at his elbow. Sue ought to think this was funny. He bent again to his writing.

Well [he continued], this Asseola looked at me and said, "If the soldiers want to surrender I will permit them to cross the river without their arms. Those we can use." At first I couldn't believe he meant it. Then I said, "Child, these troops are hungry and mad. Also, they won't give up like it was a game of ball." He didn't blink. "My people," he said slowly, "are also hungry."

Captain Hitchcock interrupted then. "What the hell is he saying?" he asked. For a minute I didn't have the nerve to tell him. Finally I said, "He says that if you stack your arms you can cross the river." He stared at that Indian like he couldn't believe it and then yelled. When he quieted down I spoke again to Asseola.

"Child," I said, "you can look at the Captain and know how he feels about surrendering." Asseola just nodded and turned around. What happened then wasn't really anyone's fault. The advance patrol of

General Clinch's reinforcement came out suddenly and saw all these Indians. Without waiting they began pulling triggers. A couple of the Seminoles were killed and the rest ran for cover and scrambled back across the river. I don't suppose anything will ever convince them that the Army didn't lure them out under a flag of truce for a massacre. It sort of left a bad taste in everyone's mouth. With General Clinch there with more men the position was too difficult to take and the Indians disappeared. Anyhow, that's how the fighting goes, no fancy charges with bugles blowing and drums rolling, just a few men dead here and there, day after day. It's like prying a wildcat out of a hole in a tree.

Clay put the pen down and called to the Spanish innkeeper for another cup of rum. When it was placed before him he drank thoughtfully, rolling the sharp, sweet liquor around in his mouth. It was all right to write a long letter but it wasn't going to fool Sue for a minute. She'd brush aside the words and get right down to the point: Why didn't he come home? He tackled the letter again.

Of course, I know you must be wondering why I stay out here instead of coming back. At first I took to the woods because there were a lot of things I wanted to forget and staying there on the Apalachicola wouldn't have done me any good. That's all over now. It has been over for a long time. If you'll still have me, I'll come home just as soon as I can arrange things.

When the ink had dried he carefully, almost absently, folded the sheets and sealed them. It would serve him right if she up and married someone else. He didn't have to stay here at Tampa waiting for a mission. He was a civilian and could walk out any time. He weighed the letter in his hand. If I had any sense, he thought, I'd get aboard a ship and go myself instead of sending a letter.

He rose and walked over to the narrow bar. The tavern keeper, Martinez, regarded him with deferential attention. He liked this tall, well-spoken American who had taken quarters in his establishment. In the evenings, when the public room filled and the concertinas were playing, the beams shaking from the stamping feet of roistering seamen and troops, this American sat drinking by himself. He never raised his voice or took part in the short-lived brawls over liquor and women. Now and then he would take one of the small, sloe-eyed *putas* to his room and keep her there for the night, but otherwise he was much alone. It was said that he was a famous Indian fighter, but, Martinez thought, it hardly seemed probable that so quiet a man could rouse himself to a great anger.

348

"You will return to eat here tonight, señor?" Martinez rested his elbows on the bar.

"I guess so." Clay handed him the letter and some silver. "I want this placed in the hands of Captain Bullet, of the schooner *Estella*. He is sailing for Pensacola sometime this afternoon."

"Be assured." Martinez bowed as though he had been knighted. "I shall attend to it myself. *Sin falta*."

Walking slowly back from the water front, through the settlement and out into the flats that surrounded Fort Brooke, Clay couldn't rid himself of the uneasy feeling that the patience of Susan Rogers was running out. If he wanted her he had better make up his mind instead of helling around in the woods.

He passed the sentry post without challenge, returning the guard's familiar wave. I must be getting to be a real shaggy character to the Army, he thought. He understood that a certain romantic glamour was attached to his person as a survivor of the Dade massacre. He was known by sight to most of the troops now, and many of them hailed him by his first name. Two other men, he learned later, had escaped from the Indians who attacked Major Dade and made their way back to Tampa. Of the entire company he and the two privates were the only ones who had lived to tell the story. Clay had told it so many times at the officers' mess that it had taken on the character of an elaborate fiction.

At a table outside Colonel Pearson's quarters he halted.

"Hello, Clay." The young orderly grinned. He was one of the two who had dragged themselves into hiding along the trail near the Great Wahoo Swamp. As a reward he had been made a corporal. This, Clay thought, was only another curious manifestation of the military mind. Why should a man be promoted for saving his own skin? As a survivor of the massacre, Corporal Thomas felt an imperishable bond had been wrought between them. "The Colonel has been askin' about you."

"Is he in?" Clay nodded toward the adjoining room.

Thomas rose. "I'll tell him you're here."

"Never mind." Clay rapped shortly on the door and then opened it. "I'll tell him myself."

Colonel Pearson glanced up. "Oh! Hammond." He frowned slightly. Civilians never wanted to be announced in the proper manner.

"How are you, Colonel? Thomas said you wanted to see me." He rested a foot on a chair and leaned forward on his knee.

The officer nodded and thought to himself that a few weeks of

349

Army discipline would do this fellow good. He was too damn easy and familiar. He had heard that Hammond was one of the wealthiest men in the Territory, but dismissed the story as barracks talk. What the hell was he doing scouting for the Army if that was true?

"I have some reports for General Jesup," Pearson said. "How soon can you leave?"

Clay rubbed at his chin. This was as good a time as any to make the break. "I'd sort of figured on resigning, Colonel," he said.

"Resign?" The officer couldn't contain his surprise. "Man, don't you know there is a war on?"

Clay smiled. "I catch a few rumors now and then."

"Well, then." The Colonel was impatient. "How can you talk about resigning?"

Clay tried to hide a smile with his hand. "Well," he said in a tone of regret, "it isn't as though I had a regular job with good pay, Colonel. I'm just on sort of a day-to-day basis without any real security. Sometimes I wonder if there is a future in it."

The levity annoyed the officer. How could any army be run efficiently when it had to depend on men like this? Hammond acted as though it were a boy's game. Soldiering wasn't a thing to be taken lightly.

"Of course," he said brusquely, "you are free to leave whenever you like. As I understand it, you volunteered for the duty." He tapped the dispatch wallet. "I'm a little surprised by your attitude. What do you intend to do that is more important than the lives of men who are fighting?"

Clay shifted uncomfortably. He understood well enough that Pearson was deliberately maneuvering him into an awkward position. Maybe the dispatches for General Jesup were important. Maybe, also, they didn't mean a damn thing. The Army was great on forms. He thought about Sue. It might be a good idea to hold off going back until she received the letter and cooled down a little.

"I was going home," he said after a moment, "but I guess it could wait if what you have there really means anything."

"I think you'll have to permit me to decide that." Pearson was having no more nonsense.

"All right." Clay dropped his foot to the floor. "I suppose I can go home by way of Fort Drane. It would be a damn sight easier to ride on a boat, though."

Pearson handed him the wallet. "It would be easier if we could all go home, Mr. Hammond," he said tartly. He leaned back in his chair.

"There are rumors that the Indians are holding peace talks." Now that things were in order again he relaxed slightly.

"I don't take much stock in rumors." Clay stuffed the dispatch case inside his shirt. "A few minor chiefs may want to quit, but I don't see how they can pull out unless the government offers a hell of a lot more than it has."

"When will you leave?" Colonel Pearson rose to terminate the conversation.

"In the morning. Tonight, if you're really in a hurry."

"That's fine." Pearson nodded curtly. "Good luck and my compliments to General Jesup." He remained standing until Clay left the room.

Outside again, Clay stared up at the sky and wondered why he hadn't said no and walked off the post. It was a long way to Fort Drane. He had made the trip so many times he could do it with his eyes shut now, but the danger remained, hiding behind every palmetto clump and each bend of the trail. One of these times he would get careless and the Army would have to find itself a new boy.

He went to the quartermaster's depot and drew the few supplies he would need, wondering whether he should leave before sundown or wait until daybreak. Walking back from the fort he decided to start in the morning. He would get a good night's sleep with one of Martinez' girls to keep his back warm. Retracing his steps to the inn, he thought of Pearson's words about peace talks. If the Seminoles had any sense they'd quit even though the Army might never be able to beat them into submission. At the end the best they could hope for would be a retreat into the Everglades around Okeechobee. What kind of life would that be, never daring to come out?

Throughout the morning Clay had the uneasy feeling that someone was on his trail. He was two days out of Fort Brooke, following a well-worn route, and had been moving steadily in a northwesterly direction since the first light of dawn, covering the ground in long, effortless strides. He still preferred to work without a horse. Headquarters, always in a hurry, tried to force a mount on him, but he refused. If I ever get bushwhacked, he argued, the first Indian bullet will have a horse as a target and I'll be on the ground anyhow and probably tangled up in stirrup leather. It may take longer this way but I like it.

As he pressed forward he wondered what was bothering him. Nothing he had seen during the morning pointed to trouble, but his instinct nagged and worried and he grew uncomfortable as a strangely persistent voice of warning kept whispering something he could not understand. Frequently, now, he turned as he walked and glanced back over the trail. In the loose earth his moccasins made a tiny whistling sound and when he halted the silence gathered about him with an eerie breathlessness. Once after turning he shook himself like a wet dog and then laughed softly. By God, he marveled, do you suppose I'm getting old enough to have nerves, peering over my shoulder every five minutes? By now I ought to have sense enough to know that if anyone is following me he damn sure wouldn't walk along in the open where I could see him if I looked around.

He debated the problem with himself cheerfully and felt better as he talked. When, however, he abandoned the questions and ready answers, the undetected menace seemed more real than ever. Now he was certain someone was following. He could feel the presence, and small nervous prickles raced along his spine. Finally, when he could stand it no longer, he began trotting, and where the path crooked sharply he leaped to one side, raced back parallel to the trail for a hundred yards, and squatted within a palmetto thicket. Now, by God, he'd find out. Whoever was behind him wouldn't be able to see where he had left the road until he was upon the turn. With the rifle across his legs he waited, motionless and alert. Through the scrub openings he had a clear view of the empty trail over which the sun poured with warm brilliance. Nothing moved upon it and the minutes gathered. Cautiously he lowered one knee to the ground, easing his weight to the support. There was a sleepy hush upon the air. A small lizard flashed across the brittle spear of a palmetto fan and halted, its narrow head lifted inquisitively. The shadow of a hawk, high overhead, drifted along the trail, veered suddenly to one side and away. There was no sound. Clay discovered his mouth was dry and his fingers crept to a shirt pocket for a twist of tobacco. It was hot within the tangled clump and he could feel the perspiration gather in sticky patches on his neck. He counted slowly up to sixty. One minute. Two ... three ... four ... five. His bent leg was going to sleep. At the end of what he thought must be fifteen minutes he rose stiffly in a half crouch. Either his imagination had tricked him or whoever had been following him was too damn smart. I suppose, he thought disgustedly, I'll have to walk backward from here to Fort Drane. Warily he pushed through the crackling fans and stepped into the open. From where he stood he could be the world's last man in this vast well of silence.

At midday he ate as he walked, cold bacon and flat pieces of hard bread, washing down the greasy mess with water from a canteen.

No longer was there any doubt in his mind. Someone was behind him, something dogged his footsteps, halting when he paused, jogging without sound when he trotted. How he knew this he could not say. The man, or perhaps men, were as real as though he had looked upon their faces or heard them speak. Having decided this, he strangely enough felt easier and even worked up a mild curiosity as to the purpose and identity of his pursuers. They were being pretty damn cagey and, he thought scornfully, a little stupid. If they wanted to jump him all they had to do was cut far to his flank, outrace him for a mile or so, and then get him head on. That was the way a white man would figure out things, but an Indian's methods were unpredictable. Maybe, he grinned, this is the trip I shouldn't have taken.

The sun began easing down the long western slope, gathering fire as it descended and tinting the pines and marshy ponds with changing splashes of color. The high clouds built themselves into billowing pyramids or writhed slowly into grotesque exaggerations of people and animals. Night would drop quickly. Clay had decided to keep moving, waiting for the darkness. After that they'd have to fire-hunt him like a buck, if that was what they wanted.

He was weary, not sleepy. It was the weariness that asks only a warm meal and a blanket on a soft piece of ground, with maybe a small fire. Well, the warm meal would have to be more salty bacon and bread. A fire would be just about the same as putting the rifle to his head and stubbing the trigger. Maybe that soft piece of ground would be so comfortable he'd lie on it forever. Then he never would get back to Sue and the Apalachicola or be around to know how this damn war ended.

It had been dark for almost two hours, the night moonless, the trail something to be followed by instinct more than sight, black upon black. This, he thought, is as good a time as any unless I want to keep moving all night, and there isn't much sense in that. He waited until he came to a spot where the worn ground was crowded into a lane between bay and myrtle scrub and then jumped lightly and crashed into the brush. Unless the bastards are following with their noses to the ground they'll have a hell of a time trying to figure out where I ducked off. They sure can't see any better than I can and I couldn't locate the print of an elephant right now. He worked his way soundlessly through the scrub, moving with patient caution for half an hour, testing the ground for silence with the ball of each foot before he placed it to step ahead. He came upon a minute clearing, all but encircled by scrub and a sapling growth, and stood within the circle, his head raised, listening and sniffing. Not even the call of a bird intruded upon the deep silence. With a soft grunt he loosened the light blanket pack. This would have to do. Of course, it didn't settle anything. If they really wanted him they'd have another chance in the morning.

He sat cross-legged and chewed on a hunk of bacon, stripping out the lean streaks with his teeth and making a sandwich with the fat between biscuits. If people would just go on and mind their business he could be stretched out beside a warm fire with a can of coffee on the coals. He pulled the stopper from a flat pint flask of rum, and drank, wishing he could have a cigar and dwelling with pleasure on the flavor of rum and tobacco. The scanty meal finished, he scooped a mound of earth together for a pillow and twisted into the scratchy wool of an Army blanket. Bedded down this way he felt as secure as a squirrel in a hickory tree. The rifle lay within his hand, and his cheek, covered by the blanket, burrowed into the soft mound. He sighed gratefully and his eyes closed.

He had no way of knowing how long he had been asleep or why he had awakened. His head jerked up from the earthen pillow and then they were upon him, diving across the narrow space, smothering him beneath their pounding bodies. He could almost taste the cloying sweetness of their stink and then something clubbed at his head and he sagged under a numbing explosion as the world disappeared.

Consciousness returned in fitful spurts and he passed from one filmy sensation to another. First: His eyes were open so he couldn't be dead. Next: He was lying on his side, his hands bound behind his back and the shoulder muscles drawn to a tight agony. His head was a great drum, thumped heavily at by the beating of his heart. Although he could not see them as he lay, he knew the Indians were there. Above the scrub the sky was thinning out with the first cottony stringings of daybreak. He wondered why he was alive. Why, when they had him, hadn't they done the job and gone on? He clamped his eyes shut against the twinging pain in his head. By God, he thought, I don't think my skull is going to last this war out. He dug with his shoulder at the ground until he squirmed over on his other side. Three Indians were placidly seated on their butts, chewing stolidly at the pieces of bacon rind and slobbering on the fat juice. His gun, pistol, and knife, together with the dispatch wallet, had been dumped on the blanket. The provision pouch was empty, and only a few crumbs were left of the small store. The rum flask was uncorked and one of the Indians lifted it, running his tongue inside the mouth for one last drop. Clay's eyes traveled from face to face; the Indians stared past him as though he were not there. This didn't make any sense. The Indians never took prisoners. Why, then, wasn't his scalp hanging from one of their belts this minute? He licked at his dry, dirt-encrusted lips and waited.

Only after they had swallowed the last pieces of rind and wiped their hands with quick sweeps in their armpits did they appear to notice their prisoner. One rose and gathered the blanket into a roll, thrusting the loop over the barrel of Clay's rifle. He waited as his companions jerked the trussed man to his feet and pushed him toward the scrub's opening.

"Where do we go?" Clay spoke thickly, half turning to look at them. He saw a flicker of interest in their eyes at his use of their tongue, but the question was ignored. One prodded him to move forward.

They traveled all morning, the Indians forcing him to a steady but unhurried trot, and he discovered how awkward running could be without the balancing effect of freely swinging arms. He fell two or three times and the Indians waited with a cold and infuriating detachment as he struggled to regain his feet, unable to use his hands to thrust himself upright. Once, at the edge of a creek, he dropped to his knees, dipping his face into the water and lapping with the noise of an animal. A blow from a rifle butt pitched him into the stream and he lay there, exhausted and not caring whether they killed him now or later. Finally they hauled him from the strangling shallows and pushed him ahead, forcing the pace.

The sun was at noon when they entered the swamp, and the Seminoles, once they were knee deep, unbound him. Here a man must use his hands, steadying himself and clinging to the trailing and matted vines. They moved slowly through the black, scum-encrusted depths. Here the sunlight was shut away and the great cypress trees strained upward on their arching roots. Thick, trailing creepers dangled like scaly ropes and heavy pennants of Spanish moss hung motionless from the branches in the perpetual twilight. On the exposed roots, venomous cotton-mouthed moccasins curled back to rear at their passing and mosquitoes swarmed over their faces in whining clouds so dense they could be scraped away with the edge of a hand. Alligators, their knobby heads barely raised above the surface, watched the intruders and retreated without a ripple. Each step was taken with care, for the swamp's bottom was tangled with sunken logs, branches, and roots. Now and then the water rose to their waists and the Seminoles sloshed forward, arms raised high as though they were leading a procession of religious supplicants.

Clay was no longer interested in their destination, wondering only why he was still alive. This, he figured, was a temporary condition at best. Maybe they were saving him for special treatment. He thought grimly of the tortured and mutilated bodies he had seen. Perhaps they had something new they wanted to try out. His anger smoldered as he went back to the stupid decision that led to his capture. He had been so damn certain he was smarter than any Indian born that they'd picked him up like a trussed 'possum. He would like to find out how they had located him. His head lifted and he stared ahead. The swamp seemed to stretch for miles, dark and forbidding. His face was a tortured, itching mask and when he wiped at the mosquitoes his hand came away smeared with blood from the squashed bodies. He wondered how long a man could live, stripped naked and bound to a tree for the swirling pests to work over. They didn't seem to bother the Indians; they probably couldn't bite through the stink. He scooped up some water, splashing it over his face. The relief was only momentary. As soon as the moisture dried the itching was worse.

He glanced back over his shoulder at the two Indians. The third was a few yards ahead. Not once had he heard them speak.

"You're damn poor company," he said in English, "and scabs on a mongrel's tits." Somehow the words made him feel better. You're getting mighty easy to amuse, he told himself.

30

THE island rose gradually from the swamp, humping itself out of the water like the spiny back of a half-submerged monster. Tall, slender pines were straight and green along the gentle ridge and the firm ground sprouted thick clusters of blue and white violets. The land was warm and dry; light sifted down from the open sky and lay in speckled puddles on the brown pine needles.

It was a big town, the lodges heavily timbered and thatched. As his captors shoved him forward Clay looked about with reluctant admiration. This was no settlement of disorganized Indians, no temporary refuge from the whites. Here was tight order and confidence. As they walked, a band of children rushed out to meet them, capering and screaming, their faces daubed with streaks of black soot as they played at being fierce, bold warriors. They thrust at Clay with sticks, racing around the legs of the guards and running backward to stare at the prisoner. From a safe distance they yelled their treble defiance, tugging at the corners of their mouths with outstretched fingers, contorting their excited faces into frightening grimaces.

As they passed through the center of the compound, between the orderly rows of lodges, women turned from their work to stare impassively and then bent again to their labors. Older boys and young men dropped from lodge platforms, falling into stride along the parade's flank. They whispered among themselves and edged forward to peer at the captive. This was the enemy, the white man, and their hatred was undisguised. The older fighting men and the ancients scorned more than a passing glance, but their sullen hostility spread out and reached for the white stranger.

Clay made no attempt to conceal his interest. Four or five hundred Indians must occupy the town. It was larger than any he had ever seen. The people were clean, well clothed and fed, carrying themselves with a quiet pride. This was how it had been in the old days. Before each lodge, skins were drying on their frames and girls worked with bone needles at moccasins and leggings. On a platform a dozen or so women were filling bullet molds, pouring the silvery metal from

357

small iron pots. Around the cooking house other women busied themselves, turning racks of smoked fish, cutting open the ugly black turtles, butchering deer and rabbits, stirring at the *sofskee* kettles, or packing the wide-necked leather pouches with rations. As Clay passed they barely glanced up, and he thought the Army would be a hundred years at the job of subduing these people.

One of the captors shoved roughly at Clay's shoulder, guiding him at an angle across the compound to a lodge where a group of men were seated on spotless mats.

"You son of a bitch," Clay whispered. There was no anger in the exclamation and his eyes were fixed on the Indian above whose head the egret plume was curled. "I ought to have figured you'd be here," he continued softly.

His guards halted before the platform and one of them passed up the captured rifle and dispatch case. Clay stood waiting. The seated men gazed down upon him without a change of expression. Asseola nodded to the three warriors and they fell away, walking back to the cookhouse for food. With a wave of his hand Asseola scattered the alert children and they turned obediently, leaving the prisoner alone with the chiefs. It was a quiet display of authority that Clay did not miss. He spat upon the ground and addressed Asseola.

"You don't have to show off in front of me," he said. "I know you're a big Indian."

Asseola regarded him unemotionally. He had changed; Clay could not mistake the scars of the years. Behind the bright eyes there was a weariness, and the mouth seemed thinner, drawn to an inflexible purpose. When he spoke the voice was impatient and accusing.

"Why do you make war against my people?"

"To hell with you," Clay snapped. "Speak English." He was weary, his body sore from unnecessary clubbings, his head a lump of pain. He glared at the Indian.

Although they did not understand the words, the angry boldness of the tone was unmistakable, and the older men seemed startled, glancing quickly from Asseola to the captive, their gaze brightening with sudden interest.

"Once," Asseola ignored the insult and continued in the dialect, "the people of my nation called you brother. Why do you, knowing well what it is we fight for, take arms against them?"

Clay shifted his weight. "I'm not fighting the Seminoles," he said, "but if I was I've a damn good reason for it. They burned my place, killed Old Clay and a couple of hundred slaves. What do you think I should do?"

358

"We are left no choice but to destroy or be destroyed. This you know is so." The Indian regarded him gravely.

There was a low murmur of approval from the others and they leaned forward slightly, resting arms on their crossed legs.

Stubbornly Clay continued to reply in English. "Well, I'm not going to argue with you about it. What the hell do you want with me, child?"

Asseola's eyes didn't change, but Clay caught an unmistakable twitch at the corners of his mouth as the beginning of a smile tugged and vanished.

"I could have you killed." He said it quietly but in Clay's tongue as though the answer were one that he preferred not to share with the others.

Clay took a deep breath of relief. If this damn Indian was going to take his scalp he wouldn't talk about it. "How did you know I was on the trail?" he asked.

"The word was brought to me after you left Fort Brooke. Your passage has been marked many times and in many different places. It is known to all that you were my brother." He paused and then returned to the dialect. "Where do the soldiers move?"

Clay shook his head and winced. "I don't know." He flipped a hand at the dispatch case. "Maybe those will tell you something." He grinned suddenly. "I'd sure as hell like to know if they're important enough for me to be beaten over the head the way I was."

Asseola picked up the wallet, turning it thoughtfully in his hand. "Go to my lodge," he said after a moment, and pointed out the shelter. "I will have food and water sent to you. Later we will talk."

Clay turned and walked away. He was almost too weary to eat, and he stumbled a little, wondering as he hoisted his aching bones to Asseola's lodge what was going to happen. By God, he thought, I may have to sit out the rest of the war here in the swamp like a captive squaw. He chuckled ruefully. Sue'll never believe this. She'll figure it's just another story I made up to keep from coming home.

A woman brought him food, averting her eyes as she placed it at his feet, and hurrying away without a backward glance. He ate eagerly, dipping his fingers into the hot mass of thick stew and emptying the water gourd. When he had licked the last of the gravy from the pot he stretched out, full length, on the mats of sweet grass. The youngsters were unable to resist the fascination of the white prisoner. They gathered about the lodge in a silent circle, inching forward, their wide eyes fixed steadily on the resting man. Clay pretended not to be aware of their presence. I suppose, he thought, they figure smoke and fire ought to come out of my ears and mouth. He sighed contentedly. He was lucky. By rights he should be lying back there in the scrub with his head bashed in. Closing his eyes he listened to the sounds of the town. They formed a lulling whisper, and beneath it he slept.

It was late afternoon when he awoke and rolled to his back, staring up at the thatching. The rest and food had been all he needed and his body responded quickly. Sitting up he glanced down the length of the street. While he had been sleeping a large body of the fighting men had moved out. Their absence was easily noted. Clay decided that the town must serve as a supply depot for the roving bands and he wondered how many other settlements such as this one were scattered throughout the swamps and in the almost impenetrable lake regions. No wonder General Scott had complained he couldn't find the enemy.

Sitting up, he removed the stiff moccasins and worked the leather between his fingers, kneading the skin. If I'm going to stay here, he thought idly, I'll have to get me a girl to chew them soft for me. He looked across the lodges to where Asseola had been sitting in council with the old chiefs. The platform was vacant and he shrugged away a feeling of uneasiness. Do you suppose, he thought, that child has gone off and left me to be carved up by the women? On the faces of the Indians who passed or looked across now and then from their work in the compound he could see the slow brewing of hatred. Here, alone, he began to feel like a turkey in a farmhouse roost on Thanksgiving Day.

He pushed his feet back into the moccasins and wriggled his toes comfortably. He was still puzzled, wondering what lay behind Asseola's order to have him brought in. If the dispatches to General Jesup were important enough to go after, it would have been a simple matter to have the bearer waylaid and killed on the trail. Anyhow, the Indians never seemed to care what the white troops were going to do. They drew up their own timetable of battle, fighting when the odds were favorable and the situation to their liking. When they didn't feel like fighting, they simply disappeared and the troops chased their own tails. No, he decided, Asseola had something else on his mind and, Indian-like, would reveal it in his own way. Until then, he argued, he'd just have to sit here and wait, hoping nothing would happen to disturb the uneasy balance of his situation.

As the time of brief twilight gathered, he watched the town prepare for the night, his eyes turning from the central fire and roaming over the compound. At the far side of the cleared section, a dozen or so children were gathered. They shouldered sticks as rifles and then fell upon their stomachs to sight along the pieces of wood, firing at the enemy. As Clay watched, they adopted stalking tactics, stringing themselves out in a slow and stealthy approach to his shelter. They wriggled and crept with deadly seriousness, enveloping an unsuspecting foe. When they were within a few yards of the lodge, they whooped shrilly and raced toward the platform, tossing pine cones as they ran, barking a simulation of rifle fire. Clay dodged the harmless shower and laughed quietly as the youngsters disappeared. They curved around to the back and then formed again at the front, staring at him. Then, tentatively, not quite certain of their purpose at first, some of the more aggressive children hurled a second barrage of cones. They bounced on the matting and rolled with a dry scattering across the mats. Unconcernedly he caught one piece and lobbed it back. It was returned, thrown with a sudden viciousness, whistling past his face. He straightened his shoulders, cautious now, the smile dying quickly. More of the boys began throwing and Clay understood it had ceased to be a game. He was in a ridiculous position; seated, his body swaying to avoid the missiles. A few older boys stopped to watch the children. Then a couple of men and a woman edged to the outside of the group. They spoke no word and the young ones, encouraged by their tacit approval, sent cone after cone spinning his way. Clay rose quickly, no longer bothering to dodge. A spiny cone struck his face and he could hear a mutter of encouragement from the elders. As he looked out over their heads, more men and women pressed into the crowd and he realized that a frightening silence had settled on the compound. Even the children had ceased their excited yelling. They threw as rapidly as their hands found fresh ammunition. Then one of the older boys stooped and picked up a heavy knot of wood. It spun through the air and crashed into the thatching. Clay planted his feet, resisting an impulse to duck and run. That was all they would need. He could see the enmity in the upturned faces. Here was the splendid humiliation of a white man, and their black eyes were heated. One of the men found a short length of wood and threw it clumsily. Out of the corner of his eye, Clay saw a fat squaw waddle up, bearing an armful of wood chunks, which she offered with quivering eagerness.

There was a frightening, slack-mouthed idiocy about the attack and it gathered violence. Soon, Clay realized, someone in the crowd would remember his knife and after that a gun. It was all so simple

361

and there wasn't anything he could do about it. They would kill him and be a little surprised later, wondering how it had all started.

Asseola didn't hurry. He walked between the crowd and the lodge, bending over to pick up a thick piece of branch and tossing it aside as though it were in his way. The gesture was one of calculated indifference and he glanced at the shifting mob with casual interest. The rising voices were stilled. Before the lodge he turned to address the children as though they alone were there.

"Go now," he said. "The white man is my prisoner." He slapped affectionately at the rump of a small boy. "I'll bring you a general to spit upon."

The boy laughed and ran, calling to his companions. Their elders backed away and the mob seemed to dissolve, taking up the even tempo of the community's life as though they had only paused momentarily and in all innocence.

Clay discovered he was breathing hard, in short gasps of excitement. It had been too close. He understood, as did Asseola, how near at hand the danger had been.

"I'm damned, child," he whispered gratefully. "You are a big Indian."

"My people have had to learn discipline. We are not savages." Asseola laid his rifle on the edge of the platform and looked up at Clay. "Have you forgotten?"

"It was kind of hard to remember for a minute there." Clay's voice was uneven. "I was wondering how I was going to fight women and children."

"Your people know well enough." The Indian's words were bitter.

"All right," Clay said wearily. "I started the war. I run the Army. The whole damned thing is my fault. Does that satisfy you? What are you going to do with me?"

"Why don't you go back home?"

Clay's laugh was short. "I've got a girl who asks the same thing. The hell of it is I haven't a home to go to."

"You could have been killed many times, Clay." Asseola seated himself, staring thoughtfully at the rifle. "Once, on the Ouithlacoochee, my own hand could have taken your life. I held it because of many things that are in my heart. Do you find that strange?"

"No, child," Clay said softly. "I do not find it strange."

The darkness came quickly and they sat within the lodge, their eyes fixed upon the wheel of fire. At the moment words had no meaning. For a long time they sat this way, leafing back through the books of the years, pausing over well-remembered passages. About

362

the compound the people moved silently to take their food from the cooking house and disappear into the shadows, and the swamp surrounding the town gave the night a voice. Asseola moved, and although Clay did not turn his head, he knew the Indian was watching him.

"My life," Asseola said tonelessly, "runs to its close. This I know is so, but if you ask me how I know I cannot say. Because of this and of the many things we hold between us I wanted to see you again. That is why you are here."

Clay did not speak, understanding the Indian expected no reply.

"We," he continued, "who were children, are now men; yet there is much in your face I remember well. That we fight each other is not bad." He laughed quietly. "Was it not always so?"

Clay found a small twist of tobacco in his shirt pocket, broke it into two sections, and handed one to Asseola.

"I remember thinking about it a long time ago," he said reflectively, "but somehow, I didn't really figure on its happening. At least," he hesitated, "I didn't think it would be like this."

There were a few moments of silence as their jaws worked over the tobacco. In his own way, each was grateful for the interlude. When Asseola spoke again, there was no emotion in his voice.

"Old Clay died quickly."

Clay glanced up sharply. "I'm glad to hear it," he said after a moment. "I wondered a lot about that."

"I was not there." Asseola shook his head, understanding well what was in his companion's mind. "The story was brought to me."

"They certainly raised hell." Clay spoke dispassionately. "Every building on the place, and only four Negrahs left out of more than two hundred. It must have been a sight while it was going on."

"Will you go back to the Apalachicola?" the Indian asked almost wistfully.

Clay grinned at him. "If you're figuring on letting me go, I'll get there someday."

"The war may end soon, Clay." The admission came reluctantly. "It will end too late for me. There is talk now of peace with the soldiers, and the whites dangle false promises before my people to catch their eyes again. There are those of my nation, old men who are wealthy in their slaves and cattle, who listen eagerly to the words of a new treaty. They would keep what they have, carrying it with them to the grave. Their blacks they must have, and to hold them they will go to Arkansas and exile. For their slaves they sell themselves into slavery. Why is it," the question was wrung from him, "the love of country grows so strong within the hearts of the poor? From them I hear no word of surrender. The government whispers well. It will pay for the cattle left behind and there are words of annuity. I can," he was angry, "fight the soldiers, but before the greed of such men as Micanopy, King Phillip, and others I am helpless. They complain of the cost and whine perpetually of their losses. Is not my life worth more than a cow?"

"I heard a peace rumor at Fort Brooke," Clay said, "but I put it down as talk."

The outburst seemed to have drained Asseola of all passion. When he spoke again his words were without strength.

"Before we go," he said, "there is one thing more I would say, for we may not meet again. There was a girl, Che-cho-ter, who was my wife. It was told to me how, at Fort King, you fought to keep her from the hands of the slave runners. I did not forget, and many times I have thought about it. Come." He rose to prevent any reply Clay might make. "It grows late. I would take you through the swamp. I will get your rifle and the foolish papers for the soldiers. You need not admit you were stupid and innocent enough to be captured. I would save your pride."

31

As THE new year turned its first quarter the war ended at the head-quarters of General Jesup, Camp Dade on the Ouithlacoochee, March 1837.

In his hand the Commander of the Army of the South held a treaty and if he entertained any doubts as to the authority of five minor chiefs to bind the Seminole nation to a compact he kept them to himself. Their X marks were made. Holatoochee, Hoeth-lee-matee, Jumper, acting upon orders from the spiritless Micanopy, Yahoolo-chee, and John Ca-wy-ya stepped forward and took the pen. No hand scrawled Asseola or Wildcat, Tigertail or Little Cloud, upon the paper, yet these were the men who had carried the fighting. If the assembled officers wondered at their absence at such an important moment they held their questions.

For all men to read the treaty stated: "Major General Thomas Jesup, in behalf of the United States, agrees that the Seminoles and their allies, who come in and emigrate to the West, shall be secure in their lives and property; that their Negroes, their bona fide property, shall accompany them to the West; and that their cattle and ponies shall be paid for by the United States at a fair valuation."

There were other articles, calling for the withdrawal of the Indians south of the Hillsborough River and their later assembly at Tampa, where ships would be waiting to carry them to New Orleans on the first leg of the journey into Arkansas, but such chiefs as Micanopy and other slaveholders would read only the words "their Negroes, their bona fide property, shall accompany them to the West."

In the swamps the empty bellies of the warriors rumbled. The fighting had been too fierce, the pressure of the troops too constant, for the planting and harvesting of even small crops. Yet they had not yielded but shut their ears to the hungry cries of children and the hopeless yearning in the sad eyes of their women. They had forced the war, seen their towns laid to waste, and yet, somehow, they could not feel themselves defeated. As the runners sent out to find them in the isolated camps brought the word of peace, they looked at each other uncomprehendingly. Was it to save the cattle and slaves of Micanopy that they had fought?

Before the fire in the big town Asseola held the long rifle of the man Powell across his arms and listened to the chiefs. Words of rebellion, of scorn and defiance, were at his lips, but he kept silent until the long talk was finished. When he spoke they understood his shame.

"By fat and greedy men we have been betrayed. It matters little that the bones of our warriors rot upon the ground where they fell so long as Micanopy and the others may keep their slaves. Yet, I tell you, this is a lie, for the whites will not suffer them to leave with so much as a single black man. When the time comes for all to board the ships you will see I have spoken the truth. Then, by this same Micanopy, you will be urged to fight again so he may keep what he values more than honor. I will fight then because I must, but it will not be to hold the black men. This is my land, my home, and I will not leave it."

Hesitantly, almost timidly at first, the men came out of the swamps and thick hummocks, standing with their women and children to look freely once more upon the high blue sky. This land, this fair and gentle place, was at peace and opened itself to the touch of a new spring. No longer must a man tread softly, and the threat of death subsided. He could walk boldly and without fear. In the small clearings they scrabbled joyfully at the earth and planted hastily. Their huts and lodges rose in many places. The children abandoned their games of war, and the women, hearing a distant shot, smiled happily at each other, knowing the sound now meant fresh meat for their pots. The terror lifted.

Once again the borders were opened and immigrants raced afoot or in wagons to claim a piece of this fruitful Territory. Former settlers, driven from the peninsula by the tides of war, bid frantically against each other to repurchase the acres they had sold. Newcomers crowded the offices of land speculators at Jacksonville, St. Augustine, Tallahassee, and Pensacola, clamoring for large and small tracts. Shrewd-eyed men who had bought in the land when it seemed valueless and overrun by Indians turned quick fortunes. In banks and taverns there was talk of railroads and new industries, of crops and cattle. Lumber mills whined the clock around and the bright yellow of freshly cut pine boards rose in many cabins. There was a lusty and heady freedom in the air and men sampled it eagerly. The treaty with the Seminoles had been signed, although its contents had not been made public. Martin Van Buren was in

366

the White House and the nation cherished the illusion of a hard-won victory. General Jesup was a heroic and astute commander.

The first murmurs of discontent were heard behind the closed doors of the War Department. They were raised in cultivated accents, deceptively cloaked and partly hidden beneath such studied phrases as "national honor" and "the dignity of the Administration." As he listened, Secretary of War Poinsett was not unduly alarmed.

At Charleston a small group of wealthy planters gathered to draft a memorial to the Secretary. They had fled from their large estates, finding a pleasant sanctuary in the studied gaiety of the South Carolina metropolis while the government dealt with the Indians. Now the war was over and they were anxious to return to their plantations. They had, the communication to the Secretary stated, learned by sheerest accident the terms of the treaty. In it there was no mention of indemnity to them from either the United States government or the Seminoles for property destroyed. Also, it appeared that the Indians were free to emigrate to Arkansas with their slaves. "We respectfully conceive," the gentlemen wrote, "that the termination of the war on such terms would be a sacrifice of the national honor."

This complaint found a ready echo, and from every corner of the Territory and in the border states the familiar cry for the return of the slaves was raised. Searching parties streamed into the peninsula and hunted down the Negroes, taking them by force and the threat of arms from the Seminole villages and encampments. An endless list of demands for the blacks mounted at General Jesup's headquarters and that harassed officer wrote Colonel Warner of the Florida Militia:

"There is no disposition on the part of the great body of Indians to renew hostilities. I am sure they will faithfully fulfill their engagements if the inhabitants of Florida be prudent; but any attempt to seize their Negroes or other property will be followed by an instant resort to arms."

General Thomas Jesup was an intelligent and capable soldier, but his knowledge of military strategy could not cope with civilian avarice. He retreated slowly from an untenable position, but the withdrawal was unmistakable. First he modified a general order prohibiting the entry of "any white man, not in the service of the United States, into any part of the territory between the St. John's and the Gulf of Mexico, south of Fort Drane." On the first of May he instructed Brigadier General Armistead to "permit citizens to visit any posts on the St. John's, and to traverse or remain in any part of the country south of the Ouithlacoochee. There are large herds of cattle in that part of the country which, no doubt, belong to the citizens."

This sop of appeasement only sharpened the appetites of the whites. The Legislative Council of Florida formally declared the right of masters to regain possession of their slaves without regard to the federal government or its officers. General Jesup retreated yet another step. "I have some hopes," he wrote to Colonel Warner, "of inducing both the Indians and Indian Negroes to unite in bringing in the Negroes taken from the citizens during the war."

Within the Indian villages the uneasiness mounted and men talked long of what was happening. Micanopy called for a high council of the chiefs and listened silently as the young men, Asseola, Wildcat, and others, denounced a treaty that already crumbled in their hands. The betrayal was there for all to see.

General Jesup made a desperate attempt to inform the citizens of what was happening and to point the danger. He wrote to Governor Call:

"If the citizens of the territory be prudent, the war may be considered at an end; but any attempt to interfere with the Indian Negroes, or to arrest any of the chiefs or warriors as debtors or criminals, would cause an immediate resort to arms. Thirty or more Indian Negro men were at my camp on the Ouithlacoochee but the arrival of two or three citizens of Florida, said to be in search of Negroes, caused them to disperse and I doubt whether they will come in again; at all events, the emigration will be delayed in consequence of this alarm among the Negroes."

The winds of suspicion played among the still hot passions within the Territory and the embers glowed fitfully. The Indians clung to their settlements, leaving them rarely as every hand was turned to planting. In the silence of their huts the men waited and listened, growing restless and filled with an uneasiness they could not name.

Indifferent to, or unaware of, the gathering tension among the Seminoles, the government went ahead with its preparation for their evacuation. Transports were moving into the harbor at Tampa and the military laid out a section in the flats, ten miles distant from Fort Brooke, where the Indians would be quartered. Runners were sent into every camp and settlement. They carried with them the chiefs' authority and the word was passed from mouth to mouth. They came without spirit, these people, only half understanding what was expected of them. The years of trouble, though, had

368

taught them obedience. If it was said they were to leave their land and the chiefs agreed, then they must go. The ragged trickles of men, women, and children from the swamps and thickets flowed together on the trail from Fort King to Fort Brooke. At nights their small fires winked and fluttered in the darkness. Surrounded by familiar sounds, beneath a gentle sky, they could imagine they were still free. It was only during the hours of day when the slow movement of many feet made a heavy whisper that they felt captive. The more cheerful tried to make a game of the trek. This was the great walk of a nation. As their forefathers had come into this country with Secoffee long ago, so they would seek a new land. The pretense was shallow and would not contain the truth.

In the camp arranged for them by the white men they were given a blanket apiece. A ration of tobacco was passed to the men. The Army had done its work well. Tents stretched in orderly rows, field kitchens were set up, latrines were dug, and a routine was established. Funneled into the main trail more than seven hundred Indians, their Negro slaves and allies, came to place themselves in the hands of the white soldiers. Within the distant harbor the transports rocked upon the tide. All was in readiness for the evacuation.

They adapted themselves to the ways of the whites. Seminole women sat before the unfamiliar tents, waiting with age-old patience. Here there was no work for them and time passed slowly. They whispered and sometimes giggled at the spectacle of men cooking and doing a woman's chores. At mealtime they skeptically tasted the food prepared by the Army cooks and wrinkled their noses in tolerant amusement at the results. The men sat apart, stuffing their pipes and fingering the issue blankets. They spoke to each other rarely, and in every mind there were the same questions. At what distance was this land of Ar-kan-sas to which they were bound? How would they find things there? They dug their fingers into the earth and allowed it to sift between their fingers, thoughtfully testing the grains. This was the mystery and wonder of all life; this soil that had fed them and their people. Would they find its like again, or was this Ar-kan-sas, as some had said, a place of barren earth, cold and frightening? Their eyes lifted and roamed among the pines, dropping to the reassuring scrub and its dusty haze. The land they had always known seemed wide enough for all. Why must they go? Were the old ways to be put aside forever?

Before a tent that he occupied alone, as befitted his rank, the fat and slothful Micanopy sat and counted his wealth. It was true, he sighed, his cattle had been scattered and roamed uncounted. His ponies were gone, the crops on his many acres destroyed. The white soldiers had promised payment for his losses and this was good. Around him his many slaves were gathered in silent groups. He was still the Pond Governor, but the young and warlike men of his people had made the title a mockery. He wondered if his prestige could endure the long journey to Ar-kan-sas. His blacks were frightened and uneasy, and even though the white soldiers did not come among them, they were worried. Three had already vanished into the woods and Micanopy had been forced to keep the others fettered at night. Over and over the words of Asseola returned to vex him. "They will not permit you to leave with a single black man." Too many times in the past had this violent warrior foretold things correctly. Micanopy bowed his head. If it came about that Asseola had again spoken the truth, then disaster would have overtaken him, for a man without cattle and slaves in a new country would be nothing.

At Fort Brooke Colonel Pearson could not shade his anxiety over the responsibility thrust upon him. The Indians were coming in as they had promised, but the men he wanted to see aboard the transports had not appeared. This Osceola, Wildcat, the flints and steel of the Seminoles, had not reported. Other important leaders were missing also. He could not help wondering whether the delay was contrived in an effort to halt the emigration. Also, he was daily harassed by the claims of slaveowners who sought permission to inspect the encampment. Only this morning he had received orders to segregate seventy-five of the Indians' Negroes and turn them over to a Lieutenant Travett who was to take them to New Orleans. The War Department seemed intent upon defeating itself. As he drew up an order for the selection of the blacks within the encampment he wondered if it wouldn't be cheaper in the end for the government to pay the whites for the allegedly stolen slaves and have done with the dirty business forever.

On the Colonel's desk there was a recent communication from General Jesup, who had written:

"If you see Powell (Osceola) again I wish you to tell him that I intend to send exploring and surveying parties into every part of the country during the summer, and that I shall send out and take all the Negroes who belong to the white people, and he must not allow the Indians or Indian Negroes to mix with them. Tell him I am sending to Cuba for bloodhounds to trail them, and I intend to hang every one of them who does not come in."

Colonel Pearson placed his signature on the order and called for his orderly. Wisely or not, he had posted no guard at the Seminole encampment. The only whites the Indians saw were the cooks detailed for the job and these had made a camp of their own outside the evacuation site. The presence of troops, he felt, would only increase the suspicions of the Seminoles and aggravate their nervousness. He felt as though he held a skittish team by a ribbon. Well, he thought, Lieutenant Travett could take his Marines and go in for the Negroes and then they'd see what happened.

32

AGAINST the morning's half-light, the rows of tents sagged limply and a damp wind sifted through the powdered ashes of dead fires, prowling around the empty shelters and bellying out slack canvas walls. A fog curled over the ground, twisting into thin spirals and whirling away to lose itself in the palmettos.

At the far edge of the encampment the Army cook roused himself and sat on the rumpled edge of a cot, scratching indifferently at his chest through the thick undershirt. It was bad enough to get three meals a day for troops who always had a gripe about the food. Cooking for a pack of dirty Indians was an indignity he found hard to endure. Rising, he tossed back the wet flaps and stood gazing morosely at the encampment. Even at this distance, he imagined he could smell the Indian stink. He surveyed the barren scene and spat contemptuously. Look at that. The lazy bastards wouldn't even get up in the morning any more. Probably waiting to be called. He turned and shouted over his shoulder to the other members of the detail.

"Roll out," he yelled, "an' get the fires started. Madam Laughing Eyes in a Pool of Water will want her breakfast." His voice rose in a falsetto of derision. "An' be sure the toast is hot an' the bacon done just right."

One by one, the other men of the squad unwound themselves from their blankets and stamped woodenly out of the tent's darkness. Mosquitoes whined about their heads, attacking bare arms and legs with singing gluttony. Even at this hour the air was thick and hot, the sticky dampness soggy enough to taste. By noontime the flats would be almost unbearable. This was a hell of a detail all right. First the Army had to fight the Seminoles an' then turn around an' feed 'em like they was guests at a hotel.

Before a low bench the men splashed their faces at wooden buckets, cursing the Army with a flat and weary lack of emphasis.

"How the hell much longer we got to stay out here, Sarge?"

The sergeant-cook rubbed at his grizzled cheeks and considered himself shaved. "The Lieutenant said they'd begin loadin' the bastards into the ships today."

"Well, the next time you're lookin' to make up a detail like this one, forget you knew my name." The soldier emptied the soapy water to the ground. "I figured we'd at least get us a piece of Indian squaw out here, but they squeal like scared rabbits when you go to grab 'em."

"You're lucky you didn't get nothin' but a yell from 'em. I've knowed it to drop right off from touchin' an Indian girl."

The sergeant stood with his legs wide apart, staring thoughtfully at the silent rows of tents. There was something queer about the morning. It was quiet and gave him the feeling of waiting in a graveyard. Finally he shook his head and started to turn away.

"I been thinkin' the same thing, Sarge." The private jerked a thumb in the direction of the Indian encampment. "Everything is so still; not even a bare-assed kid tumblin' around in the dirt. You'd figure someone ought to be up by this time. Usually they're in a line with their hands out."

The sergeant swung about for a second look at the camp, a quarter of a mile or so distant. It was funny, he decided. Usually one or two of the old men would be out, sitting cross-legged on the ground, smoking and bobbing their heads, waiting for mess call. The kids were always around, hungry and with their big eyes following the movements of the soldiers. He studied the camp for small details. The little fires before the tents weren't even smoldering. That wasn't right. The Seminoles wouldn't take fire from a white man. When they were allowed to die, the women had to strike up new ones. Mostly they were too damn lazy for that and banked them well for the night. Now the cold heaps were gray-black and without life.

"Let's go take a look," the sergeant said abruptly. "Somethin' funny's goin' on here. I don't like the feel of it."

Halfway through the camp there was no longer any doubt as to what had happened. Sometime during the night the Indians had moved out. The vacant tents gaped with the oppressive silence of open graves. The Seminoles and the Negroes had returned to the scrub, merging with the darkness, gliding on noiseless feet, shadows within the shadows until the woods claimed them. Followed by the men, who inched up to peek over his shoulder, the sergeant went from tent to tent, and his uneasy astonishment gathered. He whistled a long-drawn-out note of surprise. Seven hundred

Indians, maybe a few more. Every damn one of them gone and leaving nothing but the hush of death behind.

"It gives you kind of a scary feelin', doesn't it?" The soldier laughed nervously.

The sergeant made no reply. How the hell could that many Indians slip away without making a sound? What made them go in the night so mysteriously, vanishing like a smoke puff? The detail now moved slowly, the men edging closer to each other with unspoken apprehension as though they might be walking into an ambush. In one of the tents they came upon the stiff body of a small dog. The mangy skin was drawn tightly over thin, arching ribs and the head lay at an unnatural angle. It was pathetic in death. The sergeant stooped and examined the animal.

"Neck's broken. Somebody twisted it. What the hell do you know about that? It's wrung like a chicken." He rose, wiping his hands. Unconsciously he had lowered his voice.

Inside other tents they found more dead mongrels. This was part of the explanation. The Indians had deliberately cracked the necks of the stray dogs that had attached themselves to the camp so there would be no excited barks and yelps to betray their movements. There was something frightening in the spectacle of the thin carcasses and the knowledge that the animals had come wriggling and crawling to sudden death from once friendly hands.

"Jesus." One of the men breathed the word. He had looked upon many dead men, yet these broken dogs made his flesh creep. It was hard to say why, but he knew he was scared.

"Parker," the sergeant said to one of the detail, "you an' Harley light out for the fort an' let the Captain know what's happened. Tell him every damn Indian has gone." He walked away. "Let's get the hell out of here. It gives me the creeps."

In Tampa Bay the thirty-five transports felt the surge of the morning's tide and swung at their anchors. The early sun caught at their masts and drew long shadows across the slick decks. They could scatter now, returning empty to Mobile and New Orleans.

Two days ago the Seminoles had watched unbelievingly as the soldiers had come among them. With their rifles they had poked aside tent flaps, calling names from lists. When they received no reply they became impatient, indiscriminately hauling out a cowering Negro here and there, marching them past silent groups of Seminoles. The soft wail of terror rose as a sob from the black men and their frightened eyes rolled in appealing panic. They understood that this was a return to slavery under white masters

374

and their lament gathered volume in a threnody of anguish. The Indians spoke no word, made no protest, but the hatred and knowledge of betrayal was on their faces. Only Micanopy cried aloud as five of his huddled slaves were kicked out and forced into the group. He trembled with frustration and anger, appealing to the indifferent officer. By the treaty, he exclaimed shakingly, the Negroes were to accompany the Indians to Ar-kan-sas. It was so written and signed by the white chief. Who had set aside the agreement? On whose lips did the lie rest? To fulfill their obligation and make honorable their word the Indians had come to this place in peace to take passage on the ships. Now the treaty was being violated. He screamed his futile rage. It was as the warrior Asseola had foretold. There was no truth in the tongue of the white men.

The detail of soldiers rounded up seventy-five Negroes and marched them away. The Seminoles gazed after the straggling column. Here was the lie. What could they believe of the men who came to them with promises they did not keep? Throughout the day and long afternoon they had sat before their small fires and talked. In many little cleared patches the crops they had planted and left behind were ripened and ready to be gathered. There would be food for the coming months, and the leaders, the young and vigorous warriors, would find powder and bullet metals for their guns. No longer would they listen to words of a treaty. The women moaned softly over what they knew must come.

Later, at his headquarters, General Thomas Jesup would write to General Gadsden in South Carolina: "All is lost, and principally, I fear, by the influence of the Negroes."

At Fort Brooke, Colonel Pearson and his staff received the news of the Indians' withdrawal during the night with astonishment. Such a thing was preposterous. Hadn't they been well fed and cared for? Hadn't their chief signed a treaty binding the nation to emigrate? This was what happened when a white man was fool enough to trust an Indian. Now, by God, there'd be the filthy business of whipping them into submission and dragging them out, family by family, from the swamps. Colonel Pearson wondered if he should try to beat the scrub now for the runaways, but he gave up the idea. The troops, he thought bitterly, would only get lost, and certainly some would be killed. He had a lot of green replacements. It was a hell of a situation all right. Troops would have to be called, volunteer regiments raised. Congress and the newspapers would be asking difficult questions. Well, he sighed, he'd have to do what he could. Fort Drane, Fort Dade, and Fort King would have to be alerted. He called for information on the scouts and dispatch riders available. Damn the Indians, anyhow, for a pack of lying savages.

Clay was at Fort King when word of the Indian revolt against their removal was brought in. For six weeks he had sweated and shivered in a bed at the post's infirmary while the fever tore at his insides and sapped his strength. The surgeon pursed his lips and prescribed the usual medicines and wondered what the hell he was going to do about a malady that raged through the garrison and would not be checked. Many men died, and the fort's strength, with the release of the volunteers, was dangerously below the safety mark. Other men recovered mysteriously, although the treatment was the same in all cases. The summer months drew heavily upon the men and, the overworked medic thought, there was no way of telling what might have happened if the war had extended through the sickly season. The Seminoles seemed indifferent to the heat, bad water, and insects. The Army, he suspected, might have taken a hell of a licking this summer. The treaty had averted the test. Now, it seemed, the agreement was a worthless piece of paper, of interest only to future historians.

When his fever subsided Clay was moved from the infirmary. In temporary command at Fort King was Captain Tracey Miller, and the officer insisted the convalescent occupy part of his quarters. Miller had served with General Clinch when Clay was attached to that command and they were old friends and congenial companions.

Miller grinned down at Clay in the bed. "You're getting a lot of free treatment from the Army."

Clay was in no humor to appreciate the joke. "The Army got a lot of work out of me."

"Well," Miller offered, "you stay with me until you feel strong enough to travel. We'll have a wagon train going north one of these days. If not, you can travel with company to St. Augustine and get a stage from there. Anyhow, make yourself comfortable."

Clay grunted. "I'm beginning to think the only way I'll get home is in a box."

He was sprawled on a bench outside Miller's cabin when the rider came in. He was a lanky, sun-parched woodsman by the name of Joe Caffery, and he was on a volunteer status. His and Clay's paths had crossed many times.

"Boy," he gazed at Clay, "you better get your tail off that bench. All hell is goin' to break loose in the Territory. Them Indians cleared out at Fort Brooke an' they're makin' big medicine somewhere."

"I'm retired," Clay said. "Go tell your troubles to the Captain."

The dispatches from Fort Brooke threw the little settlement around Fort King into a panic. The garrison was isolated and unprepared to defend itself. The Indians were loose again and the more timid among the civilians made hasty preparations to leave the Territory once more. As the news spread the fear rode with it.

Later that evening Captain Miller leaned back in his chair, feet stretched on a table. He glanced across the room to where Clay lay on a bunk in the shadows.

"What do you make of it?" he asked.

"The same thing you do. The Army will have to dig them out again, if it can. There probably won't be any trouble until we start it. The Seminoles will play dead, but the minute you try to bring them in, the shooting will start. I'm damned sure I'm going home now."

"I could use you." Tracey Miller squinted at the candlelight. "I haven't a dispatch rider I can count on if something happens. Caffery left for Fort Drane. The rest of the men lose their way going to the latrine."

"Don't look at me," Clay warned. "I'm nothing but a broken-down old crock. The Army's had its last errand out of me." He felt the dry, tight skin of his cheeks. "It's sure a pretty thing I'm taking back to Sue Rogers."

"You can go by way of St. Augustine and do a job at the same time," Miller suggested.

"To hell with you and your jobs. There's a man there who's looking to kill me," he said weakly, "but it was a long time ago and I suppose he's forgotten what he was mad at by now. I just want to look at Sue an' know I'm home."

Miller smiled. "How is that girl of yours?"

Clay's short laugh was worried. "Mad as all hell, probably. Maybe she won't even speak to me when I see her. Maybe she's even gone off and married someone else. I sure couldn't blame her. I don't figure to show much profit for my time with the Army."

"It's strictly a nonprofit organization," the officer mused.

"And pretty stupid, too. You know," Clay propped himself on one elbow, "sometimes I think that if I had it to do all over again I'd fight with the Indians. I don't take a lot of satisfaction in being white right now." He dropped back against the pillow. "I don't suppose I really mean that," he continued, "but some things are mighty hard to understand. Those poor bastards want so little!"

Captain Miller pressed a thumb against the ash of his pipe. "What'll you do when you get home?"

Clay locked arms beneath his head and stared at the ceiling. He had asked himself the same question many times. It was always difficult to remember he had no home. Nothing remained but the miles of uncultivated acres, overgrown now and unproductive. He would have to start at the beginning, purchasing new slaves and stock, finding competent whites to oversee the monumental task of rebuilding from the encroaching wilderness. The plantation was in little better condition than when Old Clay staked it out many years ago. Everything he had ever associated with the place had been swept away. Gone, also, he thought a little sadly, was his youth. If Sue didn't want him he'd end up the way Old Clay had, mean, hating himself and the world. He experienced a cold fright at the idea. He was a stranger returning to a strange land.

"You asleep?" Captain Miller asked softly.

"No," Clay turned on his side, "just lying here and thinking. You asked me what I was going to do when I got home. I'm damned if I really know. Maybe Sue and I will build a big house with a wide porch where I can sit and drink mint juleps all day and watch the kids tumbling around the yard. You can come and see me if the Seminoles don't get you first."

"I might take you up on that," Miller said. "I've always hankered for the life of a plantation baron."

"It used to be all right," Clay mumbled drowsily, "before the Army came in and started this hell-raising. We all got along fine, Indians, whites, and Negrahs. I think I'll go to sleep and dream about it."

Miller rose and knocked out his pipe. "If you think of anything good," he suggested, "like sixteen naked girls in a feather bed, wake me up and tell me about it. The only thing I dream about lately is an Indian crawling through my window. That's a mighty unsatisfactory way to pass the night."

The Territory sweated beneath the strain of an uneasy and undeclared truce and the government sought to put its ponderous machinery to work again. Civilian indignation rose to a hysterical pitch. This time there would be no easy and generous treaty. The Indians would surrender or die. In the border states a call for volunteers was made, and as the unhealthy season waned fresh troops began moving into the peninsula. The Seminoles were ominously quiet. Scouting patrols reported their movements to the south and east, but there was little violence.

In a message to the troops General Jesup wrote:

Soldiers! Much as you have performed, more remains to be done; the enemy awaits you in fastnesses more difficult than any you have yet penetrated. The government has adopted the only policy that can preserve the Indians as a distinct and independent people. That policy must be accomplished and the Seminoles removed. The same energy, courage, and patriotism that distinguished you in the past campaign are confidently relied upon by your country and your commander, to accomplish in the next the object so desirable to all—the emigration of the Indians and the termination of the war. You have been exposed to the drenching rains, the noxious vapors, and the scorching sun of an almost torrid climate; you have waded rivers, made long marches over burning sands, traversed almost impassable swamps, and sought the enemy in fastnesses such as American soldiers had seldom penetrated before, and with a perseverance and energy and a courage worthy of the best era of the republic.

Along the lower St. John's River, deep within the lake country from which the waterway draws its strength, the Seminoles raised new towns and husbanded their strength. The authority had passed from old and faltering hands. Micanopy was discredited. Now the fighting men of the tribe placed their faith and future in Asseola, Alligator, Wildcat, and Sam Jones. As always, there were men of little faith and courage. Among them was a minor chief, Co-Hadjo, who went timidly to Fort King and sought a talk with Captain Miller.

Fearfully Co-Hadjo protested his good will. He spoke haltingly, and Clay, beside Miller, translated as he talked. The Seminoles, Co-Hadjo declared, would have peace, but would not accept it at the price of emigration. He, Co-Hadjo, was weary of bloodshed and would attempt a meeting between the white officers and the Seminole leaders if the council would be arranged and carried out in good faith.

After Co-Hadjo had departed Captain Miller swung back in his chair and stared thoughtfully out of the window. Finally he turned to Clay.

"What do you think?" he asked.

Clay shook his head. "You're back where you started. The In-

379

dians will stop fighting but they won't leave the Territory. That isn't going to satisfy the government or the whites, either. If it was that easy, then what the hell has all this fighting been for?"

"Well," Captain Miller stood up, "the best I can do is send a transcript of the talk to General Jesup. I wish," his smile was troubled, "he'd reciprocate and send me some men. Thanks for the interpretation."

Clay nodded. He was feeling better, with new strength flowing through him. The fever had run its course through the garrison. "That was my last unofficial or official service for the Army, Tracey. There's a quartermaster's train leaving Monday for St. Augustine and I'm going to be up ahead, pulling on the bridle of the first horse."

Miller extended his hand and there was honest warmth in the clasp. "I'll miss you, Clay. This isn't good-by. You'll stay with me until Monday, of course. I just wanted to say I'm sorry to see you go. I have a feeling this war is only beginning."

"Probably, unless you can push the Seminoles off the tip of Key West. Don't forget; any time you feel like deserting come up to the Apalachicola. I'll hide you out until it's over. Anyhow, I'll keep a chair on the porch next to mine and a bottle of whisky waiting."

33

THE pipe, intricately carved and beaded, lay on a table in the head-quarters of Brigadier General Joseph Hernandez at St. Augustine. From its long stem an elaborately decorated fringe rippled in vivid colors over the stained wood. Many times this morning the General had gazed at the pipe, and the empty bowl seemed an eyeless but accusing socket from which he turned uneasily.

He stood, hands clasped behind his back, staring out through a window at the pale daylight. Finally he sighed and swung about, looking again at the pipe with an expression of troubled irritation. He was, he thought, an honorable man and a good soldier, and the thing he was about to do caused him to cringe inwardly. He could make no easy explanation to his conscience.

Events, springing from a minor incident, had moved swiftly here, and he was unwittingly forced into a galling position from which there was no retreat. As he prowled restlessly about the room, his fingers trailing across the table, he wondered unhappily what those who would write of this war would have to say of him. At best he would appear in a dubious and unpleasant light. As the hours collected and the time remaining grew shorter he was concerned, not so much for his place in history, as to the effect his actions would have on the country and the conflict itself. Here was the bald and unpleasant betrayal of a word given.

Two weeks ago he had led an assault on a concentration of Seminoles several miles to the southwest of St. Augustine. As engagements went, the action hadn't amounted to much; a few wounded and a half dozen Indian dead. His troops, though, had taken prisoners, and among the eleven captured was the aging chief King Phillip. In confinement, certain he was to die, the feeble old man had begged to be allowed to see his son, Wildcat. One of the Indian prisoners was permitted to leave, carrying a message from the old chief. Three days later Phillip's son, Wildcat, had strode boldly to the fort. Without the supervision of soldiers he talked long and earnestly with his father. Then, leaving King Phillip, the young warrior requested an interview with the General.

As he recalled the meeting now, General Hernandez smiled to himself. The youthful chief had not come into his presence as an enemy. In his erect and easy bearing there was the jaunty self-confidence of one sportsman to another. His manner suggested that they were both participants in a deadly but exciting game and, in this moment of time out, there should be no ill feeling. Watching his gesticulations and listening to his speech, General Hernandez had found it difficult to believe this was the wild and reckless chief who had struck terror into the hearts of white settlers and soldiers alike. Wildcat laughed frequently as he spoke through an interpreter. There was a vital spark in his eyes as his thoughts played leapfrog with the words. He talked without hesitation and with unmistakable pride. As the interview drew to a close General Hernandez discovered, to his surprise, that he had been enjoying the oral exchange.

From a pouch Wildcat produced the gift pipe and a shining white egret plume. They were, he explained, presents from his brother Asseola, who would talk with the white chief. The offerings were indications of respect for a valiant and honorable foe. They signified that Asseola would come in peace and with an open heart to sit in council with the white chief. Out of the talk, to be held in good will, the letting of much blood might be spared. Many Seminoles, Wildcat admitted readily, were tired of the war. Sickened though they were of the unequal struggle, and seeing ahead only terror, they still had no words of surrender. They had fought and would continue to fight as Asseola and their leaders directed. This was as it should be. With the hope that the war might be settled with honor for all, Asseola would talk with the General if such a meeting could be arranged.

As the interpreter unraveled the message General Hernandez had listened intently. It was, he thought, a strange proposal, and in it he could find no suggestion of capitulation. For several minutes he turned the invitation over in his mind. Certainly nothing could be lost by such a talk. Much might be gained. Finally he agreed. He would, he said, meet Asseola at a place on Pellicier Creek, a few miles south of St. Augustine, on the twenty-second day of this month, which was October. Wildcat departed to carry the General's word to Asseola.

General Hernandez now paced the room with a measured tread. He was retracing steps taken many times during the past hours and understood that they did not lead to an escape from an intolerable situation. In his mind there was no doubt as to the circumstances under which he was to meet with this Powell or Osceola. He had given his word, or it had most certainly been implied, that Osceola should come in peace for the council and depart freely at its conclusion. This he knew to be so. That which had occurred this morning, however, radically altered his plans. As a soldier he was powerless to shift the swiftly running current of events. Although he could not bring himself to utter the word of treachery, the sound was there to haunt him. From Fort Peyton a dispatch rider had brought him two messages from General Jesup in reply to the one he had sent, advising his superior of the meeting. The first communication, and he thought it impossible he could ever forget the words, read:

General:
    Let the chiefs and the warriors know that we have been deceived by them long enough, and that we do not intend to be deceived again. Order the whole party directly into town. You have force enough to compel obedience and they must move instantly.
    I have information of a recent murder by the Indians. They must be disarmed.
    They can talk in town and send any messages out if they please.

Thos. S. Jesup
Major General Commanding

General Hernandez halted in his stride, staring at the pipe on the table as though it had suddenly spoken. Twist the sentences as he would, they could mean only one thing. It was Jesup's intention to violate a truce deliberately.

"Order the whole party into town." He repeated the command aloud and snorted. You didn't order a party who came to you under a white flag for council. You damn well took them prisoners and marched them to a dungeon in town. It was, he mused, an exceedingly slender thread of logic that could weave a reported killing by an unnamed Indian into an excuse for arresting and disarming a group of Seminoles who came to your camp, in an openly avowed truce, to discuss the termination of a war.

Well, he thought, there it was. He was a soldier and his orders were explicit. Osceola and those with him would be seized. The arrangements had been made, troops would surround the council and close in at his signal. With a sweep of his hand he knocked the peace pipe to the floor and bellowed impatiently for his orderly.

The second communication from General Jesup played upon an all too familiar theme. It carried instructions for the interrogation of Osceola as though the Seminole were a prisoner and not a voluntary participant at a council.

Ascertain [General Jesup commanded] the objects of the Indians in coming in at this time. Also, their expectations. Are they prepared to deliver up the Negroes taken from the citizens at once? Why have they not surrendered them already, as promised by Co-Hadjo at Fort King? Have the chiefs of the nation held a council in relation to the subjects of the talk at Fort King? What chiefs attended that council, and what was their determination? Have the chiefs sent a messenger with the decisions of the council? Have the principal chiefs, Micanopy, Jumper, Little Cloud, and Alligator, sent a message, and if so, what is their message? Why have not these chiefs come in themselves?

General Hernandez drew on his gauntlets. Always the same refrain. The war was being fought for the sake of Negro slaves. Courage in the field, the resettlement of the Seminole nation, the welfare of the Territory and the country had become secondary. When would the Seminoles return the blacks? Men, he thought wearily, had died for a better cause than this.

His staff, mounted, awaited him outside. He nodded briefly and took their salutes almost absently, swinging up into the saddle.

"Gentlemen," he said, and touched a spur to the horse.

The cavalcade moved out briskly. At the meeting place near Fort Peyton it would be joined by members of General Jesup's staff. General Hernandez fixed his eyes on a distant point, staring straight ahead as he rode. He, as much as any man in the Territory, had suffered from this war. His great sugar plantation, Malo Campo, had been raided, his fields burned, cattle destroyed. Had he desired, it would have been easy to find hatred and resentment in his heart for these Indians. He was a man of simple parentage. His family had come to this New World from the Mediterranean island of Minorca and prospered. Within him there flamed a good and honest pride that turned away from trickery and injustice. This thing that he was to do today was not good. He turned to the officer who rode at his side.

"The instructions have been carefully given, Captain?"

"Yes, General." Captain Fenton seemed grimly unhappy over the job at hand.

"Very well. Let there be as little confusion as possible. Perhaps," his shoulders drooped a trifle, "perhaps we may count on the element of surprise to spare us bloodshed."

384

At his superior's use of the word surprise Captain Fenton darted a quick glance his way but he could detect no hint of sarcasm.

"We will have the situation under control, General," he said.

From the narrow creek whose waters drained into the salt marsh the land sloped gently upward to a natural clearing, hedged by scrub and a fragrant growth of new pine. In full dress—epaulet and braid glinting warmly, leather and steel fired with a hard light—the staffs of General Jesup and General Hernandez waited.

The Seminoles came out of the woods and to the place of meeting with a solemn dignity. Asseola, Wildcat, Co-Hadjo, and Talmeco-Hadjo led the small procession and they walked with the bold step of men who went forth to challenge their destiny. As they closed the distance an involuntary murmur of surprise rose from the assembled staffs. The Seminoles came to the council in full ceremonials, from the high decorated turbans to the many scarves and ornaments of silver at their throats. Their buckskins glistened as the coats of newly born fawns and in the unhurried rhythm of their march there was a savage but compelling splendor. They came not as supplicants, but as warriors to a meeting with their peers.

When the Seminole delegation had drawn itself up before the officers, General Hernandez turned to his interpreter.

"Ask who among them is the man Powell," he directed.

"I am Asseola." The statement came firmly. "We will speak in your tongue."

General Hernandez' glance traveled slowly over the Indian before him. This, he thought, is the Seminole who has welded a nation until it questions the authority and power of the United States. He smiled to himself. That was something of an understatement. There were, he knew, formalities and courtesies to be exchanged at such a moment, but he could not bring himself to utter them. What must be done would not be cloaked in hypocrisy on his part. From his glove he drew the list of questions prepared and forwarded to him by General Jesup. Without preamble he read them aloud.

"Are you prepared to deliver up the Negroes taken from the citizens at once?"

Asseola's head stiffened. He stared at the white officer as though he had not heard aright. This, then, was no council to discuss the termination of a war. All the white men were interested in was the return of their slaves.

"Why," General Hernandez' voice sharpened, "have you not

surrendered them already as promised by Co-Hadjo at Fort King?"

Asseola made no attempt to conceal his contempt. It sprang to his lips and remained curled there for all to see. While the future of his people was at stake the whites could only mouth childish words, whimpering for their black men. Before him stood the representatives of a nation. They had met here, the Seminoles and the whites, to talk of peace and an end to bloodshed. The questions the officer now asked were in the tone of one who addresses an inferior.

General Hernandez lifted his head only long enough to catch the full impact of the Indian's scorn. "What is the purpose of your coming here at this time?"

Asseola turned to look at the Seminoles behind him; then his eyes shifted and traveled carefully over the stiff ranks of the white officers. He would not nourish this deliberate insult with a reply. He turned to Co-Hadjo and Wildcat.

"You must answer," he said simply. "I am choked and cannot."

Although he did not understand the dialect, General Hernandez could not mistake the tone. He would carry this ridiculous mummery no further or continue the farce of a council.

"Very well, Captain Fenton," he said crisply, "carry out your orders." He turned his back on the Indians and walked away.

The troops moved quickly into the clearing, bayonets glistening, rifles at ready. In rapid order they encircled the Seminole group.

Wildcat shouted his rage at the betrayal, and for a moment the Indians seemed to crouch, looking wildly about for an avenue of escape from the menacing ring. Asseola did not move. The rifle he had borne since a youth lay easily across his arm. He would not even glance at the corporal who took it from him, nor did he appear to hear the confused shouts of protest as the others of the Seminole delegation were roughly disarmed. The officers, watching him as the principal figure in the drama, were stirred and made uneasy by the controlled fury they looked upon. Cries of betrayal, accusations, and charges of trickery they would have understood. They felt no elation over what had happened. The dirty business of war had been additionally fouled. In the eyes of the Indian they could read the scorn he felt, and they turned almost hastily and attempted a casual exchange of small talk as though they chatted idly between the acts of a play.

The guard wasted no time over formalities. The prisoners were boxed within a hollow square, flanked by additional troops, and the column swung out of the clearing. The waiting officers felt better as the detachment wound down the slope and out of sight.

In his saddle General Hernandez watched as the rear files disappeared and then turned to his aide with a gesture of resignation.

"I fear we have added five years to the war," he said unhappily.

"Yes, sir." The officer shifted. It was an awkward moment.

"It is a black and unpleasant day." General Hernandez smiled a little sadly as he saw his aide glance quickly and unconsciously at the cloudless sky. "I wasn't thinking of the weather, Captain Fenton," he said.

34

THE word raced through St. Augustine's narrow streets and spread to the little settlements outside the city. To those who heard and repeated the news it seemed as though the government, with one miraculous and decisive stroke, had beheaded the Indian monster of terror. Surely, it was said, this war must end quickly now.

Throughout the afternoon and early evening groups of citizens gathered on doorsteps, at street corners, in taverns, and along the river front. Twopenny handbills were hastily struck in the print shop and people snatched at them eagerly to read the news and repeat the dramatic details. The author had whipped his imagination and the capture of Osceola and Wildcat emerged in the smudged print as a magnificent feat of arms. Those who read were given what purported to be an eyewitness account of a fierce and sanguinary battle on the shores of Pellicier Creek. There, the reporter declared, the brave troops had flung themselves repeatedly against hordes of screaming savages. Outnumbered, all but overwhelmed by the cunning and ruthless Seminoles, the soldiers had stood firm. Undaunted, and with their faith serene, they had maintained the unequal struggle until Virtue, clad simply in the uniform of a private, emerged triumphant. Stripped of their weapons and barbaric trappings, craven in defeat, the terrible Osceola and Wildcat, murderers of women and children, had been taken prisoners while the Indians retreated in disorder and panic.

As the sun hung upon the topmost branches of the high pines to the west, sputtering torches appeared to lead boisterous impromptu parades. Belligerent oratory welled from the congested parade grounds before Government House. Strangers embraced each other indiscriminately and carriages jounced and rollicked along King Street. In the taverns and pothouses men struggled for the privilege of buying drinks for all. The days of terror and uncertainty were at an end. Who could doubt that the wearying conflict must be closed now that the legendary Osceola, the renegade murderer sometimes called Powell, was safely behind prison bars?

In noisy groups the citizens moved toward the high walls of Fort Marion. On a ridge spiked with the twisted and stunted cedars they stood gazing across the moat and drawbridge as though their eyes could pierce the thick coquina blocks and see within the dungeon where the Indians cowered. Rumors sprang from the dust of shuffling feet. The Seminoles were to be hung publicly. They were to be shot and then hurled from the parapet into the river. At noon they were to be paraded through the town so all might see their disgrace; later they would be burned. President Van Buren himself would come to Florida to witness the execution. As they fed upon these morsels of gossip the people grew strong and confident once more. Many began to wonder if some profit might not be turned from this sudden shift of events. Surely the Indians must be fleeing southward, leaving behind valuable stores. More important, there would be lost and abandoned niggers, wandering helplessly as their Seminole masters scattered to safety. Smart men with dogs and guns might capture slaves with little risk. Furtively organized parties moved away from the celebration and plunged into the woods, intent upon the hunt, for the opportunity would not come again.

Dusk crept upon the river and enveloped the town. Cheerful and reassuring lights wavered behind curtained windows, and below the fort there rose the sound of carnival. The crowd on the knoll dissolved and straggled away to join the merrymaking. Within the deep square of the fort's courtyard the sentry's boots echoed on the stone flagging, and as he passed a cell near the southwest corner the man's head shifted with unmilitary curiosity to peer at the three who were locked there.

Clay entered the city shortly after nine o'clock. He had dropped from the seat of the lead wagon as the train halted at Fort Peyton, refusing an invitation to spend the night. Not until he was in the town did he hear the news or understand the reason for the noise and dancing torches.

He stooped, picked a crumpled sheet from the littered road, and read it, standing in the lighted doorway of a chemist's shop. The editor's final inspiration had been a woodcut of an Indian that surmounted the text. The features were expressionless, the cut indifferently made, but the printer blithely labeled it "Osceola." Clay chuckled. You're getting uglier by the minute, child, he thought. Where the street approached the river the crowd was densely packed. Strangers, men and women, caught at his sleeve to shout the news. Flasks and canteens were thrust into his hand. Girls, laughing with shrill excitement, linked their arms with his, danced a few steps, and then swung away to fasten upon other unattached males. As he shouldered his way through the good-natured throng Clay thought that the entire town would be drunk by midnight. Forcing his way out of the mob, he ducked down an alley and emerged on the riverbank. Here the street noise was a distant babble. He stood listening to the wash of the tide against the stones and the muted roll of the ocean. Turning his head slightly he could see the sharp outlines of the fort. He stared thoughtfully at the angles and rounded watchtowers and then smiled. Whatever Asseola's humiliation at being taken prisoner might be at the moment, he was safe. They might keep him in prison, and probably would, but when the war was over he would be released. It was a damn sight better than being in the open where some fuzz-cheeked soldier could blow his guts out. He wondered about the account he had read. It didn't seem probable that such a battle as described could have been fought. He would certainly have heard about it during the few minutes he lingered at Fort Peyton. It didn't make much difference, but he didn't believe that putting Asseola in jail would end the war. There were too many tough Indians loose, and after what had happened at Fort Brooke they'd be hard to catch again.

He dug the stock of his rifle into the sandy earth and rested his weight on it. He was tired but filled with a sense of peace. The years had brought him around in a great circle. Here, such a long time ago, he had stood with Santee and heard the sea for the first time. In this town he had looked upon the beauty of Claire Lechane and known the unforgettable warmth of a man's friendship. Many times he had wondered how he would feel when he should walk the streets of this town again. Looking upon the familiar scene, he discovered, to his surprise, that memory had no unpleasant bite, there were no ghosts to haunt his dreams. Lord, he thought, the things he had done and seen, and how the years had sped! Up there, in that fort, an Indian, a man not so long ago a boy, was locked in a cell and a town rejoiced. This, somehow, seemed strangest of all. How is a child marked for greatness? Why wasn't the sign there for all to see? Soon, in every town and city in the country, the news of Asseola's capture would be public, and people, hearing the name, would shudder comfortably. Who could convince them that this monster of their imagination had been a solemn-faced, wide-eyed youngster who had played, laughed, cried, and slept as others? That he had loved and been loved, ex-

390

periencing the same indecisive torments of youth as white boys; that he had found moments of great beauty in simple things—the bright curving of a wing, the hush at sunset, the joy of a new dawn. Could it be believed that he had experienced the same exquisite torture for the love of a maid, that his belly had been empty, his body weary, his mind confused at times? Clay did not think so, but he knew that under other circumstances this same Indian would have lived and grown old in obscurity; a simple man who would not have wandered far from the town of his people on the Apalachicola, his name unknown outside the limits of Clayport.

Clay raised the gun. In the morning he'd see if a pass could be arranged to visit the fort. The chances were that the Army wouldn't be too harsh now that its prizes were safely locked within a cell. He turned away from the river and realized he had no place to spend the night. Unconsciously he had been rejecting Slater's Tavern. Understanding this, he grinned self-consciously. Was he afraid Jamie Beulow's spook would share his table and bed, or that John Spain would walk in upon him there? It would be a hell of a note, after all the shooting he had been through, to get into a gun fight with a man whose features he could barely remember.

He slung the rifle across his shoulders, grasping it by barrel and stock. A hundred yards away the lights of Slater's beckoned, and after a moment he strode across the road and along the well-worn path. It seemed fitting, somehow, that he should return. If he had come with the same wisdom years ago, much trouble and heartache might have been avoided. He glanced down at his dirty leggings and moccasins. One thing, he thought, I probably don't look or smell any better than I did. He paused only momentarily on the threshold and then put his hand to the heavy door.

It might have been yesterday that he had stood here. The same orderly atmosphere, the sanded floor and the old tables, some laid with white cloths for supper and others glistening damply from the sweeps of rags in the hands of attentive blacks. There were the familiar odors of ale, whisky, and rum, spicing the scent of roasting meats on spits within the fireplace. Those might be the same faces at the bar, Clay reflected, only, of course, this could not be so. Time had swept many away from their favorite corners. But, he half closed his eyes, it was not difficult to see them there. His eyes strayed to a forward table where Jamie Beulow found it convenient to sprawl with indolent and provocative grace. It was unoccupied, and for a moment he was tempted to sit there and see if his presence could summon back the departed years.

The landlord, in figure not unlike Slater, came deferentially forward and halted with a short bow of welcome.

"Good evening and welcome, sir." He waited expectantly, eying the rifle and the buckskins.

"Supper and lodgings," Clay said, his eyes wandering over the room. "I'll be here for two or three days."

"Our pleasure, sir."

"My name's Hammond," Clay said absently. "Once I spent a lot of time here. Where's Slater?"

"Dead, sir," the new proprietor replied with a hushed reverence as though the passing of Slater were still mourned. "I am Markham, sir. Barney Markham, at your service. Will you drink first?" Without seeming to direct his movements, he guided Clay to the bar and tapped the counter sharply with his knuckles to summon the attendant. "Your pleasure, Mr. Hammond," he suggested, "and permit me to welcome you back to Slater's. You see," he beamed, "I have not changed the name." He lowered his voice to a confidential whisper. "Because I am an outlander, from New York, I thought it best for custom not to make any changes. Anyhow," he breathed sadly, "no one would ever call the place anything but Slater's."

"Hot rum," Clay directed, and turned his back to the bar, resting comfortably against it as he surveyed the public room.

"Of course, sir," Markham was eagerly informative, "you must have heard the wonderful news."

"About Asseola?" Clay didn't glance down.

"A rare day, Mr. Hammond, with those scoundrelly redskins safely behind bars. Perhaps the Territory may find a new and welcome peace."

"Perhaps." Clay swung about and took the pewter mug as it was brought to him. He drank with satisfaction, mildly irritated that Markham didn't go on about his business and leave him alone. He just wanted to stand here, soaking up the warmth and old memories. There Jamie Beulow had sat on the night when he kicked the chair out from beneath him. "My first inclination is to kill you, sir." He could hear the words again if he listened intently. As he looked back it seemed queer that Jamie should have used them while neither could suspect he would be the first to die. Clay shrugged away the chill and took another long swallow.

"Have you a table preference, Mr. Hammond?" The landlord made it plain that his guest's pleasure came before all other considerations.

392

"Over in the corner, near the fire." Clay nodded toward the far end of the room.

"Immediately, sir." Reluctantly Markham started to move away.

"Oh, Markham." He summoned the landlord back. "Do you know anything about the stage schedule between here and Tallahassee or beyond, to Pensacola?"

"Once a week, sir." Markham seemed to be on the point of apologizing for the delay. "Six o'clock Monday morning—God, the Seminoles, and the condition of the driver permitting. I'll arrange for your ticket, sir, if you wish, although the vehicle is rarely crowded during these uncertain times."

"Monday morning, then." Clay nodded and wondered how he would fill in the next three days. His concern to be on his way, to cover the final miles and have done with this loose and lonely existence, was something new. If, he thought, the years had taught him anything, it should have been patience. Well, he could buy some presents for Sue, and maybe get himself cleaned up and outfitted in new clothes. He'd make some inquiries as to the conditions in the slave markets. He was going to need a lot of Negrahs and some good white men to superintend the work of rebuilding. There was a hell of a lot of work to be done. Measuring the task ahead, he experienced a glow of satisfaction and an eagerness to get started. He'd turn the place into the finest and best-run plantation in west Florida.

He ate alone in the corner, arms spread comfortably on the table, eyes gazing into the fire, dreaming pleasantly of the years to come. Now and then he lifted his head and glanced along the bar at the other side of the room. There were men there he had known casually, drinking companions of other days, but he didn't feel much like talking. Now and then he caught himself wondering about John Spain and was half tempted to call Markham and inquire after the man.

When he had finished supper he walked outside and strolled along the river front. The excitement and celebration had worn itself out and the town had retired, sleeping easily for the first time in months. As he walked he wondered why he indulged himself in the pretense of having no destination. He knew where he was going and had known it from the moment he walked out of the tavern. Perversely enough, he wanted to stand before John Spain's house again and look up at the balcony.

Weeds grew within the small front yard enclosed by a flaking iron fence. Weather boards covered the windows and doorway, and vines, unkept and without blossoms, withered along the balcony railing. A sign, "To Let," hung from a nail at the side of the entrance. For a long time he stood in the footpath, looking up at the empty building, before he turned away. There was nothing here he wanted or cared to remember. The husky music of a girl's voice had left no echo to whimper about an abandoned house. This was something a man should know and be certain of before he moved on.

He returned to Slater's easier in his mind than he had been since he entered the city. The thing was done and he felt nothing but a mild regret that he had not been wiser at the time.

The crowd at the tavern's bar had thinned away. Clay ordered a nightcap of rum, hot water, and a cinnamon stick, sniffing at the vapor as it curled about his face.

"Your room is prepared, sir." Markham was at his elbow. "I took the liberty of consulting the late Mr. Slater's books and discovered that you formerly occupied the corner room, facing the river. It has been prepared for you."

Clay grinned. Why not? If Jamie Beulow howled about the place at night he could come in and sit on the edge of his bed. They'd have a good talk. Jamie would be the last, even as a ghost, to hold what had happened against him. A man did certain things, took certain chances. Jamie must have known that Clay would have to come for him after he went away with Claire. He would have despised him if he hadn't.

Replacing the mug, he glanced at Markham and saw that the man was regarding him with a quizzical interest.

"You are in good spirits, sir?" the tavern keeper asked.

"I guess so." Clay was momentarily embarrassed. "I was thinking of a friend." He paused, wondering if he should ask the question. "There was a man," he continued thoughtfully, "a John Spain who used to frequent Slater's. Does he still come here?"

Markham shook his head. "I have heard his name mentioned many times, but the gentleman had left St. Augustine before I arrived. It is said he moved to Charleston."

Clay laughed softly. "I guess," he said to the astonished landlord, "I won't have to lock my door tonight then." At the foot of the staircase he turned and saw Markham's puzzled glance. Why this should strike him as being inordinately funny he could not say. "It's all right, landlord," he called back. "Mr. Spain once promised to kill me. I didn't want to make it too easy for him." He was whistling as he reached the upper floor.

The single window, high in the wall, laced the uprights of its bars against the sky. It was a shallow cell with a broad shelf of stone occupying half its length. The door, barely wide enough to permit the passage of one man, was heavily bolted on the courtyard. By sitting on the floor Asseola could look up through the grating and see the stars as they hung just above the watchtower. He rested now, his head against the cold rock, eyes fixed on an oblong of night. Beside him the evening meal congealed in a pan. He felt no hunger and was only dimly aware of the whispers of Wildcat and Talmeco-Hadjo. The cell, during the time of Spanish occupation, had served as a small chapel. The shelf of stone, waist high, had been the altar. Wildcat and Talmeco were perched on its edge, their feet swinging, heels thumping with a muffled beat. Wildcat, proud of his lineage, a terrible and shrewd warrior in the field, accepted their imprisonment as no more than a piece of bad luck. The whites had simply been smarter than they and the result was this cell. He felt neither shame nor degradation and was unable to understand Asseola's outraged brooding. His mind, as active and cunning as a raccoon's, was already exploring the possibilities of escape. Asseola only half listened to the conspiratorial whispers.

Outside the measured steps of the guard sounded his approach and the murmur from Wildcat and Talmeco subsided until the man had passed. When he swung about to pace off the distance to the opposite side of the court Wildcat sprang up. Asseola turned to watch. Talmeco bowed his head and bent his back, hands pressed to the wall while the young chief mounted his shoulders. Asseola could hear the scraping of a knife as Wildcat dug into the soft shell stone, gouging out a toehold. When the chink was deep enough he set his foot in it and swung up, his outstretched fingers clawing for the bars. He grunted with breathless satisfaction and was at the window, resting on a knee placed within the shallow recess. Cautiously he tried to insert his head between the bars. Watching with more interest now, Asseola smiled. From the rear Wildcat appeared as a small animal attempting to burrow out of a cage. He heard a muted whistle of satisfaction as the head thrust out between the vertical rods of iron. Carefully Wildcat pulled back, slid to Talmeco's shoulder, and dropped to the floor. He and Talmeco scraped across the shelf and came quickly to where Asseola was seated.

"I am a cat," the young chief said happily. "Where my head will go my body must follow." The excitement in his eyes seemed to illuminate the corner. "Outside," he continued, "a narrow pond encircles this place. It will be necessary for us to contrive a rope with which to lower ourselves from the window. The opposite bank of the pond is not high. We can crawl upon it and away."

Against the wall was a stack of coarse forage sacks that had been tossed in to serve as bedding. Wildcat took one, tested the fibers between his strong hands, and then slashed its length with his knife.

"These strips," he said guardedly, "can be twisted into a rope and knotted together. It will take tonight and tomorrow and the result can be hidden from the guards beneath the remaining sacks. On the second night we shall disappear through the window. What do you think of that, my little brother?" He rested on his knees in an attitude of bright expectancy.

"I will not go," Asseola said, and turned his head to peer up at the sky again.

"Then you are a fool." Wildcat spoke without rancor. "I will go and for every white soldier who laid hands upon me I will kill five." He turned away and hauled a second sack from the pile. It was not in his nature to argue or intrude upon the will of another. The way was open, this he had proved. The rope should be made. When the time came he would leave this cell, quickly and without sound. If Talmeco and Asseola would come the choice should be theirs. If they were without the will to escape, then that was something a man would understand only within his own heart. He busied himself with the sacks, and his knife, as it ripped through the tough strands, made a rasping song.

Talmeco, oldest of the three, watched for a moment. His eyes sought Asseola's but the man would not turn his head. Finally he moved to Wildcat's side and with unspoken agreement held the cloth taut against the knife's blade.

Alone at his place by the door, with the damp night wind upon his face, Asseola felt himself smothered in a wave of loneliness. Why had he turned away from Wildcat and Talmeco? There was no ready answer. Why did he choose to remain here, a prisoner, when freedom was no higher than the wall's window? He could not say. His brain, usually clear and decisive, was clouded and drugged by conflicting emotions he only half understood. He was steeped in bitterness. Of all the Indians he had known the whites best. He had seen their lies mount one upon the other over the years until they formed a shield against the truth. He had wanted to believe they came to that meeting with sincerity, for if the struggle of his people was to be ended at all, it was necessary to trust someone. Yet he had been betrayed and his shame was great.

At the far side of the court a pallid light spilled from a window. He could hear voices and snatches of laughter. There his jailers sat about their fire. He wondered at their gaiety. How could men laugh at their own dishonor?

35

WITHIN the city the holiday mood induced by Asseola's capture persisted throughout the second day. Some business establishments were open only for the morning trade; others did not even bother to unbolt their doors. The townspeople strolled and gathered in the streets or paused on the flower-bordered walks of the plaza to exchange greetings and idle talk. Even the weather conspired to encourage a festive air. The southeast wind was warm and gentle and the waters of the river tossed in blue-crystal waves beneath the excited screamings of hungry gulls. It was true that reports had reached St. Augustine of a battle on the banks of the Tomoka River, far to the south, but no one was willing to consider the engagement one of more than minor importance. With the throat of its leader firmly caught, the Seminole body must perish. It was only natural it should writhe and thresh in the death agony.

Twice during the morning Clay made an attempt to gain an audience with General Hernandez. He was careful to evade the nature of his business, feeling that the military would have scant patience with a civilian who wanted to visit the captive Indians. He told the sergeant on duty he had been attached to Captain Miller's command at Fort King, leaving the soldier to draw whatever conclusions he cared to from the statement.

"You might come in later in the day or first thing in the morning," the sergeant suggested. "The General and the staff have been pretty busy." He examined Clay and saw something he liked. The lid over the right eye dropped in a slow wink. "This is a small puddle," he drawled, "an' right now the capture of them Indians looks bigger than the surrender of Cornwallis at Yorktown. You come back an' I'll get you in. What'd you say your name was?"

Clay told him again and departed. As he walked over to King Street he chuckled to himself. I'm in a hell of a hurry to get things done all of a sudden, he thought. I must have Yankee blood in me, or maybe it's just Sue Rogers calling from Pensacola.

He went first to the private banking house of Dekker and Harbord, through which Old Clay had transacted business, and arranged for funds. The senior partner greeted him warmly and kept him in the office for almost an hour while Clay discussed his plans for rebuilding the plantation.

"Naturally," Dekker said, "we heard with considerable shock of your grandfather's murder. He was a valued client and I hope we may serve you as well. I may tell you in confidence," Dekker continued, "that the nation teeters on the precipice of economic difficulties. We are calling all our large loans. You hold onto the land. In the end that is all a man can count on."

Clay escaped from the house with a feeling of relief. He didn't know anything about business. It sounded like a hell of a headache. Crops, slaves, and cattle were things a man could put his hands on.

The morning passed quickly enough. He found Linkler, the tailor, at his old address. There would be no time to make clothes for him, but the man had two completed orders on hand, clothing that had never been called for.

"The war," Linkler explained. "A gentleman selects the cloth and is measured; then," his hands spread with unhappy expressiveness, "he leaves to command a volunteer company and never returns. Things are not as they used to be."

Clay tried on one of the coats. With some letting out here and there the garments of the vanished patriot would serve well enough. When he told Linkler he was leaving for west Florida on Monday the little man seemed unusually happy.

"I would not like to have it said in St. Augustine," he apologized, "that the coat was made for you by Linkler. It will serve," he stepped back to examine the shoulders, "but more than that I cannot say."

"It'll look fine where I'm going." Clay was indifferent to the minor discrepancies, apparent only to the eye of a tailor. "Have it sent to Slater's Tavern with the other things."

Too many of the stores were closed and he gave up the idea of shopping for Sue. As a matter of fact, he was grateful for the holiday. He hadn't any idea what he ought to buy her in the way of presents; silks and gewgaws, he thought vaguely. Those were the things women liked.

The rumor was so ugly that its voice was never raised above a whisper, but it persisted, intruding in taverns, on street corners, and in the barracks. Clay heard it first that evening at Slater's. He sat at his favorite table in the corner over supper and the voices came distinctly from behind the high backs of an adjacent nook.

"Took 'em under a flag of truce, I heard. The Indians, this Osceola and the others, came in for a powwow and that was the end. Hernandez ordered his men to take them before they knew what was happening. They never had a chance."

"If it'll end the war I guess it's a good thing." There was no conviction in the second man's statement. The excuse was feeble and he knew it.

Clay laid his knife and fork across the plate. He was no longer hungry. That, he thought, was why Fort Peyton had been unaware of a furious battle. There had been no fight. Asseola and the others were tricked into the parley, which had been fraudulent from the beginning. Many times during the past years he had been ashamed of his own people as they tried to deal with the Seminole problem. Now what he felt was close to nausea. He lowered his head, unable to escape the weight of guilt that must fall upon all white men. Call it an expedient, a bloodless effort to close a fruitless and unnecessary struggle; name it as they would, the truth could not be concealed beneath shabby rhetoric. God, he thought wearily, we always know what is best for other people. How certain we are of our divine right! From the corner he looked about the room. I wish I could get out of here tonight, he told himself. I think I could get along fine for the rest of my life if I never saw another white man. I feel like building a high wall around the plantation, closing it off from the rest of the Territory until people want to be decent again.

He rose from the table, his supper barely touched, and brushed aside the anxious query of the servant.

"It's all right. I guess I'm not hungry. Bring some whisky and water up to my room and call me early in the morning."

In the darkness of his room he sat at the open window, looking out over the murmuring river. He refilled the glass twice with whisky and water, experiencing a melancholy pleasure as he felt the alcohol soften the edges of his reflections. Sometimes it was difficult to know what was right or wrong. Since the war was a senseless whittling away of men and their strength, then perhaps it was foolish to carp over the means used to close it off.

He rose and roamed about the room, undressing as he walked. Let the historians argue about it when they come to write the story of this war, he thought. I damn sure can't do anything about it. The Indians would never forget. Any hope the government might have had of negotiating another treaty or enforcing the one it had must have died on the banks of Pellicier Creek. The Indians would never trust a white man again.

He emptied his glass and stretched out on the bed. The whisky made him sleepy, blunting his thoughts. He dropped off quickly.

The deep, rolling tone of the cathedral bell spread across the town in overlapping waves, and then the single note was joined as other sections of the chimes added their voices. The city stirred and awakened. Candles glowed as men struck lights and consulted watches and clocks. The yellow points of flame were quickly snuffed, for it was not the hour of even the earliest mass. This being so, the bells could mean only trouble, and sometimes it was safer to keep a house dark.

Clay had no idea how long he had been asleep. The bells dragged slowly at him, pulling him back from a pleasant unconsciousness. He heard them dimly at first and then his eyes opened slowly and he listened. The peals seemed to be creeping upon a note of hysterical urgency. Leaning on the sill of a rear window, he looked out over the city, expecting to see the rising smoke and flame of a burning house to account for the alarm. Only a shapeless huddle of darkened buildings met his eyes. At the north end of the town, though, he could make out the erratic bobbing and weaving of torches as men held them aloft and raced through the streets. Above the cathedral's chimes he caught snatches of distant shouts and the perplexed and anxious yelping of dogs. The cries were unnaturally thin and wailing in the night. Then, as mysteriously as the uproar had sounded, it died away. The bells clashed a single sustained call and the echo lost itself, vibrating in the air for a few seconds with a bass thrumming. The barks of the dogs were abruptly broken off on a note of confused questioning. The flitting torches scattered and then drew together with a common purpose, blinking to the western limits of the settlement and vanishing behind the screening woods.

At the window Clay waited for a few moments, wondering what had caused the commotion. In the charged silence he heard the closing of doors and the dropping of window sashes as nightcapped heads withdrew cautiously. There was no movement in the street below and the town again closeted itself with the night.

Clay dug his head into the pillows, wondering sleepily what had startled the watch. Whatever it was, he thought, had high-tailed it for the woods. He went back to sleep, quickly and without effort.

With the light of day the news was cried across the town. Wildcat and Talmeco-Hadjo had escaped from their cell within Fort Marion. A knotted rope of forage-sack material dangled limply from the high barred window and trailed above the still and shallow waters of the moat. The escape was incredible enough, but the thing that caught the imagination and tantalized the curious was the fact that Osceola had been discovered by the guards sitting calmly on the floor of the dungeon. He had made no attempt to join in the jail break. With a change of sentries a routine check had been made of the cell, and with a light lifted above the level of his eyes the new guard peered into the dungeon. What he saw caused him to yell for the duty officer. There was only one Indian where there had been three.

Asseola had displayed no interest in the excited questions hurled at him. He sat on the floor, knees drawn up to his chin, scorning to make a reply. The officers measured the distance from shelf to window and declared that an escape through the opening was impossible. The swinging rope outside made their protestations ridiculous. They demanded to know the hour when the Seminoles had escaped and why Asseola had not gone with them. Wearied of the interrogation, the remaining prisoner had said, "I was asleep, and if you say a man cannot get between those bars then it must be so. White men are infallible. It has been said."

The hastily organized searching party that had awakened the town combed and beat through the woods and scrub without success. Wildcat and Talmeco-Hadjo had vanished. As the story of the flight was repeated it grew in daring and significance. Over his breakfast Clay heard several variations: Guards had been overpowered, the main entrance forced. The Indian Osceola was waiting for his warriors to assault and raze the town and effect his release. To his refusal to go with the others the citizens attached a sinister and disturbing significance.

Clay waited until afternoon before he called again upon General Hernandez. He smiled to himself as he delayed, thinking that the General would hardly be in the humor to view his request for a pass with reasonable calm.

When he was finally admitted to the officer's quarters he found General Hernandez surprisingly mild, considering the circumstances. The man even allowed a faint trace of humor to creep into his words.

"I take it," he said, "that you find nothing unusual in your petition, Mr. Hammond?"

Clay grinned. "I guess I could have picked a better time, General," he admitted, "but I'm on my way home and my stay in St. Augustine is limited."

"And your interest in this Indian, Osceola?"

"I've known him all my life. We grew up together. I'd like to see him again before I go back to the Apalachicola."

"Perhaps," General Hernandez tapped at his teeth with a thumb-nail, "since you know him so well, you can tell me why he made no attempt to get away with the others?"

Clay shook his head. "No, General. Maybe I have an idea, but it wouldn't make much sense. It's all pretty well mixed up with a lot of things I knew about him as a kid; the way the war has been fought and the way an Indian thinks."

General Hernandez nodded slowly. "We can't take any chances with him, Mr. Hammond. You understand that. For reasons of security I'm going to send him to Fort Moultrie, at Charleston."

"I'd like mighty well to see him for a few minutes, General."

Half turned in his chair, the officer gazed pensively out of the window.

"I am not unaware of your services to the Army, Mr. Hammond," he said, "and so I am overriding my natural inclination to say no."

"Thank you, sir." Clay waited and watched as the officer reached for a pen.

"You have spent a long time in the field." Hernandez glanced up from the paper. "I have heard it said that you know the Territory and the Seminoles better than any man we have. Do you think that by holding Powell, or Osceola as you call him, we can bring hostilities to a close?"

"No, sir. Now I think you'll have to kill them, cut them to pieces, push them south, and then they'll hide out in the 'glades around Okeechobee and you'll have to round them up. That will take a long time, years probably."

The officer extended the pass across his desk. "You are fortunate to be going home, Mr. Hammond." He changed the subject. "I would like to go back to my own plantation. Was your place destroyed completely? I heard of your grandfather's murder."

Clay folded the paper and thrust it in his shirt pocket. "They did a good job but the land is still there. I guess I'll have to start over where Old Clay did."

"Good luck. I wish my own way was as clear. When this is over we may meet again. I hope so."

Outside, Clay stood for a moment. His fingers touched the paper in his pocket. Maybe, he thought, it would be better if I forgot this. That child can't be feeling too good about any white man right now. Fort Moultrie, at Charleston. He shook his head. I've a notion he won't be coming back. He turned and walked slowly toward the fort's gray pile.

WITHIN the fort's north wall the narrow cell was cast in the shadowed gleaming of endless dusk. The heavy oaken portal, with its reinforcing strips of rusted iron, opened on the courtyard. By stretching a little a tall man could peer through the barred slot for a glimpse of the sun. All sound entered faintly here. The shuffling of feet, muted voices, and rasped commands, the subdued growl of the sea, faltered and hesitated before the forbidding door.

Clay arose from the unsteady bench and joined Asseola where he stood at one side of the grating. They had spoken but a few words to each other and those were restrained and awkwardly phrased. Now that he was here Clay discovered he had little to say. It would have been much better, he thought uneasily, if he had not come. The cramped and musty quarters depressed and made him nervous. Unconsciously he strained at the day's freshness as it swirled through the latticed window and across his head in feathered gusts.

"They're taking you to Fort Moultrie, child," he said. "That's at Charleston."

"It does not matter." Asseola would not turn from the window but he was not sulking. There was no anger or bitterness in the reply. He spoke listlessly and as though his thoughts were far removed from this prison.

Clay glanced about the cell. It was difficult to think of something to say. "This is a hell of a place to keep a man."

"It is good enough for a mad dog or a dirty Indian. How else should they be treated?"

Clay wanted to reach out and touch the shoulder so close to his own. His hand moved and then fell back limply. "You're making it mighty hard to talk," he finally said.

"You and I have not always felt the need of words." The voice softened.

"Well," Clay replied with an attempt at lightness, "we've never been in jail together before, either."

The shade of a smile rested for a moment in the dark intensity of the Indian's eyes and he half turned to look at the man beside him.

"Our ways have become stranger with the years," he said.

Clay leaned against the door. "You know," he said, "nobody can figure out why you didn't get away with the others when you had the chance." He uttered what had been uppermost in his mind all day.

"Let the question remain to pluck at those who have thrown me in this place. The answer isn't difficult."

Clay drew the toe of his boot along a crack in the floor. "Maybe," he suggested, "you should have gone."

Asseola threw his head up with a rebellious gesture. "I am a man," he said hotly, "not an animal to run and skulk and be hunted down. I'll tell you this." He turned and pressed his back to the wall, facing Clay for the first time. "I have no more stomach for such fighting as I have seen. The whites are not worthy to spill my blood. This thing, the honor they boast of, is tricked to meet their needs." He looked about the gloomy oblong and spat. "Would a white captain, taken honestly in the field, be treated as a captive slave? You know it would not be so. It is true I was not born a chief," the voice rose on a passionate and angry note, "yet I have led my people as one and they have followed. I am an Indian, yet I have fought honestly and in the open. Do the whites think that by hiding me from their sight here they can also bury their shame?"

Clay did not attempt a reply. His eyes met Asseola's briefly. This, he thought, is none of my doing. Why do I feel a share of the guilt? Who will answer the question?

"A long time ago," Asseola continued, "the white man Powell looked into the future for me. I was only a child, yet his words are as clear this day as they were the night he spoke them. 'They will run you out,' he said, 'or reduce you to a handful of basket weavers and cattle tenders.' Against this I have struggled. Is my offense so great? Was I born only to stand by the roadside and sell feathered ornaments and strings of beaded shells with which the women of the white men may decorate themselves? If so, I should have rotted within my mother's womb." The fury of the declaration seemed to draw off his strength and he sagged, wedging himself in a corner for support.

"Maybe it would have been better in Arkansas." Clay spoke without conviction, feeling that silence now would be unbearable. "Anyhow," he glanced about the dungeon, "there is nothing you can do here for yourself or anyone else."

The Indian's shoulders straightened and his head lifted proudly.

"I could have escaped. It was no great feat to scale the wall and force a passageway through the bars."

"Why didn't you?" Clay asked.

"You are not that stupid," Asseola mocked him gently. "I will add the power of a thousand rifles to the arms of my nation by allowing the whites to keep me prisoner. They think that by holding me they will bring an end to the war. It will not be so. Do you think the Indians will ever again believe what is told to them? They will throw the lie into each white face that dares to utter it." A scornful smile played about his lips. "To each false promise they will say: Where is Asseola? Why is he in your prison? How was he taken? To those of small heart and courage they will say: This Asseola, of our people, walked into a clearing, trusting the word of the white soldiers and their officers. He came honestly and with a desire to talk of peace, and they made him a prisoner. We will never accept their words or their treaties again."

Clay broke a section from a dark twist of tobacco and softened it between his fingers. "I guess," he admitted, "they already figure something like that. Maybe they'd like to get rid of you. But even if what you think is true, it won't do any good in the end. The government can't back down. The Army can't say: Hell, we were only fooling. Let's call it quits and go home. If it takes fifty years they'll have to whip you, child. You know that."

"Then," Asseola declared, "it will take fifty years or twice fifty. Who knows? In the final day of battle they will have to kill every Seminole in the Territory; the old and the young; the men and the girls; the women whose bellies are large with unborn children. Wildcat swore to me before he left that they would fight as long as they could find ground beneath their feet. When they have been driven from this they will move into the great swamp by the water of Okeechobee." He turned to stare out of the window and the silence between them deepened.

"For everyone's sake," Clay said, "I hope you're wrong."

Asseola appeared not to hear. He kept his gaze on the patches of sunlight within the court. He seemed to sniff at the air, tasting it.

"How," the question came with painful slowness, "how is the day outside? Is it fair and good to look upon? It is always the hour of afternoon here."

"It is a good day," Clay answered gently. "It is such a day as the many we have known together."

"This Fort Moultrie," Asseola almost seemed unwilling to speak

406

the name, "this place to which they send me; do you know it? When do I go?"

"I can't tell you. I heard only today you were to be moved."

Asseola nodded slowly. "I will not live there," he said faintly. "If you think it strange I should know this, then I also wonder at the knowledge. Yet, it must be so. I sicken inside and will not long endure a prison. Each day a little of me dies. I can feel it go." He studied his hands as though they had already become strange. "What of you, Clay?" he asked.

"I'm going back home to the Apalachicola." He had difficulty with the words. "I'll miss you there, child. It won't be the same."

Asseola's expression was almost tenderly reminiscent. "Many times," he whispered, "I have thought how it has always been between us. In my town, as you know, it was believed strange I should take a white boy for a brother. So it must have been with you when Old Clay asked questions you could not readily answer. Yet there was no time I can remember when I looked at you and said: His skin is white and mine this darker shade. So I have wondered often about this war and why we have fought it, your people and mine. It is a small thing for which to kill a man. If the people of my nation had had lighter skins there would have been no trouble. We would have raised our towns side by side, planted our fields without fences, fished from the same bank, and hunted along the same ridge. There would have been plenty of room for us all and with no question of who should stay and who must go. Why should the stain upon my face be so offensive in the eyes of the whites?"

"I don't know," Clay replied uncomfortably. "Maybe we're scared of something."

"Because of this fear many men have died. It is big medicine. How," he turned the subject easily, "how will you travel?"

"There's a stage in the morning to Tallahassee. Then I'm going to Pensacola to get my girl. After that . . ." he shrugged.

"There will be no more trouble along the Apalachicola," Asseola said. "The fighting moves ever to the south. The land in the north will be as we once knew it. I would like to go with you and stand for a moment in my town by the river."

"Maybe," Clay suggested, "I could get you out of this. Old Clay's name still carries a lot of weight in the Territory."

Asseola's quick smile was a rejection of the idea. "We both know such a thing is not possible. Besides," he shook his head, "I would not go."

They understood there was nothing more to be said and if there

407

had been they could not bring themselves to speak the words. Clay hailed the guard outside and waited as the heavy key rasped in the lock.

"Do they let you out of here? I mean," Clay indicated the open courtyard as the door swung aside, "can you walk around and get some exercise?"

Asseola nodded and stook back from the opening. "For a few minutes in the morning and evening I am permitted to look upon the white man's sky and breathe his air. Two guards go with me to be certain I do not use it all up."

"I'll come to Charleston," Clay suggested.

"No." The Indian's hand lay for a moment on his arm. "We will not meet again. Neither of us would have it so. You know that. What would we say to each other?"

Clay stood, blinking in the sunlight, listening to the cell door close behind him, and when the bolt was shot he walked out of the courtyard and across the moat's bridge toward the town below.